Full of Sound and Fury

Tonya Adolfson

Published by Fantastic Journeys Publishing,
Boise, Idaho
PUBLISHING HISTORY
E-Book released through Kindle
Soft Cover trial edition June 2015
Mass market edition/ XXXXXX

Cover art: Photo of fabric by John Farmer
Created in Gimp 2.6 by John Farmer
Cover Art copyright by Fantastic Journeys Publishing
Interior Art by Suzette Snyder
Edited by Brady Sparks and Julia Stidolph
Content copyright ©Nov 2014 Tonya Adolfson.

Published in the United States of America.

ISBN: 978-0-9855766-2-2

The characters and events portrayed in this book are fictitious. Any similarity to real persons, living or dead, common or deific, is coincidental and not intended by the author, unless, of course, I know them.
No Augustinians were harmed in the making of this book, though a few folks were roughed up a bit.

Also by Tonya Adolfson

The Souls of the Saintlands Series
Thine Enemy's Eyes
An Unpolished Gem
An Open Enemy
To Thine Own Self
Full of Sound and Fury
Determined to Be a Villain*

Other Books
Surviving Your Own Creativity
Filling Up on 500 (With Todd Adolfson)

*Coming 2016

Reviews for the Souls of the Saintlands Series

Thine Enemy's Eyes

"I loved it I stayed up late several nights because I had to know what happened! It's a great read with excellent pacing and such entertaining and rich characters. I loved the rich world she created and the details used to make it stand out. I cannot wait to read the second book to learn more about the characters and places mentioned! I highly suggest this book."
Maryanne Durant, Amazon Review

"I cannot wait for the next book, and hopefully, subsequent books to follow."
Steve Nunez, Dragonfleet Studios

"Tonya Adolfson's debut novel is incredible! Full of intrigue, wildly imaginative characters and set in a medieval fantasy world of such authenticity it blew me away. I would heartily recommend this to anyone, and can't wait until the second novel comes out!"
I. J. Smethurst, author of the *E.D.F Chronicles*

"The plot has interesting twists and turns to keep you going straight through the book. When it ends, it leaves you wanting more."
Shelley Wolf, Amazon Review

"…good political intrigue… good action scenes… Not to mention one of the heaviest cliff hangers I've seen in a while."
The William Jones Review

"This is a very well written book, and has more plot twists and turns then I could count, but each one made me all the more eager to keep reading and see where the story would end up."
Durin Boge, Amazon Review

"I've read and reread this book 5 times now, it's easily one of my favorites! The characters are well developed, the twists and turns of the story kept me guessing, and the story line easily kept me wanting more."
Chalyse Padigimus, Amazon Review

"I'm a busy professional without a lot of time to read and this book absorbed my free time quite enjoyably for the past week. It has a touch of the almost magical within an imagined realm akin to midevil Europe. It has romance without focusing overly on the taudry details as she has better things to do with the plotline. She develops several charachters including their background in succinct but inviting story telling and she juggles all of these charachters' knowledge gaps about the current situation of court intrigue quite well. I'm really curious to see what book 2 has in store for me."
Shiela Harmon, Amazon Review

"Some trouble trying to make sense of the geography at first; however, not sticking to a real world atlas got me over that hurtle. The story itself is very interesting with a nice twist at the end."
Rold DeDog, Amazon Review

"Tonya Adolfson has a way of drawing you in to make you feel like you are right there with the characters. I could not put this book down because I was so in love with the characters, I had to see what was coming next. She keeps you guessing until the very end. At times I found myself a little sad for a particular character and then later rejoicing with them. I strongly recommend this book and cannot wait to see what happens next in book two."
Kayla, Amazon Review

"This is the first book from Tonya Adolfson I have read and believe me, it won't be the last. She caught my attention for the first page and held it through all the plots and conspiracies. The setting is wonderfully imagined and the characters fully realized, and believable. A brilliantly written fantasy tale filled with exciting intrigue. I'm glad I bought this and the second book together!"
Samuel Sturkie, Amazon Review

"Tonya has definitely found her place on my bookshelf. Now have the first 4 books! Can't wait for the next one!"
Spencer Maschek, Amazon Review

"This is a fantastic beginning to a fantastic series. I could not put it down. An amazing world full of detail."
Adam Wells-Grube, Amazon Review

"Ms. Adolfson has woven a web that will catch you while you're not looking. The characters are dynamic, with relationships we can relate to and an intrigue so deep that I could not put the book down until it was over; and I was begging for more. There are few books that I have found that suck me in the way this one does."
Hannah Therrien, Amazon Review

An Unpolished Gem

"In a perfect follow through to Thine Enemy's Eyes, Ms. Adolfson continues to illustrate just how sticky the politics and personalities of her world really can be. She never lets go of you, even after the book is done. Just when I think I have a character figured out, they surprise me; I can't even tell how many sides to this story there are. I can't wait for book three!"
Julien McBain, author *Ghosts of the Past*

"It is difficult for second books in a series to have the same weight as the first. This is the rarer case of the second book surpassing the first."
Christopher Garcia, editor of *the Drink Tank*

"This book is just as captivating as the first book in the series. Again I was so enthralled with the characters, plot twists, and story line that I literally couldn't put it down and finished reading it in one day..."
Chalyse Padigimus, Amazon Review

"I love her writing style. She creates this world that becomes real to its readers. Oh and then there are these great characters with such richness and depth you cannot help but to love and in some cases hate them! She has written it in such a way you have no idea where or who, if anyone, the main character will end up with. There is such a depth in the story you just cannot put it down. I read it in a matter of hours. I know these are books I am going to read again and again throughout the years. It has to be a great book for it to have that kind of status on my bookshelf."
Maryanne Durant, Amazon Review

"Love the way the characters grow and mature. Can't wait for the next book!"
Shelley Wolf, Amazon Review

An Open Enemy

"I have flown through these books. I totally love the tangled story with so many twists ans turns. These are written by someone who knows how to keep their audience captive and I cannot wait for the 4th book!!! I have been dying to know what happens! This is definitely and awesome read every true fantasy buff should have on their shelf."
Maryanne Durant, Amazon Review

"By the time I reached this novel I knew I was going to be a life long fan. These characters hold pieces of the human experience that filled me with a sense of hope, left me speechless and at times exhausted me. An emotional journey filled with adventure that I will treasure and live over and again every time I read it for the rest of my life."
Anonymous, Amazon Review

To Thine Own Self

The whole series of these books are very cleverly written and very in depth with rich detailing and character development. I absolutely have read these books over and over again. There is a lot of action within the pages along with laughter and pain. The books tend to suck you in and show a world unlike any other.
Maryanne Durant, Amazon Review

Tonya Adolfson will take you further down the rabbit hole with this latest installment. There's only one problem. Nothing can prepare you for hitting the bottom. Riveting and jaw dropping twists that only add to the story are in store for all. Be grateful Book 5 is already out, for the wait would have been unbearable.
Steve "Warky" Nunez, Dragonsong Studios

This series is 11 stars out of 10!
With some books, it's hard to read them again once you know the plot twists. But with Tonya, she weaves her stories with such sublime brilliance that you want to read them again and again. Whether you're caught up in the beautiful dream like dialogue between two star struck characters or breathlessly page turning during the heart pounding action scenes, you will love this must-have series! Spoiler Alert: The books just keep getting better and better!
Ethan Shaw

"To Thine own Self" is a wonderful book full of love, sorrow, adventures, plot twists and turns, and everything you can imagine. Oh how it ended! After finishing the first thing I said (with a smile) was "I need to go send 'hate mail' to Tonya." In the note I told her "You're not my favorite Tonya right now." Now I wait patiently… well somewhat patiently, for book 5 to come out.

Stephanie Reese

"To Thine own Self" is book 4 in the Saintlands series that Tonya Adolfson wrote. This is a wonderful series full of intrigue, adventure, love and magic of the medieval times. This book transports you into the lives of the people and the lands to the point where you don't want to put the book down to go to sleep. I can't wait for the next book to find out what happens next. Tonya has become one of my favorite authors and deserves to have all her books read and reread over and over again. Each book is really that good. Thank you so much Tonya for giving us the Saintlands series

Tish Firmiss

"To Thine Own Self" is a dynamic continuation in the "Souls of the Saintlands" series. A delicate balance of action that moves the story forward without feeling overwhelmed or bogged down. This book in particular adds great detail to both the land and characters that have been introduced. While this is the fourth book, she has not stopped adding new mysteries and plot changes that must only be resolved in the next book. I anxiously await the next release date so I might again join the world that has created and learn how everything is resolved. A truly wonderful book and series.

Krista Wells

For Morgan and Misha, who have always
been the greatest joys of my life.

Acknowledgments:

First and foremost, I'd like to thank all the people who were inspirations for this book:

Gwen for Gwen, John for Raven, Dartanian for Alexander, Jeff for James, Misha for Emmy, Morgan for Alan and Johannes, Rod for Xeno, Shanna for Fierah, Stephanie for Belladonna, Erik for Dom, Jared for Draethen, Dave for Octavius, Morgan Wolf for Morgan Wolf, Aaron for Duncan, Adam P for Ambroise, John for Myrgen, David for Henri, Jennifer for Ce'Nedra, Daddy for Thessius, Kim for Ysabel, Joe for Nicaise, Jenn for Flora, Aggie for Aggie, and all the hundreds of friends and family that have been contributors to this book. Your work has been amazing and your lives inspiring.

A big shout out to the most amazing editors a gal could have: Brady and Julia. Brady does the technical editing but you, Dear Reader, have Julia to thank for the Skyrim-level books, religions, calendar, and appendices. Without her input, this world was far less rich.

I'd also like to thank Gwen J. and John F. for endless hours of inspiration and consultation. Thank you guys!

Thanks to Shannon Galarneau for being my agent and helping me fulfill the dream of Fantastic Journeys Publishing. I'd also like to thank Steve "Warky" Nunez for all his enthusiastic support.

And finally, to my wonderful family: Morgan and Misha, for being so tolerant of Mommy's work; to my Daddy, Ray Lamar Manley, for inspiring me to tell stories for the sheer pleasure of my audience; to my Mom, Rosemary Virginia Manley, for reading historical romances; and to the Great and Powerful Todd, for being everything a Prince needs to be.

Glarren
York
Yokotana
Papal City
Caratia
Nubia
Sea of Blood
Sea of Erasmus
Mande
The Storm Catch
Maelstrom
Yndia

The Longsword of the Orphans tells the story of the challenges of Sir Richard of Kent, a hero of the Soulless War. Richard's discoveries about the Augustinian Church and its lies and plots were told in his journal. The publishing of this book began the movement away from the Church by those who called themselves the Emilianites, after Saint Emilios the patron saint of orphans, and ultimately led to the Saint Michael's Day Massacre in Patras, Mervolingia, in 1572.

Book One

A church must build up their people, as a
country must build up their populace.
Without their people, there is no life, no
blood, no soul.
-The Longsword of the Orphans

Always remember that the crowd that
applauds your coronation is the same
that will applaud your beheading. People
like a show.
-Sir Terry Pratchett

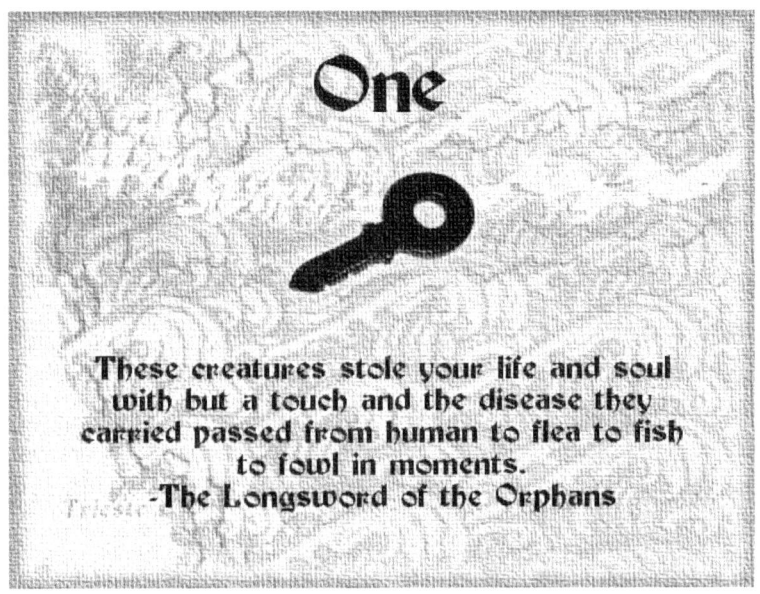

One

These creatures stole your life and soul
with but a touch and the disease they
carried passed from human to flea to fish
to fowl in moments.
-The Longsword of the Orphans

Alexander Angloume, Monarch de facto of Mervolingia, fell to his hands and knees and vomited. Black spots detonated behind his eyes as his brain tried desperately to survive what he had just done. Black slime smudged the sides of his fingers and he remembered that his palms and pants would be coated with the sludge that had oozed from the body he had held seconds before. He could smell the putrid icor, rotting flesh of something that died days ago in a swamp. The smell caused him to wretch again, successfully stopping him from remembering completely that he had just murdered probably his best friend.

Gwen was dead.

Tears fell in the vomit and he turned away and crawled to lean against a stone wall to some building. He seemed to be on a porch or something with trees and fresh air all around him. He breathed it in to steady himself. He straightened one leg, leaning his arm on the other knee and practiced just breathing.

It was beyond a challenge. Phlegm and sorrow blocked his efforts. He wiped his nose on his sleeve but got some of the scum that had poured from Gwen's eyes and ears inside the edge of his nostril. He discovered his nasal passages were not nearly clogged enough for that kind of proximity and turned to vomit again.

He just remained in that position, resigned to never eating or standing again. That was right before he heard the woman scream.

The Giver of Life screamed in her cage, collapsing to her knees. Her long, flowing hair was shimmering white-silver crashing around her and falling through the holes in the bottom of the cage. The hair and bars were her only clothing. Her lilac-colored eyes turned violent purple when she cried.

The Archangel Gabriel turned to look at her, then turned back to watching the production on the other side of the wall. The Saints in Heaven were taking the small soul globes from a clear glass-like structure and placing them in the conveyance which inserted them into newborn humans. None of them turned at the sound of her cry so he ignored her.

The colors of the globes were disturbing, cloudy or spotted or even almost half black in some cases. The more disturbing factor was the size of the glass-like container. It was smaller, and that meant it was running out. He stepped out of the room where Giver was housed and spoke to Raphael.

"The Well is smaller."

Raphael nodded. "I saw. We will have to cut back on production again." He looked behind Gabriel at the wall that was opaque from this side. "Any luck with that one?"

"She just woke again, screaming."

"So, she will weep again. Good. That will buy us some time."

"Do you ever wonder why she screams when she wakes?"

Raphael shook his head. "I don't care. The fact that she does has enabled us to continue production for the last century. The loss of souls has impacted us mightily."

Gabriel sighed. "I don't see how this has been happening. The Church is stronger than ever. It has monopolized the world. No one alive in the main continent has the option of worshiping anything but Heaven. How can we lose souls?"

"Uriel is investigating that. With Michael gone, we've been short-handed. I suspect that the Land and its allies have found a way to steal them from the Measuring Table. It's the only explanation."

Gabriel nodded. "What about the colors of those that have come to us? They are... cloudy."

Raphael looked at the glass container. "The Well has been murky for a while. But Lucifer has said he will bring the refined souls to Heaven as soon as they are ready. Unfortunately, we can't hurry that process. To do so would have souls only partially purified and that would be worse than using souls that have been deemed more good than evil. Who knows what we would get?"

Gabriel folded his arms. It wouldn't be long before they wouldn't have a choice. If the Well of Souls went dry, no more humans devoted to Heaven would be born. Heaven was only allowed the souls of its worshipers. If the human followed Karma, or the Land or any of the heathen practices, the souls of the dead went to that deity. Many of the heathen religions fell under the Land's purview in the end, and were thereby stolen from the Well. The Well was the source of all souls, and the Giver was the source of the Well. But since Heaven stole her from the ground, she had not produced a single soul unless it was a captured tear. They had a special font beneath her cage which caught the ones that fell. Over the millennia, she had wept less and less at her fate. Now, the only time it happened was when she awoke from slumber screaming.

Gabriel watched the Saints as they worked the process. There were so many up here now, it was hard to move around on the main floor. They had an area above where they received prayers and mingled with one another. There wasn't enough work for all of them in production so many of them just stayed out of the way. He looked at one, summoning it with a nod. "You. Come here."

The saint looked around, then came over. "Yes, Gabriel?"

"Where is your warlord?"

The woman glanced towards the upper area. "I believe George is in the viewing chamber, sir."

"Bring him."

The woman nodded and left. Raphael turned as a clink denoted another soul being returned to the Well. Three more came and he exhaled. "She's not crying as much."

Gabriel looked at the brand new souls, glowing like tiny suns. While they waited, five more souls appeared, then they stopped. A tall, powerful man in armor walked over to the Archangels. He bowed, hand to his chest in a salute.

"Sirs. You summoned me?"

"Yes. Where are we in the war?"

The man took a deep breath. "The fires are stoked, sirs, but there has been a lot of rebellion against the idea. The humans are opposed. They are avoiding war at the moment."

"We need a war, preferably a holy one. Make it a civil war among those who worship Heaven. That will fill the Well."

"I'll get on it." The man bowed and Gabriel went back into the room with the Giver.

Saint George entered the room with his colleagues, closing the door behind him. The place was set up with a table around a central viewing pillar. There were several smaller ones around the room currently being used by people answering prayers. Most of the time, it was a choice for the Saint to go to a Prayer Pillar, but on a Saint's feast day, they heard every prayer uttered to them, pillar or no. Many stayed in the Meditation Room on their day to avoid distractions.

George looked around and saw Giles leaning on the circular table surrounding one of the smaller pillars. He came over, keeping his voice low.

"They asked about the war again. Where's Brigit?"

Saint Giles, patron invoked against monsters and night terrors, glanced around to make sure they weren't being overheard. "Feast Day. I know she's not planning on answering many this year. She's saving her strength for Alexander."

"How's he doing?" George looked into the pillar at Alexander. He was kneeling on the porch of an inn, blackness dripping off him onto the wooden planks that were splattered with vomit.

"Oh, not good. The fool just went through the shadows again. Twice."

"I thought I got rid of that thing."

"Different one. This is the one I repelled, the one he threw over the side of the ship."

George frowned, worried. "How did he get it back then?"

"Wasn't destroyed by fire."

"They can just *return*?"

"If the wielder wishes it, but they attached themselves to the last person to use them. Previous wielders can't summon them." Giles exhaled, brow furrowing.

"What is it?"

Giles breathed deep. "Something is very different about this one."

"What makes you think so?" George looked at his friend.

"He never used it. It showed up because he thought about it on the ship. He disposed of it without using it. This one is attuned to just him."

George looked at the image of the Mervol king. "What does that mean?"

Giles' eyes narrowed. "It means this one is new."

George leaned on the table. *New?* That meant someone out there was making them again. The amulets caused the downfall of all the Inquisitors centuries before. If Alexander fell, the Angels would get their war, and it would rival the destruction of the Ascension of Clara.

Come on, Brigit. Come on.

Alexander got to his feet faster than he thought possible in his current state. He realized there was an open door near him and he smelled lemons. He ran inside and saw blood splattered on a wall near a back entryway. The building was apparently an inn, and the entryway probably marked the kitchen. He ran to the blood and saw a tall, thin man with a full head of black hair greying throughout his face. The man had a part of a stone staff that was broken, burnt as if by acid. The man was holding in his intestines with one hand and trying to wake a generously proportioned woman with red wavy hair. Her stomach had a chunk of the stone staff protruding from it and her fingers were encircling it.

From the placement of the stone, Alexander knew she would not survive the removal of the staff.

He slid on the floor to kneel beside her and put his hand on the stone. "Don't remove this. It's the only thing keeping her alive."

The brown-skinned man nodded, and Alexander looked at him. "I need to see your wound."

The man managed a slight smirk. "I don't think I'll survive showing it to you, son. No offense."

The woman opened her eyes. "Tomas... Tell him... About... Tangl..."

Alexander looked at her, then at Tomas. "Tangl? You mean Tanglwyst? She's here?"

"That monster went for her room... I... tried to deter... him..." Tomas broke out in a fit of coughing and blood gushed from his stomach wound, his fingers channeling it into a spray that misted the floor.

Alexander pulled off his shirt and tied the arms around Tomas' middle. The sleeves were full and the man was not so Alexander was able to make a strong bandage quickly. "Hold that there. I'll be right back."

Tomas nodded and the woman squeezed his hand.

Alexander looked around, trying to figure out what room was Tanglwyst's but he got an idea when he heard the crash. He ran to the source.

Duncan was blackened, shadows like ink in water billowing out from him. They formed tendrils and one of them had Tanglwyst by the throat. She had kicked over a lantern but it was the closest thing to a piece of furniture that her feet could reach. Being morning, the lantern wasn't lit, and the smell of lamp oil cut through the smell of sulfur now overpowering the room. There was a strange hint of lemony freshness still on the tall, bald man controlling the shadows, and the mixture dragged back Alexander's banished nausea.

One of the tendrils had a strange knife in it and Tanglwyst's face had blood all over it seeping from gashes from the implement. Duncan growled at her, not even noticing Alexander's arrival.

"You *used* this thing on me. Time to return the favor."

The tendril thrust the four-bladed knife between Tanglwyst's kicking legs, embedding it in her crotch. He ripped it out and thrust it again before Alexander could scream.

White light filled the room, a sphere that exploded from Alexander. The tendrils burned and retreated to Duncan, who howled in pain, shielding his eyes and face. The amulet on his neck flashed and the stench of sulfur mingled with the blood as Tanglwyst dropped to the floor with a wet thud. Duncan's second stab had gone into her womb and there was a deep gush of even more blood as the star-shaped wound splayed open. The device landed with a clang on the floor, scattering droplets of her blood across them both.

Alexander bolted towards her, all thought banished from his mind. His knees were already soaked from the people in the other room. He laid Tanglwyst on the floor to better inspect the wound. It was bad. Even if he had his Chirurgeon's kit, this was a fatal wound. Unlike the woman in the kitchen, Tanglwyst didn't have time for him to sew her up.

No matter what he did, she was going to die.

Two

The soil was finite though, and merely touching other soil did not transfer this power to it.
-The Longsword of the Orphans

"We need to burn it."

Michael looked up at the young blond man who so resembled his friend Gwen. "Pardon?"

The man did not turn to look upon the clotted sludge that was once a human being. "We need to burn it. It was touched by Shadows. The taint needs to be destroyed before it becomes something living again." The man walked over to the small chapel to the Augustinian saints and came out a minute later with a lantern and a lit votive. He threw the lantern on the ground, letting the oil inside mingle violently with the decomposing grunge trying to seep unsuccessfully into the stones. He then threw the votive down.

At first it looked like the effort blew out the flame, but the wick retained its red hot coal for a moment, which ignited the fumes of the oil. It turned out the sludge was highly flammable. That little spark made the whole thing burn like pitch on a ship's deck. Michael stepped back just in time to keep his dreadlocked hair from getting singed.

He looked at the young man, who was watching the flames, his cheeks damp. This man was a stranger to Michael, but his features decried a familial relationship. He studied the man a moment until the stink of burning hair drew him away from the sorrow. He knew the man's name only because Gwen had told them about him on the trip. Her greatest concern was that he would not approve of her rush to fight against Alexander.

"You're James, right?"

The man looked at Michael, taking in his black skin and dreaded hair with a measured glance. Michael had not shaved since they left Patras, so his two tenday growth of beard must have made him look untamed. Luckily, he had good quality clothes that had weathered the trek well, despite encountering nearly every terrain available. If he were to cross a snow-covered desert, that would complete his Terrain Checklist.

The man nodded. "Do I know you?"

Michael shook his head. "No." He looked down at the burning mound. "But I knew her. We traveled here from Patras."

James frowned and looked at the harbor a stone's kick away. "Which ship?"

"We came overland, actually."

James' eyebrows raised. "There's an overland route?" He glanced away to the nearby cliffs. "Is that route as protected as the sea one?"

"It is not an easy entry. One way in from the west. Apparently, there's another mountain pass to the north but none from the south. There you have to go by sea."

"Trust me. You can't get here that way either. Rocks and wickedly vigilant sharks patrol there. Clearly this cursed place wants no outsiders."

Michael wondered for a moment about James' words but hoped that was his grief talking. This beautiful Land would forever be tainted now by the death of Gwen. He nodded. "She saved my life traveling across the forests between here and the mountain border. Caratia is very inhospitable."

"Yeah, she did that. It was an annoying habit." James tried to sound tough but a tear rappelled down his cheek to his chin, betraying his soft interior. He rubbed his palm with his thumb, something Michael had seen Gwen do a few times. His heart broke again at the memory of the gesture.

"Do you need anything?"

James shrugged. "I don't know yet. I need to make sure this is gone, then I'm going to have to think on that." He exhaled and folded his arms across his chest. "Once I can actually think, mind you. That might take a bit."

"Do you have a place to stay?"

James looked around. He nodded to the nearest inn. "That looks like it will do. I had to leave my ship a few days from here."

Michael looked at the castle, Ashstone, where they had come from. "If I may suggest, Catriona was her patron. She will likewise be mourning. Your sister was very well loved here. Perhaps you could stay with us up there?"

James looked at the castle, his ice blue eyes more like glaciers compared to Gwen's watery blue. He nodded. "I'll probably take you up on that." He looked back at the now smoking puddle of tar. "I might be here a while though. I need to make sure this is gone."

Michael nodded, then walked over to the chapel. He found the priest just inside, coming to the door. "Father, I need more lamp oil, if you have it. And perhaps some small branches for a fire."

The priest nodded and scurried off. Michael turned to watch James. He had no intention of letting him endure their mutual loss alone.

Myrgen and Catriona stood, helping Tib to his feet as Drake and Anika hovered nearby. Many of the people in the kitchens and stables had wandered out at the sound of shouting, while others were just now arriving as the news of the battle spread. Catriona looked around and could tell the ones who saw the incident, even without using her Sight. They, too, were on their knees or crying.

As they approached the great doors through which the whole town had celebrated Naming Day the night before, several people came over and hugged her and her family. The stable hand and kitchen ladies all included Myrgen in their gestures, which seemed to surprise him. She knew that they had bonded with him yesterday during the festival, so it didn't surprise her.

The group went into the great hall and a few folks rushed off, returning with cups of water for the mourners. Everyone was silent near her, but the folks in the kitchen were murmuring quietly. Myrgen looked them over and then looked at Catriona. She could see that he was worried they would be blaming him. After all, he was the one who shot her.

The image stabbed through her heart like the arrow he fired, and she closed her eyes against it. She worried he was right. At this point, even she felt unable to divorce the two things. Then the feeling passed and she stepped into his arms. He held her without hesitation and it eased the pain and loss. It felt so very familiar, like this was his place in her world.

Like it had always been his place.

She opened her eyes and saw that this eased the negativity he had seen. Catriona wasn't holding this against him. Clearly it wasn't his fault. That brought to mind who *was* at fault, and her grief flipped to anger without notice. She stepped back from her embrace with Myrgen and turned to her Dûce and Dûcesa.

"Can you see to Tib? I need to tend to something."

Her foster parents nodded almost in unison, and Tib looked at her a moment. "Do you need to commune with the Land?"

She nodded, dropping to a knee before him. "Yes. I need to make sure the threat is out of our home."

"If he isn't, will you kill him?"

Catriona looked at her son's wet, red eyes. "No. I'll not let her sacrifice be undone. He has trapped you, and for that, I will not forgive him. But I will not destroy him and put you on the throne of Mervolingia. You are home. You will stay here."

She hugged him and stood. She turned and Myrgen walked with her. She did not think to have him stay behind, any more than she thought to take Tib or the governors of Caratia with her. She went out the doors and up the stairs. Myrgen remained silent by her side and the climbed to the top floor of Ashstone. There were two towers that rose into the air, surveying the land and sea. She turned towards the mountain and went down the hallway to a single set of doors at the end. No other rooms were in this section.

The doors were obsidian, standing out in Ashstone because they did *not* have veins of lava running through them. They were a stark contrast. There were no handles on the doors and no apparent hinges. She pulled the Onyx Key from the neck of the coat she had borrowed from Myrgen this morning and placed it on the seam of the doors.

They swung open with a balanced ease, as if they were made of balsa wood and not black stone four inches thick. She stepped in and the torches upon the wall flared to life in welcome. Myrgen hesitated at the doors, looking around, but she did not stop. If he followed her, then he would witness this chamber. If he felt it was not his place, then he would stay. Regardless, she would go.

She walked about forty feet into the mountain and turned right into a large, natural cavern. Orange glowing veins ran through the stone walls and onto the floor, lighting the way to a black obelisk jutting out of the center. The obelisk shot white light out of carvings that moved in the dark and she walked up and put her hands upon it.

Show me the monster.

Alexander looked skyward. *Dear Saint Brigit, help me.*

A light pierced the air around him and he shielded his eyes from his own Power of Sovereignty. He was in a sphere, Tanglwyst on the floor before him. A voice sounded in his head, and would have knocked him to the ground had he not already been there.

Why should I?

He blinked. He remembered a dream he had, of being trapped with statues of saints around him but he was behind bars in a prayer nave. There, the saints had shown him a path via candles lighting and snuffing out. This was far more direct, and completely unexpected. He decided not to waste the opportunity.

"You chose me. You wanted me to do something. I haven't done it yet."

Nor do you seem inclined to. You have come here, *in pursuit of a woman clearly against the laws of Heaven. A heathen. Despite all the signs against this, you continue to chase her.*

Alexander closed his eyes. That cause was irretrievably lost now. With Gwen's death, any chance of reconciliation with Catriona was gone.

Except for Alan. Alan was his heir and he could use that to get her to...

Stop, mortal. Do you not see what this course has wrought? Look around you. Look at what you have done.

The sphere turned transparent and he saw Tanglwyst in a puddle of her own blood, dying. The blood mingled on his hands with the slime that had spurted from Gwen's body. His palm hurt from where he had gripped the teleportation amulet when he took himself, Gwen, and Duncan through the shadows to the steps of the Church. But the holy ground had rejected them, shunting them to the streets instead of at the altar where he intended. He knew now that it was Gwen who had been rejected, but it was useless to think about it. Duncan, having tasted the blackness again, had responded like an addict getting an unexpected dose of his drug. He had gone mad and taken the amulet from Alexander.

Although he was gone now, Duncan had cut a bloody swath to Tanglwyst, seeking revenge for a weapon used against him. Alexander shuddered, remembering the wound the *dentate* had delivered upon Duncan, though the shadows associated with the amulet had bound his wounds in lies, pretending they were gone. The image of the man's penis flayed into quarters like a flower, leaking urine forced itself upon his mind, and he fought to shut it out.

Apparently, Duncan had taken umbrage at the offense, and sought retribution.

He looked through the open door and could barely see Tomas cradling his wife, looking at Alexander. He wife was surrounded by blood and Tomas turned back to her, his hand stroking her cheek as he waited for her to die. He, too, might, but he would bury her before that happened. He might be here all winter before someone found him.

Alexander shook that image from him as well, the despair setting in. He was nowhere near holy ground and he knew from years of practice he could not channel the power of Heaven to seal these wounds like he had upon Catriona all those years before. It took James figuring it out for Alexander to heal Duncan the first time. Here, in this heathen place, there was no Heaven.

He had failed. And now everyone here was going to die.

"I'm sorry..."

Are you? Do you see what your foolish defiance has brought to these people?

"Yes." Tears flowed again and he nodded, wiping his eyes with his hands and flinging the tears to the ground.

And what else have you done because of this obsession? Who else lies dead at your hands because you ignored my direction?

33

Alexander shook his head, images of the city of St. Marguerite on fire, of Nicolai convulsing on the streets of Rouen from Duncan's poison dart, of his brother Charles, covered in blood.

And yet, you want Heaven to serve you.

He looked at Tanglwyst. He remembered the winter, and the time they spent playing with his niece Emmy. How he had grown so very fond of her and how he had abandoned her the instant Alan had visited Emmy. Her face still showed signs of the now permanent discoloration of her skin from where Catriona had beaten her near to death. It should have healed up completely by now, but the skin was damaged. It would be years before it faded altogether.

"She doesn't deserve to die because of me." He turned his eyes to the ceiling. "Please, give me the power to save these people."

I will allow you to heal one. *Choose wisely, Alexander. It will be the last time.*

His hands glowed with a white light and he knew he could take away all the damage done to her, every slight, every illness. Even things broken in her mind would be healed. All he needed to do was touch her.

He stood. "She doesn't deserve to die."

He turned to the open door and walked to Tomas. He laid his hands upon his wife and released the energy Brigit had granted him. The inner wounds healed, the sepsis from her intestinal contents eradicated as they were restored. Her organs returned to their rightful place, causing the stone staff to push out to clatter on the floor, and he closed the wound in her stomach. He let the healing energy spread to her entire body, removing hereditary problems as well as any deterioration from her age. He made her whole again, then set back on his heels.

The glow faded as the last of her ailments disappeared, and he blinked, smiling at her as she settled into a healing, restful sleep.

"You're going to be okay, my lady." He looked at Tomas. "She'll sleep now. When she wakes up, she will be better than ever."

Tomas grabbed Alexander's shoulders, and the action caused him to wince and hold his wound again. "Thank you man. Thank you. She was my whole world. I don't know what I would do without her."

"Now, it will be a long time before you have to find out." He checked Tomas' gash again but the shirt bandage seemed to be holding.

Tomas smiled, then his eyes landed on Tanglwyst. His face sank in a manner that would be comical under any other circumstances. "Oh no." He looked at Alexander. "Is she...?"

Alexander nodded. "She will be soon enough."

Tomas looked at his wife, asleep on the floor. The blood was still around her but that was just a matter of cleaning at this point. Tomas looked at Alexander again. "Why heal my wife and not her?"

"Because your wife did nothing to deserve this."

"And Tangl did?"

"No. But she was at least involved. Your wife was a bystander, caught in an explosion of bad decisions."

"Can nothing be done then?"

Alexander shook his head. "I don't have my medical kit. I have no supplies and I can't use that ability again."

Tomas blinked. "Is that all you need? Medical supplies?"

Alexander looked at Tomas. "Yes."

Tomas smiled and nodded to a door opposite the kitchen from Tanglwyst's room. Alexander opened it and found a literal hospital's worth of linen wraps, ointment jars, bottles of potions, and surgical kits.

"My wife was a medic for the army. This was their outpost."

Alexander hugged Tomas and grabbed a surgical kit and some linen wraps. "Can you get me a basin of clean water? And some cloths?"

Tomas nodded and Alexander ran to Tanglwyst.

"Hang on, my friend." He grabbed a pillow from the bed and put it on the floor to keep the tools out of the blood.

"Hang on."

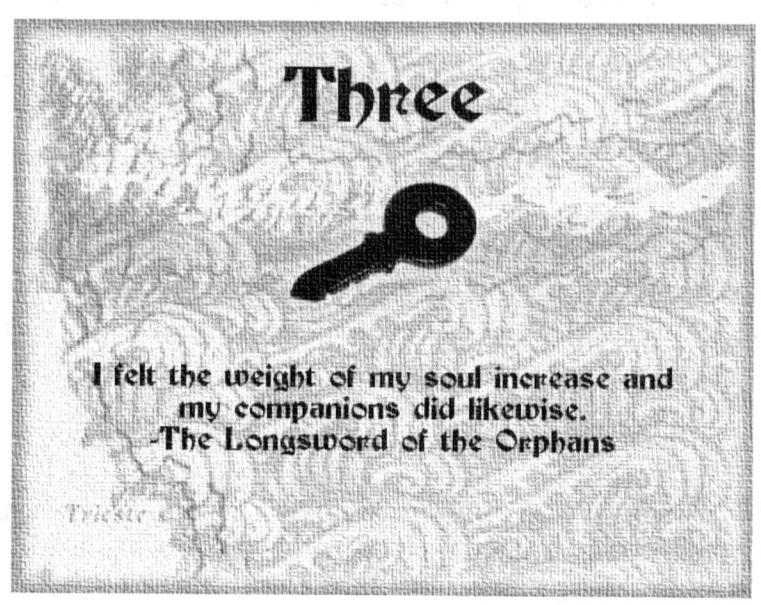

Three

I felt the weight of my soul increase and
my companions did likewise.
-The Longsword of the Orphans

Lauriel walked silently behind Raven and Octavius, his Fae-wolf form making no sound as he stalked through the forest. He and Raven had a connection to the Land, granting him the ability to walk over grass and twigs without damaging them. This made their passage trackless in the world.

Octavius was not so endowed, and he felt like he clunked through the woods of Caratia like a carrack on feet. He was a sailor, and had been at sea or on a ship for the last ten years and he still had not gotten his land-legs. The ground moved differently, as in not at all, and that stillness made him queasy. In the last ten years, he had not spent more than a night away from the *Enigma*. This was the longest he had ever been separated from his wife. He touched the cloth in his pocket, the contents of this wrapping more precious than air to him. He stroked it through the cloth, feeling the faint ridges where the color had been laid in a little thicker. He was probably just imagining it, but he felt like he was stroking her cheek, and hopefully, that was keeping her with him.

Alexander's attack on the *Enigma* had shattered more than this window. When that cannonball had come through Catriona's chambers in the bay around St. Marguerite, it destroyed Estelle's connection to the ship. According to Raven, the strange, green-haired man trotting soundlessly beside him, she still stayed a part of it only because she had this small, intact piece of the image in contact with the ship. They had found it resting behind the very cannonball that had killed her, like clutching desperately to the knife plunged through your heart to plug the hole it has made.

The image tore him apart, reliving the impact. He had felt the ship scream in pain, felt her wrack, convulse. The timbers groaned and the sails sagged, threatening to collapse upon the crew. He remembered looking up at them and seeing them recover in the wind, but he knew something was terribly wrong. When he saw the window shattered, even he had no idea what that meant. It took Raven to explain it.

He always had assumed the pitch that sealed the ship was Estelle's connection to the wood, iron, and canvas that was the body for his wife's spirit. To discover the window actually housed her soul made him feel foolish. It had never occurred to him to ask.

"Hey, how do you plan to get around the mountain?"

Raven looked at Octavius, then up at the high cliffs impeding the southern border of Caratia. This separated her from Mande and was, according to all accounts, impenetrable. "Well, I don't plan to go around. I plan to go through."

Octavius frowned. "There's a way through?"

Raven smiled. "Not yet."

Octavius looked at Lauriel. He was no help. "Okay, I don't understand. I'm just a simple Waterlogged. I don't know what you mean."

Raven's brow furrowed. "'Waterlogged?' Oh! You mean Calista follower. No, you aren't."

"I'm not?"

"No. You're a Fae follower. A..." Raven stroked his beardless chin with his thumb. "What's the derogatory term for those that worship the Fae?"

"Troll Toady."

"Yes!" Raven pointed at Octavius. "You're a Troll Toady." He resumed his trackless trek towards the cliffs. "You may have lived on the sea, but you worship that lady in your pocket. That makes you a Troll Toady." He pointed at himself. "Whereas *I* am more of a Dirt Worshiper, having actually worked as the Stâpân for the Third Dûcesa."

"You did?"

"Had to. I kinda killed off the Second one."

Octavius stopped. "You what?"

Raven turned to the blond, stout First Mate of the *Enigma*. "I didn't do it on purpose. I just let her touch a rock. Turned out that was a bad idea." He turned back, waving a finger in the air with a shake of his head. "Didn't make *that* mistake again, I'll tell you! No sir. Those rocks are *right* where they belong now."

He let a Land Worshiper touch a rock and he won't let that happen again, no sir... Octavius shook his head. Trying to understand Raven was like trying to determine the flavor of a star. "Yeah, I can see where you went wrong there."

"Hey, how was I to know? Looked like any other black rock with sparkly gold flecks. Not that there *were* any other black rocks with sparkly gold flecks. Didn't seem to matter at the time. Touch, then poof! Then AUGH-ACK! Then thud. Then *sluuurp*. Try again." Raven shrugged.

Octavius flicked a confused glance at Lauriel, but he, too, just shrugged, nodding. Apparently, that was exactly what happened. Octavius decided maybe it was a good time to stop expecting support and explanation from a Fae monster.

And his dog.

Myrgen waited by the giant, silent doors. Catriona had gone out of sight, despite the torches that lit as she passed. He felt like he was allowed this far, but no further. There was not barrier or anything, simply a *feeling*, like this place was sacred and only the most devout could go here. For some reason, he did not fit that bill, but he understood that. He had only begun to believe in the powers of the Land to interact and protect its people. He wondered if all its followers experienced things like this.

He thought briefly of Boots, and the granite sword he let her take with her. He hoped it was serving her, helping her in this time. He didn't want to think about it, lest the sword leave her side and return to his hand. She needed it, to keep her, well, *grounded*. He snorted a little laugh at the mental pun.

He heard footsteps and saw Catriona move towards the doors again. He straightened up and waited. "Well?"

She sighed, frowning. Her eyes were dark and still rimmed in red from the crying, but she was not stuffy anymore from it. She would look like hell tomorrow, yet he would still find her beautiful. Anika had been right. Catriona was the one for him.

"I tried to see if Alexander was still in the country. I thought I had him, but then, something blocked me. The Shadowwalker is nowhere to be found."

She stepped through and started down the hallway back to the rest of the castle. The huge doors closed behind them as he stepped away to follow.

"I suppose that's the important part." Myrgen fell into step beside her.

"Yes. I wish I could put up barriers of some kind to keep this monster out. If he has been here, he can return. He is not Mandian, and will not be repelled from our soil."

Myrgen blinked. Entivia "Boots" Malatesta had been shoved from the top of the mountain pass, flung by a great force away from the borders of Caratia. He had not found her body at the foot of the switchbacks, nor in the crags at the base of the path up the mountain. He hoped she had used the amulet to get to her safe place, and also hoped she was able to break free of the hold the monsters would have reasserted.

He thought again of the Granite Sword and thought again that perhaps he needed to call it back. Then he closed his fists against the urge.

No. If she is in danger, it might be what saves her life, saves her soul. I won't take the only thing that can help her.

He blinked again, realizing something. "Alexander is Mandian." He looked at Catriona. "Catherine is a D'Medici."

"I know." She continued to look straight ahead. "He should not have been able to be here. If he came by sea, he would have been eaten at the Maw of Calista. The Sea of Blood was named such because of the number of Mandians it claims."

"And the defenses at the passes would stop anyone coming here overland. So how did he get in?"

"I don't know. I'm not going to ask him."

Myrgen tilted his head, still looking ahead. "What about that man that was with him? The one who ran off after where Alexander took Gwen."

"James. She called him James." Her voice caught in her throat for a second. "James is her brother."

Myrgen stopped.

"By the Stones, Catriona, I killed his sister in front of him."

She stopped and they looked at each other. She took his hand as he realized everything that had happened. He had shot a righteous arrow through this innocent girl, Catriona's ward, in front of her, in front of Gwen's brother, in front of Michael, who traveled all the way from Patras with her. In front of Tib.

He dropped to his knees on the warm stones, pain not penetrating the fog of guilt and sorrow. He didn't know Gwen except peripherally, but he had murdered her in front of every person who loved her that he *did* know. People he would fight to the death to protect.

"I'm sorry… I'm so sorry…"

Catriona took a knee beside him, her eyes growing wet as she watched the tears fall from his. She squeezed his hand as he began to sob, and did not try to stop him as he bled that guilt onto the stone floor.

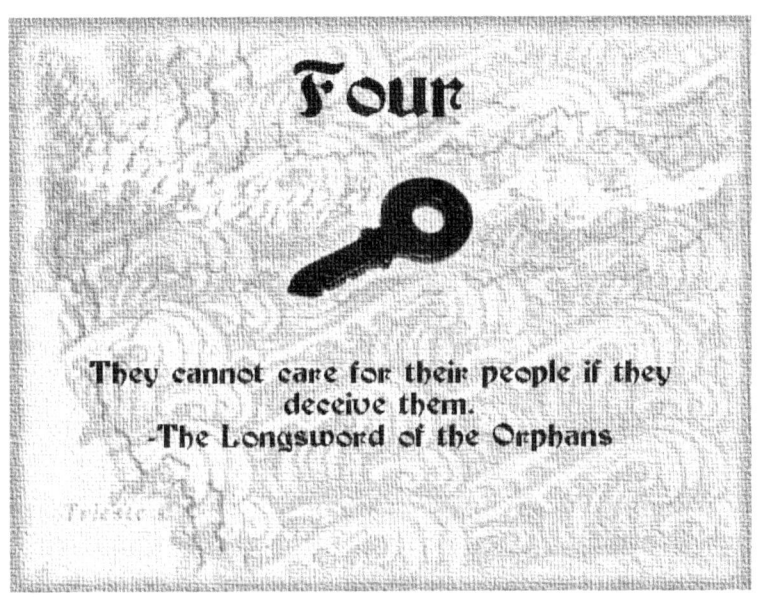

Four

They cannot care for their people if they
deceive them.
-The Longsword of the Orphans

The sun set as the fire finally went out. The priest had brought water out for Michael and James throughout the day to help them deal with the tragedy. They drank it, but neither of them had felt compelled to eat and refused food when he brought that as well. Periodically, James would coat the end of a stick in the flaming sludge, then douse it with water. He watched the ash-water sit on top of the stones in drops while the water that did not have ash in it soaked into the ground. About the eighth time he did this, some of the drops with ash also soaked in, so he took that as a sign that the ash was being purified.

It took less time that he had expected. He thought it would never be destroyed.

Eventually, as the sun left the visible sky behind the great cliff barriers towards Mervolingia, the ash was regularly soaking into the stones. He threw the last of the water upon the ashes of his sister, and they all soaked in, leaving no trace of her. She was now gone.

He exhaled slowly, breathing through the loss. Tending to her remains had been cathartic, and he felt now that she could be at peace. In Glarren, burning a body was common practice, but only because of the Soulless War three hundred year before. Prior to that, Glarrens buried their dead. Then a single touch killed you, then reanimated you, and after that, everyone burned. Probably better that way. Ashes fed the soil. Bodies did too, but no one planted crops on a graveyard. Ashes were dispersed upon the farmlands and used to nourish it. It was far more efficient.

Efficient. Wow. That's not callous at all.

He shook his head.

"What is it?"

James looked up at the large black man about his age. *Michael. His name is Michael. He had heard that...from...* Suddenly he couldn't remember. It had been too long ago. He looked around at the candles being lit in the windows of the homes and businesses.

"Efficiency. It's more efficient to put ashes into farmland than to put bodies in a graveyard."

Michael nodded, slowly. "Yeeees? It is..."

The man's response made James snort a laugh, then that snort pulled out a chuckle. Within a few breaths, he found himself laughing at the strangeness of his own comment. This man had stayed by him and handed him water for ten straight hours and all he had said to Michael all day was the occasional thank you. Now, out of nowhere, *efficiency.*

Michael watched him, smiling and yet still nervous. When James calmed a bit, he nodded. "Feel better?"

James nodded. "Yeah, but my back is sore as hell." His stomach growled. "And apparently I'm hungry."

"I think we can take care of both." Michael waved at James to follow and started walking towards the castle. "C'mon."

As they walked, James saw several people coming down from the castle. He frowned. "Was there a service and I missed it?"

Michael shook his head. "No, just dinner. But I feel safe in saying that there will still be food for us."

James watched people walk by with small baskets of rolls and fruit. "Do they feed the whole town every night?"

"Yeah."

"How? How can they afford to?"

Michael nodded towards the businesses. "Everyone pitches in. Each business makes ten of their specialty each day for the castle. The castle dispenses it to those who need it. Blacksmith makes nails, baker makes rolls, dairy brings milk. It all goes out to everyone, and everyone benefits from it."

"How do they make any profit?"

"Apparently, that's not the point. Because the community supports each other, everyone is taken care of by one another."

"What about the old, the sick?"

"I asked that question last night. The old contribute until they are called to Summerland. Then, the Bringer of Death calls them to the soil and they say their goodbyes and walk into the dirt. The Land consumes them. If a person is too sick to live, they can ask the Land to take them too. If they have fulfilled their purpose, the Land consumes them. If they have not, the Land will not take them. They return to carry on until they fulfill their role."

"They actually *see* this, or do they wander into the woods and die in the forest, torn apart by animals?"

"I don't know. I haven't seen it myself. All I can say is that, if you are not part of this Land, it will not even take your blood, much less your corpse." Michael shuddered. "That part I *have* seen myself."

"When?"

"An execution yesterday. The blood fell from both the body and head, but not a single drop soaked into the ground. They said if they dug a hole to bury it, it would be spit out by the Land."

"What did they do with the body then?"

"Burned it, at least the head. I didn't see what they did with the body. Probably the same."

"What did he do, do you know?"

"Tried to kill Catriona's son."

James blinked, puzzled. "What? Why?"

"To send a message to Alexander, the King of Mervolingia. The Church doesn't want him marrying her."

James had traveled by sea with Alexander, leaving his own ship behind to accommodate the man's obsession with this woman. He knew Alexander to be a good man, but this... this *overwhelming* drive to be with Catriona had caused the death of Gwen. James felt his rage returning.

"Well, I have the feeling that won't be a problem now."

Michael shook his head as they reached the gates of Ashstone. "No, I don't believe it will."

Tanglwyst opened her eyes, a long lingering stinging in her lower abdomen. Alexander stood in the doorway, speaking in a low voice to Tomas and Symonne. She couldn't make out the words, but Tomas saw her stir and nodded towards her. Symonne came over immediately, fetching a pitcher with water and a goblet from a nearby dresser.

"How are you doing, my dear?" Symonne sat carefully on the bed beside her charge.

"…thirsty…"

"I thought you might be. Here."

She poured water into a goblet. "Gentlemen, could one of you help her sit up a bit?"

Tomas started to move in but Alexander stopped him. "Please. I'm not recovering from a stab wound. I have this."

Tomas nodded, holding his bandaged stomach.

"You shouldn't even be up right now." Alexander nudged his chin towards the kitchen. "Get back to bed."

"Well, stop being so noisy then." Tomas smiled as he shuffled off out of sight.

Symonne shook her head as Alexander bent over and helped Tanglwyst sit up. The pain shot through her and she hissed, very much awake now.

"*Saint's blood!*" He adjusted his hold on her. "Forgive me, my Lady. I don't have any of my ointments here. I can't help you heal faster, nor even ease the pain."

"Ugh… Then what good are you?" She tried to smile away the harsh jab, but she felt she probably failed.

"That's just the pain talking, Alexander. Don't you pay it any mind." Symonne held the cup up to Tanglwyst's lips and she sipped as best she could. Some dribbled down the sides of her mouth, wetting the blankets. "Oh, don't mind that. It's to be expected. You suffered a pretty lethal blow this morning. You're lucky Alexander was here to help you."

Tanglwyst eased back, not interested in drinking anymore. "Thank… you… Your Majesty…"

Symonne smiled, then frowned. "Your Majesty?"

Alexander shrugged. "You weren't supposed to tell people that, my Lady. That was our little secret."

Tanglwyst closed her eyes. "Sorry. I guess you... should have said that... in the first place..." She breathed through the sentence punctuated with pain. "What happened?"

Alexander cleared his throat. "You were attacked. A man came in and stabbed you." He touched her shoulder and Tanglwyst opened her eyes. "He's gone now. I'm going to stay right here beside you so he can't hurt you again."

Stabbed... That's right... I was stabbed. With my own knife, by Duncan. What did he say? "You used this on me." She sighed. Yes, I did. He was... drunk. Or sick. His touch felt like he had vomit on his hands and he stunk of rotten eggs. He tried to hurt me and yes, I had the knife in... But when I saw him the next day, he was fine. I thought it had been a nightmare.

"Where did he go?" Her voice was weak in her mouth but strong in her head.

"I drove him away. He won't be back."

"How do you know?"

Alexander took a deep breath which steadied his voice. "I don't. But I repelled him before. I will do it again and again. Whatever it takes to protect you, my Lady."

Protect me. She snorted. Ha. You cast a spell on me, used my loyalty to this kingdom against me, and planned to use me to hurt my own brother. You're not capable of protecting anyone. You're scum. She turned away from him and reached out for the goblet. Her stomach and nether regions screamed again and her hand dropped.

Alexander rolled her back and walked over to the other side of the bed. He got her cup and lifted it to her lips, holding her head. After she got a few more swallows in, she moved her head, shaking it to indicate she didn't want any more. The effort of holding up her head pulled on the cut muscles in her body, and she felt something give. She winced and Alexander set the cup back down.

"I need to check on your bandages." He pulled down the covers and touched her stomach. She felt the area there getting slightly damp, and he swore. He stood and left the room, coming back a moment later with a handful of gauze. He placed it on the area where the pain was punching her and pressed down. The pain increased a bit, then dulled.

45

She grunted in response, then breathed through it again. "So, am I going to die?"

"I hope not, but I don't have any of my regular supplies with me. Luckily, your friend has an entire hospital's worth of healing herbs and ointments here. I think she has something that will work, provided I can stop you from pulling your stitches out." He was intent upon dealing with her wound. "But it probably wouldn't hurt to ask for a bit of help from whomever you pray to."

She snorted again, more gently this time. "If St. Brigit won't help you, a healer, on her feast day, I doubt I could appeal to her more."

"You might be surprised, my Lady." He glanced at her and smiled.

For a moment, his smile felt like the ones he gave her during the winter, when they played with the princess, Marie Elizabeth. She had fallen in love with him then. When Nicolai returned to her, begging for her to take him back, she almost sent him back to his wife, Catriona, because she had moved on. But then Alan came to the palace and Alexander had suddenly forgotten her. Tanglwyst now knew that Alexander had loved Catriona as well. She had never been important to him, merely nearby.

And now, Catriona had taken Nicolai from her, and killed him. Michael had been telling Gwen that fact one night on their way to this place, when they thought she was asleep. At the time, she hadn't cared. She had been under the Summoning Spell Alexander had cast. The spell only worked upon those whose fealty the Crown held and he used it to get her to come to him in Caratia. She hadn't cared then because the only thing that had mattered in the world was her love for *Alexander*.

Now, that seemed so long ago.

She coughed, and then coughed again. The contractions of the response ripped at her abdomen and she felt a gush of fluid burst beneath Alexander's fingers. White spots exploded behind her eyes and she passed out.

Five

I was given food and shelter, and asked
to go again to them the next day.
-The Longsword of the Orphans

"Symonne!"

The heavy woman ran into Tanglwyst's room. "What do you need?"

"I think an interior stitch snapped."

Symonne frowned. "I was afraid that cat gut was too stiff. It had been in there a while."

"Do you have anything else?"

She shook her head. "Sewing thread but that always causes a fever with internal injuries."

"I might be willing to risk it. She's healthy otherwise."

"Well, not right now, not after the horse threw her."

Alexander looked up at Symonne. "Horse? What horse?"

"That's why she didn't leave with her friends. A horse threw her off at high speed going down the other side into Caratia. Stumbled and killed itself, falling off the cliff. She was lucky she didn't go right with it. She didn't come away unscathed though."

Alexander looked down, then moved Tanglwyst's limp body onto her side. He had not noticed the large bruises on her back when he was operating before. The interior damage was going to have trouble healing because her body was already exhausted from healing a previous injury.

He almost cried, and gently rolled her back onto her back. The bleeding was slowing but now, he felt it was only a matter of time.

"What about that thing you did for me?"

He looked up at the innkeeper woman. "That was only something I could do once."

"Why?"

"*Because that's what the Saint who granted it to me said.*" He stood and started pacing. "St. Brigit told me I had one use, and to use it wisely."

"And you spent it on *me?*" Symonne spread her arms. "Why?"

"Because you were an innocent in this. You didn't do anything to deserve this."

Symonne gestured to Tanglwyst. "Did she?"

Alexander looked at his friend. "Well, no, but she at least knew the parties involved."

"And that acquaintance made her worth killing and me worth saving?"

"No, but…" He ran his fingers through his hair, his other hand on his hip as he switched directions, back and forth. "I just felt you were… not someone stained by all this."

"Stained by *what?*"

"*Me! Stained by me!*" He stopped and looked at Symonne but pointed at Tanglwyst. "That woman *cared* for me. She made me feel like I could get through the worst time in my life. But I abandoned her so I could pursue the woman I have loved for ten years. A woman who is, right now, being bedded by *that woman's brother.* When Brigit told me I had to stop pursuing my beloved in order to fulfill Heaven's will, I denied her. I said I didn't want to serve Heaven.

"So St. Brigit held a little baby girl hostage. A girl who had been brutalized. I had the chance to save this child, but only if I allowed Catriona to go. To leave my life and my world. I let her go, to heal this child and her village. But I… lied… I didn't stop tracking Catriona. Instead, I left a hundred wounded and sick behind and went on to commit other atrocities in the name of *love.*

"But it was all for naught. When I got there, when I spoke to her, I had lost her. I had lost this beautiful dark angel. Now, all I have left is kowtowing to the whims of Heaven and trying to sit a throne and wear a crown *I never wanted.*"

He sat down, rubbing his face. "And now, this lady will die because this morning, when the man who loved her stabbed her, St. Brigit made me choose again to leave behind Catriona. She gave me *one* chance to heal the woman Heaven had been throwing at me for almost a year. And I decided not to."

He looked at Symonne. "Because I wasn't going to do what Heaven wanted."

Symonne stood, holding her hands, her face stony and unreadable. "Alexander, you've been through a lot. You need to rest. Take the room at the end of the hall. Sleep. Tomorrow, you should be on your way."

He looked at the former nurse. "What about..."

"I'll handle them. I know how."

He looked around for something to say but she interrupted him.

"I'll make sure you can get yourself down the mountain okay. You might even contact the guard at Cliffbase and send a message to your people to come get you. But you need to leave this place."

"Why?"

She took a deep breath. "Because this is Caratia, and you just revealed an obsession with our Stâpâna. And she can find you here."

Alexander paled at the idea of what Catriona would do to him if she caught him in her country. Could she teleport around, like Duncan? Probably not. But that didn't mean she couldn't ride in here and cut him down. He stood and nodded.

"Thank you, Symonne."

The woman nodded and the King went to his room.

Raven stood before the cliff and smiled. He gestured to it. "Here we are!"

Octavius was exhausted and his feet were sore from the trek. "Yippee." He sat down on a stump.

Raven frowned. "You tired?"

Octavius just waved a hand. "Nah. Just haven't eaten or drank anything since we left."

"Oh. You should do that." He pointed to a spot directly behind the stump.

Octavius looked behind him and saw a spring bubbling through the ground into a small rock basin. He fell over himself to get to it and planted his face directly into the water. He drank and drank for several minutes, worried he would end up vomiting it all up from overdoing it. Sure enough, he felt it overwhelm him and he managed to get away from the water source before losing all he had consumed.

He decided to try again, easing into the fill. It worked this time and he was able to drink and keep it down. He started sweating within minutes and had to pee a few minutes after that. After he took care of all that, he drank more water, then went over to Raven.

"So, what's the plan?"

"Well! We open up a passage through here, then walk on through."

"Tomorrow?"

"Tomorrow we should be in Mande."

"No," Octavius pointed to the dark sky, "can we do it tomorrow?"

Raven looked up. "Oh. Um, yes, yes of course we can."

"Great." Octavius flopped onto the ground and fell asleep almost instantly. He felt the ground moving a bit later and rolled over onto his side. The ground was a little less painful this way and he almost felt like he could smell the sheets from his bed on the ship. He felt someone stroke his head and then remembered the shard in his pocket.

He rolled onto his back and pulled the leaf out. The cloth was still there and the leaf was still intact. He set it beside him, his hand upon it, and went back to sleep.

James put another bite of roll in his mouth, the only sound was the munching and swallowing between him and Michael. The clatter of pots in the kitchen as they were put on wooden tables to dry overnight coupled with the sounds of people murmuring outside in the gardens. These were all distant, out of this room. Michael and James were the only ones left in the room and the only ones at the remaining table still hosting lit candles.

The sound of footsteps on the stone near the door caught his attention and he saw Catriona escort in the man from the wall. They both paled when they saw James and stopped. The man started to turn back, but Catriona made him come in. They came over and stood across the table from them.

"Myrgen, how are you doing?" Michael's deep voice showed concern for the thinner man.

Myrgen cleared his throat. "I, uh," Myrgen glanced at James, then back to Michael, "not so good, my friend." He closed his eyes, then steadied himself with a deep breath. "You're James, right?"

James swallowed and stood. "Yes."

"I wanted to apologize. I never meant to hurt your sister…"

James nodded. "I know. It wasn't your fault. Gwen stepped in front of the arrow and saved Alexander."

Michael sighed. "Does anyone know why?"

Catriona nodded. "She was protecting my son. Alexander named Tib as his heir. If he dies before bearing an heir of his own, Tib would be given the throne of Mervolingia. A Caratian on the throne of Mervolingia would cause a civil war and even if he abdicated, the war would still erupt as nobles vied for control. Gwen saved thousands of lives with her sacrifice."

"Hundreds of thousands." Myrgen's eyes glassed over as a memory seemed to surface. "More than the St. Michael's Day Massacre."

"I can tell you her opinion of Alexander had changed from her former one." Michael picked up his goblet of wine. "I learned that on the trip overland here." He took a few swallows.

"James," Catriona looked at the young sailor, "do you know how he got here? You two were familiar with each other in the courtyard."

James gestured to the benches on the other side of the table and they all sat. "I was the captain of the ship he used to follow you here."

"How did you get through the Maw of Calista?"

"We left my ship at the mouth of rocks. They've long since returned to Naplles by now."

"Did you swim?"

"Rowboat."

Myrgen glanced at Catriona, mirroring her puzzled look. "He *is* still Catherine D'Medici's son. How did he not get rejected from the shores?"

"Moreover, how did he get past the sharks?" Catriona leaned forward. "Everyone must give their blood to the sharks to prove their lineage. Willingly or unwillingly."

"His blood was purified. He has a thing called the Power of Sovereignty that makes his blood one with the land and people of Mervolingia. He becomes exclusively Mervolingian. No other bloodlines."

Myrgen nodded. "We saw that in action as well, when he received it from his brother. It gives him the power to rule."

Michael leaned forward. "Could it give him the power to summon someone to him?"

Myrgen shrugged. "I have no idea. I knew about the Rite that transferred the power only because each chancellor knows where it is kept. It is entrusted to them and they must put it somewhere known only to them. I got it from the notes of the previous chancellor since I took office after he died. Other than that," he shrugged again, "I have no idea of the King's power parameters."

"Gwen told me on the way here that Alexander placed a Summons upon Tanglwyst. It made her obsessed with getting to Alexander. She said several times that he needed her to save him. She even told us that she was in love with him."

Catriona tilted her head. "Was that part of the Summons?"

"No. Apparently, she and Alexander spent time together this winter."

Catriona looked away, guilt on her face. Myrgen, likewise, seemed to understand something about that. James flicked his gaze back and forth between them. "What?"

Myrgen spoke up first, though his eyes stayed on the candles nearby instead of James. "Catriona and Nicolai were married a decade ago. Then she got captured and he thought she was dead. Later, she finally returned home after escaping captivity to be told *he* had passed away the previous season. They thought themselves widowed, and moved on. Catriona got together with Alexander, Tangl with Nicolai. Last summer, Nicolai and Catriona ran into each other. They decided to try to be a couple again."

Catriona sighed. "It ended up being a disaster. We didn't know each other at all, so trying to act like our lives had not moved on just made everything worse."

James sat back. "Why would you try again?"

Myrgen and Catriona looked at James. Then Myrgen turned to her, elbow on the table. "Yeah. Why *would* you do that? It had been seven years."

James scoffed. *"Seven years? Really?"* He shook his head. "I've never tried to pick things up again after one because of the time passing. I can't even imagine what it would be like after seven."

"I... he had stayed loyal to my memory... I had mourned him... we felt like we had suddenly..."

Michael smiled. "You felt guilty for being happy that each other was dead."

"I was *hardly* happy he was dead." She folded her hands in front of her. "But yes. To put it simply, I had finally let go of the guilt I felt of not being there when he died. He had finally let go of the guilt he felt for never rescuing me. We had stopped blaming ourselves and the reward was falling in love again.

"Then we saw each other and instantly, all that guilt came flooding back. We even knew it wouldn't work. When we talked in the street right after it happened, we discussed how happy we were now. If I hadn't mentioned Tib, we would have stayed with our new loves. In fact, had he not reacted like he should be a father to him, I think we still would have just joined households and had a larger family."

James frowned. "And we wouldn't be here now."

Catriona looked at James and everything grew very still. She looked at her hands, then rose. "Excuse me, gentlemen. I need to check on Tib. I'm sorry about your sister, James." She stepped over the bench and walked to the door.

Myrgen watched her go, then leaned forward his hands knitting together to press against his lips. He looked at James and Michael. "Do you have any idea where Alexander and Duncan would have gone?"

James shook his head, picking apart his roll. "I supposed they could have returned to Patras, or to my ship, though Duncan had never been there and he was the one with the amulet." He took a deep breath. "Alexander's going to have his hands full there."

Michael looked at James. "Why?"

Myrgen closed his eyes. "Because the amulets are addicting."

James stopped. "You know about them?"

"I ran across a woman in the grips of one. She walked with me all the way here. She had almost broken the hold of the thing, finally getting it off her neck, with some help. But then she had to use it again to save her life and I haven't seen her since."

"They corrupt anyone who uses them. The more they use it, the more it possesses them."

"And the more it destroys them." Myrgen nodded again, then looked over at the door Catriona had left through.

"So, you need to go take care of that?" James wasn't trying to sound snide but he worried it came off that way.

"I will soon enough. She has a real problem with blaming herself. With so many things going wrong, she's already neck deep in it. Alexander destroyed her ship and the Fae housed within it."

James blinked, shocked. "There was a Fae on her ship?"

"The ship was like her body. When Alexander fired upon the *Enigma* as it fled St. Marguerite, a cannonball shot through the stained glass window in her quarters and destroyed it. The onslaught started a fire, destroyed weeks' worth of supplies, and damaged the hull. By the time she got to port here, she had just enough energy to get in dry dock before she died, apparently. Now, it's just a ship."

"Did you ever see her?"

Myrgen nodded. "She even let me see her wounded face and bandaged body. It was horrible."

"You saw a damaged Fae?" James was stunned. "Fae never let you see their true form. If you see it, you can change it."

"I think, at that point, she didn't have a choice. She was so weak." Myrgen swallowed.

James could see the man was very moved by the situation. He wished Gwen were here to explain what Myrgen had seen. But she would have been very close to whatever Fae was on the *Enigma* and would have been devastated by this news.

Doesn't matter now. They're both gone.

Michael looked at the door, then back at Myrgen. "Do you think they have another room, for James?"

Myrgen raised his eyebrows. "Oh yeah, I am sure they do. Let me find out. I'll be right back."

"I can stay at the inn down the road."

"I doubt that." Myrgen smiled as he stood and climbed over the bench. "From what I've seen of this family, that just wouldn't be allowed. Be right back."

James watched him go, then turned back to Michael. "You said you traveled with Tanglwyst. Where is she?"

"She's probably on her way to the Papal City by now. She fell off a horse and got bruised up. We left her at an inn at the pass between Caratia and Mervolingia. Once she felt up to it, she planned to go to her grandfather's home at the Papal City."

"Did Duncan know where she was?"

Michael shook his head. "I don't think so. Why?"

James remembered Duncan's flayed penis Alexander healed and shuddered. He also remembered Tanglwyst's hold on his friend. "He was pretty close to her. I figured he might try to find her."

Myrgen returned a minute later as the two men finished their bread and cheese. He nodded. "I have one for you. Just next door to the one Michael is using. Clean linens and everything. I'll show you when you're ready."

The two men stood and gulped the last of their water almost in unison, then took their plates to the kitchen board. A couple of burly men nodded at them through the pass window and they waved their thanks to the men.

"It was delicious." Michael's voice bellowed through the kitchen and the men smiled and nodded.

They met up with Myrgen at the door. He led them to the second floor of Ashstone and turned east to the room marked with an Iron Archway. Myrgen walked past this one to another door.

"This is Michael's, that one down there is yours. It's called the Bronze Archway."

James looked at it and saw it did, indeed, have a bronze arch around and over the door. He looked at Michael's, which had a steel one demarking his.

"There's also a sizable bath if you continue down this corridor and turn left. At the end."

Michael nodded. "I can show him."

Myrgen patted Michael on the shoulder. "I should check on Catriona. See if she needs anything. I'll see you in the morning."

Michael nodded and entered his room, closing the door behind him.

James put a hand on Myrgen's shoulder, holding him back a few steps from the Steel Arch. "Look, I understand that you weren't aiming for Gwen and you didn't mean to…"

Myrgen nodded, not needing to hear the words any more than James really needed to repeat them.

"Just understand that, periodically, I'm still gonna blame you for it. It'll pass, but it's still gonna happen. I just wanted to warn you."

"I will, periodically, do the same myself." Myrgen patted the young man's hand. "I can't guarantee it will pass though."

The two men nodded, and parted company.

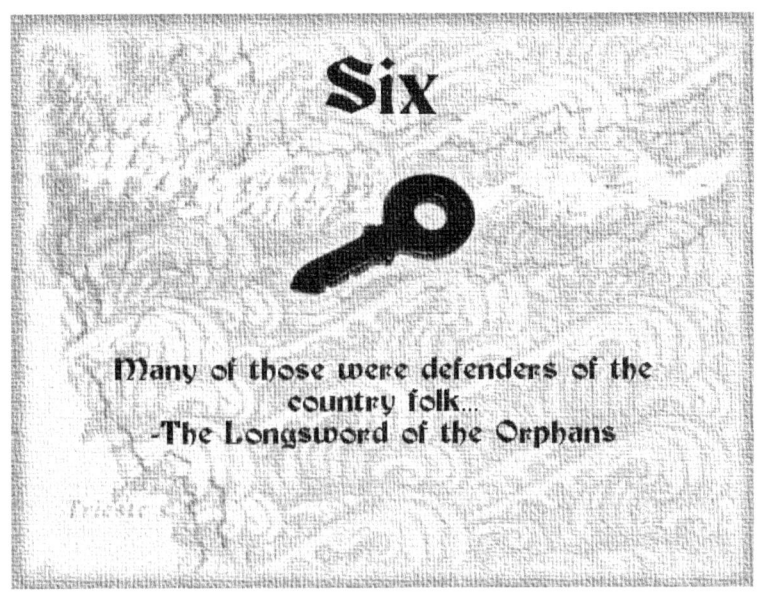

Six

Many of those were defenders of the country folk...
-The Longsword of the Orphans

Myrgen walked down the stone hallways to Tib's door and got there just as Catriona was closing it gently. She looked at him and gave a small nod.

"How is he?"

"Sleeping. I knew he would be. Luckily, the dog has learned to not bark and wake him if I come in."

"Did he wake up on his own?"

"No."

He took her hand. "Did that help?"

She leaned back against the wall. "I think he's the only one not judging me right now."

"No one is judging you right now." He lifted her chin to look in her eyes. "Except you."

"Well, that's enough."

"*Llaldeen*, you need to stop doing this. Blaming yourself has not served you even once. You keep letting guilt tie you to things you need to escape."

"*Llaldeen?*"

He smiled, and put his forehead to hers. "It's Yndian, for 'lantern'." He kissed her forehead and looked at her again. "When I have been in darkness, you have always been my light. In prison in Patras, in St. Marguerite, when the Shadowwalker held me in the dark, even under the palace, you have always been the light that guided me, protected me. I don't know the Caratian word for it, but I think it would be too mundane to those here. It wouldn't convey the magnitude with which you have changed my life."

Tears dripped from her eyes and she clutched him to her, kissing him. He welcomed her embrace, and let the darkness envelope them, dissolving in this white light between them.

Drake sat at the enormous desk in his study, the giant oak doors dark and brooding in the sizable room. He was surrounded by all the artifacts the Land had given them. A portrait of the First Dûcesa stood above the mantle of the fireplace. Her hair was long and straight, blowing behind her. Her dark jade eyes wielded great wisdom while also wielding great power, as all around her, the earth erupted in flames, killing already dead monsters that had returned to slay the living. Behind and beside her, his back to her, was a large, dark-featured man with broad shoulders, his brown shirt torn from fighting and spotted with blood. He wielded a white granite sword.

Along the wall to the north and south of the great doors were shelves that held books and scrolls. The upper half of both shelves were large pigeon holes storing scrolls, maps, and plans. Some of them were still sealed, gifts from mages across the Sea of Blood. Some were training manuals on Nubian fighting techniques. Most were maps of the world from different time frames, dating back to before the cliffs were raised.

The center of the room housed the desk, a bar with goblets and brandies, and then a sitting area to enjoy the warmth of the fire. The chairs were large and comfortable, and there were three facing each other near the fireplace, small tables by the right side of each. A larger sofa faced two more chairs of similar design, making a separate conversation area with the bar along the back of the sofa. The chairs by the fire could be moved to a more sociable arrangement easily enough, but this was where the Dûce, Dûcesa, and Stâpâna often sat and talked.

On the southern end of the room was a large window that looked over the harbor and southern borders of Caratia. Drake stood and walked over to it, leaning his forearm on the molding around the glass. The lights from the dry dock illuminated Catriona's ship, and street lanterns lit the walkways around town. He could see the Town Square where the final Trials of Succession would be held, the grass there kept tidy by sheep attended by a gardener as well as a shepherd. There were still a few folks walking around, and he was happy that people felt safe even after the attempt on Tib's life.

His biggest worry had been that the people would attack the Augustinian church near the docks over the incident. The monk who tried to kill the boy had declared it the will of the Archbishop of Patras, as a warning to the king of Mervolingia to stop his pursuit of the Stâpâna for his queen. It was a good idea. Had Tib been killed, Alexander's attempts to coerce her into that role would have turned against him. She would have slain Alexander on sight.

Drake wasn't certain that still wasn't the best course to take. Alexander had been the subject of much speculation through the years that Catriona returned home for the winter. Gwen had always come home with her, spending much of the winter here. The first journey of the year was always to Glarren to visit her family. They were probably already looking for the *Enigma* every day. He hoped Catriona or Gwen had let her family know the plans of the winter had changed their course.

The winter had been quiet and lonely around Ashstone. Tib, Gwen, and Catriona had stayed in Patras, and Anika and the rest of the folks around the keep had been a bit more somber because of it. A lot more cleaning got done as people busied themselves. Anika herself cleaned the painting of the First Dûcesa as well as the smaller one of the Third Dûcesa over on the west wall, near the southern window. Her jade eyes were the same as the First Dûcesa and the Hearthstone glittered at her neck, as alive as it was against Anika's skin now.

According to legend, the Third Dûcesa had gone to Sea and died in a storm. All on her was lost, including the Heartstone. However, she must have known this was her destiny because she wrote the Articles of Governance, the Land's instructions to her people. The Dûces, Dûcesas, Stâpâns, and Stâpânas all knew the Land's instructions for them, for the Land told them upon their choosing. However, on occasion, an outsider would ask after the traditions.

Gwen had read the articles once, long ago, but Tib had been put to bed with them more often than not, at his request. He said he got great dreams of the stories that caused the different customs to come to pass. Drake felt he would make a fine ambassador for Caratia, should the Land guide him that way.

A statue of the Second Dûcesa, her head bowed and eyes closed, flanked Drake now. Her Stâpân had carved it in memorial, since he had been the only one to ever see her alive. The Stone Bow leaned against the statue, blood still staining the bowstring.

Myrgen had been so intent on protecting the Stâpâna that he had bled down the string, not even noticing that he was holding the relic bow. He had it in his hands and he used it because it didn't occur to him that he couldn't. When Drake saw the arrow that had pierced Gwen's body, he knew from whence it had come. No other arrows in the world were made of stone.

Drake had pulled that bow once before, to protect Anika. She was already Dûcesa, having been chosen by the land when plowing her father's farm. The plow had turned up the Heartstone and when she picked it up, The Land told her that she was now Dûcesa. She ruled Caratia for three years before Drake met her. He was in the woods with some other men from Caratia's army. They had tracked a bear to a lodge in the woods and came upon the Stone Bow laying on the ground.

Drake had picked it up, shocked to find it stone, and slung it over his shoulder. He had figured it dropped from a passing rider on their way to Zara. Then they heard the roar of the bear and came upon the animal stalking a frightened child. The child screamed and Anika had run up between the two, standing her full height before it. She had not even reached the bear's chest.

But little women were frightening, and she was unwavering. The bear dropped back to all fours and walked off. At that moment, Drake realized he had pulled the bow from his shoulder and nocked an arrow, drawing down on the creature. He eased the string back, then had run up to the woman as she comforted the child.

He remembered fondly the chiding he had given her for trying to take on a bear and the vicious counter-attack she had launched. They had gone through much during that summer together and by the time the Trials came, she had cried and ran to him when he had been chosen.

Now the Trials were upon them again, and Drake could not shake the feeling that these were more crucial than ever before. That Myrgen had drawn the Bow meant he was in the same position as Drake had been, that of protector. It might mean he was not destined to be Dûce, but Stâpân. If so, then Catriona would stand on the stones during the final Trial. Drake hoped they understood their roles. If Myrgen stood when Catriona did, then he would be killed.

Myrgen rolled off of Catriona and the two sighed in unison. Myrgen looked at her, both their hair in tangled messes. "Was that inappropriate? I wasn't trying for that when I came to talk to you."

Catriona flopped her head back and forth. "I think it was exactly what I needed." She ended her gesture by rolling onto her side to face him. "You're right, you know."

He turned likewise to face her, propping his head in his hand and stroking a strand of her hair away from where it was threatening her eye. "About what?"

"I hold myself accountable for everything that happens. I have felt guilt my entire adult life, as far back as I can remember."

"What about when you were younger? What happened that you would do that? Did you lose a parent and have to take care of your siblings or something?"

She shook her head. "I don't remember my childhood. Nicolai and his mother found me in the woods of Latia with no memory."

Myrgen frowned. "None?" He looked away, thinking. "Have you recovered any of it since then?"

She shook her head. "I am completely blank before that."

"That's extremely unusual, Catriona. Most people who lose that much memory have suffered some sort of mental or physical damage. That much of your life missing means something very bad happened to you."

"Worse than all that's happened since?"

He blinked, then sat up. "No. You have lived through things that, taken individually, have broken people. I know. I broke a couple."

She smiled at him. "You're not bragging, are you?"

He smiled too. He knew she could just read him and tell everything he had done. It was something he appreciated, in fact. "No," his face turned more somber, "but it does worry me a little. You didn't just appear out of the ground. Someone put you there. When was the last time you were there?"

She stroked his forearm and shifted her head on her hand. "On our way here. We passed between Latia and the Fingers of Mande. Usually, I go by Yndia but I didn't have time."

"And you got nothing?"

She shook her head. "It has never really bothered me. I have always believed that I would remember when I was supposed to. Not before."

He kissed her. "You seem fine to me. And I can't imagine you any different. But you do need to stop blaming yourself. Gwen wasn't your fault, no matter how far back you go. It was an accident, a horrible, horrible accident. But it isn't your fault."

She squinted for a second. "How often have you told yourself that?"

"I just did." He sighed and rolled onto his back. She snuggled down into his arms. "But so far, it numbers in the hundreds. At first, I thought I needed to repeat it so I wouldn't kill Alexander. Then I did it so I wouldn't kill myself. Now, it seems like I'm trying to convince myself, which means I'm still assigning blame. It would be wrong to say it was Gwen's fault. She was protecting Tib. In the end, I come back to hating Alexander."

"Well, you kind of start there too, so that's not unexpected."

He shrugged. "Makes it an easy trick." He looked at the top of her head. "So, you went into that chamber to 'find out something'. What were you doing?"

"Talking to the Land."

"Don't you do that all the time?"

"This was more of a face to face meeting."

Myrgen blinked. "Uh…you can talk to rocks? And they talk back?"

"Mhm."

"You know, only crazy people talk to inanimate objects and hold conversations with them."

"I'm going to sleep now, Myrgen."

He lay back, closing his eyes. "It's true."

"Good night Myrgen."

"Just saying."

He felt her smile on his chest and he stroked her hair until they fell asleep.

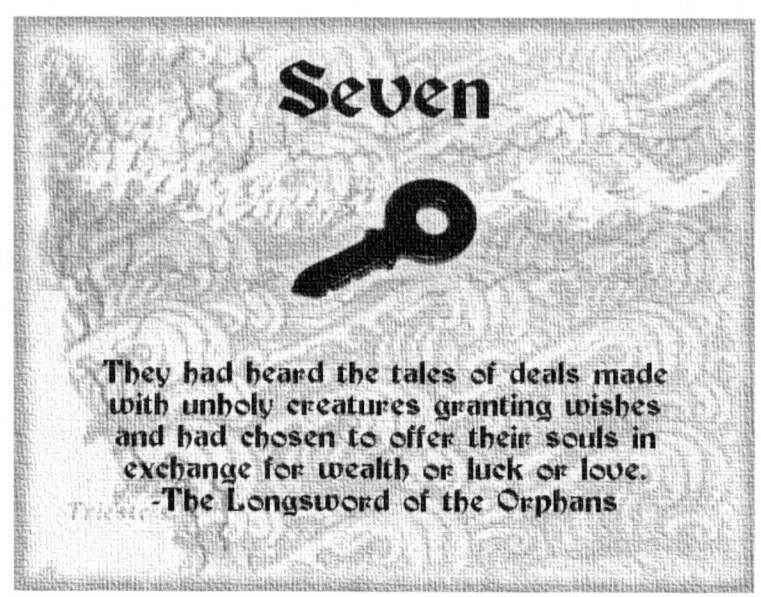

Seven

They had heard the tales of deals made
with unholy creatures granting wishes
and had chosen to offer their souls in
exchange for wealth or luck or love.
-The Longsword of the Orphans

Alexander lay in his bed, trying to sleep. Symonne's words haunted him. He knew that killing Gwen wasn't his doing, that she was only dead because Myrgen shot her. His heart thumped in excitement at the idea of Catriona coming there. If they were face to face, without Myrgen around, he could turn her against him in an hour. He could talk her into bed again, talk her into coming with him. If he got her pregnant before they got to Patras, she would be his forever. And if he couldn't talk her into it, well, he had Cyprian…

He sat up.

What the hell? Why am I turning into such a monster? He checked his body to make sure he wasn't somehow in possession of the amulet again, then turned and sat on the edge of the bed. He ran his fingers through his hair, then got up. The window showed a clear, starry night. The moon was still visible, and from here, he imagined he could see all the way to the Sea of St. Erasmus. He couldn't, not really. He could see a rather sizable forest, and glittering lights in the small town below. He saw a few more glints of light in the trees, probably hunters or woodman's cabins.

He looked to the north and could see, on the horizon, the glow of the Papal City. He could see no lights there, but its opulence caused the ground to cast a light like the first vestiges of dawn. Were he higher in the air, he was sure he could see the tall spire of the Papal Palace. That city spread out for miles, about the size of Patras. But unlike Patras, it had no waterways for trade. Everything was overland. Their water supply was all from underground springs.

In the center of the Papal Palace was the Spring of St. Brigit. It was where she had ascended into Heaven at the moment of her death. The spring was possessed of healing properties and anyone who was bathed in the water was cured of any ailment. Many vendors sold bottles of the water from the spring, but he knew the properties only worked from the source. Once taken from it, it turned into simple holy water. That didn't stop the Church from selling it, and it didn't stop people from buying it. Sometimes, all you needed was to believe it helped for a cure to work.

He thought about Tanglwyst, her injuries so severe, he wasn't sure she would survive without his help. He knew Symonne was more than capable, but she had Tomas to care for, and the inn. Before that, she had help. After Alexander's arrival, she had two patients and had barely survived an attack herself. She really didn't have the resources to handle it alone.

He got up and went into the common room. It was quiet, and he felt like he could slip out and be gone before anyone knew he was missing. For once, it sounded like a good idea. His fantasies about convincing Catriona to be with him were just past the brink of insanity. He, whether he wanted to admit it or not, was responsible for the state of Gwen's body at the end. James had told him not to touch her while the shadows infected him, but he had forgotten that in his panic. Catriona was never going to forgive him for that, and that meant that, yes, he probably should be on his way.

He went back into his room and pulled on his boots. He had no baggage to pack, no servants to corral. He could be out the door without a single preparation besides his own mind. This was a freedom he had not felt in a year, when he last escaped the palace in Patras to seek Catriona once again. He closed his door and started for the exit.

He heard Tanglwyst cough in her room, and he stopped. She coughed again, and he couldn't tell if there might be fluid building up there. Drowning from an infection was a terrible way to go, and he knew Symonne probably had a few field medic tricks to make the person more comfortable as they died. It was a painful thought, losing Tanglwyst. She had been so kind to him over the winter. He turned to look at her door.

Couldn't hurt to check in on her. I should at least say goodbye. I would hate myself if she died and I had not at least told her thank you for the tea parties.

For over half the winter, his niece Marie-Elizabeth, or Emmy as they called her, had been devoted to tea parties. She had at least one a day and the kitchens had indulged her with tiny cakes, treats, and finger foods. Tanglwyst had stayed at the palace to tend Elizabeth, the queen, and in all the free time that allowed, she and Emmy had become quite close. Alexander had somehow, in the face of all that competition, remained Emmy's favorite and he and Tanglwyst had also grown close. Even after Emmy's games moved on to other themes, he and Tanglwyst had enjoyed a few more tea parties, just the two of them.

He smiled at the memory as he put his hand on the knob to her door. *I'll just check in. No harm done. Then I'll be on my way.* He eased the door open and saw something flit across the moonlight streaming in from the window. It looked like a shadow for a second, like a bird perhaps. Then he looked at the bed and saw the figure, tall and dark, too tall to be Symonne, too upright to be Tomas.

It was Duncan.

Duncan looked at Alexander and snarled, his hand on Tanglwyst's sternum. Black claws were embedded in the flesh and her eyes were open and going glassy. Her back arched and she coughed as he drained the final gasps from her lungs.

Alexander yelled and his Power burst out, knocking Duncan hard against the wall. He disappeared and the room suddenly reeked of sulfur. Alexander put his sleeve to his nose as his eyes teared up from the stench. He turned from the stink and ran the few steps to the window, opening it to air the place out. In the glow of his Power and the moonlight, he saw his friend giving her last breaths to the night air.

"No…" Alexander was at her side and he put his hands to the new wounds. They were horrifying, oozing blackness like the slime that had come from Gwen's body. His mind forced the image of Tanglwyst decomposing in his arms and his eyes bled forth fresh tears. "No…"

Her body was brittle, like Duncan had sucked the marrow from her bones. She coughed, and he heard her ribs crack, even though the expulsion of air had been almost negligible. He remembered Nicolai

66

convulsing on the street, snapping his own spine in his last moments, and Alexander wiped away the tears with the back of his sleeve.

She turned her head and looked through him, her eyes clearing now that Duncan was gone. She blinked, and fought to focus on him. "…Al…ex…"

"Shh, my Lady. Don't try to speak." He touched her face, and the gesture tugged her skin. It tore like gossamer. He shuddered, and the spasms caused more damage. He jerked his hand away to keep from hurting her more, but she didn't even call out from the pain. He took her hand and bent down, kissing it. He didn't dare lift it lest it break in the effort.

She raised a finger to touch his lips. "…I… miss… our… tea…"

He nodded. "So do I. I never should have stopped attending them."

His Power pulsed, and he felt her fealty return. He knew she held that fealty to the Crown, to the country, but he had lost that fealty as King. It was her final gift to him. He looked down at the black stains on her skin, like Duncan's claws had been dipped in ink. He could see her heart beating in her chest beneath near-translucent flesh. He watched it slow, almost stop. The blackness was spreading, but he feared he would not see it get much farther. She would not live if it touched her heart.

He screamed. *"No!"*

He put his hand upon her and pushed all his will into saving her. He was not on holy ground, according to Heaven, but he was not going to give up until she was absolutely gone. His Power was designed to protect and save him. Maybe if he gave it to her…

He blinked. He could. He could *choose* to let it go. Charles never had because he didn't want to damn Alexander, but it was a *choice*. He looked at her eyes as they began to close a final time, at the blood barely dripping from the new gash upon her cheek. He could just pour it into her, and be done with the whole mess. He could leave her to rule, and go back to the life he had lived before.

Abandoning her? Again?

He blinked.

No. I won't leave her side again.

He touched her heart and released the Power of Sovereignty, giving it to her. As he did so, he removed Catriona's son as his heir, naming Tanglwyst. Thus, the Power shifted to her. White light flowed into her skin, mouth, and eyes, filling her up and returning life to her. He felt the strength come back to her bones, felt the air return to her lungs. Her hair and skin brushed aside the lack of shimmer Duncan had drained from her, restoring her to full health again. As the last of his Power left him, he felt the sins of its control let go of his heart.

He exhaled, suddenly exhausted, and looked upon the Lady. Her eyes closed and she breathed easy, sleep taking her. A tiny, cute snore escaped her and she squeezed his hand. It had strength and the bones did not crack. He smiled, daring to lift it to his lips this time. She stirred, her eyes fluttering open.

"Alexander?"

"I'm here, My Lady. You rest. I'll be right here."

She nodded twice and slipped back into sleep.

Eight

He had confessed, they said, and had
sought absolution.
-The Longsword of the Orphans

Octavius woke to the morning light. The surroundings smelled like home and he felt for a moment Estelle's hair was brushing his nose. He opened his eyes. He was still on the ground of the Caratian forest, near the southern border. The sound of the spring nearby caused him to have to pee. He reluctantly stood, the time on the ground reflected in groaning muscles and a limping gait.

He appreciated more than anything the sleep he got. He felt Estelle's presence, which made him realize she was still there in that glass leaf. He looked at his hand and realized he must have set it down in the night. He returned to find it near where his head had lain and he picked it up and kissed it. He felt, as his eyes closed, the feel of her lips for just a second.

This was good. She was still around. If he was getting illusions, she was still giving them to him.

Raven was perched, literally, on a large rock by the sheer cliff rise. He looked like a large bird, which was not much different from his previous incarnation as a cat. Both would have been sitting on that rock in exactly the same way.

Octavius walked up to the man, almost missing Lauriel hiding in the grass next to the large stone. "Morning."

Raven snapped around to look at Octavius like he had completely forgotten he existed. "Oh. Hey! You're awake."

"So are you. Did you rest at all?"

"Um…" Raven put his hand to his chin. "I think…" He looked at Lauriel, who shook his head. "Hm. Apparently not."

Octavius smiled, and went over to the spring to get a drink and restore his body as best he could. He tried to figure out what he was going to do for food. He had seriously not expected for them to go through the forest, having brought money for an inn and meals, but he had not brought anything in the way of hard tack or dried rations. At that point in the voyage, though, things had been so empty, they had gone the last two days on stale water and no food. They pulled into town and everyone had practically jumped off the ship to devour the nearby fruit at the market stands.

He figured Raven was probably hungry too and decided to come right to the point. "Ok, what do you do for food?"

Raven reached into a pouch on his hip and held out a piece of jerky, his eyes never leaving the cliff. Octavius took it and broke his fast.

"What are you doing?"

"Waiting, for you." He looked at Octavius. "You ready to head out for the day?"

Octavius rubbed his face. He took a deep breath, and nodded. "Yup."

Raven bounced off the stone which evaporated back into the ground. Lauriel stood, shaking the dirt off his spines. They walked up to the cliff and Raven walked right up to it, like it didn't exist. As his foot touched the wall to step through, the earth fell away, like sand pouring from a wide mouthed glass. By the time he got to his knee, the dirt was gone, revealing an opening large enough for the companions to enter in single file.

Octavius shook off the morning shudder and entered the dark hole.

Alexander snapped awake as a strong, meaty hand patted his shoulder.

"Alexander, what are you doing in here?" Her voice was a whisper.

He looked at Tanglwyst, making sure she still slept. "I heard something in here. Feared the worst."

"Well, it's inappropriate for you to be alone with the lady. I will dismiss it out of healer's courtesy. But you need to get ready to take your leave."

He stood, extracting his hand from Tanglwyst's so as not to wake her. He motioned Symonne to walk outside to the common room, and closed the door behind him. "Yes, about that. I won't be going."

Symonne shifted her weight and folded her arms across her chest. "Is that so?"

"I'm not trying to be arrogant, my lady. You have at least one patient to care for and he was your help for running this inn. So, I'm going to stay until he's better and do his work here."

She frowned. "You? A king?"

"I hope you won't hold that against me."

Symonne nodded. "Fine. The wood pile is in back. I'll expect it split for the oven fires by noon."

He bowed. "It shall be done, my lady."

He ducked back into Tanglwyst's room, closing the door behind him. She was still sleeping and he checked her breathing to see how she was faring. Her skin color was almost restored though she had some scars on her sternum from the attack. The Power of Sovereignty didn't cure that. Sadly, it appeared she would still have a remembrance of this incident.

The Power.

He closed his eyes. He didn't want it back. The weight of the entire country sat on his soul when he held it, and from what he had learned from Charles, that was part of the Power. When he saw Charles on the ship recently, he was sleeping well and easy, moving without aching, and able to take interest in simple pleasures like cooking. The weight was gone from his soul just as surely as it was present in Alexander's.

Except for now. Now, that weight was gone again, and with it the corruption he had seen forming. It was even more blatant now that the Power was housed elsewhere. From the moment he opened the drawer in Charles' desk and saw the incomplete Writ of Destruction, he had felt that darkness. He had read it, and realized that Charles had not finished it, but it was clear for whom it was. All he had needed to do was sign it.

He had spread it out on the desk and pulled the King's Quill from its resting place. The Quill was always sharp, and the inkwell always full. Charles told him that one of the servants filled it, and sharpened the quill because the quill changed regularly. There was nothing inherently magical about any of that.

But Charles was wrong. In the fall, Alexander had gone into the room and tried to write a Writ of Destruction against Nicolai, right after Catriona had chosen the man instead of him. The Quill had not collected the ink for him. But when he had tried again, once Charles was "dead", once he knew he would be king, the Quill had taken the ink and Nicolai's name had appeared on the Writ in Alexander's hand.

He always wondered if that first act was going to define his reign, and with the Power now gone from him, he knew it had been true. When Marie had stayed his hand in touching Charles' tongue, stopping him from falling prey to the same death-mimicking agent she had used to free her beloved, they had spoken about the future. She had told Alexander that Charles was being poisoned by someone here and that he was going to die anyway. There was no way for Alexander to avoid taking the Crown. He was going to have to figure out what kind of king he would be.

It had not been necessary to think about his decision. If Charles was to be killed, better to have his death faked by Marie and he continue to be there for his family, than to truly be buried, leaving them alone. The Crown and Power of Sovereignty would still be in Alexander's possession. With the power of the throne, he could also have Catriona.

Alexander sighed.

That was not how it had worked out. With the stain of Nicolai's death on his soul, he had let more and more corruption, more and more selfishness fill him. Every act had been to serve his own ends, with precious few exceptions. He had healed one village, but set fire to another. He cured Duncan only to destroy Gwen. He had pursued an unwilling woman and forced another to...

He felt something on his cheek and brought up his hand to touch it. He looked upon the tear deposited there and looked again upon Tanglwyst. He could not put this burden upon her. She had been an unwilling pawn in this already. He put his hand upon hers and willed the Power of Sovereignty to return.

Nothing happened.

He frowned, and tried again.

Still nothing.

He put both his hands upon hers, closing his eyes and squeezing, trying to drain the Power from her. Still nothing filled his body.

Why isn't this working?

Then he realized what was wrong. The transfer of Power depended upon two things: One Willing Participant, though it did not matter if it was the giver or the receiver of the Power, and that the Recipient be the Heir of that Giver. Tanglwyst had not yet awakened. She did not yet know she possessed the Power. And she had not yet chosen an heir.

He opened his eyes and looked into hers.

"Alexander? What are you doing here?"

This is going to be awkward.

"You *what?*"

Alexander was on one knee before her. "I only did it to save your life."

Tanglwyst paced back and forth in the common room of the inn. Symonne poured hot water in mugs while Tomas rested in one of the hearth chairs. Their eyes did not leave the couple.

"Was that *truly* the only option you had?" She pointed to Symonne. "Was her skill insufficient? Or were you simply too impatient?"

Alexander chose wisely not to speak further but Tanglwyst was not yet spent in her ire. She stormed around the room, her booted feet punctuating her anger.

"And you have the *worst taste* in heirs, Alexander Angloume! Catriona's son? Have you truly been so amazingly obsessed with her that you jeopardized our entire *populace* by naming Alan your heir?"

He looked up at her. "I'm afraid so, my Queen."

She wheeled on him, her hand up as she pointed to him. "No. You don't get to call me that. Not now. Not ever. You *used* me to get out of ruling this kingdom so you could scamper off to chase that poor woman. I know her well enough to know that if she hasn't embraced you by now, she has a good reason not to. Right now, I'm willing to bet it's that she's married."

"Not…" Alexander stopped.

Tanglwyst lowered her hand. "What have you done?" She stepped towards him. "Tell me."

He swallowed. "I… My Lady, I beg you, do not make me reveal my sins."

"Tell me."

She felt the command concuss from her, hitting him right in the fealty. He had given it to her, and had not yet dismissed it in his heart. He closed his eyes.

"My first act as Sovereign was to sign a Writ of Destruction against Nicolai Moriarity. The assassin of the King was Duncan McVryce, and he carried out the Writ in the streets of Rouen."

Tanglwyst's face broke, her breathing became labored. Her eyes reflected instant sorrow. "Why?"

"He was a monster, drunk and damaging, and he did not love her. He was a danger to her and her son. He was a danger to you as well. It was only a matter of time before he turned upon you in a rage."

Her gaze cast to the floor and she closed her eyes. He was right. She had even seen it on more than one occasion, though never against her. She had felt her heart warm to Alexander over the winter, and remembered a sense of relief that he would never raise a hand against her. He would elevate her, not belittle her.

She had no idea at the time how true that statement would become.

"What else have you done that would shame your country? That would shame this Crown?"

Alexander flinched, resisting her question, but she had given him a command. "In my obsession, I left a number of people who needed my help to pursue her. I also let a village burn instead of letting the guard put out a fire, because I tried to stop her ship from fleeing."

"Why did she flee?"

He swallowed. "Because I tricked Myrgen into leaving her ship and her protection. She did it to rescue him from the headman's axe."

She could tell he wasn't telling her everything.

"What else?"

"My Lady…"

"What else?"

"I so angered the Stâpâna of Caratia that her protector felt the need to fire upon me. In attempting to save my life…" Tears fell from his eyes as his throat tried to choke the words from his lips. He swallowed their tethers and let the confession pass. "In attempting to save my life, Gwen… took the arrow meant for me. To stop Catriona from learning my crime of Nicolai's murder, I took Gwen through the shadows, knowing that their touch would kill her."

"You killed Gwen? On purpose?"

"I panicked, my Lady. I forgot that her Fae lineage would be attacked by the darkness."

"Why did you do it then?"

"I needed to get her to Holy Ground. To heal her wound. Using the amulet would get me there in an instant. I thought I could heal her before the damage was done."

"Amulet?" She drew a steadying breath. "Those horrid things that take your through the shadows in an instant?"

Alexander's eyes grew puzzled in a single blink. "You know about the amulet?"

"Yes. Duncan used his to take me," she glanced at Symonne and Tomas, remembering they were not her subjects, "out of Patras. They are the containers for monsters that feed upon your soul. What does that have to do with the Fae?"

"Her brother told me they destroy the Fae-touched upon contact. I didn't realize what he meant until she was disintegrating in my arms."

Tanglwyst dropped to her knees, the image feasting upon the fluid behind her eyes. She remembered the caress of the vile creatures and the way they affected Duncan. She remembered his attack before, when he tried to rape her and she stopped him. Now she knew it had not been a dream. The Shadows had done something to him. She had thought it a nightmare, especially since he had no debilitating wounds. She could not imagine the price they extracted for that service.

Duncan was clearly not Fae-touched, having gone through the shadows more than once, but she could feel the Power of Sovereignty starting to glow as she felt the touch of their slimy tentacles again. She shook it off. "How did the Power allow you to even go into that place?"

"It shielded me from being touched by the things, but it still scarred my soul. The power it offered was addicting."

She looked up, eyes narrowing as she shook her head, baffled. "How could you find that addicting?"

He shrugged. "It was easy, convenient."

She wanted to vomit. She stood, her anger returning. She strode to where he knelt and grabbed his hair at the back of his head, yanking his eyes to meet hers.

"*Easy?* Do you have *any* idea how *easy* it would be for me to execute you right now?" She looked at Symonne and glanced at the knife near her. She nodded to it. Symonne looked at it, picked it up, then took a deep breath. She tossed the knife to Tanglwyst and she caught it like this was choreographed. She put the knife to Alexander's throat.

He did not waver in his gaze. Neither did his fealty. She could feel it in his chest, in *hers* as well. She could *see* him in her mind when she looked for him. She knew where he was, just like she knew where everyone else was whose fealty held the Crown. A small weal of blood sneaked onto the tip of the knife.

He wants to die.

She pushed him away and walked over to wipe the blood off the knife.

She was not going to give him his wish.

Nine

He made a table of stone for himself.
-The Longsword of the Orphans

"Uh, has this always been here?" Octavius looked around the tunnel Raven was making.

Raven didn't break his concentration. "Well, no. The First Dûcesa made it."

"How?"

Rock fell away before him as easy as wiping dust from a mirror. "Um, well, she was mad."

A few more feet of rock disintegrated before them and Lauriel made a light on the wall by putting his paw on it, which left behind a paw print with a yellow glow about the strength of a torch.

Octavius cleared his throat. "That's a full explanation to you, isn't it?"

Raven looked back at Octavius. "It isn't?"

Octavius looked at Lauriel, who shrugged, then back at Raven. "Let's try this: Raven, why was *this* woman being angry different from any other woman being angry?"

"Because she could control the earth."

"Like you are?" Octavius waved to the regularly vanishing stone.

Raven stepped back, putting his fists on his hips. He took a survey of the area around them. "Huh? Yeah, I guess so." He looked at Octavius, holding up a finger. "But she wasn't a mage."

"What was she?"

"She was the Dûcesa." Raven went back to blasting the wall.

Octavius sighed. "I'm pretty sure there's a sizable gap between what that word means to you and what that word means to me. Isn't Anika the Dûcesa?"

Raven stopped. "Not the same."

"Why not?"

"Her memories are not the Dûcesa's."

"Uh, the Dûcesa has different memories?"

"Wouldn't you?"

Octavius looked at Lauriel again, who arched an eyebrow and nodded as if that was simple logic. The Fae wolf put another light on the wall. "Is there a chance this is written down somewhere?"

"Oh no! That would be *very* bad. Then just anyone could know what happened."

"Yeah, that would be horrible. Does anyone else know this story? A bard, perhaps?"

Raven stopped again, his mouth twisting in thought. "Calpurnia would be the best person to tell the story because she's really smart and can understand how to explain things. She's kind of unconscious right now, so that's not much help."

"No, that wouldn't be."

"There's Merrick, who's attending her."

"Yeah, so he? She? It? Is kind of busy watching the unconscious lady?"

Raven nodded, not acknowledging the lack of pronoun. "That's probably best. He is her friend."

"He! Merrick's a he!" Octavius took this victory and his excitement about it as proof he was delirious and that he might have head trauma. *I'm probably still on the ship and we are becalmed at sea. We're all starving to death and I'm unconscious with Estelle telling me a story about her insane brother who can destroy mountains.*

"Merrick's a mage. He does *mentus* stuff."

"Still a victory." He smiled at Lauriel, who acknowledged the win. "Hey, does Lauriel know this story?"

"No."

Octavius pouted. He reached into his pouch and took a bite of jerky, which was strangely filling. He worried it was Fae jerky or illusionary jerky and he was still actually starving to death. He tried to brush aside that thought. He would know soon enough. They would be travelling through the mountain until dark.

"Well," Raven touched the smooth rock ahead of him, "looks like we're done."

Lauriel and Octavius looked at the polished stone before them. Lauriel put a light on it. It was smooth as a calm sea. "We're done? We're still inside."

"Yeah, but this isn't a barrier I can break. It was put here by someone far more in their power than I."

Octavius felt some clarity. "This is the border of Mande, isn't it?"

"I imagine so. I didn't realize cartographers could be so precise."

Octavius looked up. The ceiling of this cave was about five feet above their heads. He suddenly realized that there was an entire mountain of rock directly above him. His throat started to close off and he was having trouble breathing. He fell to his knees, gripping the dust all over the floor. Despite the lights and Raven's sense of complete competence, Octavius felt like he was about to suffocate, as surely as if he was drowning. He pictured the ceiling crumbling and giving way, collapsing on the fault line Raven had created to get them in here. Dirt fell from above him and he tried to scream.

The impotent croak that his throat allowed was unsatisfying and scared him even more. He was going to die under a mountain of stone and not even have a voice. He reached into his pouch and pulled out the leaf, trying to recover his wits. He rubbed the glass through the cloth but it didn't help the feeling of claustrophobia.

Raven knelt beside him, and tried to speak but the roar of his fear defeated the attempt. Raven looked at Lauriel and then fetched Octavius under the arms. The mage did his disintegration magic up at an angle, following the Mandian border and going east. He moved through the rock like an eel through water, Lauriel running behind them.

They burst from the stone over a swath of sea, jagged rocks a thousand feet below them. Raven was caught off-guard by the lack of rock beneath them where they came out and grabbed a handhold in the cliff face. Octavius fell, finally finding his voice in the open sea air.

Lauriel scrambled, clawing his way back into the mountain opening, back claws breaking off chunks of rocks.

Raven reached out his hand and a spur of stone the size of a table jutted from the cliff. Octavius hit it hard, the wind knocked out of him and the edge of the table bruising his sternum. His arms fell on either side of the spur and his hands went limp.

The fabric unwound and fluttered away, and the shimmering leaf spun in the mid-morning sunlight, casting its green rays across his face for just an instant before it fell out of his reach. Above him, Raven shouted to him but Octavius couldn't hear him. Octavius saw another spur of rock jut out just below the leaf and for a moment, his heart had hope that she would be saved.

Then the glass shattered against the stone, the impact staining the grey with glittering dust. Wind blew the fragments and fine pieces into a mist and he blinked. He felt her light leave his heart and then, she was gone.

Myrgen awoke, feeling Catriona getting out of bed. The daylight streamed through the window, making a ballroom for the dust mites in the air. The day was beautiful, the sun warm and relaxing. She put on her dressing coat and left, returning a few minutes later. He realized he, too, needed the facilities and reluctantly dragged himself from the comfortable bedding. He took his own long coat from the hook by the door and padded down the hall.

Upon finishing, he noted James and Michael talking in the hallway across the stairs. He nodded and waved. Michael and James nodded in return and walked towards him. He met them at the stairs.

"Good morning. Did you sleep well?"

Michael and James nodded. James looked around the hallway. "These stones are very strange. They give off light and heat without burning. It reminds me of a Fae trick to light up passageways."

Myrgen nodded, looking around as well. "I think it's molten stone, to be honest. I thought I saw a similar glow in a room at the west end."

Michael touched the floor. "You think there's a source there, like a water pump?"

Myrgen shrugged. "Either that or it's Land magic."

James nodded. "That sounds likely. This is the heart of the Land, this country. Like Glarren is the heart of the Fae realms."

"And the Papal City is the heart of the Augustinian lands." He folded his arms across his chest. "What are you going to do today?"

James glanced down the stairs. "I need to sort that out. I'm going to have to return to Glarren but my ship is days from here. I could go overland faster that I could to go get it."

Michael nodded towards the docks. "What about Catriona's ship?"

Myrgen shook his head. "Dry dock, repairing Alexander's damage."

James bristled at the name, but breathed through it. "Regardless, we should eat beforehand. I might be more level-headed if I am not hungry."

"We'll meet you down there." Myrgen returned to Catriona's room and knocked on the door.

She opened it, her face becoming curious. "You knocked?"

"Not my room. Speaking of which, Michael and James are heading downstairs to the dining room. I was going to change, since my clothes are over there." He gestured to his room at the Iron Archway. "I didn't want to just disappear on you."

She smiled. "Thank you."

"So, I'll get dressed and be back in a few minutes?"

She nodded and they parted company.

It took him about ten minutes to get dressed and he returned to stand outside her door. It was simple having only one or two outfits to wear. He shook his head at his lack of caring. He knocked on her door and then heard her talking to someone. She opened the door and revealed Anika as her companion.

"Good morning Myrgen."

He bowed. "Noble Mother."

"Drake and I were wondering about the plans for Gwen's memorial service."

"Her brother is downstairs now. I know he plans to return to Glarren."

"Tib would like to do something for her here."

Myrgen nodded. "I would expect no less. He is a kind young man."

"Well," Anika patted Catriona on the shoulder, "I'll see the two of you downstairs." She left them alone.

Myrgen walked over to Catriona, touching her shoulder. "Are you alright?"

"It still seems like a horrible nightmare. I keep thinking she's right around the corner, just out of sight. I can still feel her."

He wrapped his arms around her and held her until she released him. "Have you looked for Alexander?"

"I haven't. I don't care to. If I find him in Caratia, I'll just want to hunt him down and drop a boulder on him. Gwen gave her life to save him. I can't undo that by seeking vengeance."

"What about the other one, the Shadowwalker?"

"He is not here, but he can return anytime. I do not yet know how to counter that. I hope James can help me with that."

"James?"

"He is Gwen's brother, and from Glarren. He knows about the Fae."

He stepped towards the door and she followed. "Are the Shadowwalkers Fae related?"

"I don't know. But I was told that he beat Alexander in the street for letting one touch her, and apparently, Alexander knew the danger. I believe that means they talked about it."

Myrgen nodded as they walked to the stairs. "He definitely knows about the amulets."

"Amulets?"

"The things the Shadowwalkers use to get around."

She looked at him. He felt her gaze infiltrate him and he had to admit he was a little worried about what she would think of Boots. She flinched at that thought, and delved down that line. He held nothing back from her, showing the fight with the Mandian woman, her capture of Myrgen, the fact that she wanted Catriona's help. He showed her The Granite Sword and what he did with it, how he broke the amulet's hold on her. He even revealed Boots' attempt to kiss him. There was no point in concealing it.

She blinked out of the reading. "Thank you for your loyalty."

He took her hand. "It's not loyalty, Catriona. I love you. I have no interest in any other woman. Proximity didn't change that."

She relaxed, smiling. "I can't tell you how relieving it is to be able to see you."

"It's mighty handy on this end to. I don't fear you misunderstanding my intent. You do need to restrain yourself if you ever expect to be surprised by a present."

She kissed him. "I'll never let on that I know."

"That's the most I can hope for."

They went to the dining room and found it filled with the usual numbers. Drake and Anika were walking around, refilling water goblets and talking with people. They went over to James and Michael and sat across from them. They all ate and drank, listening to the chatter around them. As the eating wound down, Drake rang a bell in the middle of the hall.

"My family, as you know, we lost a loved one yesterday. Our grandson Tib had requested that we have a memorial ceremony for her. Many of you knew the lady. I hope you will all attend. It will happen at the height of Embertwist's reign."

Myrgen leaned over to Catriona. "When is that?"

James leaned over. "Embertwist is the Fae Lord of Spring. His power is strongest mid-season."

"That would be the Feast of Uriel the Archangel to us, Myrgen. The Church set the Archangels' Feast Days across from the solstices and equinoxes to battle the Fae Lords."

"Ah." Myrgen remembered the teachings of the church like they were fairy tales from childhood, even though he was technically a member of the Church until his Naming yesterday. Although he had not stood the same ceremony Tib and the other children had, the Naming Quill had written his name to be read, and when it was, he had felt a connection to the Land. Moreover, he knew who he was more than he ever had before. He kind of wanted to go through the whole process, so he could know his place in the world as well.

"So, we have a month?" Michael looked at his companions.

Catriona nodded. "It's tradition for the family and friends to make gifts to Go to Ground with the interred. They place they gifts around the body and when the Land takes them, it takes the gifts too. This is so they have tokens of love in Summerland, the place beyond."

"Summerland?" Myrgen took a sip of water.

"When the Land claims you, it filters your soul of the pain and wrong you had in your life. Once it has been cleaned, it is returned to the world in another, newly born. The experience takes a while and during that time, you live in Summerland."

"Do you return with your memories?"

She shook her head. "No, the Land keeps those. It holds everyone's memories from every life."

James leaned back, ripping apart a sweet biscuit. "I wouldn't want the memories of every life I ever lived. It's hard enough to get over the challenges of this one." He took a bite and chewed, his words filtering through the food. "So, we gotta have you guys back by mid-Spring."

"Back?" Myrgen looked at James and Catriona.

"You're coming with me, right?"

Catriona took a deep breath and nodded. "That was my plan."

Myrgen leaned an elbow on the table. "When exactly were you going to tell me this?"

"As soon as we had a plan."

"Is that a good idea? You've already been away all winter."

She swallowed. "Yes. That's why I was going to ask a favor of you. I need you to stay here and take over as Stâpân."

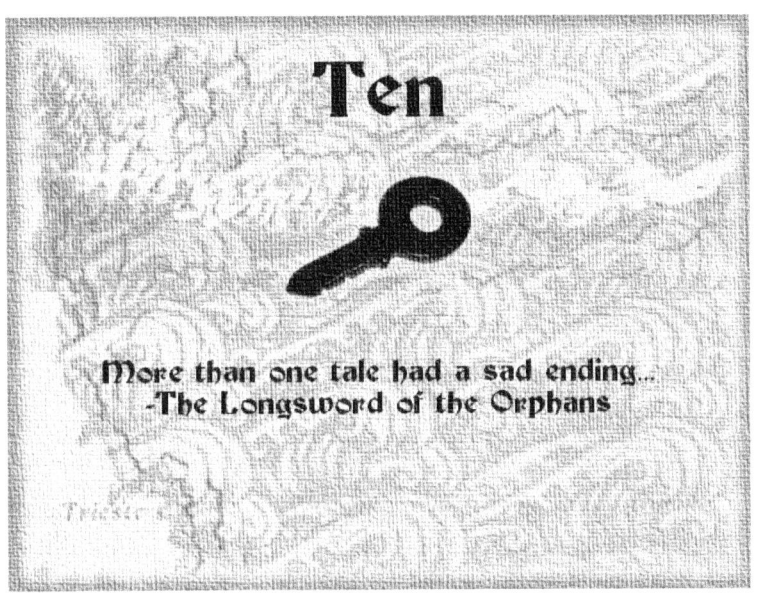

Ten

More than one tale had a sad ending...
-The Longsword of the Orphans

Raven dropped to the spur with Octavius, the table widening to accommodate him and Lauriel. The wind was strong at this altitude and Raven reached out as the fabric from the leaf came back at them. He looked at the fabric, then down below at the other spur. "Oh no."

He dropped down the twenty feet and knelt beside the splatter of glass. He touched them, but Octavius could see his body go limp from sorrow. Raven looked up at him.

Lauriel walked to the edge of the table and looked down at the lower spur, his grassy fur rippling in the wind. He laid down, nose still off the edge, and whimpered. Octavius couldn't move.

Raven cupped his hands over the remaining pieces and light bled from between his fingers. He opened his hands and picked up a clear stone with the leaf bits floating in it. He made steps into the mountain and walked back up to Octavius.

"I'm sorry."

Octavius looked at him. "What were you thinking, making a rock platform?"

"I thought you dropped the jerky. I didn't know you were holding her."

Octavius opened his mouth to yell at Raven, but the man's tears stopped him. He reached out and took the clear stone in Raven's hands. He had fused the leaf back together, but Octavius could tell it wasn't the same. He closed his hand around it and took the fabric Lauriel was holding for Raven. He wrapped the stone in it and put it back in his pocket. He looked below them at the sea and thought about falling so he could join Estelle. He would enter death in the sea, fulfilling his service to Calista. He knew this area was filled with her dire sharks. He would be accepted into her embrace.

He felt a hand on his shoulder. "Don't."

"Why not?"

"Because you need to return her to her father."

Octavius snorted. "That's also suicide. It will just take longer to do it."

"Yeah, probably. The alternative is for him to get your body and soul from the sea and demand reparations."

Octavius frowned and looked at Raven. "He can do that?"

Raven shrugged and Octavius tried to decide if it would be worth it. Dying right then felt like the best thing to do, especially since he was the reason she was gone. If he hadn't pulled her from his pocket to counter his fear in the mountain…

Lauriel brushed Octavius' other hand. Raven looked at his companion, then back at Octavius. "He says it isn't your fault."

Octavius shook his head. "How can you say that? How can you? I had her in my hand. I *knew* she was fragile. But I needed her. I was such a coward, so *overcome with fear* that I couldn't breathe, I couldn't stand. And I pulled her out in that horrifying situation. *I was afraid I would die from the mountain collapsing on me, and I took her from her safety. And now she's gone! And I dropped her! I killed her!"*

His tears were ripped away by the wind, denying him even that solice, and he could no longer stand. Raven raised a wall against the biting wind, making an enclosure for them, and Lauriel put a light on the wall to chase away the dim. They didn't interfere with Octavius' tears as they puttered around the growing shelter. They didn't bother him after they moved him to a comfy chair before a fireplace, didn't force the tea upon him that they set beside him on the table.

They let him mourn, and for that he was eternally grateful.

"The hell you do." Myrgen looked at Michael. "Did you know about this?"

"First I've heard of it."

Myrgen looked at James. "You?"

James shook his head, raising his hands.

"This wasn't their decision, Myrgen. It's mine. I can't leave the people unprotected but I have a duty to Gwen and her family. They need to know what happened."

"Can't you write a letter?"

Catriona frowned at him. "Would you want to find out in a letter that your child has died?" She shook her head and he glanced away, silently agreeing. He swallowed the lump forming in his throat. "No, I need to do this. I was her employer. I took her from her home and let her stay with me. I brought her back each year to visit her family. They are expecting us."

"But…" Myrgen tried to work through her logic but in the end, he recognized the futility. "What do I need to do?"

"Drake and Anika will help with that. There are books that explain it."

"Is it permanent?" He looked at the key on her neck.

"You will be able to return it to me when I get back, should you be told to."

"Told to?"

"By the Land."

He sat back. *Ah. So, the Land is telling her to give this up.* "And the Land is good with you not having its Power as you travel?"

She smiled. "I am a servant of the Land. I always have its power." She touched his hand. "But now you will be its protector. We will do this later today. I think we will want to be on our way tomorrow."

James nodded.

Myrgen looked at Michael. "I'm going to expect you to keep me in line."

"I'll be going with them."

Myrgen's jaw dropped. *"I'm doing this alone?"*

"I traveled with her right up to her death. I have to tell her family what she did, what she learned. James and I were talking about it earlier today, in the hall. They need to know what prompted her to give her life."

Catriona squeezed his hand. "You will be fine. This is an important trial for you."

Then he understood. Trial. He closed his eyes and nodded. *Of course. The Trials of Succession. This is probably some test of responsibility or something.* "What am I supposed to do while you're gone?"

"Well, you'll be expected to take care of the people, enforce the laws of the Land, help folks."

"Will I be able to communicate with you?"

She looked saddened. "It doesn't really work that way."

Myrgen shook his head. He didn't like this.

He didn't like this at all.

Tanglwyst hung the cleaned sheets on the line out back as Alexander cut the wood. She only had three rooms and five beds to make but it was a bit more than she had done before. Her parents always made them take care of their own rooms, changing their beds and cleaning their sheets, but that had been years ago. She hadn't changed a bed in at least five years.

It's not that she didn't remember how. She just forgot how sore her back got. After making all the beds, she realized it didn't matter. Her *muscles* sure did. She had been out back, washing the sheets when Alexander came out to chop the wood. He sounded like he had a good rhythm but she had also seen the stack of logs out back to be split. She did not envy him at all.

She smoothed the last sheet on the line, and picked up her empty basket. She walked past the wood, smiling, ready to tease Alexander about how he must be feeling by now. She was grateful he so far had not yet chopped anything off himself.

"So, regret giving up the Power ye...t...?"

He was leaning over to pick up the half log, which proposed a nice enough view, but when he straightened, his long hair flipped back and she saw he was shirtless. His white shirt was currently being scrubbed by Symonne. He lifted the ax and swung it down with ease, actually hitting where he aimed. He turned to get another log and looked up at her.

"My Lady, did you say something?"

Tanglwyst swallowed, and Symonne cleared her throat.

"Tangl, you might want to sit, girl. You're turnin' a bit red."

Alexander dropped the ax. "My Lady?" He stepped over to her and took her hand.

Tanglwyst came to her senses, her face hot and flushed. She shook off the reaction. *What's wrong with me? I've seen a shirtless man before. Especially, a well-toned one.* Her heart just kept thumping though, much harder than she authorized.

"Sorry, Your Highness. I got lost in my own thoughts for a moment and forgot to breathe."

"You...?"

She swallowed. "Not important." She walked past him, retrieving her hand in the process. "Symonne, I have the sheets hung. I'll be inside washing dishes. Let me know when you are done with those things there." She nodded to Symonne's wash basin, then walked inside and stood just by the door, trying to calm down.

"My Lady?"

Tanglwyst almost jumped out of her skin. She turned to look into Alexander's far too nearby eyes.

"Symonne needs that basket." He nodded to the laundry basket still in her hands. "For the wet clothes?"

She felt the sudden urge to kiss him, her mind replaying the image of him asking her to a ball back in the palace. Then she remembered that he never showed up to that ball. She remembered that he stopped talking to her past a random acknowledgement in the hallways of the castle. She remembered that he decided to place a summoning spell upon her when he could have just *spoken* to her. The urge bled away.

She blinked and then handed the basket to him, then turned to the sink to do the morning dishes.

Eleven

Raven was sending envoys with the stories far and wide, for it turns out he is, well, not the best at conveying information.
-The Longsword of the Orphans

"Tell me about the First Dûcesa."

Raven looked up from the fireplace where he was turning the seagull on the spit. Lauriel had caught it when it flew into the building Raven had made. The birds were huge, often sent to becalmed ships to help them survive. Raven knew of one tale that the captain made harnesses for several birds that the crew caught, rather than kill and eat them. The grateful birds dragged the ship to shore, saving them all.

"What about her?"

"Who was she?"

Raven knew he could tell the tale. The problem was in getting Octavius to understand it. When it came to teaching, Raven apparently had a speech impediment. Everyone told him he spoke in nonsense and riddles. He didn't know what those people were talking about. He knew Alistair always seemed to understand him.

He smiled at the thought of having Alistair tell the tale instead but it wasn't possible to conjure something like that. Besides, his magic didn't work that way. He decided to try and keep it simple. He didn't want to frustrate Octavius and cause him to shut them out again.

"She was a large woman, very well built. Sturdy. She felt like the strength of the Land had governed her whole life."

Octavius nodded, but didn't seem much livelier than he had been the couple of hours before. He had not even flinched when the seagull had entered the hut.

"Her Stâpân was named Slade, and he was even sturdier built. He made her look small."

Octavius nodded. "I've seen her portrait in Ashstone."

"There's a portrait? Oh wait. Yeah, there would be. I did it."

"There's also a statue."

"Oh? No, that's not right. I didn't do a statue of her. I did a statue of the other one. The *sluuurp* one. Pity."

He saw Octavius starting to glaze over and remembered. *Focused sentences.* "Sorry. Yes. Um, where was I?" He looked at Octavius. "What were you asking about?"

"Were you there when the cliffs were raised?"

"Ah. No. That was before my time."

"Do you know how they were raised?"

Raven swallowed. "Kind of. The power of the First Dûcesa was… different. She was… she had…" *Focused sentences.* "She had a stronger connection to the Land than anyone since."

"Why?"

Raven glanced down at the fire. "Because she had her Stâpân with her."

Octavius took a deep breath but didn't say anything at first. After a minute, he moved, sitting upright in his chair. "Why did that matter?"

"Because the Stâpân holds the stones." He remembered when he touched the black stone with the gold flecks, holding it in his hand as he offered it to the Third Dûcesa. He knew it would give her all her memories, without a filter. But his wife had been ill and he had been gone too long already. By the time he returned to Canterbury, Wilgefortis had been on her death bed.

Time had not passed for Raven, but it had passed for her. It had been fifty years since he had seen her. Their children were grown, with grandchildren, and all of them had gathered to bid her goodbye. She had been so happy to see Raven, and he had known it was her the second he saw her. He touched her, restoring her. The disease ravaging her disappeared and she had sat up.

But she was still old, and he decided to make up for his absence. Mages often brewed longevity potions back then. More time to study.

Raven had gone to the labs and mixed a few for her. Within the year, the half a century was gone from her body. They played with their children and grandchildren and beyond, into the greats. It was another hundred years after that that she faded from him. She had stopped taking the potions, he knew not when, but one night she kissed him good night and did not kiss him good morning.

It had taken him years to recover. Her dream dragon, Escalleon, had stayed with him for a few decades after, but in the end, he, too, faded back to the ether. When he went to Caratia to visit, he found that the Third Dûcesa had recovered her memories and left him a note. It said what she planned to do, and hoped he would find her again in Nubia. But he never did. Her ship went down at sea and she never was reborn.

"Alistair said she was here. He said he thought he met her."

Octavius perked up a little. "Alistair? Alistair McGlarren?"

"That was the name he chose, to hide. It's funny to think about it now. He was a thief, a rogue at our covenant. The Prince of York shoved him out the door when the Soulless attacked, and the Prince was touched by one of the monsters. He was drained in thirty heartbeats, and right as he turned into one, I managed to kill him. Our rogue knew that the kingdom would destroy itself without a royal line. So he had me cast a disguise spell upon him, and made it permanent so he could look like Alistair. He told everyone that the rogue died saving him, and went on to become a very great and interesting man. It's because of him that York is now a matriarchy."

Lauriel padded over to the hearth and flopped down with a fart. The stench filled the hut within minutes and Raven and Octavius stood outside the stone hut in the misty wind, drinking in the unpolluted air. Octavius snorted a laugh, and Raven looked at him. Another chuckle broke from Octavius' chest, then the laughter started in earnest. Raven joined him, not entirely certain why the mirth was so prevalent, but after the stress of the day, it felt good to laugh.

Tanglwyst stepped into the back. "Symonne, we have customers."

Symonne looked at Alexander, then stood and went into the inn. She greeted one of the people by name but Tanglwyst did not hear it. She instead went to check on the sheets. They were dry and she got the second basket from near the wash tub to put the laundry in. That meant passing Alexander three times in his shirtless splendor and she was glad she did not feel the pangs she had before. Maybe, she was finally getting over him.

She folded the sheets instead of just dropping them in. It meant they would not be wrinkled and would not require ironing. She had also not ironed anything in five years but she definitely remembered hating that.

Alexander came around the wood shed as she finished. "Can I carry that for you, My Lady?"

She looked him over. "You must be exhausted."

He smiled. "It's the good kind, from work."

"I was surprised to find you... competent at chopping wood."

"Is that so? I feared it was finding me half-naked that startled you." He took the basket and started walking with her to the kitchen. "When was traveling, I would often offer to chop wood or work in the kitchens to pay for my passage."

"You were the Prince. Why didn't you just have your own money?"

"Too dangerous. Rich pockets make for rich ransoms."

She smiled. "That's actually wise." She picked up the other basket, full of clean, wet laundry and took it to the line.

He came back a few moments later, pulling on a blue shirt. "My Lady, it seems Symonne needs us."

They went inside without delay. Tanglwyst saw three people near Symonne, each with letters. One man had several, the others only one each.

"Can you help those folks?" Symonne gestured to the three others in the inn.

Tanglwyst and Alexander walked up to the others. "What can we do for you?" They looked at each other, startled by their question in unison. All parties looked at the pair, then the demands started.

"I need a stable for our horses."

"Is there a place I can rest?"

"Do you have any food here?"

Alexander took care of the horse inquiry while Tanglwyst took care of the resting and food options.

She listened to the talk around the common room to figure out why this place was suddenly so popular. They were so high up, but apparently they had a rather impressive messenger service so people made the climb. One man came in carrying several messages with fifty silver per message to send them. Another man came up to send a will to his children. A final message was from a young girl to her mother regarding her wedding. Symonne took care of these while Tanglwyst and Alexander handled the food and got people settled.

At first, she and Alexander got in each other's way. Then she realized he was very good with the organizing of the kitchen, so he stayed back there and she worked the floor. By the time the meals came out, they were working so well, one of the customer's asked if they were married. Alexander blushed a little and returned to his kitchen, and Tanglwyst was pleased to find she had no desire to be intimate with him as she had that morning.

When the rush was over and folks were out the door to return to Cliffbase, Symonne came over to them. "Thank you for your help today."

Alexander bowed. "It was the least I could do."

Tanglwyst smiled. "He beat me to it, but yes. I'm glad we could help." She looked behind Symonne, towards the innkeeper's chambers. "How is Tomas doing?"

"He's at war with himself. He likes being able to relax, but he hates that I'm doing so much without his help. He would be impossible if you two weren't here."

"Good."

Tanglwyst turned away, her throat starting to close up. She went to the tables and started gathering up the final bits of discarded utensils. She did the table farthest from Symonne and Alexander first, to give her emotions time to come under her control again. She didn't want to start sniffling where Symonne could hear her.

A few minutes later, Alexander came over to her, a cloth in a bucket in one hand, a broom in the other. He set the bucket down on one of the tables.

"My Lady?"

"Yes, Your Highness?"

He put a hand upon hers. "What is it?"

She glanced over her shoulder to make sure they were alone. "We need to get you out of here."

He looked down. "I know. But I'm not going to leave these people without help. She's right. She needs us, for at least several more days."

"Can I heal him? The way you did me?"

"With the Power?" He shook his head. "No. The only reason that worked was because the sickness killing you was supernatural in nature. Had it just been the stab wounds, you would have still died."

She shuddered at the memory.

He set the broom aside. "You're fine now, My Lady."

She looked down at their hands, still touching. "Not entirely."

He nodded and took his hand from hers. "Forgive me."

She smiled, though not with her whole face. "That's not what I meant. I meant that I should not be holding this Power. It is not my right." She leaned on the table with both hands. "When I was in school at St. Agnes, Elizabeth and I always dreamed and talked about what it would be like to have Mervolingia be a matriarchy, like York. When Beth…" she closed her eyes against the emotions, "when she needed someone to enact her will, to slaughter the King, she chose me.

"And all she had to do was put some Fae potion in my wine and I was ready to cut your brother's throat." She turned away from him, ashamed at the admission. "She duped me, Alexander, and with ease. And all because you and I grew close."

"What?" Alexander leaned on the table as well, looking into her face.

"It's true. I found a journal of hers in a secret lab in the palace. It had not just the formula for my control potion, but a love potion meant for you." She looked at him. "She was going to make sure you married her."

"I'm not so easily swayed."

"Well, apparently I am. And if a simple potion made me almost murder my sovereign, I truly shouldn't have this Power right now."

"That Power is in the best hands possible right now. If Duncan comes after you…"

"What if Catriona comes after you?" She was worried, and he seemed to just be dismissing this threat. "I haven't designated an heir yet. If she kills us both, and she has no reason not to, our kingdom will eat itself in civil war."

"Why haven't you designated an heir?"

"Because the only proper choice is Emmy. And she's four years old. Who would regent? Your mother? You? You discarded this Power in favor of a peasant woman's life."

He smiled. "You're hardly a peasant woman."

"You're right. I'm worse. I'm a traitor and a fugitive. You should be killing me instead of saving me. Why spare my life when it's slated for the hangman's noose?"

He looked down at the table. "You can't give it back. Duncan is still out there and without that Power, he will kill you if he gets his hands on you."

"And Catriona will kill you if she gets her hands on you."

He looked at her, smiling. "That's why you have my fealty, My Lady. I know you will protect me."

She searched his eyes, trying to emphasize how vulnerable he was. "I was *tricked* by someone I thought was a friend. How can I possibly be trusted? I was going to kill your brother and if she had wanted it, I would have raised a hand against you. She could have had me covered in blood." Tears were coming down now and she turned away from him.

He put his arms around her, hugging her, and despite her best efforts, she sobbed into his chest.

"Myrgen, it's time."

Myrgen looked up at Drake, who stood in the doorway to the Iron Archway room, and nodded. He got to his feet and followed the man. They went downstairs to the courtyard where Anika and Catriona waited. James and Michael were with them. The courtyard had many people from Ashstone standing around and he expected the procedure to be done there. Then, Drake took Anika's hand and everyone started moving towards the city.

Catriona kept her head bowed and did not talk to anyone, nor did anyone approach her. She stayed right behind the Dûce and Dûcesa. He was still sorting out how he felt about this but he knew this was not the wrong choice. He wondered if this was just prep work for standing in the Square to be the Dûce. Perhaps holding this position would teach him valuable lessons regarding being a servant of the Land.

The people at Ashstone followed the group to the Town Square and to the stone slabs that were present in the grass. They were made of similar stone to the lava ones at the castle, except these were smoky black instead of grey. Catriona stepped over to stand upon one of them. Drake gestured for Myrgen to stand on the other one.

Anika nodded to them and took a deep breath. "My Family, our Stâpâna has a task that will call her away. She does not wish to leave our people without their protector as she makes this trek. Thus, at this time, she is requesting to step aside as Stâpâna in favor of another."

Catriona took a breath. "Land, I offer myself to you. Please take this from me and give it to the one you find worthy."

The stone key she wore fell from her neck and disappeared into the ground. Her sword pommel fell off as well, disappearing when it touched the stone beneath her feet.

Myrgen looked down at the stone around him, and waited. At first, nothing. Then he saw a shape forming in the smoky clear stone. It rose like it was coming through oil, and finally surfaced. He knelt down and touched it, picking it up from the stone. The earth solidified underneath him and the stone slab disappeared. He looked up and the entire town breathed a sigh of relief. He saw it in every face, including Catriona's.

He walked over to her and held up the Onyx Key. "I'll take care of this," he looked at the assembled folks, raising his voice, "take care of all this," then back to her, "until you return."

"I'll be back as soon as I can."

He touched her hair. "You'd better."

As the crowd came up and congratulated him, he nodded to them, holding onto Catriona's hand with his left as he thanked people and accepted hugs with his right. Every person he saw, he *knew*. There were truly no strangers here. Suddenly, he realized what everyone else had been saying all along. Drake and Anika were Father and Mother, and he was now the oldest sibling. Each of these were his blood.

He looked at Catriona and saw her a little different. She was not exactly his sister. She was... He couldn't place it, but he was glad he didn't get the sibling feeling from her. *Once was enough.*

When most people had left and the processional started back to Ashstone, he leaned over to her. "Why was everyone holding their breath during the ceremony?"

"Because they didn't want either of us to die."

Myrgen smirked. "Was that a possibility?"

"Yes."

The smirk faded into seriousness. "Really?"

"Yes. Every time the Stones appear, anyone who steps upon them is offering themselves for sacrifice. If the Stones judge you unworthy, not just for the task you stand for, but for anything, you are consumed."

He stopped. "Really?" He thought about everything he had done in his life, and swallowed. "Like… kidnapping your son… or… you know, stuff like that?"

She squeezed his hand. "You're still here." She tugged at him and they continued up the hill.

"When do you leave?"

"Tomorrow at dawn. We are going overland, since neither of our ships are available."

"Yeah, I was thinking about that. I want to accompany you, at least to the border. I just got you, I don't really want to let you go."

She smiled. "That would be wonderful." She glanced down at the ground. "Would you be willing to stay with me tonight?"

"Under one condition. We spend the night in my room. You're going to be gone for a month. I want my pillow to have your scent as long as I can."

"You can always stay in my room."

"And I might, when I'm missing you. But that's your room, and I want it still yours when you return. If you decide to combine our rooms after that, then we'll do it together. I don't want to start scattering my things around your space."

She stopped and looked into his eyes, then kissed him. "I love you. I can barely believe it's happened, but I do."

He smiled. "Without reservation?"

"Without reservation."

He kissed her again and they returned to Ashstone.

Twelve

It was here that I encountered the
missive from Raven, brought by a very
peculiar bird.
-The Longsword of the Orphans

Duncan leaned against the wall of the room, breathing hard. The sound of someone hitting a chisel with a hammer had completely unsettled him. He looked at the amulet and removed it, setting it on the desk. There were so many things different about this room that he could barely count them all.

First, it was darker than the previous one. There were no lighted runes on the lower wall.

Second, there was no furniture. The only reason he had a lantern was because he brought one with him this time. His first visit here had been horrifying. He had not been able to leave due to the scorch marks from the Power of Sovereignty. But there had been absolutely no light, and his eyes never caught the faintest glimpse of the room the entire time he healed. Luckily, that factor remained the same. Within a few hours, he had healed nearly all the damage, more than enough to kill the woman.

The woman. She's not 'the woman'. She has a name. At the moment, he simply could not remember it. The second flash had blinded him completely and he believed it no longer mattered that the room was completely dark.

Once he could feel his eyes in his sockets again, regrown, he had left, to test his sight. He managed to make it where he wanted to go, which was a back room at the cathedral rectory in Patras. He took a lantern and disappeared again. He had lit the lantern and discovered the absence of, well, everything.

Now, this sound, echoing from outside but nearby. That meant someone was near him. It had gone on for quite a while and he was able to pinpoint it about thirty feet away on what was to him the west wall. That was when he found the number.

LVII

Fifty-seven. Fifty-seven what? Was that how many of these rooms there were? He studied the amulet in the lamplight. The base plate was solid gold and the stone was very unique with a strange reddish-brown hue. It was very different from his. The gold was newer and shinier, not antiqued like his previous one. He found an engraving on the back of it.

LVII

Someone marked this. It belongs to this room, or vice versa. It made his stomach roll to think there were fifty-seven of these things. He knew he could only take the amulet off and be free of it in this room because he couldn't leave without it. The amulet would go dormant, so to speak, once it wasn't needed for healing. Activating it only required picking it up with the will to use it.

He remembered listening to the hammering, and thinking. The carving had paused once for about a minute. The rest of the time, the longest pause was about twenty seconds. That pause happened six times and then the longer one. Then six times from farther away, and then no more. That meant seven numbers.

He looked at the numbers in his room. They were Old Mandian from before the War. He touched the carving, thinking. If there were seven numbers, then there were far more than fifty-seven of these amulets. Whoever had these was building a very mobile army. Worse, they had someone who knew how to make these amulets.

He looked back at the amulet he held. This was something Alexander just called to him. It wasn't on him. It appeared in his hand. Duncan realized that this room was a trap, that he could be abandoned in here at any time if Alexander called it to him. Duncan gripped the amulet and willed himself away.

Catherine D'Medici looked at the sealed envelopes in her hands again. The first one had flowing script, elegant and clean. The second one was crisper, more curt. The third one was sharp, angry. The biggest concern was not just the writing on the outside. It was the fact she knew to whom it belonged.

The Queen of Krakte was clearly upset, and Catherine could figure out why. Elizabeth was Sovereigna's only child, having lost the other children to "natural causes". Granted, what passed as natural in that country was far from what it meant here. Krakte was governed by Fae worshipers and surrounded by the Black Forest. According to the Church, the Black Forest was filled with monsters.

Catherine had not gone there, even in her youth, but she had to admit it had always fascinated her. In Mande, fairy tales were illegal but here, they were simply something frowned upon, something for which a child might get a spanking. Instead, the tales of the Saints were presented to children as entertainment for their role playing and games. Even fantasizing about contact with the Fae could bring it about, and those encounters were never positive.

Still, she had selected Elizabeth on purpose out of the hundreds of daughters vying for status. She was hoping to get access to children's books in Krakte and hide them away to read for herself. Unfortunately, the Church officials had gone to Krakte to prepare the princess before Catherine had a chance to meet her. Her desire to see this magnificent place had been extinguished in its infancy.

That did not stop her from corresponding periodically with Sovereigna, but recent events had proven distracting. She had not sent or received a letter in almost three years, and she was too afraid the Church would read any mail she sent from the Papal City. Trucking with the Fae was an executable offense there. To see her friend's handwriting so distressed was more than upsetting, it was frightening.

She shifted between the three envelopes again, the heavy wax seals still intact. Unlike Charles, Alexander had not given her permission to do as she pleased. Quite the opposite, in fact. He had expressly forbidden her from getting involved. If he had not known of Charles' previous decree, she could have gotten away with it. Unfortunately, their relationship had been beyond strained since the St. Michael's Day Massacre, when Charles revealed that the letter had been written by her and not by Plantyn. Her ruse had worked. Plantyn had died as she desired so she had not cared that they figured it out. However, the resulting disintegration of her family had left a chasm of distrust.

Now she held these envelopes and was forbidden from reading them. To do so would be treason. So all she could do was shift between them, hoping to find a way to learn their contents.

A knock at the open door revealed Dominic, his skin a little darker and his temples turning grey. He was barely past his twenty-fifth birthday, but this job was aging him. Since he took over for Myrgen, Dominic had been in contact with Mande and had overseen the damages of a fire in St. Marguerite, as well as taken charge of the country's finances. The coronation would be expensive, as would the wedding. Luckily, they could be combined into one celebration and the gifts from other countries would offset the expenses. Caratia's goods were beyond price. A country devoted to Land worship must have gold and gems as common household items.

"Your Majesty, you sent for me?"

"Yes. Is there any word on His Majesty's location?

Dominic sighed. "No, Your Majesty. I'm afraid not."

"Caratia is not far enough for him to still be there."

"No, but getting into it is possible only for a select few. The Lady Tanglwyst never managed it."

"She seems to be quite the negotiator, judging from her current whereabouts. I still fail to see how house arrest was chosen for someone accused of treason."

"His Majesty insisted."

She straightened, disapproving of this information. "Of course he did. As was his right."

She shifted between the letters again, pacing.

He walked over to her and extended a hand. "Your Majesty, can I see those?"

She looked at his outstretched hand and paused her pacing, noting his coat. The style was Mandian, of course, but she realized she knew the tailor. He was exclusively out of Mande and did not export his work. This style was current, as she had seen in the latest dolls sent for the

Coronation. This tailor would make the clothes for Alexander only if the King came to his store. The fit was so precise, it must be done in person.

She looked at Dominic and he flinched. She resumed her pacing.

"These need to be handed directly to the King himself. If he is not going to show up here, then we simply have to go to him."

He bowed and stepped back into the hall, clearing the way for the Queen Mother. Catherine strode to the Royal Messenger's office. The servants inside all stood and bowed when she entered.

"I need to get a message to the King. How do I do it?"

The oldest man, she believed his name was Josephus, gestured to a pile of missives behind him. "I'm sorry, Your Majesty. If we had that answer, we'd all be a lot busier."

"All those are for the King?"

"They are, Your Majesty. Reports from all over the country, missives regarding taxes, marriage proposals, I imagine." He looked at the three missives in her hands. "By the Saints, have those not been opened?"

She looked down at them. "No. They are foreign correspondence. They are for His Majesty's eyes first. Once they are opened, he can delegate them a he sees fit." She took a deep breath. "Unfortunately, that is how he has chosen to handle things during his reign."

Josephus leaned on the counter. "Is there anyone with the authority to open them? Any of them?"

"I'm afraid not. So unless you know of some magical way to get these to him…"

"I might."

The two older people looked at the young man standing off to the side of the room. Catherine looked him over as Josephus gave him a stern look. "Don't make the Queen Mother wait, boy. Tell us your idea."

The young man looked nervous and glanced around at the other messengers. Catherine turned to them. "Could you give us the room, please?"

Although she phrased it like a question, it wasn't, and everyone knew it. Josephus even motioned if he should leave as well and she nodded. She thought the boy might be afraid of losing his job if he said the wrong thing. With no other witnesses, that would not be a problem. Josephus closed the door behind them.

"What's your name, young man?"

"Charles Read, Your Majesty."

The young man was blond with a barrel chest and strong legs. He was no taller than her, being eye to eye. He wore the Royal tabard here but the sun marks on his neck indicated a different garb when outside.

"An excellent name. What's your route, Charles? Where do you frequent?"

"Papal City, Your Majesty. I've delivered messages for you about six times."

She nodded. "What is this potential messenger you spoke of?"

He glanced at the door and she followed his gaze, looking beneath it for shadows. There were none. He returned his gaze to her. "There's a service near Cliffbase that can deliver a message to anyone alive in the world."

"Where is Cliffbase?"

"At the bottom of the pass on the Mervol side," he swallowed, nervous, "the one going to Caratia."

Catherine frowned. She had already lost one son there. "How do you know this?"

"It's a common rumor at that end. If you contact the service there in Cliffbase, they take a run regularly up the mountain to send them. They are expensive, but according to every messenger in the east part of the kingdom, they work."

She looked at the letters in her hands. "Anyone alive? No matter where they are? How long does it take?"

"I don't know. I've never used them personally. I just know when a letter *must* get to someone, that's the only sure way."

She frowned, thinking. If Alexander was coming from Caratia, he had to leave over that pass, the northern pass, or by sea. There were no other ways in or out of the country. It made them all but impossible to invade. However, that worked in her favor. If he was returning to Mervolingia, wouldn't he do so coming from there?

"How long does it take to get to this place?"

Charles squinted at the ceiling. "About a tenday, Your Majesty."

A whole tenday. She turned from him, angered. Her son's impulsive attitudes had always been prevalent and she remembered how he had infected her own Charles with that wanderlust. She had no idea how long it would be before he contacted them. Before, he had been gone for months at a time.

"Fine. I'll get ready. We'll head out at noon."

"*We*, Your Majesty?"

"Yes, we. I am done sitting around here, doing nothing."

He bowed and stammered something as she opened the door and left.

Anibal Cipriano Malatesta, the King of Mande, wiped the sweat from his brow, leaving a bloody streak in its place. Getting the heart while it was still beating was the key. The person had to be alive, not causing their heart to race, and not feeling the pain. With the right drugs and the right cuts, a person could be awake and alive right up until the point where he used their heart to make a room underground. True, by the point he did that, they were grateful to die, but the fun part was striking that critical balance.

Dealing with infernal forces was always a messy business.

He liked to pretend he was doing the world a favor by killing these people, but in the end, he would have done it for the fun of it. These were the worst criminals, the ones who were destined for Hell: Violators, murderers, monsters.

He took criminals just barely getting into the task, people who were dipping their feet in, and gave them a taste of success. Few ever chose to stop after the first time. Once he had them committing their third, more terrible act, he would "discover" them and they would be put to death. If they got *good* at it, then they were used even more.

This was part of the bargain he had to get the power for his project. One corruptible soul for one truly despicable one. He didn't care what was done with the souls he sent. He just knew this part of the work was the part he enjoyed.

The man under his knife could still feel pain. He was feeling a lot of it right then. The important part was that he wasn't making his heart beat too much. A steady, even rhythm was essential to this part of the spell. The pulsing of the heart was the pulsing of the power. Too fast, and the power made the wielder insane quickly. Too slow, and the wielder became slothful, dying in the secret chamber.

The heart was the part that made the power center of the amulet, the secret room somewhere in the world. Cipriano had figured out a way to word the ritual so the rooms were all directly underneath the Mandian royal palace. He had gone below and checked. It was a mausoleum down there, a chamber of chambers with no doors or windows. He tested every amulet once it was made and carved a number in the wall. He wished he had figured out a way to do them in numerical order, but alas! It was not to be. He would try destroying one in the future, but he believed as long as the amulet was intact, the room would be.

The heart was set upon an ornate golden platter, with sturdy prongs that held it in place. The entire ribcage had to be removed to accommodate this, but it was worth it. Then the lungs could be just flopped to the side, out of the way. The skin was already gone on the torso anyway. He looked up at the mirror overhead to make sure the plate was properly centered, then cast the final incantation.

The man's eyes grew wide as he watched his heart whither into a solid black lump, the platter shrinking with it until it completely housed and protected it. Cipriano looked at the man and watched the light go out in his eyes. He smiled, pulling the new amulet from his rattling chest. He looked behind him and went to see where the new chamber had appeared.

Cipriano took a lantern and walked the mausoleum hallways. The lantern wasn't for this part. The chamber had sufficient lighting. He got to the one that was without an exterior number and looked at his ledger. He took the hammer and chisel and went to work. Once he was done there, he used the amulet to teleport to the chamber. The dark tendrils felt welcoming now, and the purpose for the lantern was revealed.

The amulets made by the Church had been filled with runes that offered light at the base boards but his did not. He had not figured out why, but his plan didn't allow for too much experimentation. He had a goal. He figured out where he wanted this mark, and got out his hammer and chisel again. Thirty minutes later, he lifted the lantern and admired his work.

CXCVIII

Two more to go.

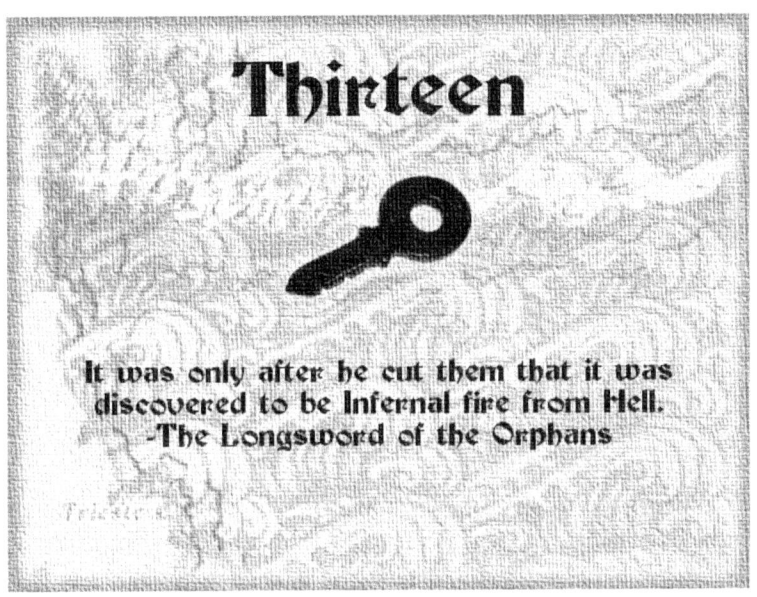

Thirteen

It was only after he cut them that it was discovered to be Infernal fire from Hell.
-The Longsword of the Orphans

Alistair blinked. It was the first thing he had done since the room he was in went blank. It was infinite and a neutral grey shade, which was appropriate for the realm of Karma, so to speak. It was definitely better than the shattered kaleidoscopic glass shards and shredded sunset-colored silks soaked in blood. The sound of crimson fluid hitting the marble floor had not lasted long, but it had lasted long enough to drill into Alistair's memory.

He did not understand a lot of what had happened. He had watched Gwen throw herself between Alexander and the arrow, the entire scene projected through a crystal pillar onto the nearby wall. At the time, there had been a wall, and a large bed with curtains of silk in orange, gold, pink, and blue. The floor was scattered with textured pillows in every color and woven rugs of Yndian design. He had fallen to his knees upon some of these pillows when he saw the arrow pierce her throat, spraying blood all over Alexander.

He screamed, but even then, a tiny glimmer of hope kept his own heart beating. A throat wound from the side could sever her life as surely as cutting could, but a hole through the center of her neck, where it didn't hit anything outside of her voice, that she could heal from.

Maybe Alexander could take her to a church to do that. He definitely owed her that.

Then Alexander had done exactly that, but in the worst way possible. He took her through the shadows. Alistair had watched the shadows leap upon her, attacking her soul and body. They invaded every pore, consuming her with ravenous passion. They excreted their pollution into her skin, so her entire body was filled with its putrescence. It was the ultimate destruction while also being the ultimate insult. Worse, she had still been alive during the entire process. She died only after he stepped back into the world.

Alistair had dropped to his hands and knees in shock, trying to control the revulsion in his body. He heard a scream near him and had glanced up at the wall in time to see a nude woman with long silver hair in a cage. Behind her, an angel turned to look at her over his shoulder, then returned his gaze to a large window overlooking a hundred people working in rows with their backs to him. The wall went blank and Karma had knelt beside him.

"I'm sorry."

He had looked at it, housed in the body of a lovely woman he knew in Rouen. It wasn't Xannu. It was a façade, like this whole room. He was just essence. The pillows were illusions, the rugs, the wine and food. The paintings on the wall, the silks on the bed, just color for color's sake, plush for plush's sake, spice for spice's sake, scent for absolutely no reason at all. None of this was real.

But that girl, his daughter, she had been real. She had been strong and alive and loving. She had been brave, beautiful, selfless. She had been powerful, connected, experienced. Alexander had stripped all that from her and allowed her to be feasted upon by monsters. He felt part of him die, and part of Gloriana die. Her death was real. Now her brother had to burn the last essence of her because the disease of the shadows destroyed her, leaving *just enough* behind to infect James.

He had closed his eyes, trying to block out the sounds of them feeding, the sounds of her screaming, the stench of their breath. It only amplified it. He had vomited, but nothing came out. There was nothing in there to begin with. He couldn't even get the relief of this indignity. He watched in a haze as James tended the body, not wanting to leave his side. He couldn't be there for him, he couldn't even leave this place because Karma did not want him to. He was a prisoner, condemned to only watch events in the world, impotent.

No, he remembered thinking. *Not impotent. I can influence things. I can change things. I can't bring her back, but I can make sure he suffers for this.*

He had stood and grasped the crystal Pillar, willing it to show him Alexander. Karma had watched him but had not interfered. He saw Alexander sitting in his room at the Drum and Nightingale Inn, saw him almost leave. He had watched him give the Power of Sovereignty to Tanglwyst to save her and had swallowed, irritated. Alexander seemed to be trying to balance his own soul against what had happened in Zara. Karma had smiled.

That's when he realized Karma was rooting for Alexander.

"Are you *favoring* him?"

Karma had looked at him. "Perhaps just a little. He has a value here you don't understand."

"Enlighten me."

Karma had looked at him a moment in silence, then, "No."

Alistair had been stunned. "Why not?"

"Because I don't have to. Nothing is compelling me."

Alistair was dumbfounded. He had just lost his daughter and this creature was defending the person who put her through that pain. "No. Nothing is. I was asking because it seemed as though you were protecting and defending the person who just murdered my daughter."

Karma tilted its head. "I suppose I am. But, then again, I have to maintain a balance. I did, after all, let Michael survive the trip to Caratia."

"Let him?"

"Well, I didn't interfere."

Alistair had frowned. "How could you have interfered?"

"The Hand of Karma can step in at any time. The person will simply be in our debt afterwards. If they don't balance themselves, we'll intervene again."

"So you could have stepped in and stopped Gwen from being killed."

Karma bit its lip. "Yes. But I would never have stepped in to protect that girl."

Alistair didn't remember what happened after that except the feel of the illusion solidifying under his fingers as he strangled the life out of Karma. He didn't even figure he had done that. Karma wasn't a person. It was an entity. It didn't have substance. When he came out of it, Karma lie lifeless on the ground. He exploded in rage. He drew a sword and shredded the silks, shredded the pillows, systematically eliminating everything in this prison. None of it was real anyway, so he just went on a spree. He plunged the sword into Karma over and over, casting off blood across the room.

When he finished, he stood over Karma. Its eyes opened and it folded its hands underneath its head. It crossed its feet and looked at Alistair. "You done with your tantrum yet?"

"No."

He had grabbed the illusion of Karma and threw it at the Pillar in the room. It was the only thing that always remained, no matter what the scenery change. Karma hit it hard, and was dazed. Then he picked it up and threw it onto the sharp tip of the Pillar. The crystal shard rammed through it, the body making a strange, realistic *schlock*. It twitched, blood dripping down the obelisk until it flowed to the lip on the pedestal and dripped onto the floor. The entity twitched until the room faded into grey. Once it did, his rage bled out and he dropped to the ground, leaning against the Pillar. He just went numb, waiting.

Now he was coming through the numbness and he was a little confused to find the entire realm still grey. Was this his punishment for his tantrum?

He looked down at himself and found he was clothed in a white outfit with black embroidery. Elaborate scroll work dominated the cuffs and waistband of the outfit and cascaded down the front of the doublet and breeches. His boots and gloves were a contrast, black with white embroidery, as was his shirt. He wore no hat, but there was one beside him, white on top, black underside, complete with matching feathers that began white and faded black, and vice versa. He picked up the hat and saw a piece of paper beneath it, white on black paper.

Can we talk?
~Hell

He looked around, then picked up the note. It was real. He got to his feet and looked behind him. The Pillar was still there but Karma was gone. When he had been shown the true nature of the realm, it had been stark white and he had been nude. Now it was nondescript and he was resplendent. He couldn't understand. He looked down at the note.

Hell? How was he supposed to get to Hell?

A square opened up in the floor and a white spiral staircase descended into the space beneath it. It went to a room with a door of black ironwood set in a white wall. He walked over to it and twisted the handle. It opened, showing a corridor that opened into a large room about twenty feet away. Wide stairs led into the area that had books lining the walls and a large fireplace behind some elaborate carved chairs.

In one of the chairs was a man in beautiful black clothes with a long, fitted coat nearly touching the ground. He stood as Alistair entered, setting down a black glass mug of some beige liquid. There was a tray of similar liquid in a bowl next to an empty cup, and a tall tower of tiny, opulent cakes. The man was beyond handsome.

"Alistair, you got my message. Please come in."

Alistair looked around, coming over to the man. "What *is* this place?"

"I'm afraid it's Hell."

Alistair frowned. "Sure it is."

"No, it's true. I can demonstrate, should you need it."

The man waved his hand and the room was devastated by heat. The scent of sulfur in the air made Alistair gag, and he felt like he was drowning. Behind the man was a mountain of tiny glowing white balls and as Alistair began to drop to his knees, something fell from the ceiling that looked like a filthy rag. It screeched and twisted, turning upon itself into another tiny, glowing white ball and fell onto the mountain of its kin. The man glanced behind him, then returned the room to its previous incarnation.

Alistair stopped gagging and drowning. He panted a moment, then stood. He waved a hand at the room. "Thanks. This will be fine."

The man smiled. "Good!" He gestured to the elaborate chair. "Please, sit. I'm sure you have lots of questions. Can I offer you something?"

Alistair waved, not certain he yet felt comfortable in this place. "Perhaps in a minute."

The man smiled and nodded to Alistair's clothes. "Excellent choice."

Alistair looked and nodded. "Not quite sure where they came from. Last time everything went away, I was nude."

"Ah yes, Karma's little power play. Never cared for that jackass."

"I feel like I already know the answer to this question, but I'm going to ask it anyway. Who are you?"

"Archangel Lucifer."

Alistair nodded, feeling a strange disconnect. He could tell that was indeed who this was, though he didn't know how. "You're right. You are. And that truly fills me with wonder. Archangel?"

Lucifer nodded. "I'm afraid so. Not a title I'm especially proud of but it tends to set others at ease."

"Forgive me, but this is vastly confusing to me."

Lucifer winced. "Yes, it should be. There's a lot to understand and Heaven isn't going to tell you. I don't know if Karma is one to leave a journal. Frankly, I don't know enough about the Land to give you an insight there. It's fairly insular."

"Why are you telling me this?"

Lucifer leaned forward. "Because you have been denied answers long enough. You have questions. Let me see if I can answer them."

"Okay, what happened to Karma?"

"Oh, you killed it."

"I… killed it?"

"Yes. You used the only thing that actually existed in the realm. It's truly the only vulnerability we have. Those Pillars are not from here, or rather, are older than anything else in the entire world or realms. None of us can remove them, break them, bruise them, shatter them, etc. Each realm has one."

"Just one?"

"Just one. Heaven has duplicated the effect, as have I, but in reality, there's only one Pillar in each realm."

Alistair mulled this over a moment. What did that mean? Was Karma no longer a religion? Was the world going to lose its capacity for balance?

Could he go home?

"What does that mean to me?"

"Well, as far as I can tell, it means you are now in charge of that balance."

"Me?"

"Mhm." Lucifer sat back and picked up his mug. He drank the contents.

"Why? Because I killed it?"

"Because you were there. The realm of Karma is not easy to enter. In fact, so far as I know, you are the only person in history to have ever seen it. Had Karma died with no one there, I think it would have disappeared from the world."

"Did Karma *know* it was going to die soon?"

Lucifer shrugged. "I have no way of knowing that. But I can't imagine it would have acted the same way if it had, being as you were the foil."

Alistair thought about this. If Karma was ready to die, perhaps it chose to let him in. But Karma was not precognizant. It reacted. No. Karma had not foreseen its own death. The chaos of the day replayed itself in his mind and caught on an image.

"Who is the woman in the cage in Heaven?"

"Ah, yes. That is Heaven's great secret. That is the Giver of Life." Lucifer gesture to the empty cup before Alistair. "Hot chocolate?" He poured some hot chocolate into his cup and dropped a crushed chili into it. Alistair frowned at the action and shook his head.

"They keep her there to add to the Well of Souls," his host continued. "They harvest her tears, when she sheds them. They could probably harvest much more, were they willing."

"Like what?"

"I suspect every part of her would give life. Hair, skin, fingernail cuttings. They don't want to risk it though, being as she is the only source. So they take the small things she gives, puts her in painful mental and physical agony, and hope she cries."

"That's horrible."

"Why do you think I walked away?"

"So, now you're the good guy?"

"Oh no. Make no mistake, I am a villain. But I am a villain quite aware of what will bring about my undoing. And I'm working towards that end."

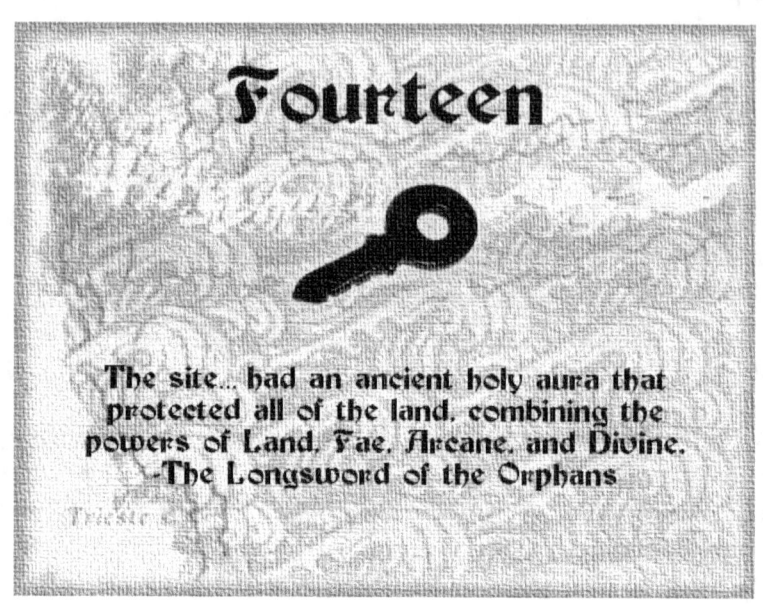

Fourteen

The site... had an ancient holy aura that
protected all of the land, combining the
powers of Land, Fae, Arcane, and Divine.
—The Longsword of the Orphans

Alistair stared at his host. "What? Why would you try to take yourself out of power?"

"Do I need to show you Hell again?" He took a sip of hot chocolate.

"Oh. So you were trapped here."

"No, I'm here quite by choice. It keeps my brothers out."

"Because you love them?"

"Because they're monsters." Lucifer took a petit four from the stack. "I hardly want them having access to this place. The destruction they would wreak." He reduced the cake to half its size with his perfectly even teeth.

Alistair's face scrunched in confusion. "I... don't understand."

He finished off the cakelette. "Karma really told you nothing?"

"I got some sort of babble about the Death Bringer but none of it made sense, of course. I tried to puzzle it out but it implied that the First Dûcesa was the Death Bringer and that, once Slade entered the realm with the Last Child, she disappeared."

Lucifer narrowed his eyes. "So she *was* back. Interesting. I helped create a situation that I hoped would return her to the world." He looked disappointed in his hot chocolate. "I never knew she actually got here. Then again, nothing was getting in or out of York that summer."

Alistair sat back slowly. "You... created those things on purpose?"

"Well, I added my part. Didn't expect it to go so well."

"Thousands *died* from those things." Alistair gripped the arms of the chair and felt like he could rip them from their moorings.

"Yes. That was what Heaven wanted."

"Wanted?"

"Utterly. It *chose* that plague."

Alistair wanted to ask why but his mouth just didn't want to work. It just kept opening and closing like he was gasping for air. Finally, he managed to get his brain and his tongue to compromise. "And Karma just let that happen?"

"It had really no stake in the matter." Lucifer cocked his head. "Karma really *did* keep you in the dark, huh?"

Alistair shook his head. "An understatement, to be sure."

"Okay, there are three forces at work here: Heaven and its associates, the Land and its associates, and Karma."

"And its associates?"

"Karma has no associates. Nothing is like Karma. There is a thing called the Great Wheel, which is actually not a wheel at all. It's more like a plate balanced on a fulcrum. If the person believed in Heaven in life, the soul drops onto the Wheel and is measured.

"Now, sin makes the soul go towards the Hell side, while sanctity makes it go to the Heaven side. If it's more good than evil, it returns to the Well of Souls in Heaven. Otherwise, it comes here for purification.

"Of course, originally, the souls all went to the Well, regardless of who the person worshipped. Then Heaven decided to bring people up whole, stopping their soul from being weighed at all. My brothers claimed these people would have put in Heaven anyway because they were so pure, but all that really did was keep the Well from getting muddier.

"Because of this action, the Land decided that it would use a different method for its followers. Now, no worshiper of the Land or its associates is returned to the Well. That's why Heaven put out the directive to destroy the other religions. But first, it needed a catalyst for this or people might rebel."

Alistair paled. "The Soulless."

"Indeed. These monsters were *very* effective and frightening. It was easy for the Church to charge the entire thing to the worshipers of every other faith. People were kept uneducated, mages were hunted to extinction, Fae were burned. And people turned to sin quickly and easily. Heaven didn't mind because, technically, Hell is part of Heaven. It's not like the souls were actually *not* going to be put back in the Well eventually, and they desperately needed those souls.

"It's like the Well is a bowl of paint. Good is white, bad is red. If a soul is fifty-one percent white, it's also forty-nine percent red. When it drops into the clean, white Well, the paint becomes a little pink. Add more like that, and it becomes a LOT pink. As each person is born, they get their soul from that Well."

Alistair nodded. "I get it. Because the Well has that pink, then the soul already has sin at birth. So it's easier for it to fall to Hell. So, how was it supposed to get less pink?"

"Purification. The fires of Hell burn away the sin, restoring the soul to its original white."

"Ah. Then those get added to the Well and that counters the red."

Lucifer nodded.

"So, what's the problem?"

Lucifer leaned in, glancing from side to side as if checking they weren't being overheard. "Hell hasn't been returning the souls."

Alistair blinked. "Why not?"

"Cuz I'm a little mad at them."

Raven looked down the cliff to the sea and sipped his tea. The sunrise was just getting going, brightening the sky with gold, pink, orange and blue, laid out like Yndia silks. He heard stirring inside, and Octavius came out, also holding a mug with tea. He looked at the sky and took a deep breath.

"Wow."

Raven nodded. "Yeah, I know."

Octavius' face scrunched a bit, his brow fighting his thoughts. "Seems rude, you know, having such a beautiful day after such a horrible yesterday."

"The sky doesn't do it for us. It does it for itself, for its own pleasure. We just get the benefits."

Octavius took a deep breath. "That's probably for the best. Then us people don't get arrogant, thinking the sky had our pleasure in mind." He took a sip of the tea then looked around from their perch. The wind was cold and constant, but they had a wind break from the bulk of it. He glanced down.

Raven looked as well. He was concerned about what he saw.

Octavius looked sideways at his travel companion. "Why are the juts of rock only down one side of the cliff?"

It was true. The rock tables Raven had thrown out yesterday had stopped as if cut right at the center line of the mountain.

Raven nodded back at the hole they had made the day before to escape the cave. "Apparently that barrier we encountered down there wasn't just through the mountain." He nodded toward the stone spires that bisected the ocean to the east. "If I recall right, that goes all the way to Nubia, then becomes a barrier across the entire continent."

"I guess whatever made it didn't want anything getting here from Mande."

"That's a safe bet."

Octavius looked at the glimpse of countryside beneath them not blocked by the mountain. There was a bustling dock city about five miles away. He pointed to it with his mug. "That's Naplles over there. We could get to it by noon if we have a way down this cliff."

Raven rubbed his arm. "There's a little challenge with that. I can't touch Mandian soil."

"Why not?"

"For the same reason Mande can't touch here. The magics are incompatible. Specifically, Lauriel will burn if he goes there. I mean, I can walk there and survive since I'm not one hundred percent Fae. But he is."

"Can he stay behind?"

Raven glanced at the doorway to the stone hut. "*Can* he? Probably. In fact, this place is probably the safest country he could be in outside of Glarren. Just don't know if he will."

"Well, what other option is there?"

Raven blew out a long exhale, creating a dragon breath of icy fog in the chilly air. That entertained him and he played with the swirls by breathing slowly, like he was filled with smoke. This went on for several minutes until Octavius tapped him on the shoulder.

"Oh. Yeah. Uh…" Raven stroked his chin because he thought it made him look thoughtful. "Oh! I can make a ball of earth from Caratia!" He gestured out his plan. "Lauriel sinks into it, encasing him fully. Then I just roll him across the country." He smiled, triumphant.

"Roll a person-sized ball of earth across the entirety of Mande?"

"Just to the docks there. Then we get a boat to Galadorn."

"That shouldn't draw any unwanted attention at all."

"Exactly!"

"I was being facetious. A person-sized ball of earth rolling along will catch a lot of unwanted attention. Especially one asking to go to Galadorn."

"Well, what do *you* recommend?"

Octavius looked down to the giant shards of vicious rocks at the bottom of the cliff. "Well, first we need to get down from here in one piece."

"I can do that."

And he pushed Octavius off the platform into the crisp salty air.

Catriona opened her eyes and looked into Myrgen's. The sun was coming up over the horizon of the Sea of Blood and bathing his room in the early morning light. She smiled as he stroked her hair.

"Have you been awake all night?"

He shrugged under the covers. "Not *all* night. I'm sure there was an hour or so when I nodded off against my will."

"That's going to haunt you later when you end up riding back here alone."

"I know. But I really can't tear my eyes away from you."

She smiled with her mouth but her eyes frowned. "I know the feeling."

He hugged her. "What am I going to do without you?"

She returned the hug as best she could with one arm pinned under her pillow. "I have the same thought."

He leaned back and looked at her. "You don't know what I will do without you?"

"Nope. Probably fall apart, crying in your paint brushes."

He flopped onto his back, feigning hopelessness. "I'm lost."

She likewise flopped across his chest, making sure her hair covered his face. "Oh Myrgen, my love!"

"Catriona dar…" He puffed her hair out of his mouth. "Darling." He puffed again and sputtered, then moved her hair aside to breathe. "I cannot live without you. Please, don't go."

"But I cannot stay. The *world* hangs in the balance."

"Then I shall accompany you."

"You cannot. The *world* hangs in the balance."

He lifted his head. "How can it hang in the balance for both of us?"

"One of us on each side." She raised her head and sat up. "What do you think maintains the balance?"

"Ah. So it's an equal weight sort of thing." He nodded, stroking his unshaven face. "Now I understand." He pointed at her. "Wouldn't a really big rock solve that?"

"The horse doesn't care for that plan."

"Ah." He exhaled and sat up as well, returning to seriousness. "We probably need to get moving then."

She, too, returned to the seriousness of the situation. She was not going on a trip to gain a new merchant or crewmember. She was delivering the worst news possible to an unsuspecting family, and she would not even have the man she loved with her for it. She felt like she was abandoning him to this country, completely unprepared.

"Look," she reached out and took his hand, "Myrgen, I trust that the Land will guide you, and you'll have Drake and Anika here to help you. I just… I hate that I have to leave you already."

"You worried about the trip?"

"Yes. I've been in York only on the port side of the Wall. This is an overland trip. The northern pass only goes into the wasteland."

"Do you have the equipment for the trek?"

"Yes, we'll be fine. The Land there never recovered from the War, but I don't think the soil is actually dangerous. The trouble will be bringing enough food. There are no villages and nothing grows on that side of the Wall."

Myrgen frowned. "How long is the trip?"

She swallowed. "It will probably take a couple tendays."

He drew back and she read his apprehension easily. She put her hands up.

"Don't worry. There's several places where the wall has gates to the wasteland. We'll have access to the coastline. We'll be fine."

"Then why are you worried about bringing enough food?"

She looked down at their hands.

Myrgen drew her eyes back to his. "Don't lie to me, Catriona. I don't have your gift and I might accidentally believe you."

She closed her eyes. "Yes. I'm sorry. The trip will require an extra horse so thank you for being willing to walk back to Zara."

"I didn't..." He sighed. "Of course." He kissed her forehead. "Whatever you need."

James met Michael at the stables as the hand finished saddling all the mounts for the trip. The fourth horse was getting packed with lentil and chick pea cakes for the animals in sizable numbers. The people could eat them as well, so they didn't need other food. Still, James hoped they would get some things from the kitchen like jerky and dried fruit.

The biggest problem would be water. There was no way to transport that much water for three people so the hope was that the abominable weather in that part of the world would provide fresh rainwater. There were pans for collecting it being added to the pack horse as Myrgen and Catriona arrived.

Everyone was dressed for long distance travel, with coats and good boots being worn. York was known to be inhospitable, with fog that lingered until often after the sun reached its zenith. The ground in the great cityscape was all cobblestones because the weather made the ground muddy and impossible to navigate. James had no idea how they would counter that in the wilderness.

"Are we ready to go?" Catriona looked at the stable hand and the horses.

James nodded. "I was hoping for some provisions for the trip that were perishable for the first leg. We have no idea when we'll see fresh food again. From what I've heard, there isn't even game to hunt."

Catriona shook her head. "No. It will be a desert, for all intents. Hopefully, there will be access to the city if we simply travel near the wall. We are bringing climbing gear, yes?" She looked at the stable hand and he nodded. "Then we can always climb the wall if we must."

Everyone nodded and mounted up.

Fifteen

With every victory, we took the amulet corrupting my brother and burned it, for Gerard did not have any skill with flame.
—The Longsword of the Orphans

Raven dispelled all the rock slabs going down the face of the mountain to protect Octavius, despite his screaming. Couldn't have his companion and brother-in-law smacking his head on a rock plateau and dying, now, could he? The drop was far, but he hoped Octavius would at least enjoy it a little. Raven leapt off and brought the wind up beneath him, allowing him to fly.

Then he crossed over into the Mandian side of things, and the magic holding him aloft disappeared. He looked down and Octavius had tumbled to the Caratian side, so Raven twisted until he got control of his magic again. That barrier was far stronger than he expected and that was going to cause problems.

The wind caught Octavius and stopped his fall gently, allowing Raven to catch up to him. They were about halfway down the cliff now and Octavius' blond hair looked a little paler than Raven remembered.

"What…was…that…?" His eyes were wide and his breathing labored.

Raven smiled. "We're heading down. I thought we'd take the fast way."

Octavius looked at Raven and punched him in the face.

Raven was knocked over into the Mandian side and they both began plummeting. Raven was a little more nervous because he was farther away this time, but he streamlined himself, like a diving gull, and got back over to the Caratian side. Octavius stopped right beside him again and reared back his fist.

Raven threw his hands up to catch the blow this time. "*Stop, stop.* We're too close to the bottom this time. I won't be able to save us if I go to that side again."

Octavius kept his arm cocked to throw the punch while he measured his desire to stay alive. Finally, he dropped the held blow and relaxed. "Fine. What's your plan?"

"We get down there and ask one of the sharks to take us to Galadorn."

Octavius cast a casual eye at the giant fins cutting through the water near the Teeth. He returned his casual gaze to Raven. "Oh. And that's supposed to work?"

"Of course. Why wouldn't it?"

"Well, let me think. Is it perhaps possible for them to say no?"

"Oh peh. I…" Then he thought about it. "Well, I suppose they *could* say no and eat us…"

"Gimme another option."

"Um, I can make a stone platform about twenty feet from the water and we can dive to the Mandian side of the Teeth. Then we swim to that port city."

"Five miles?"

"Is that hard?"

Octavius took a deep breath. "Raven, do you know how to swim?"

"There's no better time to learn."

"No better time to learn than after a long plummet into probably rocky, shallow, flat water right before a *five mile* swim?"

Raven squinted at Octavius and raised an accusing finger. "You don't sound like you're being supportive."

"Gimme a new option."

"We fly…"

"New option."

"We run along the Teeth…"

"New option."

"We make a ship of stone…"

"New option."

"We make a ship of *glass*…"

"New option."

Raven folded his arms and pouted. "You're being unreasonable."

"Yes. New option please."

"Fine, we'll slip into the water here and swim over to that sand bar over there that goes to the mainland. Then we'll walk along the beach until we reach the city and charter a ship to the main island of Latia."

"Ne…" Octavius gave it a moment to muddle through his brain, then nodded. "That works. Alright."

They drifted down to near the base of the cliff and Raven looked up at the little hut way up at the top. He put his hand on the cliff face and the entire hut reappeared around them. Octavius glanced around at the cozy building, noticed Lauriel just now stretching, completely undisturbed by the trip, and punched Raven in the face again.

The path up the Caratian North Face was about as steep as the one going up the Western Face, with a few switchbacks. The horses took it in stride but Myrgen was grateful he would not be going uphill to return to Zara. He had done a lot of walking in the last month, but he still didn't feel like he could have taken this climb in less than a full day.

There were trees along the way that he had never seen before. White trunks and heart-shaped leaves that were almost white themselves, fluttering at the slightest movement. The passing of the horses disturbing the air or the tremors of their hooves on the ground caused quaking. Myrgen decided to break the silence that had settled on the group.

"What kind of trees are these?"

"Sentinels." Catriona smiled. "They respond to the environment. Touch one."

Myrgen brushed a few of the leaves and painted them a warmer green with the contact. When he stopped, they faded back to palest gold after a moment's contemplation. "Interesting."

"I know." She reached out and touched them herself. They turned almost blue at her passing. "They detect if you are friend or foe. Friends and allies go to the blues and greens, the cooler colors. Foes are warmer and the colors remain until a friend touches them again. That way, they can identify a path through the trees as well as features like height and numbers."

Michael touched one and it went green. "These were not on the other pass into Caratia. That was just very heavy switchbacks."

"Well, the Fae cats patrol the western wall and forest. Once, long ago, we got trade from our northern neighbors. That time has passed now."

"Why?" Michael's deep voice caused the sentinel leaves to shudder.

"They have nothing to trade overland."

Silence settled upon the group again as this fact sank in. Myrgen worried again about his friends traveling in a place with no resources. He wasn't sure if bandits would be a bigger threat, or if starvation would.

Tanglwyst sat up, her eyes wide and the Power of Sovereignty flared around her. Alexander looked at the sliver of open door to her room and got up from the stool across the bar from Symonne.

"My Lady?"

She looked at him as he entered the room, her breathing still heavy from what was clearly a disturbing dream. "Alexander…"

He hurried to her side, sitting on her bed. He had been worried when he got up and heard her tossing and whimpering. In light of the recent days, he had opened her door to check on her, but it was just a dream. He had left the door ajar just enough to see her from the stool.

"Alexander… we need to go."

"Why?"

"We can't risk Duncan coming back." She glanced at the slightly open door.

He nodded. The idea of Duncan returning and destroying Symonne, Tomas, and this inn was a heavy burden. Their unnecessary kindness was sweet, but he could tell that Tanglwyst's heart was more noble and the idea of keeping these people in danger was worrisome.

"I can't envision him returning. He was wounded by the Power. Even if he can heal that, he won't want to return and get another dose. You're safe."

"I don't care about *me*. I care about *them*." She nodded towards the foyer. "Duncan cut them down without any remorse to get to me. Yes, he may not be able to touch me, but that won't stop him from touching you. If he can cut you down, our country goes to war." Her eyes wandered a moment, then got instantly frightened. "By the Saints, *Emmy*. What if he goes after *her* because he can't get to you?"

That did it. He had been selfish enough all this time. Now that she reminded him that his attitude could hurt a true innocent in this, he couldn't let it persist. If the amulet were no longer in his possession, Duncan could withdraw from the shadows again, like before, but this time without the benefit of Alexander's assistance. That broke his heart to have caused Duncan to return to the shadows when he could not be there to pull him out of them.

But the danger was too great.

He took a deep breath and stood. "That will not happen, My Lady." He held out his hand and summoned the amulet to him.

Black tendrils flowed up his arm to his chest and his heart beat faster. Before, he had the Power to keep its murderous shadows away but right then, he was vulnerable. Everything Tanglwyst feared was about to come to pass.

"Alexander?"

He struggled, trying to push the shadows away. "The... Power... It protected me before..."

She narrowed her eyes at him. "Fine."

She put her hand on him and made him her heir. He felt it the second she willed it. She then willed the Power to return to him and, in his present situation, he accepted it. He was afraid of what the Power had done to him before, but he couldn't let these people be hurt again because of his inaction. The Power surged through him and took hold of the shadows. There was a struggle for control, but the Power pushed the darkness back into the amulet, the shadows screaming in pain. Then it cast a glow around the amulet to keep them enclosed.

"What do you need?" Tanglwyst seemed smaller now.

"A fire. Fire is the only way to destroy it."

Tanglwyst looked around but the fire in the hearth had got to ash overnight. She looked at Symonne. "Is the oven going?"

"Of course." The two women ran to the kitchen and Tanglwyst came back with a burning log held in tongs. Symonne came in with kindling and a few smaller pieces of wood. It took about half an hour to get the fire built up enough but eventually, Alexander approached. He threw the amulet in the fire and collapsed to his knees. Sweat dripped from his temples and his heart was beating hard, but he kept his eyes on the screaming blackening gold until the whole thing dissolved in a flash.

Once it did, he leaned forward on his hands and knees, exhausted. Tanglwyst put her arm around him. "Let's have you lie down, okay? Symonne, can you get him some water or wine?"

"Aye, that I can."

The robust lady returned to the kitchen as Tanglwyst helped Alexander back to his room. Symonne brought in both libations as Alexander fell back onto his bed. Tanglwyst took his boots off him and Symonne offered him the water. He drank it and waved off the wine.

Tanglwyst shook her head. "You drink that too. It will make you feel better."

He sighed, but did as he was told. The wine did taste better than he expected and he lay back after gulping it. He closed his eyes and fell asleep before he even knew it.

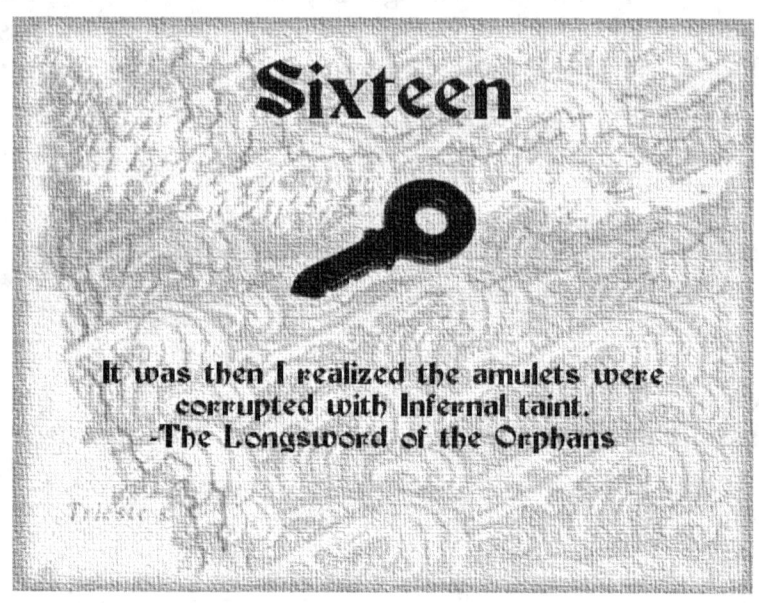

Sixteen

It was then I realized the amulets were corrupted with Infernal taint.
-The Longsword of the Orphans

Duncan dropped to a knee in the woods outside St. Andrew. The absence of the shadows had not fully hit him yet, but he knew it would. At least this time, he wasn't going to have any flayed or removed parts to worry about. Still, he was glad he had figured out the previous night not to stay in the accompanying room. Instead, he had decided to return to St. Andrew and reach out to Henri and Ce'Nedra.

Once he arrived in St. Andrew, the shadows were far too excited to be near his friends. He had instead gone into the woods and found himself near the barn where they had fought the goblins not long ago. He had gone to Caratia to find Alexander to bring him back to his friends to heal Henri and instead had ended up in far worse trouble than he expected. The rush of damage hit him all at once and he had passed out from the stress.

He awoke this morning to find the amulet gone from his person, and he had taken a knee to give thanks to the Saints. With the amulet back in Alexander's hands, maybe he could return to find Duncan himself. Or try to reach him. Either way, he was too grateful to be rid of the thing. He looked around and got his bearings, then walked toward town without going too near the manor house.

At first he was fine, but a few steps later, he felt nausea building and his head started swimming. He threw up, black sooty ink drenching the ground and his boots. He did not remember this from before, but then again, he had been unconscious when he was cured. Before, Alexander had purged it all from him through holy fire with a touch. This time he was on his own. This thought caused sweat to pop out on his skin. Though he did not remember the healing, he most definitely remembered the pain right before.

It took a few minutes for him to assess his condition, and he ended up vomiting a couple more times before he could move again. He was hoping he would be able to get some water to restore himself in town, but he worried he would be unable to get that far before dying a merciful death.

He felt tears roll down his skin and he took off his gloves to get a look at the color. As suspected, the tears were oily ink as well. His vision was blurry and he thought better of returning to a populated area. He would be burned as a witch if he showed up leaking black tears. Though that might truly be the best choice for his ailment, he was really hoping to live through this.

He looked down at the vomit on the ground and saw parts of it wriggling. He pushed aside the idea that the shadows were manifesting as worms inside his body, and instead tried to steady himself by kneeling near a tree stump. With his eyes blurring and his consciousness already iffy, he couldn't trust himself to tend a fire in the woods to destroy the shadow worms. He also didn't want to leave the damnable things unattended while he sought help. He heard a noise behind him and saw a woman from the manor house near the barn. By the time he remembered her name, it was almost too late.

"Angela!" His voice was rough and thick with vomit but he saw her turn at the sound of her name.

She looked for the shouter and he waved to her. She set down the pieces of wood she carried and came closer. "Hello? Who's there?"

"My name is Duncan. I was here a few tendays ago… at the barn…"

She stopped.

"My lady, can you send someone for Henri?"

"Henri, the city official?"

Duncan nodded, almost worn out. He looked down at the vomit, and saw the worms were eating each other. He looked up again and saw that

Angela had come closer. "My lady, I need assistance here. I can't move from this spot but I need a few hands with shovels and a fire."

"Fire?" She looked confused and started to come closer.

"Yes. Please, stay back." He knew he couldn't save her if she became infested with the larvae, not in this weakened state. Her curiosity was dangerous to them both. "It's goblin waste."

That stopped her, as he was gambling it would.

"I'll be right back." She scurried off to the house.

A few minutes later, she was gesturing to Duncan as he leaned against a nearby tree. Two men came over with shovels and another carried a lit oil lantern from inside. They looked on guard and focused. A sturdy one with a full moustache looked him over.

"Where's the goblin spoor?"

Duncan gestured to the black writhing mass on the ground. The other one with the shovel, a wiry young man with a fully shaven head showing the day's stubble, blinked repeatedly, his movements jerky. "What are we doing?"

The younger man stepped up to look at the inky worms and stopped. His muscles twitched in an involuntary, frenetic way. He stared at the blackness, silent. The older man looked at him. "Hackbardt, do you recognize this?"

Hackbardt took a moment to study the worms, then shook his head. "The good news is that the little monsters are eating each other. The bad news is that the survivors are growing." He looked at Duncan. "How bad did they getcha?"

Duncan shook his head. "One crawled in my mouth when I took a nap. I woke up and bit down on it. The taste…" He shuddered. The revulsion was true, even if the story wasn't.

Hackbardt looked Duncan over, going twice over his cheeks. "Yeah, you got goblin piss all over your face."

Duncan wiped his face with his sleeve but the tears would have only shown damp on his clothes, not color.

Hackbardt looked at his companions. "Cheston, keep that lantern ready. Bruno, help me dig a fire break real quick."

The older man with the shovel and moustache nodded and they got to work. Duncan stayed clear, but watchful. The worms didn't seem to be aware of anything outside their private battleground and Duncan was grateful. In a few minutes, the men had a trench dug around the goo and were starting on making it deeper and wider when the larger worm opened a large mouth lined with needle sharp teeth.

"Uh, fellas…"

Bruno and Hackbardt looked at Duncan, then at the worms. The toothy one grabbed one of the slightly smaller ones and Hackbardt hit it over the head with his shovel. The *clang* rang through the woods and Duncan thought he heard a woman's voice some distance away respond to it. He looked back at the worms. The blow had stunned the bigger one, the worm in its mouth now in pieces on either side of it. The two men with shovels worked as quick as they could until the larger worm was fighting the last of its brood mates.

They got a wider deeper trench finished just as the final swallow occurred. Hackbardt hit the worm with the shovel again and this time, the worm reared up and caught it in its teeth. The needles went through the shovel blade, shredding it like vellum. The four men looked at the splayed metal, and Cheston took the cue to throw the lantern on the monster.

The screeches were deafening and the flash of light caused them all to shield their eyes. By the time the women arrived, the monster had tried to move away from the circle but the fire had worked fast enough to sap its strength. It squirmed in the circle, and finally died. The oil on it continued to burn, producing a dreadful smoke. Duncan looked at the women who had arrived.

"Ce'Nedra?"

The blonde woman ran the Black Cat and Anchor Inn and Tavern in town. She was also Henri's beloved. "Duncan! What happened?"

"Ran afoul of a goblin spawn. How is Henri?"

She swallowed, turning from the burning mess. "Uh, he's healing. The greatest danger is gone now. He scared me a few times." She looked at the tall, bald pirate. "What about you? Did you…" She glanced at the others and stepped back, motioning him to follow. He did. "Did you find the king?"

Duncan glanced at the others to see if they had heard. Unfortunately, they had. He nodded. "Yes."

"Is he coming back?"

He didn't want to lie, but he also didn't want to ruin Alexander's reign. Catriona was not going to be a problem. She would never marry him, no matter how much he begged. "He's returning from Caratia now. I was able to get ahead of him to see how things were going here."

Angela looked back at the pile of burning waste, but she spoke to Duncan. "The mistress has returned to her family in Patras. She couldn't face the shame and hostility of the townsfolk. She left us behind to care for the manor."

Ce'Nedra glanced at Angela, then back at Duncan. "After you left, things got ugly. The families of the children who were murdered came after the lord of the manor. The tore his body apart. He was burned, alongside the goblin. Then people started to believe the mistress couldn't have been blind to her husband's activities. Before they could come for her, she left in the night."

Duncan looked at the ground. "I'm sorry."

Angela didn't look up. "She knew, but like the rest of us, she couldn't do anything about it. The lord was too strong. He had everyone frightened, believing we would be killed. We had all reached the breaking point after the King came through and healed the town. We weren't going to let him kill again. When you came along, when Anthelme…" A tear left Angela's eyes.

Hackbardt spoke up. "That's when I got here. The mistress sent for me from St. Giles. She knew my family had dealt with these creatures before. They were waiting for me to arrive before attacking."

"Volkard's family is from Krakte. The Hackbardts left their lands for Mervol soil after the Yorkish lands became barren. They have farmed the border between Bordeaux and Krakte ever since."

Duncan looked at the twitchy young man. Dealing with Fae would cause a person to grow up with a few tics, that's for sure. Tanglwyst's vineyards were in Bordeaux but she was south from the Krakten border. So far as Duncan knew, her lands had never suffered a Fae attack, but he also knew her lands were blessed and had church symbols all around the perimeter. One of the benefits to having the Pope as your grandfather.

Duncan nodded to the pile of burnt shadow. "Is it dead?"

Hackbardt poked it with his shredded shovel blade. The dead worm crumbled to ash. Hackbardt and Bruno started to bury the ash, but Hackbardt's shovel was all but useless. It was more like a rake now than a spade. Ce'Nedra gestured to town and Duncan hesitated. The stomach worms were gone, but he was still going to be a mess. He turned to Angela.

"My lady, I don't want to assume I'm safe to be around people yet. The barn had a locking trap door, did it not?"

She nodded and Ce'Nedra looked at Duncan. "We cleared out the bodies, but there's still a lot of... unpleasantness down there."

Duncan felt small cramps in his lower abdomen and he took a deep breath to settle them. The women saw the distress and Angela nodded again.

"This way."

They hurried to the barn.

Cipriano didn't look up at the servant who came in with the reports of the day. He never gave away his excitement at the court proceedings but with his situation downstairs, he had to actively calm himself. When he wasn't going to squeal with glee, he finally looked up at the servant.

"Come."

The servant bowed, then placed the documents on his desk. Cipriano dismissed him quickly, not tolerating any offers of wine or food. Once alone, he picked up the letters and shifted through them with a purpose. He almost threw the papers on the ground in disgust. Nothing but minor infractions, released after paying a fee.

What was the world coming to when he was two people away from completing his invasion army and no one was being cooperative? He shoved the papers off his desk, scattering them on the floor. If criminals were not going to present themselves, he would see to this himself.

He put on a very rich merchant coat and a white shirt with gold embroidery on the collar and cuffs. Gold and blue breeches of Yorkish design matched a doublet of the same style, and he chose gold hose and shoes for his legs. The accompanying hat sported several imported feathers dyed gold, held secure by a large sapphire. He put on a gold full-face mask, pulling it snug to his skin via a button on a short string held in his teeth.

He pulled on a cord that summoned two guards and he pointed to a black cloak. They nodded and put it on his shoulders, raising the hood, then did likewise with their own hoods. Cipriano guided them out the back of his room to a hidden passage. A winding staircase led to a chamber near a sealed door. He passed the floor and came to another one. This door led into a back street behind the palace, but a few turns and nods past the perimeter guards, and he was into the city.

Cipriano cast off his cloak and one of the guards picked it up. They let him get ahead of them before following and he was certain to make sure they stayed in sight of him and vice versa. Now for the hunt. Dressed as he was, he spread some money around, being certain not to speak or remove his mask. He kept his pouch of gold in his doublet, next to his chest, making no pretense to cover that motion. When he walked through crowds, he was conspicuously holding it with a gloved hand upon the bag.

This had the effect of making him a wise buyer incapable of being pickpocketed, and eventually, he bid farewell to the market and started back through the streets. He saw two people starting to move a cart from one of the stalls down a street and turned down a side street to continue on his way. A little way down from there, he saw a prostitute draw a customer down another side street, then stop to service him.

Cipriano took another detour, slowly maneuvering back towards the palace. He glanced behind him and saw that the guards were now nowhere to be seen. He looked around, worried and saw two men come into another alley ahead of him. He ran, spooked by their sudden presence, turning and twisting until he found himself in a blind alley. His motions were frantic and he turned to see two thugs enter the alley. He put his back to the wall as they advanced.

"You seem to have made a wrong turn, my friend." The thug on the left, dressed in well-made leather in a darkened black pulled a dagger from his belt. "And after being so careful too. I almost thought our ruse wouldn't work. But you seem to have an abundance of money in that carefully guarded pouch at your chest. Hand it over or we'll take it from your dead body."

Cipriano shook his head, holding out a gloved hand to ward them off while clutching his doublet and pouch with the other.

The second thug sighed. "Looks like our Yorkish friend here has chosen to do things the more unpleasant way."

The thugs leapt at him and grabbed Cipriano's hands. They each punched him in the stomach, doubling him over, and he dropped the button from his teeth, the silk-covered mask hitting the alley stones silently. Cipriano looked up at his assailants.

The second one started to kick Cipriano but the other one stopped him, his own face turning to horror. "*Leo, no.*"

Rough hands were put upon the two thugs and the guards had daggers at their throats.

"You are charged with high treason, laying hands upon the king with ill intent. The penalty for this is death."

Cipriano nodded and the thugs were forced to their knees. He pulled a pair of coins from the pouch and stepped forward. "Hold these in your mouths."

The thug in black shook his head but Leo just looked confused.

"You wanted my money. This is so you can taste the gold you sought."

Leo opened his mouth, glancing at the first thug. Cipriano put it on the man's tongue. When nothing happened to his partner, the first thug looked back at his king.

"Come on now. This is going to go to your family, but only if you have it on you when you are executed."

The first thug shook his head. "I have no family."

Cipriano looked genuinely saddened by that knowledge. "What a tragedy. Well, then maybe you can bribe a guard. Or pay the headsman to sharpen his axe. You really should take it."

The guard pressed the knife into his neck and the thief winced, spreading his lips. Cipriano seized on the action and grabbed the man's hair through his head covering, shoving the coin in his mouth. The thug apparently decided to go down swinging and thrust his dagger into Cipriano's leg.

His face was very satisfying when it met with a *tink* against the tight scale mail woven into the breeches. Cipriano also had the same in the doublet, built between the lining and the outer cloth. It wouldn't stop a sword blow, but a dagger at close range was not likely to have enough power behind it to penetrate the mail.

Then the poison acted. Leo flopped over and the one in black being disarmed stopped struggling for a moment, giving the guard on him the chance he needed to punch him to the ground. The thief scrambled away and got to his feet. The guards turned to watch him run, and he turned back to see this. He slowed, stumbled, then fell a few feet from the mouth of the alley.

Cipriano smiled, then turned to the wall. He moved the catch and a secret door swung open in it. He waited for one guard to retrieve the unconscious thief from the end of the alley, while the other slung Leo over his shoulder and entered the passage. He ushered in the second guard and then followed them to the passage that led to his underground torture chamber.

Seventeen

...For the Prince Alistair Yorkthrone had
run to Persephone pursued by monsters.
-The Longsword of the Orphans

Tanglwyst shouldered the satchel Symonne handed her, both of them careful to avoid the nightingale board on the front porch. They had not said a word to each other since Alexander passed out. Tanglwyst had gone straight to her room and began to pack. Symonne had seen this, nodded, and went to the kitchen. By the time now-former Sovereign of Mervolingia was ready for the road again, Symonne had food for her journey in the satchel.

They had a quick hug goodbye, then Tanglwyst went silently on her way. She knew Alexander would be upset with her, but frankly, she didn't care. That horrible amulet was destroyed and Alexander had the Power back. She also knew from holding it that it would be just power with no agenda when he received it.

She thought about what he had told her and, with the Power inside her, she felt several important things. Because Alexander's first acts with the Power were selfish, the Power was likewise selfish. When he gave it to her to save her, it came to her as a healing thing. Since she did nothing to alter that while she held it, it had remained helpful.

She felt Alexander was a wonderful man. He was strong enough to weather this storm, if he stayed in his healing mindset. With the loss of everything driving his obsession, she hoped that was also cured.

However if it wasn't, then, from the sounds of it, Myrgen and Catriona would kill him. She only hoped he would be smart enough to name Emmy his heir this time.

She knew she also felt that the best thing she could do for him at this time was to leave him. She had a place to go and she needed to be on her way. She had slept for almost a full day when the Power came to her. She hoped he would do likewise. The danger was passed, outside of the Stâpâna of Caratia showing up, but she also got the impression that maybe Myrgen was with Catriona by choice. She wouldn't come after Alexander.

She wasn't quite so sure about coming after her though. Tanglwyst had been the orchestrator of the kidnapping of Alan, not Myrgen. If she was with him, she knew this. If Michael was with them, and since Gwen made it to Zara, Michael undoubtedly did, then Catriona would read him and know the rest of that story. She didn't really know how Catriona would take the knowledge that Tanglwyst had fallen in love with her beloved, but she took it as a good sign that her passage down the mountain had not been interrupted by Caratian soldiers or patrols.

Besides, that had passed. If she looked at Tanglwyst now, she would have seen only a woman apologetic about the kidnapping, saddened by the loss of Nicolai and Alan, and whose heart had come to its senses regarding Alexander. The Prince had been a sweet dalliance, one that helped heal her heart. The problem had not been in the return of Nicolai, but in Tanglwyst's own weakness, spurred by Elizabeth's machinations. She had been lonely, and so had Alexander.

Nothing more.

She felt tears on her cheek. They were not tears of sadness as much as tears of release, remorse. She needed to do penance, to get her head and heart clear. The tears were a good start so she let them go untethered. It was a good feeling.

The road down looked like a few people had tried to make a path that went straight down the mountainside. It was not visible from the bottom but was all but obvious from this side. She took a chance and started down the straight path. It was far easier than she thought it would be and she made it down with little expenditure of resources about mid-day. She looked behind her to make sure Alexander hadn't awoken and decided to chase her, but she was still alone.

She gave herself a moment out figure out how she felt about that. She pictured him doing just that and wondered if she would run or stand still to meet him. Would she hide in the village, sneak into the woods and leave a message to the guards that he was there, impairing his chase? Or would she stand there, waiting for his embrace? Another moment passed and she sighed. Luckily, she didn't have to find out either way.

She saw a messenger shop and thought about sending word to her grandfather, but that seemed silly. The messenger would have to go overland just like her. The message would get there when she did, if not after. Nope, she was just going to have to get there on her own. She wasn't even sure she could afford a horse to make the trip easier. With no horse to trade, she would effectively be buying a horse and her money was depleted. She would be on foot, but these boots had proven good traveling companions.

She passed an inn with the smell of bacon and sausages filling the air, and she realized she was hungry. She had not gotten the chance to eat before the ordeal of the day and she was feeling it now. She checked her pouch and found enough money left to get breakfast and be on her way. She also found that Symonne had been more than generous with her rations. Tanglwyst pulled out a biscuit and a carrot and began eating.

"There's an inn up here?"

Myrgen's question as he looked at the building seemed funny. The sign swinging in the light but chilly breeze said BrewHa House. The inn had a sizable garden spot on the side with at least ten different things planted. An old and well-used well supplied water and a compost pile in the back left a faint smell of rotting foliage. Two blond children were tending the garden and they looked up when the party of travelers arrived.

One of them leapt up and ran inside. "Ma! Ma! There are people!" The girl's voice was nasally and strangely familiar to Catriona. Catriona dismounted and the others followed suit, grateful to stretch their legs. She looked down the other side of the mountain to see what they would be up against as the child announced their arrival.

Myrgen came over by her, removing his gloves. "Wow. That looks... desolate."

Michael and James tended to the horses as the young boy from the garden came over to ask what they needed. There didn't seem to be a stable.

Catriona folded her arms across her chest. "Yes. Well, that's what the Soulless War did to this country. It destroyed it." She pointed to the eastern edge, which glinted in the sun. "Their entire surviving society moved there, to the ocean."

The city stretched the entire length of the country, one long, endless series of houses and factories. On the landward side, a tall wall separated York from an almost desert.

"I've been to York several times. Tanglwyst has a few manufacturers of some note there. I've always seen it from the seaward side. But that's not where you'll be going, is it?" He pointed to the more desert-like wilderness. "You're heading there."

"At least at first. We'll head into the city if we need to."

He looked at her, his worry fairly clear. "How much have you studied that place?"

"Well, like you said, Tanglwyst has manufacturers in that city. I, too, have dealt with them often."

"Okay. Just..."

She put her hand on his. "I know. And I will."

James and Michael came over. James whistled. "That's... barren."

"Yes, but still dangerous." Michael's baritone echoed around the top of the mountain. "The city wall was built to protect the survivors of the great wars but in fact, it was assumed nothing else could be done with the land, so they made bricks from it. There are secret doors in the walls to get in and out and the homeless have built hovels all along the wilderness side of the wall."

"So, there will be bandits." James took a deep breath.

"Yes," his new friend replied. "Most certainly." Michael looked at James. "What's your plan?"

"This." James held up a journal. "It's Alistair's."

Catriona and Myrgen both frowned at the object.

James answered the unspoken question. "He left it for me and Gwen." He opened the book and showed a map. "This is what York used to look like. And this," he pointed to a grand tower, "is Persephone."

Myrgen frowned. "Persephone. Raven mentioned that."

James looked surprised. "Raven Grasshair?"

Myrgen bobbed his head. "Probably, judging by his appearance."

"Huh. He's in here. I met him a few days ago in cat form. He," James smiled, despite the circumstances, "sank Alexander into the ground up to his neck."

"What?" Catriona was shocked.

Myrgen nodded. "Yeah, I can see him doing that. But cat form? How did you know it was him?"

"He said he was leaving 'Lauriel' there to guard Alexander. My uncle wrote about Raven and Lauriel. I don't get the impression he would be traveling without him. If Lauriel was still around and with a Fae, he was likely with Raven."

"Where do you encounter him?"

"South of Zara, in the woods. He and another fellow from your ship, Catriona, was with him. He said Alexander shot his sister and he didn't have time to deal with him right then."

Shot? Sister? Catriona felt a strange pang, like she did when she stepped through the Church to Father Benjamin. There felt like a memory that could not be a memory.

Persephone.

She looked at the map. The area with the tower was well east of the Wall. Going through there would make it more dangerous since bandits, desert, and who knew what else would be there. There was another word on the map by Persephone: Covenant. She knew from Galadorn what a "covenant" actually was. Persephone seemed to have a lot of answers, at least potentially. The First Dûcesa fell near Persephone. She very much wanted to go to this place to look at it.

She looked at the area below, then went and got her telescope from her horse. Since the ship was in dry-dock for the summer, it made no sense not to have it on this trip. She opened it and looked in the area of Persephone. It took a moment to find it, but she found something that looked like it could have once been a tower.

"I think I see it. It's just a ruin now. A few stones." She handed the telescope to James.

He looked and nodded. Then he moved to scan the wall. "Hmm. There are a lot of buildings down there. It could mean maybe the soil is healing."

She smiled. "I would like that."

"Me too. It would mean we have food on the outside." James handed back the telescope.

Myrgen looked at the inn. "Shall we…"

He stopped and Catriona looked at him, then followed his gaze. Two older folks, a man and a woman, came out onto the porch of the inn. She had on an apron and her hair was pulled out of her eyes into a muffin cap. She put her hands on her hips. Her voice had a nasally pitch to it.

"Hello there."

She gestured to the older man next to her. He was white of hair and beard and wore an apron covered in flour.

"I'm Cecelia and this is Lawrence. Welcome to BrewHa House."

Alexander opened his eyes, stretched and figured out he needed to pee before remembering that he had the Power of Sovereignty again. The thought was very sobering. He had needed to do it. If he hadn't, he would have had to hand the amulet to Tanglwyst and, especially then, he could not put her in jeopardy. Even now, the thought of her in danger was…

He shook off the path his thoughts were taking. Just because he was King again didn't mean he was more worthy. In fact, he now saw that he was the servant for his people. It was odd that he had that mindset now. He reflected upon what he had done before and how strangely good he had felt after confessing his crimes. He had turned dark because of an obsession, an addiction to a memory. Last time, the Power had fueled that obsession in the most unhealthy way.

But this time, he had taken it to protect the current Sovereign and save people. That was a very different act and he could feel the difference in the Power. It had changed. He wondered what had been his father's first act, what was Francois'? He knew Charles' had been to say their mother Catherine never needed to bow to him again. Tanglwyst's first act was to demand the truth from him, which meant, if she had decided to hold onto it, her search for truth would have governed her reign.

He got up to relieve himself in the chamber pot, then went into the common room. Tanglwyst's door was closed and Symonne was out back, pinning sheets on the line. Tomas was in the kitchen, stirring a stew. Alexander realized Tanglwyst might be resting. Dealing with the Power could be an ordeal and he didn't want to disturb her. He went out back and chopped wood for a while without having to be told.

With every chop, he worried he might awaken her, but part of him *wanted* to wake her, to talk to her and thank her for her insight, her sacrifice. Holding the Power was exhausting, feeling the weight of the entire country upon you. Still, he owed her. He was clear of the megalomania that had clouded his mind for so long. He was glad he hadn't actually gotten where he wanted to go with Catriona. Had she become pregnant, it would have been disastrous.

This was better and he could feel it. He was okay and his heart felt lighter, the weight of the populace not as great. He could still feel them, like before. He could feel the people whose fealty he held. He smiled at the idea and looked for Tanglwyst. He felt her and knew instantly she was miles from this place.

The axe thunked hard into the chopping block and he stopped. He looked at Symonne, who he now realized had been watching him.

"No. You didn't let her..." He didn't finish the sentence. Instead, he ran inside and threw open her door.

Tanglwyst's room was empty.

He turned on Symonne and Tomas. "You *let her go?*"

"She's a grown woman, Alexander. She wasn't a prisoner. Of course I let her go."

Tomas shrugged, then nodded. "It seemed she was ready."

"She's out there *alone!* There are bandits and beasts and she's out there near a wood right now. She doesn't even have a hunting knife to protect herself."

Symonne sighed. "She's going to be fine, Alexander. She knows where she's going."

"Did she tell you?"

Symonne looked at Tomas, then shook her head.

Alexander knew she was either heading to Patras or the Papal City, and she really had no reason to go to Patras. With him missing and her a fugitive, the patrols could arrest her if they recognized her and he wouldn't be able to stop it.

"I have to go." He went to his room, looked around, then realized he didn't have any baggage. He threw some gold on the bed and stormed out.

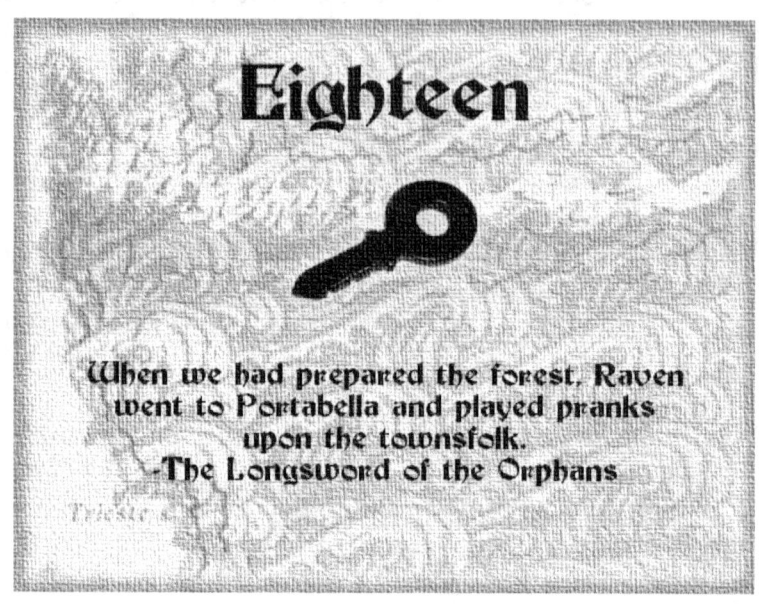

Eighteen

When we had prepared the forest, Raven
went to Portabella and played pranks
upon the townsfolk.
—The Longsword of the Orphans

Myrgen was about to ask the innkeepers if he knew them but Catriona put her hand on his arm and stopped him. James started discussing the mundane arrangements for a simple meal before heading down the mountain, and Catriona tugged Myrgen a step back.

"It's not them."

Myrgen looked at her. "You recognize them too?"

She nodded.

Michael looked back at the couple. "Twins?"

She shook her head. "I doubt it. They are identical to the kitchen servants in Patras. I can honestly see no difference in the details."

Myrgen looked at Michael. "When was the last time you saw Lawrence or Cecelia?"

"I think when you were at the castle."

"You didn't see them there after we parted company?"

Michael shook his head.

James walked over to the group. "What's so important over here?"

Myrgen nodded to the inn. "Those folks work at the palace in Patras."

"What do you mean?"

Catriona looked closely at James. "You saw something."

"I saw something I expected."

Michael frowned. "What?"

Catriona breathed in. "Fae."

James nodded. "Not unexpected. It *is* an inn."

"Can you speak to it?"

James shrugged. "Yeah, I could, but that would be redundant. It asked to talk to you."

Dominic D'Medici stepped out of the Chancellor's office, his latest report in his hand. He had managed to clean up all the information regarding the fires in St. Marguerite, but in doing so, he decided some arrests and prosecutions were in order, preferably beheadings. St. Marguerite had an executioner on site. Dominic felt it might be time to give him some work. After all, lies about the Crown destroying the village could hardly be tolerated. Especially when he had another report that Alexander was in St. Andrew at the same time.

"Lord Dominic," a young servant named Felix bowed before the Acting Chancellor, "Lady Rochefort is here seeking an audience with the Queen Mother."

"Why are you telling me?"

"Well, because…" Felix averted his eyes, not wanting to break whatever news he had to Dominic, "she's not here."

"Where is she?"

"I believe she left to return to the Papal City. She left yesterday."

"Without telling *me?*"

Felix shrugged.

"Well, I suppose I'll see her then. Send her to the King's Chamber."

Felix left and Dominic went into the King's Bedchamber. Alexander had still not asserted his presence here but with Gomez de Santander out of the castle, the place was practically Dominic's. He sat in the elaborate desk chair and set his reports on top of the sizable stack of other reports he had assembled during Alexander's absence. It had been several tendays since Dominic had last seen him and there was still no word regarding his whereabouts.

Dominic was glad Catherine was gone now too. With everyone else gone, he could govern this place properly. The King would return to a well-run kingdom, and would have little or nothing to do but read reports to catch up. Since Alexander had never trusted Catherine, he would be looking for someone to be his power behind the throne, and Dominic was making sure the logical choice was him.

The door to the Chamber opened and a noblewoman of middle age entered. She had dark hair and pale skin, not uncommon amongst the nobility of Patras. Her eyes were the standard blue and she was wearing clothes that indicated a horse, not a carriage. He found it odd that a noblewoman would come to an audience with the Queen Mother in riding clothes.

"Forgive me, Your Lordship. I was hoping to see the Queen Mother." She curtsied.

"I'm sure you are glad she was not available, with this attire."

She glanced up but did not stand. "Qu…quite possibly, sir. I…" She wobbled and fell to a knee.

He stood and called out for a guard. One entered the room, bristling, and Dominic came over to her. He looked at her a bit more closely and saw she was exhausted. He saw now she was not advanced in years. In fact, she was likely closer to his age than Catherine's, but she seemed to have some wear on her. Her complexion was clear but her eyes were weary and her skin had a slight sag to it, like she was too thin. He looked up at the guard.

"Bring the Queen's handmaid."

The guard nodded and rushed from the room. Dominic reached out a hand. "Here, sit."

He helped her stand and glanced about for a proper chair. The desk chair was too elaborate for a mere noblewoman and besides, that was Dominic's chair. He looked at the large overstuffed chair that replaced the one Charles was in when he was killed. That one was too regal for her too. There were chairs around the table, and they were appropriate, but then *he* would be sitting in one and that would put them on even footing. Definitely *not* appropriate here.

Then he remembered this woman requested Catherine directly. "What business did you have with the Queen Mother?"

"She told me to seek her out if I ever found myself in trouble."

A personal friend?

"Here, let's do this." He took her over to a padded trunk at the foot of the King's Bed and then moved his desk chair to be near her. "This way, should you need to, you may lie down."

"Oh, thank you, Your Lordship." She looked at the surroundings. "Your office is resplendent."

"Yes. It is. Now, what brings you to the palace?"

She looked down at her hands. "A few tendays ago, the King came through St. Andrew. While he was there, he... healed people."

Dominic sighed. "Well, he's a generous person. He frequently treats others in pain. His physician's kit is legendary around the palace."

"Physician's kit?" She looked askance at the young Chancellor. Then she glanced around the enormous room, apparently wrestling with something. "I'm sorry, when will Her Majesty return? This is truly a conversation I should have with her."

Dominic decided his time was far too valuable to be bothered with some useless woman who didn't realize her place. "I don't know. However, why don't you write her a letter and I'll have a messenger take it to the Papal City. Then she will be able to respond to you personally."

She smiled. "That would be a very good idea."

"Come then. I shall take you to a chamber where you will have some privacy."

He turned to leave and waited at the door for her to follow. She seemed less fragile this time which meant he wasn't going to need a guard to carry her. He took her downstairs to the antechamber and gestured for her to enter.

"I'll send in our messenger. Wait here."

He closed the door and went to the service office in the palace. He had one boy he used specifically, a Mandian, and he beckoned him. "Uberto, there is a woman in the Antechamber that needs to send a message. Please take her the supplies to do so. Bring the message to me when she is done. I need to add some things to the package."

"Of course, Your Lordship."

Dominic returned to the bedchamber and stopped, annoyed again. "Officer Richelieu. What are you doing in here?"

Nina Richelieu, Lieutenant to Grande Guarde Gomez de Santander, turned to face Dominic. She was six feet tall and willowy, with dirty blonde hair and almost Fae-like features. Because of this, and because she was very loyal to Gomez above anyone else, Dominic didn't trust her.

"I was turning in the guard reports, Lord Dominic."

"Fine. Anything useful?"

"Other than the Archbishop's death? No." She started for the doorway.

"Wait, what?"

She turned over her shoulder. "It's in the report. I figured you wouldn't find it to be of importance because it wasn't about you or money."

"*Lieutenant Richelieu.* Need I remind you that I have the King's authority to run this country as I see fit until he returns, and that includes getting rid of any employees of the palace I deem useless?"

"I quiver with fear. You actually *don't* have control over the guard because that is the purview of His Majesty Alexander and I have felt absolutely no transfer of that power to the likes of you. So return to your petty bribes and hissing from the shadows, *Lord Dominic*. Your snarls mean nothing to the Guarde."

She turned and left, not rushing, but not storming. She left like she had the *right* to.

Dominic fondled the amulet through his tunic. He looked around the room.

Soon enough, that power will be mine.

Nina closed the doors to the King's Bedchamber behind her, annoyed as usual at Dominic. He was so *pretentious*. Taking over the *King's* bedroom, where His Majesty Charles had been murdered, and acting like *he* was entitled to be there was beyond infuriating. She couldn't wait for the Prince to return.

Besides, she had a question or two about something. She was lying in there just now, but she was also testing. She actually *had* felt a transfer of Power happen recently, transferred to someone she knew but who wasn't *well* known to her. Then, a day later, it transferred back to Alexander. She could tell it was him, but even so, she could tell it was different.

Before, his power and directions were turning more sinister every tenday. The sensation wasn't a daily thing and was gradual, but when Gomez left for St. Giles, she had felt Alexander's mental state to be passionate. Then, as time passed, it had turned controlling. As someone whose loyalty to the Crown and the State was part of her rank, she felt these differences more than apparently anyone else.

Except Gomez. Gomez was closer to Alexander and as such, could be a part of such rituals as a Summons or a Writ. She was not ready for a bond that close. That level was part of the office of Grande Guarde so she was perfectly happy with her position as Lieutenant. It was more than enough of a connection to the person holding the Power of Sovereignty.

She saw a messenger, Uberto, waiting outside the Queen's Antechamber downstairs as she passed the hallway on her way to the Guarde office. She was immediately suspicious. Uberto was a favorite of Dominic, which pretty much meant the young man was either suspect or at risk. She stepped back to where she could watch the end of the hallway and waited until Uberto left with the message. She expected him to head towards the messenger office near her but he instead turned towards the upstairs chambers.

She knew at once he was taking the note to Dominic. There was no one else up in the royal quarters except him and Emmy. This irritated her, but she decided to check on something first. She went to the room Uberto was monitoring and opened the door. A dark haired girl was sitting alone, waiting and looking anxious and haggard.

Nina bowed. "Can I assist you, my lady?"

"I'm waiting. I am Sylvaine Rochefort, from St. Andrew."

"St. Andrew. The King was recently there. There was also a problem with a noble." Nina then remembered the name of the nobleman who was recently killed. "You... you are his daughter?"

"Wife, actually. Widow now."

"I'm sorry for your loss."

Sylvaine shuddered. "Please, don't be." She suddenly seemed to realize she was not speaking to a friend or confidant and her eyes snapped wide in fear. "I mean..."

Nina held up her hand. "I read the reports. I'm Lieutenant Nina Richelieu of the Grande Guarde. Please, don't fear speaking around me. It's my job to protect Mervolingia's people."

Sylvaine relaxed.

Nina stepped over and knelt beside the young woman's chair. She was younger than Nina by probably a decade, which put this girl about fifteen years old. "Why don't you tell me why you're here? I might be able to help."

Sylvaine frowned and Nina realized the girl was on the verge of tears. "I was married to my husband four years ago, arranged by a man in Mande. My mother was Mervol but my father was Mandian. They arranged my marriage, with part of the bride price being that I move to Mervolingia and be educated. I was to marry a young man named Felix, whom I met here a few years ago, after I was out of school in six years. His family had him as a valet to King Charles.

"Then my parents died. I still don't know what happened. Suddenly, a different man was at our house. He said my parents owed him a lot of money and that my marriage rights were forfeit. He nullified my contract with Felix and married me to Rochefort to settle my family's debts. He did not want me to be educated and kept me at the manor house in St. Andrew.

"Then the children started being hurt."

Nina looked away. She knew about the reports of dead and maimed children. "Did he hurt you?"

"No. For some reason, he never touched me. Ever. But I was so afraid, I didn't know what to do. I made sure Angela and the others I hired didn't have children, and sometimes, that bothered my husband. I kept children from the house as much as I could, but he still got his hands on a few every couple months.

"Then, a couple tendays ago, some people came to the house and managed to stop my husband. They came upon the barn he used as a lair and got inside the basement. They managed to save some people, but it turned out there was a monster in the basement with him, a demon Fae. It was killed but so was my husband."

Nina patted the girl's hand. "So, was there something new? What brought you to the palace?"

"Catherine told me if I ever needed her help to come here. She knew the man who sold my marriage contract and she didn't like him. She liked Felix and me together."

"What help do you need?"

She looked down at her hands and realized she had been squeezing them. She relaxed, her hands having small indents in the flesh from her tension. "The town was starting to act suspiciously. They seemed to think I knew about my husband's proclivities and that I should have stopped him."

"You're barely no longer a child yourself. What did they expect from you?"

Sylvaine shrugged. "I just felt like I wasn't safe. My staff did as well. They told me to leave. So I came here last night."

"You traveled at night?"

"Better than dying burned at a stake."

Nina nodded. There was that. "Where are you staying?"

"I don't know. I don't have any family left."

Nina thought for a second, then smiled. "I have just the place."

Dominic set down Sylvaine's letter. *Magical healing from Heaven?* The fact that he did this was disturbing, worse because it was apparently so public. He looked at the stack of reports on the desk from the Guarde. He felt there would be nothing useful in there except the crimes of Lord Rochefort.

He felt a shudder of conscience, like a part of him was fighting the rising shadows clouding his view. He tried to remember the feelings he had when he spoke with Catriona in the catacombs and the honor in Myrgen's plea to save Catriona's son. He had felt good, whole. Gwen had hugged him and he felt something *real* for a while: Camaraderie. Friendship.

Then he found the amulet Tanglwyst had dropped and it all faded away as suddenly as it had appeared. He fingered the amulet now, and decided to stop wondering about it. His ambition now was to advance in the world and he was not going to alter that course. He had gone to St. Marguerite to investigate the reports they had filed. He would do likewise with St. Andrew.

He gripped the amulet and pictured the council hall in St. Andrew.

Nina knocked and entered the Bedchamber, not much of a pause between the two actions. "Dominic, I'm taking Lady Rochefort to Holloway Manor…"

She looked around and went to the desk. A horrid stench of rotten eggs befouled the air and she covered her nose and backed away. *By the Saints, Dominic. What have you been eating?* She imagined he was undoubtedly in the privy after such an emission so she decided that asking permission, even for a house under seizure by the Guarde, was simply not going to be the best course. She'd leave a note…

She saw the letter Sylvaine had written on the desk, open and walked over to it. She picked it up, then folded it in fury. A letter to the Queen Mother and Dominic had the audacity to read it before it was sent. Well, Nina would make sure that it got to Catherine personally, with full disclosure of how she found it. She was also going to get a similar notice off to Gomez, who would be able to get this news to Alexander. This was going to be his undoing.

A woman who Nina recognized as one of the former queen's Ladies in Waiting was heading down the stairs. She nodded to Nina. The Queen's Ladies had nothing much to do with Elizabeth dead and Alexander off in search of a wife. They had made all the preparations they could in anticipation of the unknown, but in truth, there was only so much pillow fluffing one could do when the identity and proportions of a person were still undecided. As it stood, everything was decorated in blue and gold as a default.

Nina joined her a she made her way towards the Antechamber. "Sabine, how are you doing today?"

Sabine was a lovely woman. Long dark hair with lots of waves and dark brown eyes. She was very sweet but had that ability to govern children and sycophants with matronly ease, despite being no older than Nina, and unmarried. "*LORD* Dominic has sent me to the Antechamber to tend to someone. That's all I have."

"Ah. That's actually good. I'm on my way there now. She's Lady Rochefort."

"The child molester's wife?"

"She's almost a child herself. She left St. Andrew out of fear of being burned out of association. She's so glad he's gone and the town is safe again, but she is also very tired and scarred by it all."

Sabine's eyes softened. "The poor thing. What are we going to do?"

"I'm going to put her up in Holloway Manor. The Grand Guarde has jurisdiction over it at present. She has no family." Nina thought for a moment. "She's going to need some people she can trust around her. Please take her and Felix to the Manor and take care of her. I'll send for you when the Prince returns."

"Felix? Why Felix?"

"He was her betrothed before Rochefort bought her marriage contract. As far as I can tell, she's still intact so their marriage might still happen. I know he has never entertained any other opportunities."

Sabine frowned. "*Intact*. Disgusting. That a woman must be *intact* while a man can alley cat about at will. A woman who has had sex is hardly 'ruined', but men seem to think they can control the birthing process if their seed is the only one deposited. It's like it never occurs to them that if she has his brother as her lover, the child will look the same."

"The only certain parent is the mother. That's why men fight so hard to control them. No proof."

"Well, I know Felix. He's a good boy. He has stopped some of the other boys from bullying and foul behavior. In the last year, he's been a great influence upon the new charges that have come to us."

Nina smiled. She was glad to hear that Sylvaine's first love was a decent person. Nina wanted her to have a good person by her side after the nightmare of the last four years. She honestly didn't believe that the girl was intact, not when her husband was hurting children. Then again, she might have been too old for his tastes.

Nina opened the door to the Antechamber and saw Felix sitting next to her, holding both of Sylvaine's hands. Nina and Sabine stopped and Felix looked up. He didn't start, like he was doing something wrong. He instead looked like Sylvaine's comfort was worth any chastisement he would get later for impropriety. The two women exchanged a look and a smile.

Sabine stepped forward. "Do you need anything to eat or drink? I can have something brought."

Nina nodded to Felix. "And I'll be letting the Chatelaine know that you are being reassigned for a while."

He glanced at Sylvaine, who looked nervous. "Reassigned?"

Nina smiled. "Yes. Lady Rochefort needs someone to help her transition to living here in Patras."

Felix lit up, as did Sylvaine. They hugged as the two older women backed out of the room to attend to their tasks.

Nineteen

When they used the amulet, a terrible
stench surrounded them, like rotten eggs
and brimstone.
—The Longsword of the Orphans

The door to the St. Andrew Council Hall office opened and Dominic D'Medici stepped in. He looked surprised to see not just Henri, but two other people in here. Then he recognized Duncan. He reached up to his neck and Duncan saw the amulet. He hit Dominic in the chest, knocking the wind out of him. Duncan was afraid that would prompt a jump to the secret room and he grabbed the amulet. The thought was in his head of the secret room when the amulet teleported.

The room had a light blue glow around the edges of the floor. There was furniture in this room, similar to the kind in the room associated with his previous amulet. *This amulet is from the Church.*

Dominic staggered, but Duncan grabbed the amulet to stop him from escaping. The chain was strong and just yanked Dominic's head forward and Duncan stepped back to get more leverage. Someone grabbed him from behind and he felt a sharp stab in his lower back, then another. The amulet slipped from his grasp and he slumped to the floor as Dominic disappeared.

The man above him had a nasty scar across his face and a wicked knife in his fist. He looked where Dominic had been seconds before and bellowed in rage. His eyes had the crazed look of someone who had been trapped alone for far too long. His eyes widened and he plunged the knife into his own neck, covering Duncan in a spray of gore.

He fell back and landed on the floor at the foot of the bed. The shadows started to whisper towards him but Duncan shouted an ancient sound and the glowing symbols around the room flared, banishing the shadows. He watched as the scarred man bled out onto the floor, his own blood starting to stain his fingers.

Duncan looked at the chest across from the foot of the bed and crawled over to it. This was where he had stored bandages and things to repair himself before he realized the shadows would heal him. He hoped that the scarred man had done likewise, but when he opened the chest, it just held wine. Not a bad use for a room that had no light coming in, but not what he needed.

He remembered the shadows still within him from the new amulet and shuddered. *No. Not that. The amulet is gone. I can't call it back. I tried. I'm going to have to sweat this out.*

A writhing voice whispered in his head, and he knew its source. *That won't matter if you die from these wounds. You only have a few minutes before you bleed out.*

Duncan was tempted, but he knew if he accepted the help of the shadows, that as soon as he was purged of them again, he would be just as injured as he was right now. There was no benefit to accepting their help. They only served themselves.

Then what will it hurt to be healed? At least that way, I can survive long enough to find a way out of this room. I can't heal in here with no bandages or herbs.

Duncan leaned against the wall by the chest. He didn't want to give in to the shadows again. They had taken him over, made him hurt a woman he cared about, and justify killing as the solution to any problem. Better to die free than live as a slave to an addiction. The shadows would lose, and that was enough for him.

He could still feel the pull of the monsters, though. He knew he had to act immediately if he wanted to get through this without their help. He was going to defeat this. If he healed up…

His eyes fell upon the scarred man.

If I heal up, I'll still go mad. I'll live forever in this prison, never aging, never eating, never drinking after the wine ran out. Why would Dominic ever return here now? If this man didn't kill me, I would kill

Dominic. The only way I get out is if someone other than Dominic gets that amulet, and the way those things work, no one gives them up willingly.

He looked at the wine and pulled out a bottle. He realized he had no way to remove the cork and looked at the desk and dining table in the other part of the room. It was a dozen feet away and he really didn't feel like trying to move that far. He looked at the knife still stuck in the neck of the scarred man. That was much more accessible.

He crawled over to the foot of the bed and pulled the knife out. More blood than before coated the body and he ended up wiping the blade on his own sleeve. Then he used the back of the blade and hit the neck of the bottle. It chipped and his stab wounds threatened to put him under. He shook it off and hit again, this time breaking the neck against the cork. A few more whacks and the neck came off, the glass from it embedding in the cork. He pulled the top off, unseating the cork and poured some into his mouth.

The wine was a good vintage and he took pleasure in what was sure to be his last meal. He was glad because he was hungry and this way, he could sleep as well as die. He had trouble sleeping on an empty stomach. The thought made him giggle and he laughed despite his pain. He took a few more drinks and waited for the wine to numb the pain.

Hungry.

He swallowed, his laughter fading.

I've never been hungry in the Room. It was one of the benefits to being in the Room. One could stay here as long as they needed to avoid patrols, heal, or be in prayer. That's what the symbol of a wheat sheaf was for, or was it one of the others...

His head started swimming from the blood loss, lack of food, and the alcohol and he thought he might pass out. He also thought that might be better. He was hungry, which meant *this* room was not *his* room. He had gone to the default safe room for that amulet and it was not the one he had used. He listened for clanging like he had heard in the dark room, but he could tell by the size and feel that this was not in the same place, only prepped for habitation.

He was not *attuned* to this room. And therefore, it did not need to keep him alive. Black spots formed at the edge of his vision and he looked at them, expecting them to stay in place, but they didn't. He felt weak, and tired. He took another pull on the wine and looked at the scarred man. *How did Dominic get this man's amulet?*

He looked around, his blinks getting longer. He wondered if he would be able to haunt this place or if the divine connection would simply send him elsewhere. Either way was fine. He tried to lift the wine bottle to his lips again, but it had somehow become very heavy. The shadows crept in from the edges a little further and this time, they did not go away. He could feel them waiting to clean the room. He knew he could still call out to them, but that was the point of the wine. When he drank, he got depressed, suicidal. The empty stomach helped speed that process along.

They wouldn't claim him again.

He slumped to the floor, putting his head right where the bottle could tip easily into it. His hair got wet in the mixture of blood pools. He was able to get two more swallows in before he closed his eyes.

Henri and Ce'Nedra ran outside the open door but could find nothing but the horrid reek of sulfur. Henri held his still healing arm, protecting the stump. After Duncan cut it off to save his life, Ce'Nedra had cauterized it with a torch brought by the staff of the manor house. He had passed out from the pain and awoken later as he was moved into the manor. He was here in the council house for the first time since the attack.

"Did you see who that was?"

Henri shook his head. "Not precisely. I may have seen him before, but I see so many people, I can't be sure."

"What did he do with Duncan?" Ce'Nedra looked around, scared.

Henri felt his own heart thumping. "I don't know. He was here and then…" The idea that someone could just appear and disappear was frightening, especially if they could take someone with them. He looked around at the council office with fear. "We should go."

Ce'Nedra stared at him. "What if he comes back?"

"That's exactly why we need to leave. Duncan caught him by surprise. He wasn't here for him. He was here for something else."

Ce'Nedra looked worried. "Henri, Duncan was fighting some dark thing in the woods. What if the man who grabbed him served that darkness? His eyes were swirling with black."

Henri looked at his lady. Without his hand, he was more of a burden than a help. He had been fighting with the idea that she would be better off without him, but that was a discussion not even tolerated by her. Unfortunately, she seemed to sense that he was about to say something to that end.

"Don't you even think it. I'm not going anywhere while you wait here in case he returns."

Henri swallowed. "Because I'm a cripple?"

"By the Fae, *yes*. You're still healing, you haven't gotten your second wind to fight your feelings of inadequacy yet, and you haven't gotten your balance under you on how to operate without your hand. And you're insane if you think I'll abandon you because of some male sense of protection. If Duncan returns, he'll find us."

He nodded, grateful for her bluntness. Duncan was a good fighter and more than capable of taking care of himself. He would find them. Henri nodded for the door and they hurried out.

Dominic dropped to the floor in the King's Bedchamber, his breeches wet from fear. *What was that place? How did we get there? Who was the man in the room?* Dominic felt certain he was about to be divested of the amulet and that thought was more frightening than anything. He had replaced the amulet's damaged chain with a heavy, non-breakable one and it had saved his life, he was sure. His fingers were clutched around it as he steadied his breathing.

He hadn't expected there to be anyone at the St. Andrew council office. When he appeared, he was thrown off by the presence of people, but he had no other place he knew. Tanglwyst would usually pull into St. Andrew really early or really late in the season so his duties were focused upon tallying totals and planning stops. The only time in seven years he went into St. Andrew proper was to file a financial report at the Council Office. It was preferable to appearing in the harbor.

The thought came to him to return to the room but the other man had stabbed Duncan. There was no chance Dominic would have been able to overpower him if Duncan fell. He would return later to see if Duncan killed the man.

Unless Duncan is dead now.

Dominic had no idea what that place was but that man was waiting for *someone* to arrive. He obviously planned to take the amulet from whoever wore it in there. Which meant he knew about the amulet, and he knew Tanglwyst took it. He was expecting *her.*

That made Dominic's mind rebel even more at the idea of returning there. He had not met a man in several years who would hurt her, at least not a man who preferred women sexually. The man in that room was crazed enough to attack and kill the first person who arrived there.

No. Duncan's body would just have to be discovered by someone else. Dominic was too fond of his blood exactly where it was at present.

He took a few more minutes to calm himself and change his breeches. He still had to deal with the situation with Lady Rochefort. He needed to confirm the whereabouts of the King during the fire. Though the idea of spending the night in the arms of a beautiful woman in a resort spa was far more *royal,* the tale of Alexander healing children in a fishmonger village was far more in keeping with the Prince's behavior. He thought about simply sending a letter to demand information from the council member…

Dominic stopped.

Henri. That was the name of the councilman he was looking for, the man in the hall in St. Andrew. Dominic closed his eyes. Henri and the blonde woman had seen him teleport with Duncan. They would ask questions. Or worse, they would look for Duncan. If *they* knew of that room, if they were the ones to discover the body, then they could tell Gomez. The thought made Dominic sneer.

Gomez would have no problem telling Alexander that Dominic was trucking with magic if he got word of it. Dominic needed to get rid of the witnesses, *before* they filed any reports.

He fingered the amulet and closed his eyes. Better to get to work while the killer was still murderous.

Nina opened the door to Holloway Manor and escorted Lady Rochefort inside. The guards here were using it as a local office and she could see why. It was very luxurious. She felt a pang of disapproval. Using the Lady's home while she was still alive could look bad on the Guard. If they damaged anything, that could be a problem. She gestured to a chair in the foyer and went to find the sergeant in charge.

"Sergeant Chaput? A word please."

A young man a little older than her looked up and stood. Rodolph Chaput had always had a good head but he also seemed to behave better if there was a woman around. With this outpost being all male, he had fallen into the practices of neglect common in an informal setting. He seemed to realize this instantly upon laying eyes on Nina.

"Lieutenant Richelieu, how may help you today?"

"I have a noblewoman from St. Andrew who is in need of a safe house. I had hoped to utilize this facility while Lady Tanglwyst was gone." She glanced around. Many of the staff looked quite exhausted. "It looks as if your men have been having the run of the place."

He followed her gaze and saw discarded socks and boots in a greeting area. Mud was currently being swept from a floor leading to what surely must be a stable, judging from the manure in it. He swallowed.

"I fear we might have gotten a little too settled, Lieutenant."

"Need I remind you that the Prince, soon to be the King, was rather *fond* of the Lady Tanglwyst this last winter? He will have a problem with her home being treated like a barracks."

Rodolph straightened, nodding. "My apologies, Lieutenant. I shall see to it right away."

"Good. Now, to Lady Rochefort. She has already been through a terrible ordeal at the hands of a madman. I do not want to put her in a house full of ruffians. You will maintain *professional* appearance at all times," she glanced at his couple day's growth of unkempt beard, "as will your men. You represent the *King's Guard*, by the Saints. Start acting like it. I will be checking in on her regularly. If I see *one* sock or boot print the next time I inspect this place, you'll all be on street patrol. Are we clear?"

"Yes, Lieutenant."

"Is there a clean bedroom upstairs?"

Rodolph glanced around for a moment and Nina sighed in anger.

"I'll have one cleaned immediately, Lieutenant."

"See to it, and make sure your men do it, not this staff. I feel certain you have taxed these people like a tyrant already."

"At once, Lieutenant." He bowed, then went to the greeting area and started barking orders at his men.

Catriona stepped into the common room and looked around for the Fae. James nodded to a table where Cecelia was bringing mugs of ale for the others and Myrgen and Michael drifted over to it, chatting merrily with the innkeeper. Then he guided Catriona over to a hidden corner near the ale casks behind the bar. He nodded to the pale shadows.

"Captain, this is Khud. He lives here."

She blinked and a small bear-like creature wearing a blue tunic and brown leg wraps nodded to her.

"Stâpâna." His voice was resonating, deep, and cheerful. He sounded like he probably snored.

"Khud. 'Tis a pleasure to meet you. I understand you wish to speak with me."

"Indeed. Word has reached my ears you plan to head down to Persephone."

She looked at James, then nodded.

James frowned. "What do you know of Persephone?"

"Well, I had a brother who lived there, back in the day. He took care of the ales and beers. Persephone was a good one. Not all the covenants were like that."

"Were there a lot of covenants?"

"There were a lot less after the War."

Catriona and James exchanged a glance, both a bit worried by the topic of the Soulless War. "Is there anything left there?"

Khud shrugged. "I don't know, but if there is, I need you to do something for me. Look for my brother Mikhail. Tell him where I am. I don't know if he's still in that area, or if he died in the War. If he did, pour out some of this onto the ground." He reached behind the cask of ale and pulled out a wineskin, holding it out to Catriona. "I made it myself. Raise it to him, and dump it out."

She nodded, taking the wineskin. James stood and Khud went back behind the cask, his business with them concluded. She looked at it as she stood as well.

"I wonder why he had to give it to me. You are more attuned with the Fae."

James stroked his chin. "There must be a reason. It will become apparent when we get there and do this." He shrugged. "Or it won't. That's the way of things with Fae."

She nodded, then caught something in James' eye. "What is it?"

James licked his lips and rubbed his thumb on his palm. "Most women can't see Fae unless they're Glarren. But you don't appear Glarren at all. Even the Midlands Glar, who have black hair, don't look anything like you."

"It's my connection with the Land. It gives me access to all the Land's kin."

"So, this isn't a Caratian thing then?"

"Oh, many Caratians can see Fae. Again, it is the connection with the Land."

James continued to frown. "I wonder why the Fae only let women see them then in Glarren."

She smiled. "When we get there, I'll ask them." She looked at Cecelia as she brought in a tray of cheese and meat to the table. "Let's eat and get on our way. I'd like to be off the mountain before dark."

The four friends ate, sharing stories of their time apart. James asked about Gwen's trip and nodded whenever Michael told of her wisdom or stubbornness. Catriona was glad to see him seeking stories of her last days and smiling. It made the loss easier for them all to handle.

She they finished, she looked at Myrgen. "It is time."

Myrgen sat back and exhaled, his face turning sad. "I knew you'd be the one getting things on the road."

James slapped Michael on the shoulder and nodded toward the door. The two men gave the couple their privacy and Myrgen took her hand as they closed the door.

"Catriona, I love you. I really can't think of a life without you in it. It's not one I'm going to want. There's no point where I'll be able to hide

163

anything from you so I figure being honest with you is going to be the smart thing." He looked at her eyes. "I'm going to marry you. I decided not to marry the last woman I loved and I lost her to my arrogance. I'm not going to lose you.

"I understand that the Land kinda makes those decisions for us now, but I saw you. I saw you through the Heartstone. I am to be with you. I hope you'll consent to be with me."

"Does this mean you are looking to step out of the Trials as well?"

He took a deep breath. "I was thinking about it. If you don't stand and I don't stand, then Drake and Anika just keep ruling, I think."

"Or they get consumed and we get a new selection."

"I like my way better."

Catriona laughed. "I do too."

He smiled. "No, I don't know yet if I'm going to step out. That's what I'm going to be doing while you're gone. I'm going to speak to the Land and to the people, learn the histories, listen. I need to do that anyway."

"Yes, you do."

"When I see you next, I know I'll have an answer."

They kissed and she knew he meant every word.

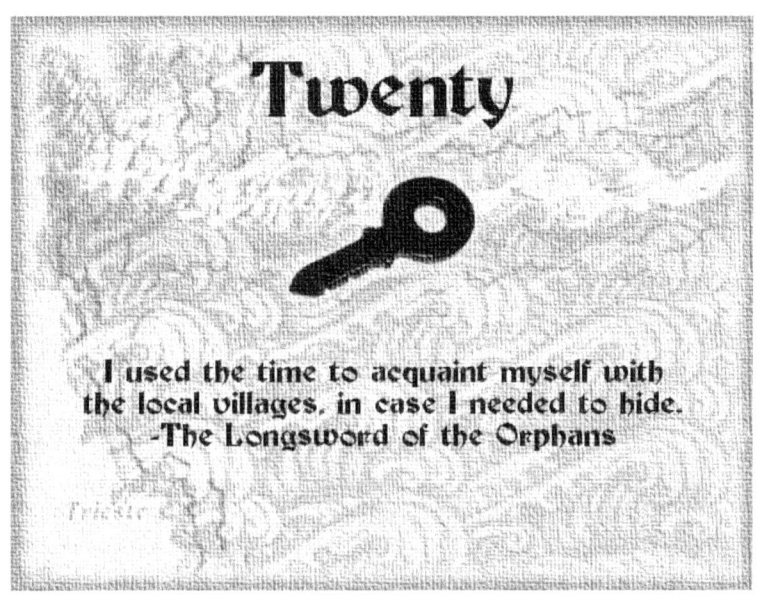

Twenty

I used the time to acquaint myself with the local villages, in case I needed to hide.
-The Longsword of the Orphans

Felix helped Sylvaine to her feet. Sergeant Chaput picked up the saddlebags one of his men had brought in from her horse and led them upstairs. The discussion with Lieutenant Richelieu had led to all the men on the grounds cleaning the bedrooms with the staff helping by getting fresh linens, handing out cleaning assignments, and gently taking back their home. The main bedroom was offered by Chaput to Lady Rochefort but the Chatelaine, a portly woman named Glenna, told him that was off limits.

Thus, they took Lady Rochefort to the next grandest room in the house. It had been empty for several months but all it needed was freshening up to make it suitable for her. The window overlooked the gardens which were spectacular in bloom. The window was opened to air the chamber out and a multitude of floral scents rose from the ground to greet her.

"Felix! Come look!"

He joined her at the window and leaned out, taking in the view. From this height, the layout of the garden was clear. There were privacy nooks and well-kept hedges hiding benches within enclosures. Roses in several colors were budding alongside broad leafed bushes of fragrant purple flowers. There were so many colors and varieties, she was overwhelmed.

His foot bumped a long-empty, clean chamber pot right by the window. She looked along the wall outside and frowned. "It looks like whoever lived in this room made a habit of emptying their chamber pot here."

Felix looked, nodding. "Their aim was really good. There's a little staining but not a lot."

She frowned at the practice. "Still, to befoul such a beautiful garden with this practice is inexcusable."

Felix picked the chamber pot up and sniffed it. "It hasn't been used in a while. Maybe it was a child."

She nodded. "That would make sense. A child would just think it was good for the plants."

He nodded to the plants growing under the sill on the ground. "They might be right. Those plants don't seem to be any worse for wear."

She looked out at the plants below. "Huh. Those are Mandian. I saw them there in family gardens all the time. I don't remember what they're called but they are common among the nobility."

She scanned the entire back yard and the view of the city. They were on the second floor and that put them out of reach of much. One of the things in the center of the back yard was a well, with a nice, wide path to it from the house. She pointed it out.

Felix whistled. "I'm jealous. I draw from the well near my family's house and it's often got debris in it from having so many people use it. We boil it, just in case. It's something my brother said the natives did in Yndia. He said it stops people from getting sick. He's right too. Since we started doing that, no one in our house has been sick once, where it used to happen at least once a season. It does make it taste a little different though. My mother strains it through cheese cloth. Sometimes it feels like a lot of work."

"I don't think they'll have that problem here. Those plants right around the well are good herbs for healing. We grew them at the Manor." She blinked at the mention of her old home, then got solemn.

Felix took her hand. "I'm here for you, Syl."

She smiled, a little weak for the effort. "For how long? You have a very important job at the palace. You need to be there. And as a messenger, that puts you on the road, and in danger."

"I'll ask for a city position."

"Can you?" She looked hopeful. "Can you do that and not get in trouble?"

"They only use single men for the overland trips."

"*Single* men?" Her eyes twinkled.

He blushed. "Well, I'm seeing a path down which I may not be available for that work anymore."

She put her hand on his. "Felix…"

He kissed her hand. "I will do it if only to make sure I'm here for you. And Lieutenant Richelieu will help. I know it."

She smiled, genuinely this time, and it was the difference between a cow and a cake. "I'm so glad you are here. Did…" She looked down at their hands. "Why didn't you marry?"

He laughed. "When have I had time? I started working as a delivery boy around the time we met. I have been running all over the city and eventually the country for years. I barely even know my neighbors anymore. Besides, when you've met perfection, it's tough to settle for anything else."

It was her turn to blush. "How did you get so sweet with words?"

He smiled, leaning on the window sill. "I listened to the Prince. He and the lady who lives here got close this winter. I thought they might actually become a couple. He's a nice man, and he told me that once."

"Was this lady the perfect one?"

He frowned. "I don't think so. I had asked him why he never married, and that was what he told me."

"*He spoke to you?*"

"Well, yes. He's a very nice man. A little sad. That's why I was hoping he would get together with the Lady Tanglwyst. It was the first time I saw him genuinely smile since the summer."

She looked back out over the garden, then pulled him from the window. "Let's walk in it. I think I see a place I want to try out."

Catherine and Charles the Messenger pulled up to an inn as the afternoon was winding down. They were still a couple days from their destination but the mountains were looming larger. She also recognized the road. Tomorrow, they would be traveling a road she did not know, the one towards Caratia. The messenger nodded to the building.

"This is the last Inn for a while, Your Majesty. We made good time."

She nodded towards the north. The road rose and fell in this part of the world so she couldn't always see where they were going, but this inn was on a small hillock so she could see the tops of trees a half-day away.

"Isn't that the road to the Papal City up ahead? We always stay at an inn there, the Benevolent Friar."

"That one is not far, but it would mean backtracking in the morning, if you would prefer it to this one."

"I would. I'm not sure about this one. I'd rather not stay where I'm not known. One never knows if there are bandits nearby."

They spurred their horses on. The Crown's horses were good, able to travel longer and farther than common horses. They were from a line of sires and dames that originated in the Papal City. The pope's own stables supplied the Mervol Royal line. That had been a contract long in the making, but well worth it right then. She was far more accustomed to carriages than steeds, but she was grateful to her Matron-in-Waiting for the willow bark that made the trip bearable. She didn't want to appear weak in front of the child.

She reached into her pouch and fished out the final piece of willow bark. When she had realized she had gone through half her supply the first day, she cut back. The trip was going to be long, and she had hoped to become acclimated to the discomfort by now. Unfortunately, it had gotten worse and she knew she would not have the luxury of the remedy for the entire trip. She did think she could replenish her supply at the Friar, though, making another reason the extra riding was worth it. She put it in her mouth now and chewed.

The sun was making long shadows in the road by the time they made it to the Benevolent Friar. When she dismounted, she practically dropped. Charles caught her and steadied her.

"Thank you, my boy. I fear I am not the spry filly I once was."

"We've been pushing ourselves pretty hard, Your Majesty. Don't worry. We'll get you inside and resting. We'll carry on towards Cliffbase when you're ready to leave. You said they know you here?"

"I pay for a room by the year, my boy."

They smiled at the extravagance and he helped her stand straight so she could walk in of her own volition.

Tanglwyst stepped back into the trees. She had just about intercepted Catherine as she rode up. Had Tanglwyst not stopped to use the privy first, she would have been in the Benevolent Friar in full light and view of the Queen Mother.

Cliffbase? Why is she going to Cliffbase?

Then she remembered the messenger service Symonne offered and realized what was happening. Alexander hadn't told Catherine where he was going. Tanglwyst put her hands on her hips and shook her head. His obsession with Catriona had made him so careless. And thoughtless. He couldn't just run off when he was in charge of the country. Too many people had to fill in the holes. She was glad to be rid of that burden.

She looked behind her at the woods. She had already walked the length of the forest to get here, not wanting to venture in. She knew of at least one set of bandits in there and wasn't about to assume there was only Tulio's band. The patrols on the road were too prevalent. Her horse was still with them as far as she knew. She had left it there when Alexander put the Royal Summons upon her. She could probably track them down and reclaim it.

She peered into the woods. There were no fires yet, but it wasn't completely dark. If she were attentive, she could hear the bandits gathering wood before they saw her. Worst case, she would invoke Tulio d'Or's name and hope that would stop them. She took off into the woods, angling slightly towards the Papal City.

When Alexander arrived down the mountain, it was getting late. He focused upon Tanglwyst's fealty and could sense her about a day ahead of him, going west. He remembered her having a vineyard in St. Giles and figured that was where she was heading. He hoped she was stopped for the night to give him time to catch up to her. He was more annoyed that she had left than that she had left *him*, but in the end, he could see her reasons. Giving her the burden of the entire kingdom was a pretty harsh move. He had been prepared for this his whole life. Putting that weight upon someone unsuspecting was rather cruel.

Still, he couldn't regret it. It was desperate, but effective. She was alive and he was now furious enough to kill her. Well, figuratively. It would seem quite a waste to confess so much only to be abandoned because of it. Not that the additional burden of his confession wasn't justification. He took a deep breath and stopped.

It *was* justification. She had left him because, frankly, he deserved it. Had she confessed such atrocities as he had, he would have left too. He wanted to chase her down but, in the end, her leaving was the best choice for her. She was going someplace safe, with people she could trust. He had no right to stop her.

He looked around the small village and saw an inn. The sign above it called it The Whole Pig, and showed a pig on a spit. He walked over and was hit by the aroma of roasted pork. The whole place smelled of it with various vegetables and smoke. He pushed open the door and stepped inside. The place was almost wall to wall. It looked like half the town was here. He found an empty chair at the bar and filled it, the dirty dishes from the previous owner empty and cold while the seat was still warm.

"What can I get for you, sir?" The bartender cleared away the dirty dishes and he wiped down the bar.

"First off, do you have any rooms available tonight?"

The man frowned. "Let me check." He looked under the bar and came up. "Sorry, no. But there's a couple more inns in town. You're more likely to get a spot at the Next Day's Agony, next to the Pickled Patron."

"That doesn't sound very appealing."

The man smiled. "That's why you're likely to get a room. Might want to hurry though. They have a habit of getting booked before the night's drinking begins."

A barmaid brought a plate of food to the patron next to him and it smelled amazing. Pork roast, roots, onions, mushrooms, and a large piece of buttered bread made his mouth water. He tried to decide if he should risk it, then made a decision.

"I'll have that. Here's my money." He handed the man a gold ducat. "Save me a plate."

The man smiled and nodded. The barmaid held out her hand for the coin and took note of Alexander's face, then nodded. Alexander took off down the street to get a room for the night.

Catriona, James, and Michael set aside bedrolls in the pair of tents and settled in to sleep. They had stopped at the foot of the mountain, the descent not something to be rushed. The road from this side was steep and treacherous. It seemed the First Dûcesa had not been interested in visitors.

The plan was for one person to be on watch throughout the night, changing shifts every three hours. She had first watch and was glad for it. It would give her a chance to try a few things with this land. She had never tried to work with it but she could feel the *wrongness* in it. It was as if there was no life in it at all.

All land, from swamp to desert, had a life to it. She had never felt land with nothing growing or alive in it before. This was land only in name. It had no memory. So, she decided to dig down and see how far it went. One of the things they had was a masonry drill, in case they needed to peek through the wall for patrols. She thought it a better choice than the clunking thuds of shoveling. She got the tool kit off the saddle and brought it out, careful not to clink it and bother the men trying to get to sleep.

She chose a patch where she could go deep but not put her back to the open area. She knelt down, touching the ground with her palm, trying to feel the terrain under the soil. She found a place where she could get the most depth, but it wasn't very deep. She put the tip of the drill down and started turning.

At first it went easy. The top soil seemed arid and powdery. Then she started hitting harder soil and stone. She had to shift the drill more than once to get enough space to move on, but far too soon, she encountered solid rock. It wasn't unexpected. She was at the base of a mountain. Still, it happened too quickly.

She pulled the drill out and pulled the soil from its bit. The core had a few layers to it, but for the most part, it was all dead. Whatever attacked this soil was very thorough. The only indication of "color" was at the tip where it had encountered rock about three inches down. Still within reach. She stuck her finger in the hole and touched the stone. Then she called out to the Land.

Tell me what happened.

She was met with silence.

The Land, which touched everywhere, was no longer in this place.

Myrgen got halfway down the mountain and saw a strange little spur from the road that looked almost like a reverse path. Instead of dirt showing through grass, grass was mysteriously growing on top of rocks, roots, pretty much anything where someone might have stepped to go to a different place on the mountainside. The sight was so curious, he decided to follow it.

The footholds were easy enough to follow and he felt safe when he walked where the grass grew. At one point, he thought he had lost the trail, but then he saw a patch of grass a little ways away large enough to be two feet standing. He put his foot down to walk to it and the ground crumbled beneath even the barest step. He looked, calculated, then took a breath and jumped.

He made it, but only by grabbing the tree beside the patch of grass. Had it not been there, he would have fallen, well, hardly to his *death*, but probably to his *severe injury*. He went around the tree and encountered a familiar sight: The cave Raven had shown him. This was something he had wanted to search for during this absence. Apparently the Land approved of this endeavor.

He looked behind him at Zara, glittering by the sea. It looked so peaceful, so welcoming. He was glad he had come here. He felt like home had found *him*. He wondered how long it had searched for him. That was how it had to be, since he had not known he was missing it. He had seen too many things to assume the Land was not the one in control here. It was too old and wise, and knew too much. He thought it interesting that he did not feel a personification of the Land. It was neither male nor female, simply an entity. He thought about it and no one had ever assigned a gender to Heaven either, so that wasn't odd.

He looked into the cave and moved along. He saw a torch on the wall with a flint and steel beside it. The light from the mouth of the cave would last only so long. Better to prepare. He didn't expect to be out past dark since it was spring and it stayed light longer.

And he couldn't believe he was over-analyzing lighting a torch. Maybe he wasn't ready for this cave.

He lit the torch and moved into the cave. It went deep, as he remembered. He thought they were in the center of the mountain when they found the sarcophagus. That could take an hour to get to, but he was willing to make the trip. Raven had said there was something important for him to learn there. He might as well get to learning it.

As he walked, his mind wandered to the previous night. He and Catriona had shared that intimacy when a couple dreads a long, inevitable separation. Not entirely desperate, but wanting to have as much closeness as possible. He could still feel her embrace from their parting above. They had not really spoken, and now he rather wished they had. He wanted to ask about the Trials, her feelings about this trip, what she wanted from him and vice versa. In Zara, she was in her element, literally. Her ease and comfort here was enviable and he wanted to explore it with her.

He realized he knew so little about her. He could not count on an abacus all the things he had experienced, but he could cite everything he knew about her in the time it took to walk an hour into a mountain. He felt the cold air around him and was glad it retained some freshness this far in. The light from outside was far from visible, the tunnel apparently having a small curve or something somewhere.

He saw the cave widen up ahead and he stepped into the room with the paintings and large, rectangular crypt with a lid. Upon the wall, there were the renderings of several different artists. The lid to the sarcophagus had marks on the top, a dozen from the count. There was no indication as to what they were for.

On one wall, someone had drawn a woman with several other people with her. The people seemed to be smiling. Then the story moved to her touching a woman in a bed while others cried. There was a man with the woman in the bed, who then was next to a child in a bed when the first woman reappeared. He then stabbed the first woman. The man took the first woman's body to a cave and dropped it in a fissure. There were similar pictures after in smaller form, like an addition after the story was told.

The next wall had a lot of writing on it. Unfortunately, the script was something he had never seen. It *almost* looked like a root alphabet for ancient Caratian, something he had put some time into years ago. It had served him earlier in the season when Catriona had spoken in her sleep.

Don't let them kill me again...

He looked at the third wall, where there were pegs hammered into it. They might have held lanterns or tools once. He couldn't tell why they were there but there were several. He brought the torch close to inspect them and thought he saw discoloration, like...

He stepped back.

Like blood.

This was some sort of detainment, or torture chamber. He looked to the ceiling and near the top of the wall was a large hook. Scrapes in the stone indicated a chain was hung from it and someone was there for a long time. He stepped back and realized the pegs in the wall looked like a person, their arms stretched to the sides. Three down each arm, four in the torso, two in each leg. The hook was directly above this formation.

They were hung here, then staked in place.

He looked closer and touched one of the pegs. The patina on the iron was in streaks, like blood had dried there.

He swallowed and looked at the sarcophagus. He pushed on the lid and it stayed right where it was. He looked around and saw a shadow in the corner near the entrance. He inspected it and found a burlap sack of tools. There was a hook on a length of rope, and a long chunk of wrought iron. He took the iron bar and planted it against the base of the crypt, then hooked the bar with the rope.

The bar flipped and slid towards him while the bottom slid away, and he realized he needed something to put it in. He looked around the base for a wedge or hole and found one. He jammed the bar into it and tried the hook again. He went to the other side of the lid and pulled. The lid shifted and he hauled harder, bracing his foot against the sarcophagus. The lid opened enough to get the bar in and he moved it to get different leverage. It took some effort but he got the lid off and it fell to the side.

He looked in and saw a natural cavern, a drop that went out of his vision. There were things sparkling on the bottom but he couldn't make out what they were. However, though the torch wasn't bright enough, the drop wasn't too far. He took a minute to secure the hook to the side of the box and made sure the rope could hold him. Then he got into the box and dropped the torch.

The fall was about forty feet, still a lethal drop but not further than the rope could reach. It coiled on the floor amongst the glittering items. He had not used his arms for something like this in a long time and figured he might need a rest at the bottom before returning. As he got closer, he saw the things on the floor were stones, but clearly not ones indigenous to the cave. These were polished, smooth.

He dropped the last few feet to the cave and picked one up. He brought it close to the torch to shine the light through it. It remarkably resembled the Heartstone Anika wore as Dûcesa. The Heartstone had been lost for a century before being found in a field by Anika as a young woman. This was especially bizarre since the stone had been lost at sea but according to the hundred year old portrait in the ducal study, they were identical.

These almost looked like the one on Catriona's pommel. He picked up another one, and cast the torchlight through it as well. It had fewer flecks of gold in the stone but was pretty similar to the first one. He gathered up the stones and was kneeling to grab the last one when he realized he had subconsciously counted them.

A dozen.

He remembered the marks on the outside of the lid and the smaller pictures. Then he grabbed the torch and inspected the ground here. It was stained with blood. He stood and looked. There were multiple splatter marks in the blood, but it looked at once long ago and all too recent. He could see the edges of the stains, even make out a few drag marks where the victim had survived the drop only to die in a different place.

What kind of horror is this? Why is this here? Why has the Land not purged this place from its core? And what were these stones? He looked at the handful of them. They were essentially the same size, but had a marked difference in the number of gold flakes. A couple only had a few, easily less than a dozen. One of them was practically overwhelmed with gold.

He put them in his pouch and shook out his arms. He put the torch in his mouth, noting how far it had burnt down. He wasn't sure he'd have enough time to get out of the cave, given how long it took to get there, but he was at least lucky enough to know it was a straight shot out. The hardest part would be the fear he had gotten turned around in the dark.

Twenty-One

Other knights tried to assist Michael but
succeeded only in cutting his wing, for
Irazan was tricky and would move the
shadows to hide them.
-The Longsword of the Orphans

Dominic couldn't eat. He was too worried about Duncan and what happened to him. He worked up the courage to do something drastic: Return to that room and see what transpired. Dominic had popped from his room at Tanglwyst's to his palace bedroom several times, getting the hang of the amulet. He felt he could get in and out and only take who he wished. He took a deep breath and closed his eyes.

He went to the room.

He was wary, half expecting it to be empty, half expecting to be jumped and stabbed. The room was quiet, and he exhaled. The lights were dim but his thinking about them made them brighter. The light came from runes glowing on the wall near the floor. They were the symbols of different saints. The room had a desk, a table, a bed, and a chest. He also saw something near the foot of the bed on the floor and it took a moment to register that it was two partially-devoured corpses.

Shadows were coating the corpses of Duncan and his assailant and they were munching, the sound filling Dominic's head more than the air. It was so sickening that he popped back to his bedroom at Tanglwyst's house. He went to the window and took a deep breath, shaking off the experience.

Those were monsters. Monsters cleaning up the mess in that room. That is handy. There were also no windows or doors in there. That place is the perfect prison. Anyone who gets dropped in there is never getting out unless I get them. And if they die in there, no body to deal with.

The idea was *very* appealing. And now he knew what to do with witnesses.

This time, he appeared in St. Andrew well after dark. He hoped the offices would be empty and quiet, and he was not disappointed. He wore clothes that were black and close-fitting, but still rich, in case anyone recognized him. He was becoming known, which was what he wanted, but in this situation, he was more interested in finding his quarry and not getting caught. He figured the councilman who was in this room belonged there, which meant he had a room nearby. Honest men rarely made enough to afford a good home.

He looked around, peeking in windows. It took only a few before he found a room with a bed in it in the Council hall. He was annoyed to discover the bed empty. He didn't have all night. If the man was honest, he was probably not rich enough to stay the night in a brothel either, which meant a tavern. He went to the front of the building and looked right. Most right handed people looked right first, so that would be his main inclination.

From this vantage, he could see the bright doorway of the Black Cat and Anchor.

He was pleased, as he approached, to see an alleyway near the kitchen. With any luck, he would be able to watch the door for the man to leave. Then he heard the conversations from down the alley, at the back door to the kitchen.

"Any sign of Duncan?" The blond woman was standing near a rubbish bin, talking to a short man with a stump.

"Not yet. I've checked everywhere but frankly, he wouldn't have gone to the Red Sky or the docks, not when he disappeared from the chambers. He'd find *us*."

She folded her arms. "I suppose you're right. I guess I was just…"

The man touched her arm with his good hand. "Hoping?"

She nodded and he hugged her.

Now's my chance.

Dominic moved up to the couple and touched each on the shoulder. In a puff of lemons, he and his two victims were gone.

Tanglwyst moved through the trees, trying to stay quiet. The trees gave enough cover that she felt safe enough walking, expecting that the light from fires would be visible from far enough away. She also didn't expect them to be near the edges. Patrols would find them too easily. She kept moving until she started getting tired, and since she still had not found anything to reveal any camps, she decided to call it a night.

She sat down under a tree to rest and thought about settling in right there. The ground was soft here and she noted it was pretty late. No reason not to go ahead and sleep.

Alexander closed his eyes but the sound of revelers next door was obnoxiously loud. He now understood why this was the inn for drunks. They could sleep through anything. He reached out and felt the fealty of his world, just to keep from feeling alone. There were so many people for whom he was responsible. They filled the space behind his eyes with bright pinpoints of light.

He looked for Gomez and found he was west, apparently up at St. Giles. He felt for Emmy, but she didn't have fealty, exactly. She trusted and loved him, and the Power of Sovereignty saw that as the same thing. He could tell she was home, probably in her bed. It *was* pretty late. He almost felt for Gwen, then he remembered.

He reached out for Tanglwyst. She was closer than she had been before, and he wondered for a minute if she might have changed her mind. Then he realized that, judging from where he was, she was in the woods. That made him sit up.

She had been past the woods. Why would she be in them now?

He had a bad feeling. He could really think of no reason why she would be in a dark forest, populated by bandits, of her own volition. And bandits weren't known for their courtesy towards women. He got out of bed and got dressed, grateful that the weather was warm. A cloak would have slowed him down and caught on branches as he ran, and he needed to be quick. Her life might depend upon it.

179

He followed her little bright light into the darkness, the moonlight filtering through the leaves. He barely paid attention to where he was going, his focus was so intense, and he didn't notice the trap until it was sprung. His foot caught on something and yanked his foot out from under him. The snare was attached to a small sapling but he was not a raccoon or badger. The tree was incapable of lifting him into the air but it was definitely capable of immobilizing him.

He looked up and the loop around his ankle was not rope he could snap. He needed a knife to get himself down quickly and he didn't carry one. It was stupid to travel the world without this simple device and now that he had been reminded, he would remedy that. The trouble was that his ankle was higher than it was easy for him to reach and because of this, he couldn't give it slack necessary to get his foot free. Even if he stood on his head, the tree had enough height to keep the restraint tight.

He needed to get slack on his leg. He curled up into a ball, bringing himself directly under the rope. Then he snapped himself up, grabbing the rope by his ankle on the jump. He pulled himself up the rope until he was effectively standing. The rope finally got some slack to it and he kicked his foot to get it free.

He dropped to the ground, trying to land on the uninjured foot. He rolled and stopped. He checked his foot but it was asleep and he rubbed it until it was done with the pins and needles. When he felt he could move again and not risk a twisted ankle, he stood and was grabbed by two very large hands. An arm went beneath his head and pressure was put on his windpipe. He struggled as the world became black around him.

Sylvaine looked up from the bench hidden in the privacy hedge. *"Felix,"* she whispered, *"someone's in my room."*

Felix looked up as well and as the man stepped away from the window. He stood, slipping from the enclosure. "Wait here."

"What are you going to do?"

"I'm going to see if it's one of the guards."

"Why would a guard be in my room?"

He glanced at her. "That's what I'm going to find out. Wait here."

He walked out and moved into the manor. He saw three men by the stables, two in the kitchen talking to the Chatelaine, and one in the greeting room. That left two unaccounted for. They could be asleep or out front, but someone was in the room. He thought about grabbing a guard but he didn't want to have three against him. Better to have it just be one on one.

He crept up the stairs and was annoyed when he stepped on a squeaky one. He worried that alerted the man to his presence, so he moved faster. He listened at the door but heard nothing. He opened the door just enough to get a look at the area and saw no one. He pushed the door open more but still found no sign outside of a very faint rotten egg smell. Whoever had been in here had passed gas, but that was the only presence in the room from what he could tell.

He lit a lantern and another, then looked outside to wave up Sylvaine. She wasn't in the privacy hedge and he turned to find her right behind him. He almost jumped out of his skin.

"What are you doing? I told you to stay there."

"And risk you getting beaten by a guard?" She took his hand.

"I was never at risk. I think it was someone who came to check on you or something. They probably looked for us in the garden."

There was a small pop by the window and then the reek of sulfur. A man was suddenly next to them and he looked shocked that there was someone in the room. He put a hand on each of them and they disappeared.

"Your Majesty, they're ready."

Cipriano turned to look at the General in the doorway and nodded. He glanced a final time at the mirror, confirming his regal appearance. He walked to the door and followed the General to the Council Chamber. The dozen citizens present quieted as he entered, bowing as he proceeded to his throne. Once he was seated, he nodded to his herald, who announced the attendees make themselves comfortable. There were no chairs in the room for them, so there was only so much they could do.

General Benedetto Traversi was in charge of the elite forces in the room, and he stepped forward to speak. "You have been gathered from the entire military array of Mande, from the naval forces to the City Watch, because you are in charge of the best combatants in the country. You are here to perform the singular task of infiltration and conquering of the country of Caratia."

This brought about a murmur of discussion from the ten men in the hall and Cipriano stood, bringing the room back to silence.

"You are probably wondering how we will do this thing when no one from Mande has set foot in Caratia in centuries. I have been working on this task for years, and the problem is access. If we get access to the country, we can control it. Caratia has no standing army. They have no need of one. Their access is completely limited. Thus, their army has long since disbanded, going about their lives as farmers and miners.

"But thanks to the Church, I have acquired two things that will give us this victory."

He nodded to a servant holding a long wooden chest, who then stepped up to the dais to stand beside Cipriano.

"The Land has servants, special individuals that are marked by items the Land has given them. These artifacts are a Letter of Marque, granting access to anywhere the Land holds sway, including Caratia. When Caratia is about to undergo a change in regime, these artifacts begin to show up to designate the people who are to attempt the trials to become ruler. One of these items is the White Granite Sword."

He opened the box and pulled out the Granite Sword, holding it aloft for the populace to see. This caused a gasp of appreciation and wonder to ripple through the gathering. He put the sword back in the box and the servant backed away but stayed on the dais.

"That item will get us through the Teeth and into the Sea of Blood."

The General looked at another man of similar importance, who stepped forward while murmurs populated the group again. General Traversi stepped forward with him. "Your Majesty, Admiral Conti."

The Admiral bowed to the king, who nodded acknowledgement before sitting again on the throne.

"Now, we all know the treacherous nature of the Sea of Blood, and that is part of this plan. The Sword will get the ships carrying your men past the Teeth. Then we will drop anchor. Once inside the Maw, we will be able to see Caratia. That's when the second step in the attack will occur."

He waved to another servant, who brought over an ornate wooden box. He opened it, and took out an amulet. He removed his hat, offering it to the General, who took it as the only person in the room of equivalent rank. The Admiral put the amulet on, then disappeared. Several cries went up, surprise, shock. Then a voice came from the back.

"These amulets, made by His Majesty, were a dispensation from the Church. They allow the wearer to go anywhere they have been, or anywhere they can see."

He disappeared again and reappeared at the dais. He removed the amulet as the group's conversation grew excited. He replaced the amulet and turned back to them. He raised his hand and the room quieted instantly.

"Each of your men will be issued an amulet and will be trained in its use. Have them report to the docks tomorrow at dawn for their assignments. They will be trained on the ships."

Cipriano nodded as the Admiral bowed to him, then retrieved his hat. The king stood and the people became quiet again.

"We will no longer be vulnerable against the threat to the north. In less than two tendays, we will be raiding the treasury of the former Dûce of Caratia. And anyone who stands in our way will be expendable. You and your men will not be alone in this.

"I will be on that mission alongside you all."

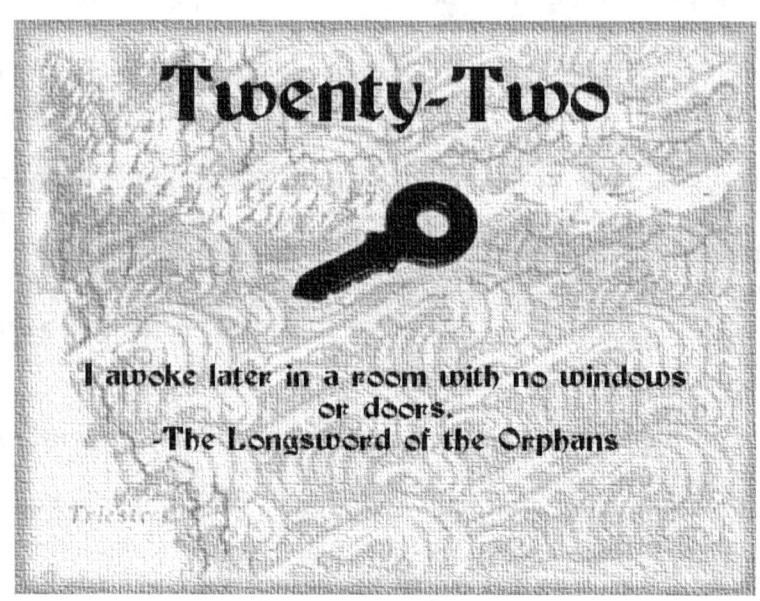

Twenty-Two

I awoke later in a room with no windows
or doors.
-The Longsword of the Orphans

Alexander opened his eyes and moaned, his head throbbing. He moved to rub his temple and was struck to find his hands bound. Panic flared in him.

If someone had recognized him...

He took a breath, calming himself. First he needed to figure out where he was. He was sitting on the floor in a single room pavilion with a center pole. A large, redheaded man was in the tent with him and looked up as Alexander became aware of him. The tent flap moved and another man, with dark hair pulled back into a ponytail, looked into the tent.

"Tulio! He's awake."

A few seconds later, a Toledan man of robust form and easy smile entered. He wore elegant clothes of black, a coat that flared at the waist, and a head cloth that bore subtle black on black embroidery and covered dark brown hair that fell in gentle curls. Even his supple gloves had the common hue of the Toledan country. As the main source of multiple natural plants for the color, Toledans often showed off the expensive dye common in their area. He smelled of campfire and confidence.

"Ah, so he is!" His smile was genuine and shone in his deep brown eyes. "I am so glad you are alright. You had quite the little adventure earlier. Allow me to introduce myself. I am Tulio D'Or. Welcome to my forest." He bowed with a flourish of showmanship.

"An honor to meet you, Tulio. Lovely home you have here."

Tulio looked around with pride, nodding. "It is grand. I am so very glad you accepted my invitation. I've been meaning to talk to you for a while," he looked pointedly at Alexander, "Your Majesty."

Alexander stifled a wince at the title and tried to play it off, raising an eyebrow, "You always treat people you kidnap like royalty?"

"If they were not royalty, we would not kidnap them. No money in it. But you, you are special to us. You are not any random royal. You are one who can settle this issue of disputed territory."

Alexander blinked. "Oh?"

"Why yes. You see, you are under the impression that this forest is part of Mervolingian soil while I believe it is, in fact, just mine."

Alexander frowned, his best political face on. They both seemed to be ignoring the fact that he was bound and sitting on the floor. "I see. And what evidence do you have that this claim is just?"

"Just? I doubt it is just, per se. More like, I think it is indisputable. After all, you would not try to tell someone in their own home that it was not theirs, would you?"

Alexander decided to test the waters. Kidnapping a king, even before his coronation, was an act of war. It seemed foolish to believe anyone would do it for land. If Tulio was willing to risk the Mervol army invading the area over a mile of forest, he was either crazy, or actually territorial. Time to see which.

"It would depend upon how many others claimed it for their own as well. I might be willing to believe I was in error if there were no others to disagree with you."

"You mean rival groups in this forest?" Tulio shook his head. "I can assure you, no one else lives here unless I have said they may."

"That's easy for you to say, but I know of at least one other person here."

"Here?"

Alexander nodded. "To the west. I couldn't tell you if there were numerous folks in that area, but there is at least one. Therefore, unless you can bring them here and prove they do not also claim ownership of these woods, I cannot, in good conscience, hear your case."

Tulio gave a dismissive smirk. "That sounds unlikely. Exactly how do you know they are in my forest?"

"I persued her here. She's a fugitive who escaped. I've been hunting her for weeks and I have tracked her to this forest. So, if *one* outlaw is here without you knowing it, I worry that there could be more. But I shall hear your case, *if* you bring her here."

Tulio folded his arms across his chest. "Well, if an outlaw has invaded my forest, I will solve your problem for you and kill her on the spot."

"No." Alexander breathed the panic out of his voice. "Please. She is in part responsible for the murder of my brother but she knows the names of others involved in the conspiracy. If she dies without revealing those names, well," he spread his hands apart, the wrists still bound, "then my life would be in jeopardy as well. And my death would *interfere* in any land holding awards I might wish to impart."

Tulio stroked his beard. "Seems like an awful lot of work to go through for a woman."

"She is an exceptional woman." The words were out before he could think about them, and they caught him a little by surprise. He glanced away for only a moment, then returned his gaze to his captor. "Bring her to me and allow me to question her. Once I get the names from her, I shall let you decide her fate."

The bandit king looked at his hostage for what seemed like days, then gave a slight nod. "West, you say?"

Alexander looked in the direction of the fealty light. "There. About a mile."

Tulio looked that direction, then nodded. "If she is there, I shall retrieve her. If she is not, I shall assume this to be a ruse and will no longer trust anything you say."

"I accept these terms."

Tulio disappeared from the tent and Alexander relaxed as he heard the hunting party move out. He kept his mind's eye upon her light and prayed she was alright.

The noise faded away and Henri looked to where the bodies had been when he and Ce'Nedra arrived. There had been just enough of the bodies left to recognize Duncan, and the scarred man. Henri, having read the letter from a woman in St. Giles, believed this was the perpetrator of a murder there. Duncan had killed the man, which was preferable to being trapped in here with him. The cost of that safety, however, was rather high.

When the young people had been shoved at them and the man disappeared again, Ce'Nedra had reacted quickest. They had seen the bodies and knew that shadows were devouring them. This had frightened her intensely, mumbling something about the Fae. The shadows had stopped, and she had stepped back, quieting, and the shadows had returned to their activity. Thus she was right next to the spot when they appeared.

Neither of them had been able to grab their jailer before he was gone, but Ce'Nedra moved the girl to a corner away from the monsters and turned her away from them. The boy had pushed to see what was happening and instantly regretted it. Now, with the noise ceasing, Henri felt he might be able to open his mouth without screaming.

"I think we need two things right now: Introductions, and to pool our knowledge. I'll start. I am Henri de Porthos, Chancellor of St. Andrew. I have no idea where we are nor how we got here. Who's next?"

"I'm Ce'Nedra. I own the Black Cat and Anchor in St. Andrew. I don't know where we are or how we got here, but I know what those things were in that corner. They're Shadows, and they are deadly to Fae. One touch and they will destroy one, turning it to black sludge. The one who brought us here is apparently a Shadowwalker, something I overheard some customers talking about. They can move instantly from one place to another, but the act corrupts them the more they do it."

"I'm Felix. I work for the Royal Family in Patras as a messenger. And I know who brought us here. His name is Dominic D'Medici. He's the acting Chancellor for the Kingdom, now that His Lordship Myrgen the Grey is gone. The Queen Mother left to find the Prince, Alexander, a few days ago. Alexander went to travel the countryside looking for a wife and Gomez, the head of the Grande Guard went with him. With

Gomez, Alexander, and Catherine out of the palace, he has all the power in the kingdom. This might be a test, to see if he can dispose of people in here that get in his way."

Henri frowned. "How did you two get in his way?"

The girl piped up. "We saw him appear in my room. I'm Sylvaine Rochefort."

"I couldn't tell if that was you. I'm afraid I was not coherent when we met."

Ce'Nedra smiled. "You had passed out from the pain. It was truly for the best." She looked at Sylvaine. "I want to thank you for opening your home that dreadful night. I heard you were in the Manor still."

"I feared for my life with the way the town was acting. I left a few days ago under cover of night. I thought the townsfolk might burn me at the stake for my husband's crimes."

Ce'Nedra patted her hand. "We never would have let that happen."

"I had no way to be sure. My husband hurt so many of those children. Had I children of my own, I might be likewise inclined. But my husband was never interested in me."

"Can you tell us anything we don't already know?"

She frowned and sighed. "Yes. I can tell you about that amulet."

Tanglwyst felt a hand on her shoulder shaking her awake. She opened her eyes and saw Tulio crouched beside her, his kind and ever-present smile as bright as the torch in his hands.

"My dear, what are you doing out here? You are more than welcome in my encampment."

She yawned. "I couldn't find it. I decided to just take a nap and look tomorrow." She sat up, creaking. "Ugh… You probably just saved my life. I doubt I would recover from such kinks in my body as I was about to have had I slept all night there."

"Well, there is a bed and food, should you need it."

She took Tulio's hand and squeezed it. "Saints protect you, Tulio. I shall take you up on that."

"I need to warn you though. I was sent to fetch you, by a young man very intent on your arrival in camp. He tried to pretend there was some legal interest in you but I suspect you might have influenced him, shall we say?"

Her heart froze in her chest. If Duncan had found her friends... "What did he look like?"

"Handsome, intelligent... Wait, I think I've seen him before." He reached into a pouch on his hip and pulled something out. "Yes, this is him." He handed her a small, round piece of metal.

She looked and saw a minted coin with Alexander's face upon it. She relaxed, and handed the coin back to Tulio, smiling. "I see. Allow me to reassure you that I have not done any such witchery upon this man. I'm pretty sure he'd be immune anyway."

Tulio pressed his fist to his chest, alarm in his face. "Blasphemy!"

She put up her hand. "No, no. 'Tis no myth. This man has protections the likes of which mortals do not." She put her hand on her heart, her other hand pointing to the sky in an oath. "I have seen these protections first hand and felt them upon my person. I have no control over him nor his plans."

"What a tragedy."

He helped her onto the horse and then climbed on behind her. He steered the animal back to the east.

"He said you have the names of others who were in on the conspiracy to kill his brother."

She sighed. "Well, there are none he doesn't know. I fear that was a ruse. He already killed the one responsible for Charles'death."

"Oh I do enjoy a juicy bit of gossip. Who was the culprit?"

"The queen, Elizabeth of Krakte."

Tulio stiffened and his tone became somber. "Really?"

She turned to look at him. "Did you know her?"

He blinked, then smiled. "My dear lady, how could I possibly? I am a humble bandit in a wood days from Patras. I'm hardly the type to hang about in castles."

She told him of the horror of Elizabeth's execution as they rode. It didn't take long but it did make her feel more tired. She didn't tell him of the discovery of her sorcerer's laboratory in the closet. She was still dealing with that betrayal herself.

He nodded to the area where lights were starting to glitter through the trees.

"Oh by the Saints, you mean I was this close the whole time?"

189

He pointed. "There's the guest pavilion, but he's in it. Will you be safe there? I don't truly have a better place to offer."

She thought about it a moment. "Let's wait and see what kind of reception I get. I'm actually kind of mad at him."

"Why?"

She thought about telling Tulio about the last time she was here and the fact she ended up killing an innocent animal trying to get to Alexander. Then she remembered that the horse brass was probably a gift from Tulio and she didn't want to cause him pain as well at the thought of it killing the beast.

"He played a trick on me. But that's behind us now. He's better, I think. He doesn't do that sort of thing anymore. He's learned it is too upsetting to people."

"Good."

She snorted as the horse trotted into camp. They dismounted at the edge and she made sure she stayed quiet so as not to disturb the other people sleeping. Tulio handed his horse to a person, Raoul, she thought, as she went to the guest tent. She looked into the tent through the open doorway.

Alexander was lying on his side, his hands tied. He had them tucked under his head and he was snoring. Apparently, he had worn himself out. She nodded to the guard outside and he smiled and nodded back. She leaned in to whisper to him.

"He's asleep. We'll be fine."

"Are you sure?"

She nodded. She looked behind her at Tulio, and nodded to him as well. He wordlessly dismissed the guard.

The man pointed to a nearby bedroll on the ground under a tree and pointed to his chest, indicating where he'd be if she needed him.

She nodded and went inside.

Alexander didn't stir when she knelt beside him and she couldn't untie his hands without waking him. She decided to let him rest. They could talk in the morning. She went to the bed, removed her boots and dusted herself of any debris before climbing onto the floor mattress. This was considerably better than the forest floor and she fell asleep before anything could disturb her.

Felix looked at the others, then back at his beloved. "What amulet?"
She nodded to the walls and ceiling. "The one attached to this room. This amulet is an artifact of the Church. Very old. My father is a goldsmith in Mande and worked for the Church for decades, like his father. Our whole family line is dedicated to this service. Several years ago, he got a commission for an amulet of a specific style. As a model, he got another one. But I tried on the amulet one day when he went to get a delivery of gold. He was coming back and it caught on my hair. I didn't want him to see me with it so I panicked.

"It took me to a room exactly like this one."

They looked around as she pointed to the features.

"The low lights came on bright when I became afraid of the dark. The amulet fell off of me and I tried and tried to get out. I screamed but no one heard me. I looked around, opening the chest, the desk. Checked under the bed. No way out, though someone had put some food in the chest over there."

She got up and walked over to it, opening it. The others went with her, glancing to the sides for the flesh-eating shadows. She felt inside the chest and looked up.

"This is it. This is the room."

She stepped back and they looked in. There were gouges in the wood inside, fingernail marks.

"Finally, I calmed down enough to realize the amulet brought me here. I picked it up and held it, thinking of my bedroom. It took me there, with a flash of lemon smell. I was so scared, I ran to my father's room to return it. He thought I was lying, so I told him to try it. He did and he disappeared. He returned, but his smelled like eggs. I recognized it the instant I smelled it in my room, when Dominic, you say? When he arrived."

"What happened?" Felix took her hand, trying to assuage her fears.

"He refused to make the amulets. He said he would not be a part of such witchcraft. Shortly after, he was killed, and a man took the design, and married me to Rochefort. I remember overhearing him telling someone they would get a new gold smith, but that person said to use the designs my father produced. The thing is, they were not complete. My father had mentioned to my mother he still had to finish the back. Then I took the amulet and he never touched the replica mold again."

"Do you have any idea how many of these he was making?" Henri's face reflected the concern on everyone else's.

"A lot. The amount of gold my father ordered was sizable. In fact, that's the 'debt' I was sold to cover."

Ce'Nedra scoffed. "It's gold. It's not like it depreciates. I take it the man didn't know you discovered this room?"

Sylvaine shook her head. "Father said he discovered it."

"That lie probably saved your life."

Sylvaine looked down, eyes tearing up. "I know."

Felix hugged her.

Henri and Ce'Nedra looked into the chest. She counted the bottles. "That's enough wine to help keep us alive for a few days, but that's all. If we use it sparingly."

Henri snorted. "Maybe they refill. It *is* a Church relic."

"With things like those Shadows to clean up the mess? No. That's probably how they are fed. This is less a prison cell and more like a kennel."

Felix looked at the adults. "What are we going to do?"

Henri looked at Ce'Nedra. "Can you do something?"

"Like what?"

"Well," he looked around, "this room isn't very large so privacy isn't going to be possible. So, I'm just going to say it. Ce'Nedra, is there anything *Fae* you can do?"

She glanced at the younger folks, slightly panicked, then sighed. "I'm *so* glad I'm not an actual Fae or extensively Fae-touched. If I had been, that trip here would have killed me." She looked at the symbols on the wall. "Hm. I doubt it. This is the symbol for St. Giles, the protector against nightmares. This is the one the Church evoked to drive all Fae and magic from the cities. I worry, if I make the counter symbol, it will turn off the rune here."

"Counter symbol?" Sylvaine came over to the same one Ce'Nedra was inspecting.

"When the Church came to rebuild the cities after the Soulless War, many tavern owners were scared. They all had Fae helping them."

"Really? They had monsters helping them?"

Ce'Nedra shook her head. "Fae aren't generally monsters. Many are actually very helpful. They do things like keep weevils out of the flour, keep the beer and ale good, keep away rats. Things like that. If they were driven away, many taverns would be in danger of closing their doors. Plus, they become like part of the staff. We care about these Fae. We take care of them, and they take care of us and our customers.

"So, when our Fae told us there were magics being erected to repel them, we began to carve counter symbols in the walls and rafters of the inns. Some are subtle, part of the décor, like in my inn."

Felix nodded, pointing up. "The woodwork up at the ceiling. I've been to the Black Cat. It's always been very homey and welcoming. Is that why?"

Ce'Nedra nodded. "But most people carved them into the bottoms of the tables or under the bar where they wouldn't be seen. After all, they were on a deadline and with the Church running a lot of the construction companies at the time, there were no extra contractors to do the work."

Henri crouched by the glowing symbols. "Did they work?"

Ce'Nedra nodded.

Felix looked around. "What would we have to do?"

Ce'Nedra touched one of the symbols. It sparked at her and she backed away, falling on her rear. Sylvaine touched it and it didn't respond. He looked at the innkeeper.

"It knows."

Henri glared. "Then it will work. It wouldn't be trying to protect itself if it wouldn't."

Felix helped Ce'Nedra to her feet. "Do you have to be the one carving it?"

"No, I don't think so, but if there's counter magic to be done, that probably will fall to me. I just don't know if the spell will work. Still," she rubbed her arm where the spark struck, "Henri's right. The symbols are here for a reason. They fuel this magic. If this one protects against non-Church magic, what do the others do?"

"That's Walburga, the wheat sheaf. Protection against starvation or famine." Sylvaine pointed to another symbol. "St. Nicholas the Wonderworker, patron of travelers, the book and pall. St. Brigit, mortar and pestle, healing. Raphael, bringer of light. That's probably why these shine." She pointed to another one. "I don't know this one."

She looked around the room, Felix and Henri helping her move the furniture so she could see the symbols.

"That's the only one. The others just repeat." She pointed to the symbol. "I remember something else. This was on the amulet my father made. The design was these symbols overlapping. The third one down was this one."

Henri looked at it. "Are you sure?"

"Yes. He drew them all separately, figuring out the order by what parts were covered by other lines. He said it was the hardest part. He actually separated out the other symbols he could identify, leaving this one behind."

"Then that's the order we need to counter them." Ce'Nedra crossed her arms. "And I have a feeling I know what part of this room that symbol represents." She looked at Henri, then to the end of the bed where the corpses had been.

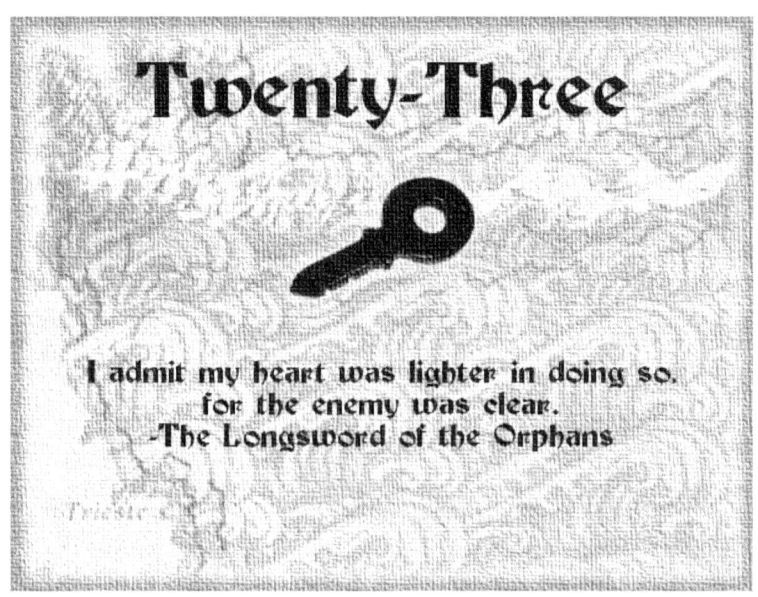

Twenty-Three

I admit my heart was lighter in doing so,
for the enemy was clear.
-The Longsword of the Orphans

Myrgen confirmed his trajectory as going towards the air before the torch finally sputtered and went out. He set the burnt out torch aside, and dusted his hands on his breeches. He wanted both hands to make sure he didn't wander into something important. In the catacombs beneath the palace in Patras, he was completely comfortable, partly because he knew there were only so many pathways, and because there was a whole palace right above him. Inside the mountain, it was the opposite. He was alone, but with literally only one way out.

He didn't remember any offshoots or fissures on the way in, but in the now total darkness, his mind was imagining yawning maws of teeth forty feet across and twice that deep. He pushed back the claustrophobic thoughts after the torch went out by thinking about Catriona. He started counting and figured he had been there a few hours. He squinted, searching for the pinpoint of light that showed the exit and he thought he could make it out. However, he realized he was in the cave longer than he anticipated and the distant light was already fading to the dusk of nighttime.

The intelligent thing to do here would be to stop for the night.

Of course, he had no bedding, no flint and steel, not a thing to pass the night. The most he could hope for was an uncomfortable bed that left him with bruises and no rest. Better to get out before stopping. After all, he was only about an hour in.

He felt in his pouch for the stones he had found. They were smooth and strangely comforting. He was careful not to rub them against each other, somehow worried about damaging them. The Land, and Raven, had gone to a lot of trouble to let him know that place was important. He wasn't sure if it was the stones or just the knowledge of the torture chamber that was significant, but he was going to bring back something to study. Those stones seemed the most portable objects.

His foot hit a rock and it was only because his hand was on the wall to keep him steady in his course that he didn't fall and scuff himself up. He did, however, strew the stones from the pouch when he pulled his hand free to stop his fall. He sighed and dropped to his hands and knees, feeling about for the stones.

He found four right away, then felt in the pouch to find how many he was missing. There were six in the pouch so he put the four with those and felt around for the other two. He picked up a stone but it had sharp edges so he tossed it aside. This happened a couple more times and he started to lose hope he would find them in the dark. He looked up towards the opening to gauge how far away it was, and his hand touched something soft and furry.

With claws.

Breath blew onto his face and he carefully moved his head back from it. He felt the snort of something sniffing his hand, then a tongue nearby on the ground. He heard teeth click against stone, and then two glowing rings about the size of his palm rose to meet his search. The gold eyes looked at him, then moved behind him. He got slowly to his feet and the animal stepped up, putting its head under his hand. He jerked his hand away, but the animal leaned against his legs. He looked down and could see an outline of a Fae cat, darkness against shadow.

His eyes caught a glimmer on the ground by his feet, and he saw one of the other stones next to the wall. He knelt down carefully, his hand going to the Fae cat's shoulder. It was large enough to pin him against the wall if it chose, so he picked up the stone, hoping not to startle it. He stood again, and the cat moved forward. It was silent, but between the darkness and the adrenaline, his hearing was heightened. It was heading towards the cave mouth and he could hear the breathing of the large cat. He followed it, keeping his distance, until the adrenaline bled out.

What felt like thirty or so days later, the mountain opened and Myrgen almost fell out of the cave opening, he was so tired. The Fae cat had disappeared at some point and he thought for a second he might have imagined it. He stopped, sitting at the mouth of the cave and breathing in the air. The position of the moon confirmed his suspicion it had been hours since he had entered the cave. He leaned forward, resting his head on his arms. He didn't realize he had fallen asleep until he pitched forward and slid down the mountain.

He lay on the ground at the base in pretty much the same spot he landed the last time he took the fast way down the hill. Well, at least he was consistent.

The stars were lovely and he closed his eyes, just relaxing and feeling for any injuries. He dozed off again, and when he started awake, the sky was starting to get pale. He sat up and rubbed his eyes, then looked around for the lights of Zara. The pinpoints he saw cleared from the blurry dots into reflections and he realized he was looking into the eyes of the Fae cat.

The cat looked at Myrgen, relaxed. She didn't look predatory at all but Myrgen wasn't about to take that as fact. He knew cats. No matter their size, they were effective killers. Majestic, adorable murderers. The Fae cat did a slow blink at him and began to purr. It sounded like personal thunder.

He got to his feet, careful not to startle the cat. She watched him stand, then looked between her feet at the final gold-flecked stone. The cat picked the stone up in its mouth and Myrgen watched its eyes go from gold to emerald green. He was struck by how similar they were to Catriona's eyes in that moment. Then they turned less crystalline, and became more like jade.

Myrgen blinked, certain he was imagining things in the growing light. The Fae cat put the stone down, then walked off into the forest, away from town. Myrgen looked at the stone and saw it was one of the more infused ones. He looked behind him but there was no sign of the cat, no sign that any of this had even happened.

Myrgen then looked up the mountain from whence he had come. This place had more mysteries than trees had leaves, and the animals were among them. He picked up the stone and put it back in his pouch, then moved on towards town.

Catriona woke in the brightening light, struck by the absolute silence. No birds, no bugs. No wind rustling grass. The air wasn't stale, but it likewise had no life in it. It was merely mobile. She crawled out of the small tent and stood, stretching. She looked toward the sea and listened, hoping the sound of seagulls would come to her. She was rewarded with a hawk from the mountain, but it did not circle or fly much over York.

James looked up and nodded. "You hungry?"

Catriona nodded. He handed her some of the bread they got from Cecelia and she took it, happy to eat something still pretty fresh. "So, what is the plan?"

James nodded to the northwest. A plates"Persephone is that way. We have a delivery to make and frankly, I'm very curious. Alistair talked about it often." He took a steadying breath and let it go, temporarily releasing whatever weight he was carrying. "You need to go there too, to deliver Khud's message."

"True. What does it say?" She nodded to the book James had on the rock beside him.

"A lot. First off, when the last mages came to Persephone, it was only a few years before the War. There was a mage's council back then, one that actually governed them because mortals couldn't. If a mage went bad, no guard or baron or king could stop them. Only another mage could. There were mages that were just for that purpose. They were called Exûlicars. They would come in and investigate crimes perpetrated by mages and prosecute them. For the mages, this was the only authority they heeded."

Catriona felt something behind her eyes, like she was searching for the right word to describe something but could only get the first letter. "That sounds very arrogant."

James nodded. "And dangerous. These people wielded the forces of nature. One of the mages was Yokotaman. They couldn't pronounce her real name but because of her abilities with water and air, she called herself Snow. She could affect the entire county with her weather control. And Aidan, the leader of Persephone, had tons of power over nearly everything. Merrick controlled people's minds. Wilgefortis was among them, though she wasn't magically endowed at the time. She was the new seneschal. The old one passed away. Raven controlled earth and when he used his magic…"

"Things grew…" Catriona blinked, not really understanding where the comment came from.

Things grew. Plants bloomed, fields matured, grass covered the area. She could see things growing at an accelerated rate and she saw him standing on a battlefield, distributing dirt that stopped creatures from fleeing. And one child in particular… with a strange shadow, reaching for her…

"No!" Catriona scurried backwards and the stone from the mountain behind her thrust forward, walling her away from the emcampment.

James jumped up, standing back from the eruption. Michael yelped in his tent. A couple seconds later, he was standing next to James, looking over the top of the enclosure. Catriona got to her feet, looking around for the child before realizing it was not real. The three of them stood, staring at the wall of stone. She put her hand on it and willed it away. The stone *obeyed*, which did not have the same calming effect upon her companions that it did on her.

"My apologies, gentlemen."

"What the hell was that?" James seemed a bit more rattled than Michael, who was pale to an ashen tone and apparently speechless.

"I'm… not sure…" She cocked her head. "I… *remembered* something."

"And it did *that*?"

Michael seemed to regain his voice. "Captain, what did you remember?"

"Something I can't explain. I've experienced this before."

James frowned. "Like *déjà vu*?"

"No. Not this incident. I remembered something that's never happened to me."

"Uh," Michael looked at James, then back at Catriona, "like you read it somewhere?"

"No." She shook her head, meeting their eyes. "Like a memory of a life I never lived."

"Reincarnation?" James relaxed and lowered himself back on the rock.

"Maybe." She nodded. She knew of the belief practiced by those who worshipped Karma in Yndia. "But I don't follow Karma. Just like I would not go to Heaven if I died on this trip. I am a servant of the Land."

"But the premise behind reincarnation is that you lived before. So perhaps your previous life was a Karma worshiper."

Michael nodded. "What did you remember?"

"Battle. Seeing a man with green hair distributing dirt on the ground to curtail the movements of a child. But the child was reaching out to me. It had a Shadow attached to it."

"A child?" James picked up the book and leafed through it to a picture. "This one?"

He turned the book towards her and there was the image she had seen, but from a different angle. The green-haired man, *Raven,* had surrounded the child and a few others around him with a ring of dirt. There was a black hole opening in the air behind him. A large man was pushing a woman out of the way of the child's reach and the child's finger was upon the man. Where the child touched the man's back, there was a grey sickness spreading across his skin.

The caption below it read, *Slade Stormchest saves his beloved Dûcesa from the Last Child.*

She heard the scream in her head of the woman in the illustration and her heart shattered. She fell to her knees, weeping.

"No... don't leave me... Not after..."

Michael and James flanked her, arms around her shoulders. They were speaking but she couldn't hear them. She knew the story. She knew the First Dûcesa loved her Stâpân, she knew he retired from the position so they could be together. She knew the War rose and she and Slade went to fight the threat in York. She knew Slade died in battle and that she died within a day of him.

But *this,* this was something else. She *knew* him. She knew who he was, *what* he was. She knew he was more than a lover, or a protector. He was her *companion.* He never left her, not for good. But this time was different. She felt the hole closing around him and knew she would never see nor feel him again.

She also knew herself, and that she was far older than anyone else knew. Slade had always been there, just as she had always been there. There was no time without him. Or rather, *there was,* but it was too far back, too far gone to remember. She had asked for him to be with her and he was. It was simple. He also held something for her, something that would destroy her if she beheld it. Without it, she would live, could laugh and be happy. Without him to hold it, she would be... a monster.

"No wonder she died." She sat back, her tears slowing. "She lost everything." Her eyes felt cloudy from the crying, and red and puffy.

James' face grew concerned. "Catriona. Your eyes..."

Myrgen saw Drake and Anika in the dining hall just sitting down to eat. Many of the other folks were finished with their own breakfasts and were starting to leave. Myrgen smelled the eggs and fresh biscuits and almost lost his entire courteous upbringing in his assault on the food. He managed to get a plate's worth but was not able to stop himself from biting into the biscuit before he actually got seated. Drake and Anika waved him over and he sat just as he swallowed that first, succulent bite.

"We were worried about you." Drake glanced at his wife. "Well, Anika was. I knew you were fine."

"You liar. You checked his room every hour last night."

"Not *every* hour..."

Myrgen smiled, so happy to be home. "I went by that cave I mentioned before, the one Raven Grasshair showed me."

"I thought you were gonna have me go with you?"

"I thought so too, but the Land had other plans. I found some things too. There were a bunch of stones in a pit, much like the Heartstone." Myrgen looked at Anika's necklace. One of the flecks in it was glowing. "Hey there. What's that?"

Anika looked down at it. "I have no idea." She looked up, perplexed. "It's ever done that before."

Myrgen pulled the other stones out of his pouch. None of them were glowing. The couple looked at the stones he produced.

Drake touched one. "Are these them?"

Myrgen nodded.

Anika picked one up, but it didn't change.

Myrgen squinted, trying to remember something. "Anika, has Catriona ever touched the Heartstone?"

She shook her head. "No. I was wearing it before she was made Stâpâna. The only stone like this she's touched had been her pommel on the Onyx Sword."

"Onyx? It never looked like onyx to me."

"It disguises itself."

He nodded. "But not even to find her true love?"

Anika shook her head. "She refused. She didn't want to know."

Drake compared the stone in his hand with the stone at her neck. "These are almost identical. The only difference is the number of flakes in the stone."

"Same with the others." Myrgen picked up another. "The stone you wear is rife with them. The most populated stone here doesn't have half the flecks yours does."

"What does that mean?" Anika looked at the men.

They shrugged.

"Maybe there's something in the books in the study." Anika looked at the stones again. "I never thought there would be more than one of these, but if there is, it will be in the histories. We'll look after breakfast."

Myrgen wanted to add to that but his stomach demanded he stop using his mouth for talking. He instead nodded and finished his biscuit.

Twenty-Four

Alexander awoke to people talking outside, realizing he had fallen asleep when the search party left despite his efforts. He had fallen on his side, which meant that he was not actually attached to the center pole of the tent. The sky was lightening and he was able to make out colors around him. There was a bed in the room and he realized that there was someone in it. His hands were still bound behind him and his arms were beyond sore. His arm and hands were asleep from his position and his cheek hurt from resting so long on his knuckles. The blood and feeling returned to his appendages as he let his eyes adjust.

He sat up and crawled to the bed. Red hair cascaded across the pillow and Alexander smiled. *They found her. Thank the Saints.* He sat back, relieved. He didn't yet know if she was unscathed but at least she was here and he could protect her. He sat back, relieved. He didn't yet know if she was unscathed but at least she was here and he could protect her. He shook out his arms, then frowned.

Yeah. I'm a pillar of salvation. I won't be able to stop anyone from taking her away if that's their aim.

He listened to the encampment and heard mostly snoring. Despite the light, everyone seemed to be asleep. Now was his chance. He put his hand across Tanglwyst's mouth and she started awake, as he expected she would.

"My lady, we need to get you out of here."

She sat up, looking around. She opened her mouth to talk but he put a finger on her lips to silence her. He leaned next to her ear to avoid being overheard.

"There's no time. The camp is asleep. They don't need you. You have to escape. Run to the Papal City."

She touched his chest, her eyes questioning.

He shook his head. "I'll be fine. They need me for the ransom."

She closed her eyes, sighing. She leaned to his ear. "This is ridiculous. You're..."

"Papal City. Don't go anywhere else. I need you safe. I insist." When he said that past part, he pushed her fealty with the Power of Sovereignty to make sure she did as requested.

She nodded and got out of the bed. Her boots were on her feet in moments while he kept an eye on the door. He was pleased to hear the snores continuing as she came to the pavilion entrance. She looked outside through the door flaps in the tent, then slipped out. He listened close for any sign of discovery and was happy when he heard not a single alarm. After about ten minutes, he breathed again. He moved the blankets and sleeping furs to look as if someone were still in the bed, then went back to lying on the floor. He closed his eyes and concentrated on her fealty light. He watched it closely, imagining her running through the forest.

She looked behind her only once, her path set on the northeast. The glow of the Papal City had been visible from the inn on the mountain and he wondered if she would have been able to see it through the trees if it were still dark out. If he were released or to escape, he imagined that would be the path he took. No one seemed to pursue her and she slowed to a less stressful pace.

He opened his eyes, confused. Had he just *watched* her? Could he *do* that? He tried to conjure up visions of Gomez but the same thing did not occur. For some reason, he could follow her.

Or I fell asleep and dreamed it.

He closed his eyes, making sure he was fully awake now, and concentrated upon Tanglwyst. He didn't see her like he had before and concluded that, yes, he must have fallen asleep while following her fealty light. He didn't much care. He remembered the dream and it was comforting.

She was going to be alright.

Catherine came downstairs from her room, happy for the rest in a familiar bed. The money she paid annually afforded a real bed of down and wool instead of straw like other patrons. The blankets were comfortable, not itchy, and the linens were always clean and of the finest cloth. All the accoutrements were imported from the Papal City, employer of the finest tradesmen in the Saintlands. If you were considered the best in your craft, you lived in the Papal City. And it showed.

"Good morning, Your Majesty."

Charles the Messenger bowed. She found she had an easier time not feeling affection for the lad if she reminded herself of his role in the world. Her motherly instinct was to favor him like he was her murdered son.

"Good morrow, young man. Did you sleep well?"

"As good as at home, Your Majesty."

The innkeep came over to Catherine and bowed. "We have a multitude of delights this morning, Your Majesty. Shall I bring you a sampling?"

"Please. And do likewise for my companion."

The innkeep bowed and returned to the kitchen.

Catherine waved Charles over to her. He politely joined her, waiting for her to speak and direct the conversation, should any arise. She had not yet decided if one would, but after a minute, she found something to discuss. "Young man, tell me of this messenger service. How does it get the messages to the recipients?"

He nodded. "I do not know, I'm afraid."

"What are the rumors?"

He shook his head. "It is a secret. If someone were to spy upon them, they would likely have them killed."

"Killed? Why? Are they Mandian owned?"

He shook his head again. "Not that I know, Your Majesty. They are, however, the only service which does this."

She took a deep breath and glanced behind the young man at the approaching innkeep and his server. They bore two large trays with multiple small plates. "We shall find out today. I'll not risk a letter to the King of Mervolingia without knowing precisely with whom I am dealing."

Charles bowed in his seat and then became lost in the feast of breakfast food.

Tanglwyst walked through the forest until she saw the sun peek between the leaves directly above her. She realized then she had been walking for a couple hours and finally felt like she could stop to rest. She sat upon a root and felt her feet cry out in relief. She pulled some willow bark she got from Symonne and chewed it, feeling the relief in her back and legs out of anticipation more than the remedy. She checked her heading and figured she was about a day out of the Papal City.

Well, at least she spent one night in a real bed. Come the morrow, she would sleep in another. Had she gotten a horse from Tulio, she would be doing so tonight.

She furrowed her brow.

Why didn't I get my horse from Tulio? I'm sure he would have returned it to me.

Insight passed across her eyes. Alexander had *geased* her. Again.

She kicked the ground, which caused an ache to course through her foot again. She erupted in obscenities.

"My. That's unexpected."

Tanglwyst turned to the voice and saw Tulio standing there with her horse.

"Oh Tulio. I am so sorry. I had no intention of leaving without saying goodbye."

He raised his hand. "Fear not, my good Lady. I simply figured you might like your animal back. He's been misbehaving since you left."

She walked over to the horse and petted his forehead. "Bedlam, why have you been so rude to your host?"

"He was probably jealous that you rode another horse here before and left with it. He was so happy to see you last night. Nickered for half the night." Tulio smiled at the interaction, stroking the horse's shoulder. "What prompted the exodus today?"

"Alexander." Tanglwyst sighed. "He compelled me to run. Here, I hoped he had changed but no. The first chance he got, he spelled me again."

"He spelled you to flee?" Tulio leaned against the animal. "It sounds like he was trying to protect you."

"Remember when I was here before? That was the result of his *last* compulsion." She shook her head. "He has to control things. If he sent me away, it was undoubtedly to get me to do something for him."

"Well, what are you feeling compelled to do?"

She opened her mouth but in the end, she really didn't have a compulsion at the moment. The one getting her to safety was gone. She had no idea how Alexander's spell would have known Tulio was not a danger when it seemed to think he was one in the encampment. Perhaps this particular spell had a range or time limit. She shrugged.

"Nothing. Right now, I just feel…" She had trouble finding the right word.

Tulio looked at her. "Betrayed?"

She looked at her friend. "Yes." She let her gaze fall to the ground. "I'm afraid so."

"How did he compel you?"

She rolled her eyes. "It's something he can do to anyone whose fealty he holds."

"If he has done this harmful thing to you, twice, why does he still hold your fealty?"

She looked through the woods towards the encampment. She had gone into that tent to thank him, to make sure he was uninjured. She had wanted to make sure he was safe. After all, he had sent Tulio out to find her. She did it out of concern, not out of any compulsion. After the trading of the Power, she believed he thought of her as his equal.

But that had been naive. When he told her to leave, she was about to tell him that it was ridiculous, that they were in no danger. But he had decided to force her to run instead of giving her a chance to speak. How could she respect someone who didn't respect her?

Tulio knew people's hearts and she trusted his judgment. With this comment, she also knew what he meant. She may be loyal to Mervolingia, and to the Crown by extension, but that loyalty was far from mutual. As long as she was loyal to her country, Alexander had control over her.

"Tulio, how did you find me last night? How did you know where I was?"

He pursed his lips. "My omniscience about my forest and trespassers within it?"

She frowned at his joke. "*He* told you, didn't he?"

"He seemed to know right where you were. I followed his directions and practically trod right on you."

"So, yes. He can find me and compel me no matter what, as long as he has that hold over me."

She sighed out her anger. He was far from here. He was in no danger with Tulio but she would be able to get away. No one in that camp would be loyal to Mervolingia. She closed her eyes for a moment and, for the second time in her life, released her fealty to the Crown.

Now, no one who even knows of its existence is, either.

Tulio patted the horse on the shoulder. "You have supplies for the road in the saddlebags, should you choose a different path than the one he put you upon."

She looked at the bandit leader. "Well, in truth, he didn't put me on this path. I did. When we last parted company, I was heading to the Papal City. My grandfather has a house there."

"That's probably for the best. But remember, I didn't come to find you on my own last night. He sent me to find you so nothing would happen to you."

"Of course not. He needs his pawn."

"Well, I've never really thought of you as that piece on the chess board, and judging from the lies he was telling himself and me, he doesn't either." He tapped his forehead with his fingers in salute. "Safe journey, my friend."

Nina opened the door to Holloway Manor and looked around. Chaput was in the greeting room, his beard trimmed and the house pristine. She smiled, glad he took her seriously. She bowed when he looked up. "Sergeant Chaput."

"Lieutenant." He smiled, gesturing to the improved manor. "How does it look?"

"Much better. Thank you. Is Lady Rochefort about?"

"I haven't seen her today."

Nina frowned. It was past midday. "At all?" She looked up at the stairs.

Chaput looked outside like he was just realizing the hour. "No."

He and Nina looked at each other, then went together up the stairs. He stepped up to the door to Sylvaine's room and knocked. After a few knocks, he tried the knob and found the door locked. He pulled a ring of keys from his pocket and put one in the lock. They got the door open and entered.

The air was fresh, filled with the flowers in the garden through the open window. The fire in the hearth was long dead and the bed still made.

Nina looked at Chaput. "When was the last time anyone saw her?"

"Last night. She and the young man, Felix, were in the garden." He looked at her. "Perhaps they left together?"

"The bed has not been slept in. There are wrinkles from someone having sat upon it. The fireplace has not been stocked for the night and the ashes removed. And the door was locked."

"Maybe they went to his house, or returned to St. Andrew?"

Nina looked around. "No. See?" She pointed. "Her things are still here. She would not have gone on a journey without changing into her boots." She walked over to the wardrobe and opened the door. "And these are her clothes she wore to get to Patras. She wouldn't have stolen a gown from Lady Tanglwyst. She would have put on her own clothes."

"Nina, she only *had* those clothes. She might be out shopping for others. You said she was uncomfortable borrowing Lady Holloway's gown."

She nodded then exhaled, forcing herself to relax. "You're right, Rod." She looked around once more. "I'll return to the palace. Hopefully, Felix will know where she is."

"If she returns here, I'll let you know."

"Thank you." Nina took another look around the room and left.

Book Two

Trivote

The Child sought a bridge between the
two worlds to walk again and breathe air.
—The Longsword of the Orphans

Twenty-Five

She cast the spell through the feather and drew them both into the sword.
-The Longsword of the Orphans

Catherine and Charles the Messenger opened the door to the messenger shop and stepped inside. Catherine was rested from staying overnight in the master bedroom of the mayor's home, exiling him and his wife to guest quarters. Charles had suggested she lay low, but there had been no rooms at any of the inns by the time they arrived. She could either buy a room from a current resident, or go to the guard office and introduce herself. She chose the latter.

There were four other people ahead of her. The Captain had insisted upon having one of his guards with her at all times, for her protection, and he took in a breath, preparing to speak up. Catherine put her hand on his shoulder, stopping him. If he was interested in her safety, alerting these people would not help.

She pulled him down to whisper in his ear. "Prevent anyone else from coming in instead."

The man nodded and stepped outside. Charles smiled and she felt strangely validated by this boy's approval. The others took several minutes to conclude their business but she definitely knew the procedure by the time it was her turn.

The young woman behind the counter smiled to the Queen Mother and her companion. She had long brown hair with a blue streak through it. It was a fashion common in Mande and a holdover of Nubian culture. Slaves often had brighty colored hair thanks to secrets of stripping the color from hair and replacing it with floral dyes. "Charles! Hello! I haven't seen you in a while."

"I've been stationed in Patras for the last two seasons. You look lovely, Magdelena. When last I saw you, you and Anthony were expecting."

She smiled. "She was born at the beginning of this season." She stepped into the next room and picked up her daughter from a small enclosure on the floor. She came out around the counter, a little girl on her hip. "This is Aubrielle."

Catherine was surprised to see the child was of mixed race. This was common in Mande but not so in Patras. She reached forward to touch the child's hand. "She's lovely. Congratulations."

Charles gestured to the Queen Mother. "This is Catherine." They had discussed to whom he would inform about her true rank. She said she would make the decision.

Catherine shook the tiny hand that grasped her finger. "Catherine D'Medici. Are you from Mande?"

Magdelena nodded. "My husband is Nubian. We came here from Pardua."

"You're a long way from Pardua. That's in the Storm Catch, at the thumb of Mande. Did you flee here?"

The young woman swallowed. "Not exactly. I'm a cartographer. We got here and were going to map Caratia but I can't get in."

Catherine blinked. "Ah yes. I thought that was a myth."

Magdelena shook her head, then bounced her baby a little. "Oh no. I can get to the top of the last turn of the road up and no further. Anthony has to go the rest of the way."

"For what?"

Magdelena smiled at her baby. "Deliveries." She looked at Charles. "What can I do for you?"

Charles leaned on the counter. "We need the Infallible Messenger."

Magdelena inhaled and kissed her baby's forehead, then set her back in the enclosure. "Well, he took a delivery up the mountain a few days ago. It could take a while for the Messenger to return."

Catherine frowned. "How long?"

"It honestly depends upon the previous message and how difficult it is to deliver."

"And there's only one of them?"

Magdelena nodded.

"How much is it?"

"Depends upon how difficult the person will be to find."

Charles glanced at Catherine but she nodded. "What do you need to know to find that out?"

"The full or unique name of the person to whom the letter goes."

Catherine narrowed her eyes. "Unique?"

"Yes. Name and nickname, or origin location, description, last known whearabouts."

Catherine smiled. "Will a title do?"

"If it's unique enough, possibly."

"Then he should be very easy to find."

Octavius hauled the ropes from the rope locker to the man sewing the mainsail and dropped them to the deck. It was good to be at sea again, but he had almost forgotten how to be just a deck hand. His bed was also incredibly uncomfortable. Estelle had really made his life a wonder. He caught himself thinking about her more often now that he was back on a ship but after three days, he was finally not crying every time anymore.

Raven came over with a second set of ropes and set them beside the other stack. The Sail Master looked up from his task and nodded to the other side of the ship.

"That set goes over there."

Raven looked at the rope, then at the opposite deck. "Oh."

Octavius picked up one of the stacks of rope Raven brought and helped him haul it to the other side. They set it down by a cleat and Octavius put his hands behind his kidneys and stretched his back. Raven did likewise, then stretched his hands up and did his arms as well.

"Hunh. A parade."

Octavius looked at his companion, then to the sea where he was pointing. Several ships were sailing perpendicular to the route this ship was on. He frowned as about five ships in a line seemed to be heading east. The sails were nondescript, and they flew no flag. They clearly weren't pirates or this ship would have been stopped. They would have easily won a race. He thought he saw something on the deck of the lead ship and looked at the Crow's Nest.

He climbed to the Nest and took the spyglass from the watchman. He looked through it and confirmed what he saw. Fighting. There were about forty men on each ship not helping sail the thing. Instead, they were training in battle. He did a quick count.

Two hundred. That's if there are none below decks. What in the world are that many soldiers doing on ships going east?

He looked down at Raven who was looking up at him. They couldn't get off the ship just yet to investigate. They had to get to Corrigan. Octavius exhaled, handing the spyglass back to the watchman. They must be going to Nubia because the Teeth blocked the way anywhere else. He was glad Catriona was not at sea now. She would have taken them on.

No doubt about it. That many soldiers was an invasion force. He shuddered to think of the poor village that was about to be claimed.

Nina looked into the messenger office at the Palace and gave the dispatcher a questioning look. He shook his head, his reply mirroring her mood. Felix and Sylvaine had been missing for three days now and he had yet to report to work. No one had seen them, including his family, who had actually sought *her* out to investigate his disappearance. They had no knowledge that Sylvaine had even been in town. Their disappearance had occurred before he had managed to return home that first day of her arrival.

Dominic passed her in the hall and had a strange lingering stink of digested eggs. He seemed to be covering it up with perfumes but whatever he was eating was clearly not agreeing with him. He was, however, amazingly smug and always busy. She found it frustrating and annoying. She had given him a report about Lady Rochefort's disappearance (leaving Felix out of it because she didn't want to get him in trouble) but Dominic had just dropped the report on his desk and ignored it.

She decided to get a report off to Gomez. She had no idea what he was doing in St. Giles, but it was time to come home. Alexander needed to be home too, so this scampering off in search of a commoner bride was done. Dominic could not be allowed to dig in like a tick, which was exactly what he was doing. She watched him go into the King's bedroom again like it was his personal office and it angered her.

She decided to make him read the report. He needed to take this seriously. She turned and went to the door and put her hand on the knob. The guards at the door stayed her hand.

"The Chancellor is working, Lieutenant. He is not to be disturbed."

"I have business..." She frowned, looking at them. "Who are you?"

"We are Lord Dominic's personal guards."

"I am in charge of the Royal Guard. I do not know you."

"No. As we said, we are his *personal* guard. He hired us directly."

Her mouth dropped. She looked at the door, then back at the guards. *He would never have done this if Gomez were here.* Then she gave it a second thought and realized yes, he would have. Dominic had an adversarial relationship with the guard, believing he was above the law. This was simply yet another example of this.

She really wanted to get in to see him now, and realized the benefit of his choice of room. There was another entrance into it and she hoped he didn't have a guard there too. She went back downstairs and to the back of the palace. She looked around from a hidden spot and saw an unknown guard at the exit to the King's Bedchamber. That made her even more determined. If Dominic was not only hiring outside the guard to protect his activities, but also stationing them so no one could sneak up on him, that meant he was definitely in there doing something he shouldn't.

She needed to draw off the guard somehow and hope he didn't have another guard in the tunnel. She was going to need some time to think about this. Gomez would just go right up to the guards and walk past them, but then again, he had no problem cutting down a private guard that was interfering with his duty. Dominic was playing upon Nina's personal belief against unnecessary killing. If she wasn't willing to do the same as Gomez, she needed an alternative, and soon.

If Dominic was in fact the source of Sylvaine and Felix's absence, there was no telling how long before their situation became critical.

Ce'Nedra closed her eyes. The symbols around the room which granted sustenance now sported a Fae rune above them. It had been at least a couple days since they were placed in this prison but there was really no way of telling. If this didn't work, they would be dead soon enough. This rune was supposed to do what the symbol of St. Walburga did. She spoke the spell and destroyed the last of the Saint's symbols.

The Fae spell flared when Ce'Nedra finished, but then the other Saints' symbols flared as well and the Fae spell was squelched. She frowned and put her hand upon the faintly glowing symbol. To her surprise, she felt her hunger fade. She took her hand away and the feeling of hunger returned, but she felt like it wasn't as strong.

She looked at the others in the room. "I think it worked."

The two men looked at her from the table and chairs. Sylvaine lay on the bed, resting, and didn't stir. This worried Ce'Nedra. She knew what would happen if the girl died here.

"I don't feel any different." Henri looked at his hungry stomach.

Felix shook his head. "Me neither."

"Touch one of the symbols. I think it's like a bucket with a very slow leak. If you put your mouth, or in this case hand, right on the symbol, you can get what you need from it."

The men got up and moved to different symbols around the room. There were only four, one on each wall, so she was grateful they had no other mouths to feed. She put her hand upon the symbol near her and let it rest there for a few minutes. When she pulled her hand away again, she *definitely* felt less hungry. She looked at the men and they nodded, feeling the same thing. She looked at Sylvaine but she still had not moved.

"We need to prop her up against one of these."

Felix stood and picked her up off the bed. "Which one?"

"The spell will help us once a day, but only one of us, so she needs her own rune." Ce'Nedra pointed to the one on the other side of the bed.

Felix set her down so she was leaning against the symbol. She started to fall over and he caught her, then sat with her. It took about a minute for her to start looking a little less haggard but it was about thirty minutes before she opened her eyes.

"Did it work?" The young lady's voice was small and weak.

Ce'Nedra nodded. "It's faint and you have to be touching it, but that's just because the Church's spell is so prominent. Once I break those runes, we should be fine. For now, just lean against the rune."

Sylvaine nodded and rested.

Henri put his hand on Ce'Nedra's shoulder and nodded toward the farthest spot from the couple. He kept his voice low to avoid being overheard. "How long will this work?"

"I have these runes around my inn. Have you ever left my home feeling hungry?"

He glanced at the floor. "No. But you also actually had food there."

"True. But this will work. This room is designed to enclose and protect the inhabitant. I saw the body that was next to Duncan. Part of why it took so long to devour was because it was healthy. That means this room keeps you fed. Also, look around. No waste removal system."

Henri looked and nodded. "You're right. Not even an old chamberpot."

"Now, it could be that any waste is devoured as well, keeping this place clean. But it's also likely the body is sustained by the anti-famine runes. The healing runes also mean that if the person in here is injured, they will have time to heal. Remember when Duncan came in with all those horrible wounds? I think he healed up in a place like this. That's how he knew about it and tried to stop that man."

"So, the shadows are… *helpful?*"

She shook her head. "Far from it. Those are monsters."

"Then how are they here, in this holy place?"

"Because they are from Hell. It's the only explanation. Hell is under the purvue of Heaven. Can't have one without the other. The Infernal has only ever been counteracted by the Divine, and that's because they are one. It's easy to control your own arm. Hell is the punishment part of Heaven. It's not separate."

Henri looked around at the room and the young couple on the opposite side. "Proximity is the greatest threat, according to the Manifesto of the Saints. The closer you are to Hell, the more likely you are to sin. Those shadows…"

Ce'Nedra nodded. "I know. I need to get to work."

She kissed Henri and returned to her chanting.

Twenty-Six

I took the information to the Papal City
and was granted a meeting with the
Cardinal Counsel.
-The Longsword of the Orphans

Tanglwyst rode her horse through the woods, the sky lightening through a yawn. Occasionally, she saw flickering lights through the trees, like ground-level stars. The road to the Papal City also went west along the border between the wastelands of York and the upper edge of Bordeaux. Bordeaux was the uppermost region of Mervolingia and was unique because it had no baron, count, or duke to rule it. Her home port was St. Giles, the main city, and she missed it so much. If she had not had a mission to accomplish, she might have turned west and just gone home.

But Alexander's compulsion last night reminded her he was not a good choice to lead Mervolingia. Besides, she was still wanted for murder there. She was sure her assets were captured for the Crown by now. After all, Dominic was in charge of all that, and no one knew as much about her holdings as Dominic. He had reported every speck of gold to her because she told him he could embezzle three percent from her and she would never interfere.

Her bodyguard Othon had told him he was allowed two-point-eight. No one ever challenged Othon. He was known in song to have seven weapons you saw and six that you didn't.

That had been years ago, but the figure became a point of trust and status amongst her staff and household. She had let him know embezzlement was expected in a Mandian financial manager, and the only way to keep them honest was to make sure they were vested in making the business do well. Dominic had not aspired to anything more, so she had recommended him to be Myrgen's assistant. He had never betrayed her so she did her best for him.

There's that word again.

She must have felt it more than she thought. Now she was noting it in just about everything. Then again, she was entitled to feel betrayed. He used her trust to force her to flee. It didn't matter that he feared for her safety. He used it too easily. The Power was like a pile of petit fours. Each use seemed so small and harmless, but it had weight you would have trouble releasing if you indulged too often. It was *easy*, like that amulet was *easy*.

That was what made it dangerous.

Alexander looked up at the man who stepped into the tent. He was a large man, and Alexander was pretty sure he was the one who carried him to the encampment. He remembered the breadth of the shoulders under him. He also vaguely remembered Tulio calling the man Raoul. The large bandit glanced at the bed Tanglwyst was supposed to be in and Alexander was glad he had bunched the blankets to look like a person beneath the covers. The guard didn't seem to pay the "body" much attention outside of confirming its presence.

Raoul stepped back and motioned to someone outside. Another man brought in some venison and Alexander was about to ignore it when he caught the scent. His stomach growled loud enough to startle all three of them. The newcomer smiled and Alexander cursed inwardly. The meat was tossed to Alexander, and he caught it, then dropped it because it was still hot. His shirt caught a dose of grease and soot from the cooking.

He managed to retain his dignity just long enough to get that first bite. Luckily, the others turned and left him to eat unsupervised. The meat had the bone carefully removed so the chance of fashioning a weapon to enable an escape was not available at this time. He tried to be resentful and "strong" but the idea of ignoring food while here was not beneficial. If he *were* to escape, he would need his strength. Likewise, for him to keep his wits or continue to deflect attention away from Tanglwyst, he was going to require food.

He glanced at the bed, then at the edge of the tent. He could see boots outside the walls but Raoul and his companion kept their voices too low to hear without going closer. He decided against that course. It was better at this point to not attract attention. The longer he kept quiet, the more time Tanglwyst had to get to safety.

He closed his eyes and thought of Gomez. He had strangely not been able to "see" him like he had Tanglwyst and Alexander had not yet determined why. He decided this might be a good time to try and sort it out. He had a theory. Tanglwyst had held the Power while Gomez had not. He decided to test this theory against others who had reigned.

He thought about Charles and sought him out, but although he knew Charles was alive, and even about where he was in the world, he could not see him. That surprised him for a second, then he realized he had not given Alexander or the kingdom his fealty. To do so would require Charles to return and become King again. He sighed, again dealing with the mixed emotions this brought. He was glad his brother finally had his heart's dream, but doing so had cost Alexander his. The love of his life would never be his Queen.

He searched for his mother and was disturbed to not see her in Patras. He broadened the search and was shocked to find her very close by. He frowned. *Why is she in Cliffbase? If she's here, who's guarding the throne?* Part of the reason he had left was because Catherine would make sure everything was handled with royal dignity and fire. She may not want the Power for herself, but she would run through hell after anyone who tried to usurp it.

He sighed. *Probably looking for me. She indicated in the crypts that she had heard the rumors. Unfortunately, she never gave up her Mandian heritage so she will not be able to enter Caratia to look for me.*

He tried to "see" her too, but to no avail. Her light didn't have the same... He couldn't place it. There was something not a part of Catherine that was a part of Tanglwyst. Then he "looked" at Tanglwyst. Her light had an almost blue aura around it. He flicked back and forth between the two and then he realized what it was.

Tanglwyst's aura had the same glow the Power of Soverignty held.

Alexander opened his eyes. The Power saved her life and she had given it back, so that was probably it. Catherine had never taken the Power for herself. That actually went farther than any other argument in her defense. He remembered something Catriona had told him, that Catherine had always had Mervolingia's well-being in her heart, and that every course she had taken was to stop civil war over religious differences from destroying the country. That's why she had killed Plantyn, and why she had gone to the Papal City to protect the Mervol lands. It was also why she had never given up her heritage. She needed the blood ties to Mande in case Mervolingia ever needed her. Mande meant money and influence, and she was cousins with Cipriano.

The insight into his mother was exhausting and with his hunger quieted, he felt the wear of the day's activities upon him. He climbed onto the bed next to the lump in the blankets and lay down on his back. The mattress was far more comfortable than he wanted it to be and he fell asleep before he realized his eyes were even closed.

Octavius looked at the ceiling above him, unable to sleep. They would be in Galadorn within a day and he was not sure how to handle the task before him. To tell the Midsummer King that his daughter was dead...

Octavius wiped a tear from his eye before it got too embedded in the process. He still had yet to come to grips with the idea. He felt like he had been scooped hollow and magically filled with excess tears. Working on the ship had helped pass the time, but when it came to sleep, he still felt inexperienced. Without Estelle to accompany him into it, it all felt like such a waste of time.

Part of him expected to be killed for his transgression. After all, the man *was* the warrior king of the Fae. Another part wanted to offer himself to be executed for not taking better care of Estelle. If Corrigan took his life, that would mean Octavius would no longer live in a world without her. He would go to Summerland, the afterlife of those who served the Land. There, he would meet her, and they would live together for eternity.

"Raven?"

The mage had turned his hair brown for being in public, and he looked up from the elaborate sculpture he was making with string between his fingers.

"Yes?"

"Is Estelle in Summerland?"

"Oh." Raven set his hands on his chest, still ensconced in the string. "Well, I imagine that's possible. Fae don't really... have souls, like you and I do."

"What do they have, then?"

"Essence. They are made up of Magic, you see. The great Father, Sovereignlumin, discovered Magic and fell in love with her. Together, they made all the great and magical creatures. Dragons, and Fae, and giants. Pretty much any amazing thing out there. But then something happened and now Fae just dust."

Damn... for a second there, he almost sounded like he could be coherent. "'Dust'? What do you mean 'dust'?"

"They become kind of a shimmering powdery stuff that catches the light. It *glitters*, for lack of a better term. Comes in every color, which is nice, but the stuff gets everywhere. Once I had some on my face and no matter how often I washed or chased it with magic, I somehow always missed a spot. I think it's gone, then suddenly, I catch a shimmer in a reflective surface."

Octavius' face pinched in concerned disgust. "You have dead Fae on you and it never goes away?"

"I wouldn't put it like that m'self."

"Why not?"

"Because that just sounds horrible."

Octavius decided Raven must have been being obscure again. When the leaf had shattered on the rocks, of course there had been shimmering flecks, but that wasn't supernatural in nature. It was glass.

...the shimmering leaf spun in the mid-morning sunlight, casting its green rays across his face for just an instant before it fell out of his reach... the spur of rock jutted out just below the leaf... the glass shattering against the stone, the impact staining the grey with glittering dust...wind blowing the fragments and fine pieces into a mist...

His heart heaved again at the memory, still so fresh. At about midday, they had finally sailed to the point he could not see the site of her death. He had caught himself checking repeatedly during the day, his eyes catching upon the cliff face. He knew he would never be able to cross into Caratia from the south again without reliving that horrible moment.

"So," he swallowed to allow the phlegm to clear from his throat, "then what becomes of her? If not Summerland, then what?"

"She is reabsorbed."

Octavius closed his eyes. *So, she just dilutes, then? Back into the ether like a breath in a breeze?* He stroked the stone holding the leaf fragments, but in the end, it did not comfort him. It was too depressing to think of the flecks of color in a stone being all that was left of her. If so, what was he going to do?

He raised the stone to his lips, the overflow of tears once again draining into his ears as he lay back on the floor of the lower deck. They didn't have the hanging nets like the *Enigma* did here. That was probably for the best, but the alternative was parasite-infested bedrolls spread on the floor of the gun deck, pretty much anywhere they could fit a human. Octavius had almost refused to sleep but then Raven had cleaned the bugs away with some subtle magic.

He hoped it hadn't been illusion to make him *think* the bugs were gone. That would bite them both, literally, later if true. Yet another thing Estelle had saved him and the entire crew from experiencing. He had no idea all the things she had done for the ship until he was on this one. Half the men had scurvy sores, many had bad teeth, and several had limps or missing fingers from working the ropes. He had been extra careful when he remembered this ship wasn't sentient.

Well, tomorrow would come and his fate would be decided. Regardless of the method of his execution, he was ready to move on.

Tanglwyst looked up just as she left the border of the forest and found herself on the broad road to the Papal City. The center of the Augustinian Church was designed to impress dignitaries. It was almost an excess of the wealth of the continent. Tanglwyst had forgotten how amazing the city looked. Her travelling season was spent at sea and winters were spent in Patras. She never even thought about traveling here until a few tendays ago. Now, here she was, like the end of a pilgrimage she hadn't known she was on.

The city was encased in a tall, strong wall, though there were lots of areas around the outside of the city that sported farms, vineyards, or stables to spread the girth of it. Inside the city, because of the containment wall, the buildings had grown up instead of out. Spires with Mandian gold glinted in final remaining starlight and she could only imagine how beautiful it would be in the sun.

In the center was a glittering, white marble castle, towering over the city. It was lit by blue glowing lights that she had never seen before. They must have been new and there were other spires that she did not remember from before either. There was so much light, it looked like daytime, despite the hour. It was striking enough to make her forget she had been travelling all night.

The giant gates stood open, golden archangels wielding their signature weapons flanking the archway that marked the entrance. Even the guards wore white and gold. They were the first encounter for travelers and needed to be bright but imposing. There were six guards on either side lining the walkway, street lanterns hovering above them on poles. A gatehouse with a single guard drew her attention and she approached him.

"Good night, My Lady. Can I assist you tonight?"

Tanglwyst nodded, getting off of Bedlam. She stumbled as her feet hit the ground, her balance off and muscles deeply sore. The guard stepped forward, catching her arm.

"Forgive me. I've been traveling all night."

"So it seems. What is your business in the Papal City, my Lady?"

"Visiting family. My grandfather lives in town."

"Is he expecting you?"

She blinked, not realizing she might have to have someone vouch for her. "I… I'm not sure…"

"What is his name? We can send someone to get them."

She hesitated, not certain she wanted someone to go to the palace to get the Pope.

A voice from behind the row of guards interrupted their conversation. It was deep and crisp. The man was in deep red, his face a cross between a scholar and a horseman, bespectacled eyes of chestnut brown with lush hair to match. He had what seemed like twice the teeth of a normal person and was nearly six feet tall.

"Cardinal Caiaphas." The guards bowed before him.

"Caiaphas?"

He embraced her, to the surprise of all involved. "Yes, sister. It's me."

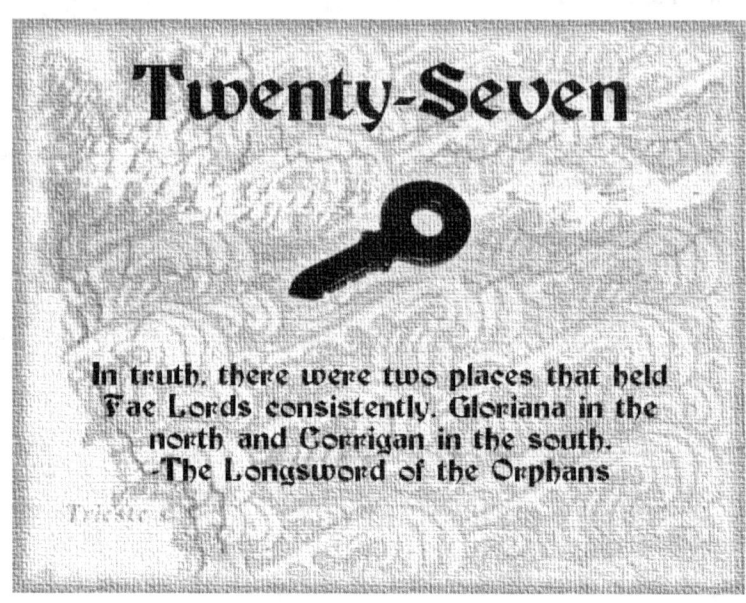

Twenty-Seven

In truth, there were two places that held
Fae Lords consistently. Gloriana in the
north and Corrigan in the south.
-The Longsword of the Orphans

Trieste (

   Alexander walked through a wood, the leaves and flowers striking in the mottled sunlight dancing through the foliage. The breeze was gentle across his skin, almost loving in its caress. Gone were his fancy clothes, replaced by his humble travel attire. Browns and greens helped him blend with the surroundings and he was wearing his comfortable boots and gloves. In his hand was his healing kit, the one he used on Catriona in Cheryb.

   A familiar scent came on the breeze, spice and sandalwood. He closed his eyes, breathing deep this perfume. It heralded his beloved, and he felt soft lips upon his, familiar and needed. His eyes opened and he confirmed her to be the one. Her dark hair and black clothing complimented her mocha skin, all enhancing her sparkling emerald eyes. The green had little gold flecks in them, catching the light and making them even more cheerful.

   He kissed her again, reveling in this moment. He was happy, and she loved him. He had no doubt. He opened his eyes to take her in again. She stepped back and took his hand, leading him through the woods. A sea breeze filled with the sound of gulls and he realized where they were.

   The cabin on the Cliffs near St. Giles.

He squeezed her hand as they entered the house. Gwen passed by him, her dress bloody and her eyes crying black. He looked at her, disturbed, but Catriona tugged his hand and he forgot about Gwen. His beloved led him to the bedroom and he entered the room to see another person on the bed. Myrgen reached out for her and she let go of Alexander to go to his enemy. He sat up in the bed, clearly nude. Catriona kissed Myrgen with great passion and her eyes changed.

She looked at him with jade-darkened eyes, and she drew her blade from the ground beside the bed. Myrgen lifted his chin, noticing Alexander for the first time. He turned to Catriona and she nodded to her new lover. Myrgen drew a bow that was suddenly in his hands and a great marble arrow flew at Alexander with alarming clarity, directly toward his chest...

Alexander awoke when firm hands grappled him, dragging him off the bed. His shoulders was sore from having his hands bound and being jostled with such anger was making the pain flare like he was being branded. He felt the horror of the dream sear his mind in a similar manner. The men didn't seem to care. They dragged him from the tent and threw him on the ground near another large tent.

Tulio stepped from the tent and stood, his arms crossed over his chest. The Toledan looked him over.

"Are you in love with her?"

Alexander blinked, wondering for a moment how the man knew about Catriona before it dawned on him he likely meant Tanglwyst. He felt the dream from earlier, not *remembering* it as much as just feeling what happened there. He had almost put aside his feelings for Catriona, put aside the grief. He had forgotten the pain of Gwen's death, his hatred for Myrgen. When he had given the Power to Tanglwyst, that rage had fled with it. When the Power was returned to him, he had felt free, purged of the anger.

"I left the woman I love in Caratia."

Tulio nodded. "Ah. A broken heart?"

"More like an inappropriate match. I was not the one for her, and she was not the one for me. It was... *ill fated.*" He had not quite abandoned all emotion regarding Catriona but he did not feel the obsession any longer.

"That explains it, then. We were curious why you were not fighting the kidnapping, or declaring your rage at such a disgrace to your person. But you left your beloved in Caratia? Clearly, it was her choice. Another man, perhaps?"

Alexander's face twisted in pain at the thought. Tulio had found a wound, and he was poking it. "It doesn't really matter now, does it? She's made her final choice, and it wasn't me."

Tulio cocked his head. "Such a difference from what Tanglwyst said. She gave me the impression you were a very self-serving creature."

"Despite what you think, I have no desire or motivation to harm or impede the Lady Tanglwyst. I saved her life in Caratia, healing her wounds." His shoulders sagged and he sighed at the memory, Brigit's voice echoing in his head.

Is this your choice?

Tulio leaned forward. "You healed her? She was hurt?"

"Near death. She was attacked by a," he shuddered, against his will, "monster."

"How long ago?"

"I healed her a couple days ago, before we left Caratia"

"She was in that state *a couple days ago*? And she ran away today? What kind of healer are you?"

"Is someone in your group injured?"

Tulio looked about, pursing his lips as if thinking carefully. "Nope. We're all well and healthy here."

"Then I highly doubt it matters at all to you."

Tulio smiled, but it wasn't the gentle kindness his face settled into naturally. This smile was strange, like the source was from an unholy place.

"No, I don't expect it does." He looked at the guards who brought Alexander. "Return him to the tent and tie his hands behind him this time. He may claim he holds no ill will towards our friend, but I think I'd rather hear it from her mouth than his."

Ce'Nedra opened her eyes, listening. Henri and Felix were sleeping on the floor on the far side of the room. The table and chairs had been moved to the center of the room to give the men a space to sleep. She and Sylvaine had been given the bed and the girl had spent too much time sleeping. Ce'Nedra caught herself getting annoyed with her. There was going to be work needed soon and the girl was going to have to get used to contributing.

She sat up and looked around the room. She had managed to get the sustenance runes in place and removed the grain divine symbols. The next step had been to replace the traveler's symbols. Ce'Nedra had surmised this was the symbol that allowed the amulet to access the room. It was the only reason for a symbol like that. She had replaced it with a rune to Tooele.

Tooele was the Keeper of the Ways, and was the only Fae who changed. He did as the reigning Fae Lord needed when it came to roads and pathways. During the winter, the roads were closed and impassable, requiring healing and family unity as per Gloriana's edicts. During the summer, the roads were wider and level, as would be preferred by a Warrior King like Corrigan. All the taverns held his runes at the compass points of the exterior.

Ce'Nedra's hope was to tap into the ability of Tooele to help lead them from this place of divine control. With any luck, invoking the Fae Lord of Pathfinding would provide a way to escape this prison. At the very least, it might reveal a door. However, it would not happen until the divine influence over the room was defeated. She also hoped that exchanging the runes would seal this room from a return visit from the man who imprisoned them.

The next phase was removing St. Brigit's symbol. The "healing" offered by the shadows was not real healing. It was infernal. She needed to remove their influence before it became a problem. If any of them were hurt, that could spell the end of them all.

She got to work.

Catherine looked up at Charles the Messenger as he entered. "Your Majesty, are you ready?"

"Yes, my boy."

She gathered up the message she had written to Alexander, demanding his return to Patras. Her traveling clothes had been cleaned and returned to her, so she was ready to go. Even her boots had been polished. Her golden hair was streaked with grey, the bleaching treatments helping it all grow out without showing her age. She had it braided into a practical style for the trip up the mountain.

They left the mayorial manse and got on their horses for the trip to the Drum and Nightingale Inn. The trip was going quickly and it looked like they would make it to the top well before midday. It took just over an hour before she began feeling uncomfortable. It started as a pinprick of nausea in the pit of her stomach. She noticed it, but dismissed it. It was undoubtedly from breakfast.

When they took the next turn in the road, the nausea asserted itself and became more evident. She would not vomit, not being able to tolerate the concept of indignity. Instead, she swallowed and focused upon the road. The next turn brought a greater wave and she barely managed to stop the wretching. She stopped her horse and looked up the mountain.

No Mandian shall pass into Caratia.

Sweat popped onto her forehead and breast, heat rising from her core. The idea came to her to renounce her Mandian heritage and embrace her Mervol marriage, but she did not want the binds she had to her homeland to fade. Certain rituals had been performed when she became Henry's bride, so that if she changed her blood to that of the Mervols, her family holdings would drop to the next heir in line. She would be as poor as a street beggar.

"Charles… wait…"

The messenger turned, reining in his steed the moment he saw she was not following. "Your Majesty?"

"I can't approach."

He blinked, then nodded. "I suspected as much. I knew you were from Mande. Do you wish for me to take your message up there for you?"

The message was innocuous. It told no secrets, gave no information that an enemy could use against her country or family outside of the idea that the king was not in Patras. Since this was common knowledge, it was not dangerous. The only value it had was in the nature of the messenger.

A spy could follow the messenger to Alexander.

There was nothing of value in the note beyond the chastisement of a misbehaving child. She shook her head.

"No. In the great scheme of things, there is no hurry, young man. My son will return when he is ready."

They smiled at each other and he looked off into the distance. His face fell into a confused frown.

"What is that smoke?"

Myrgen closed the book and rubbed his eyes. There was no real documentation for the stones in his possession. The only thing close to it was the history of the Heartstone. Nothing explained this. He looked at the stones again. They made no sense to him. The number of flecks in the stones glistened in hidden meaning.

The Fae cat's eyes had changed to jade when it touched the stones. What did that mean?

He hesitated to do so, but he finally picked up one of the stones, the one with the fewest flecks in it, and put it in his mouth.

Nothing happened.

He frowned.

Ah well.

He spit it out and looked up at Drake coming into the room. Drake looked at the rock in his palm, then back at Myrgen.

"Make sure you wash that before you put it back with the others."

Myrgen nodded, pouring some water into a goblet then dropping the stone in it. "Do you need your study back?"

"What exactly do you think I do in here? Race horses? This room is sizable. Anything I need to do will hardly be interfered with by your presence." He nodded towards the door. "Anika is downstairs asking for you. You came in at dawn, then didn't sleep very long before coming in here. She's worried."

Myrgen got up and stretched. He realized how sore he was as he heard his bones and muscles pop and groan.

Drake looked at the book before Myrgen. "Any luck?"

Myrgen shook his head. "There's a little about the Heartstone and the pommel of the Protector's Sword but that's all. Both of those are unique."

"Do you think touching them to one of those stones would help?"

Myrgen shook his head. "I doubt it. They've been clunking around in that pouch for a day now, but," he shrugged, "nothing else is working. I'll head down, then maybe rest for a while. Maybe something will come to me after a nap."

Drake nodded, taking a seat at his desk.

Myrgen found Anika in the courtyard, on her knees alongside two men and another woman, weeding the gardens. He nodded to the helpers as he tapped Anika on the shoulder.

"I hear you're looking for me."

"Ah, yes." She stood and wiped the dirt off her knees. "How is your research coming?"

"Not well. I'm not hitting anything in the books."

"Hm." She frowned, nodding, then took him by the arm and led him away from the courtyard. "Have you considered going to the Meditation Chamber?"

Myrgen glanced down, not wanting to seem foolish. "I thought about it but, I really don't feel comfortable going in there. That's the Protector's chamber, their opportunity to talk with the Land. I feel it's... *sacred.*"

"Is that respect talking? Or fear?"

He smiled. "Or?" He sighed. "Truth is, I don't want to check in there because I don't feel I'm ready yet. I don't have that calling."

"But you're participating in the Trials for Succession?"

He shrugged. "Not *successfully* at the moment."

She laughed, then patted his hand. "Make sure you don't starve yourself. And get some rest."

He kissed her hand and nodded. "I'm actually going to do that right now. I'll see you at dinner."

Octavius stepped off the ship and looked over the port where he had sailed away with his beloved. It had changed over the years, gotten bigger, but he could still see the tops of the forest from here. Raven stepped up next to him, surveying the view. They saw a road leading along the edge of town and Octavius and Raven both headed towards it. Octavius thought about going into town for a moment but in the end, he had no reason. No store-bought gift would appease Corrigan after this news, he didn't need to get a new shirt for the meeting, and no profession was going to be able to take the edge off the punishment. No need to put off the inevitable.

The walk to Galadorn was beautiful, and with each returning memory, he realized how much he had missed this place. He rubbed the stone with the glass embedded in it, then decided to bring it out. If he were going to walk through their memories, he wanted to share that walk with her. He held his hand open, the stone resting there, offering up the magic around them to his wife. A small part of him glimmered in hope that she was still there and that returning home would revive her, but the entire trip to the covenant garnered not a glint.

By the time they rounded the bend that looked into the grounds of the covenant, Octavius was close to tears. He had always known she would return here, but he never expected to outlive her. She was *Fae,* by the wisp! She was supposed to be damned near immortal. Raven pointed to the area beyond the Galadorn tower and Octavius saw a tall, golden tree about twice the height of the rest of the forest. It was in the center of it.

"That's her." He looked at Raven, his eyes brightening. "It's *alive.* Maybe she didn't die after all."

He started running to the forest, and Raven decided to run along with him. They charged past the workers in the fields, Raven laughing as his hair returned to green. When he released the magic, the fields along his path matured to full term, much to the shock of the workers. One of the workers ran to the tower but Octavius didn't care. He entered the forest and slowed a bit, getting winded. Raven scooped him up and they rode an earth sled towards the center.

There were twists and turns in the path, but Raven seemed to be very determined. Octavius saw the path diverge and the tree was most definitely in another direction entirely. He tapped Raven on the shoulder.

"I think you missed it."

Raven smiled, not taking his eyes from his task. "No I haven't. This is Embertwist's time. Any path is not designed to get you there, but to make you enjoy the journey. It's the scenic route."

"How do you know?"

"Because I can sense my father," Raven pointed, "and he's over there."

Within a few minutes, Raven stopped the earth sled and settled before the golden tree they had seen. Corrigan was sitting on his throne nearby but the ground around the chair was worn. He looked at Octavius and ran over to him. He hugged the very surprised sailor.

"You made it." Corrigan released his son-in-law. "Did you bring it?"

"Bring…"

A Fae near them pointed to Octavius' hand. "There, sire! She's there!"

Corrigan opened Octavius' hand and took the rock with the fragments. He held it up to the light. "Good. Smart thinking to encase it." He looked at Raven. "Do you mind?"

Raven waved his hands, muttering a few words. The stone dissolved, leaving just the glass fragments. Corrigan moved over to the tree, drawing out his knife. He pulled up some up the bark, careful not to pry it off, then slipped the shards inside the opening. He stepped back, his eyes watching, eager. Raven stepped next to him, watching as well.

The tree shimmered, the bark around the cut moving, as if swallowing the shards. The leaves fluttered, and all the Fae in the area sighed in relief.

Octavius looked at Corrigan, then Raven. "What happened?"

Raven smiled. "She remembered."

"Re… huh?"

Corrigan clapped Octavius on the shoulder. "We needed the shards of her former self to remind her who she was. Otherwise, she was going to forget and just become a tree. Now, we just need to change her back."

"Change? Change her back?" Octavius was stunned. "We can do that? She isn't dead?"

"By the wisp, no, my boy. She went dormant, and we worried she would forget who she was. If she turned into a tree, she would die."

"But, she's already a tree."

Raven shook his head. "She couldn't be. Remember? Changing a Fae will destroy it. Look."

He waved his hand in front of Octavius' eyes, then pointed. The tree became transparent and he saw Estelle in the trunk of the tree, sleeping. He ran up to the tree and touched it. He felt the trunk, but not her. He kissed the tree, then turned to Corrigan.

"What do we need to do to change her back?"

"You need to travel to a port nearby. I sent my Second to attend to some things there. Preparations for the summer. You need to get him because he has to break the spell."

"Great. Where is this port?"

"Not far. It's in a place called St. Giles."

Octavius blinked. *"St. Giles?"*

Raven looked at him. "Oh, you know it?"

Octavius stared at the young mage. "You might say. It's that way about four tendays."

"Great! We'll begin now."

Octavius closed his eyes. "Why don't we rest first? We'll leave in the morning."

Raven pointed to Octavius, then to Corrigan. "Or that. Let's do that."

Corrigan nodded.

Octavius looked again at the tree and smiled. He needed a night next to his wife.

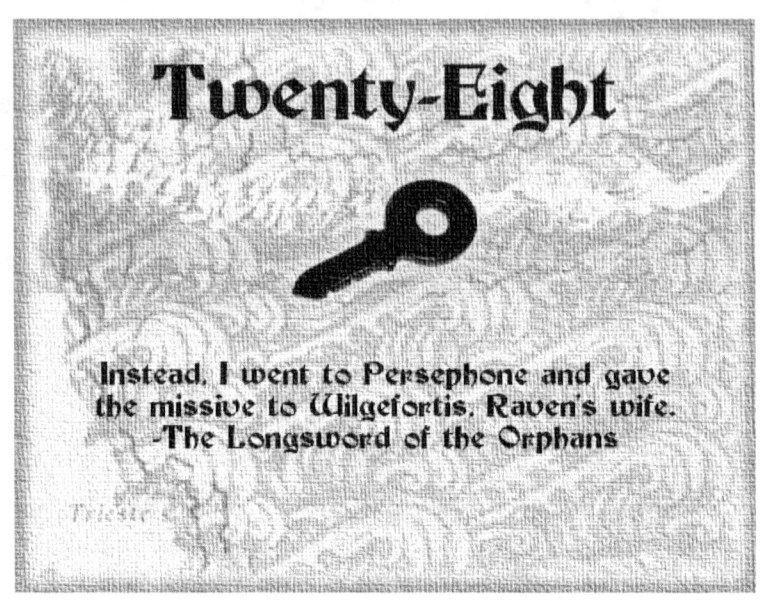

Twenty-Eight

Instead, I went to Persephone and gave
the missive to Wilgefortis, Raven's wife.
-The Longsword of the Orphans

James looked up from the book in his hands and pointed. "I think that's it over there."

The three companions looked at the lump in the horizon, and nodded. They started riding again. Michael found the whole landscape disturbing. They had come upon a signpost about an hour from the mountain camp that pointed the way to Kent. The covenant had been in Kent, with ties to Canterbury, which had governed it. They knew that because James had read it out of the journal Alistair had left behind.

"I get the feeling there should be, I don't know," Michael looked around, "vacant farms or something. But everything is dead."

Their boots and pants were covered in pale mud kicked up by the horses, whose legs were white as well.

James referred to the journal. "Yeah, it says here this was all farmland." He pointed to the north. "Up by Glarren, that was sheep country. The royal palace was that way."

"It is on the other side of that wall now." Catriona nodded towards the east, where even at this distance, there was a thin line visible.

James patted the book. "Yeah. Apparently, the successor got help erecting it from the mages of Persephone. Otherwise, it might still be accessible from this side. That was something to be avoided."

Michael nodded toward a stone roadside trough, the only source of water they had found regularly. "Let's give the horses a drink. I need to stretch my legs."

"This is the third one of these we've seen." James led his horse to the trough. "Where do you think they came from?"

Catriona dismounted, splatting into the white mud. "I suspect they were always here. York gets a lot of fog and these used to be major roadways. It's far more economical to have water collectors than to dig wells with this much moisture."

It was true. It took until well past noon for the fog to dissipate from this morning. She was glad they packed the food in oiled leather to keep it from molding. She looked around. The amount of damage to the ground on this side was overwhelming, even with the moisture in the air. She felt no connection with the stuff beneath her feet. She could have been walking on air or water. There was no life.

Except...

She stopped. There was a tiny, distant vibration, like a wheel turning far away, grinding flour. There were no windmills or water mills here, at least not in the direction the vibrations were shaking the ground. She knelt down, putting her hand on the earth. Sure enough, the vibrations seemed to be coming from the ruins. She looked up at her companions.

"There's something at Persephone."

They watered the horses then moved on to the ruins and found what must have once been an active village. Houses and shops still stood inside the low wall around the complex, which was more than could be said about the rest of York. Everything else had long ago been harvested to build the city by the sea. But here, the homes were not dismantled, at least not by scavengers.

Michael looked behind them. "We aren't far from the coast. Why is this place still here? They have re-consumed every other item in the country."

James shrugged. "I can't imagine. Even allowing for superstition, desperation always outranks it."

The vibrations were even more prominent here. Catriona knelt again. "Can you feel that?"

The men stooped to touch the earth but after a minute, they both shook their heads.

She felt around. "It's definitely coming from inside the wall. But it's deep, like below it."

"Could it be a message or trail just for you?" Michael's voice carried through the wasteland, resonating almost as much as the hum in the ground.

She stood. "That would be very unusual. No one in York knows I'm here."

"Then it obviously wouldn't be from York." James looked at the small buildings that had collapsed under the weight of the centuries. "Come on. Let's look for Khud's relative."

They went to the archway leading into the walls. There was a flicker of light and a voice, faint and feminine, whispered through the dead air.

"You are from the Land. You have stood here before. You may pass." Catriona turned to look at James and Michael as they met resistance entering. She stopped.

James and Michael stood outside the wall, hands upon some sort of barrier. James looked at Catriona. "Are you alright?"

She could hear them and see them, and they could hear and see her, so although the barrier was magic, at least it wasn't solid. "What happened?"

James shook his head. "Dunno."

They all put their hands upon the air of the archway. Catriona's stopped on this side. "It's a trap."

Michael and James tried pounding on the air while Catriona looked around for some sort of lever or catch.

She found nothing. "I don't see a way to deactivate it."

James pulled out the journal and opened it, scanning the text. "It says here they repelled attackers on more than one occasion by erecting a barrier. It's connected to the magic source here."

"Why would it feel you two are threats?"

James looked up from the book. "Why would it feel you are not?"

"It said I have been here before."

Both men exchanged a glance then returned their gaze to her. James spoke first. "You heard a voice?"

She nodded. "You apparently didn't."

The voice came from behind her. "They cannot hear because I do not let them."

She looked behind her but saw nothing. "Who are you?"

"I am Persephone."

James and Michael watched Catriona and she stepped to the side to be able to watch the area as well as her friends. "Why can't they come through?"

"I do not want them here. That one is a minion of the Fae, and the other is a minion of Heaven."

"Minion of Heaven?" She looked at Michael. "The voice says you're a minion of Heaven."

"Really?" He shook his head. "I have been a practicing Augustinian since I was captured, but I have never felt devotion to it."

James shrugged. "It may not matter. Did it say anything about me?"

"That you're a servant of the Fae."

"That's true."

Michael shook his head. "Why would that be a problem?"

James took a breath. "Well, the Church became aggressive during the years after the War. They sent inquisitors all over the world to destroy anything that didn't worship Heaven. Covenants were destroyed, cities rebuilt to house divine energies and repel Fae ones. I understand the rejection of anything holy. But the Fae were allies of magic in the War. Why is it repelling me?"

Catriona looked into the complex. "Why are you keeping out the Fae servant?"

"He has never been here before. This gate only allows access to those who have been accepted by the Covenant."

James looked past her, pointing. "What's that?"

A glint caught the light in the courtyard. She looked at the men. "I'll go see."

Michael hit the barrier. *"No."*

She looked back at the glint, then at Michael. "I'm sorry but, you can't stop me."

She walked down the road, keeping her companions in sight. The glint was between a few buildings but it was moving. Catriona stopped and waited to see what it was. She felt her heart thumping in her chest and tried to control the fear.

There was a strange humming and clanking, like someone walking in full plate armor while running their finger around the rim of a crystal goblet. A few seconds later, a woman made entirely of gold stepped around the building. She had long, curling hair and wore what looked like a peasant dress from long ago. She wore a heavy leather apron and boots and gloves, like a blacksmith's wife, but every inch of her was gold. She clanked and moved like a rusty wagon wheel. She opened her mouth to talk and a screech filled the area, like a fork scraping on an empty plate. Michael and James winced from it.

The woman bowed to Catriona. "Old One, welcome back."

Catriona tried not to react to the sound of the voice and focused upon the contents. "'Old One'?"

The woman blinked. "Oh, you have gone through a transformation. I did not realize it at first. I am the Gold Wife. I am a servant of the Land."

"Did you raise this barrier?" Catriona gestured to the archway.

"No. These were the automatic defenses of the Covenant." She looked at James and Michael. "Ah. I see my manners are not in effect yet. Forgive me." She cleared her throat. When she spoke again, her voice was smooth and as soothing as warm water. "Is this better, Old One?"

Catriona raised her eyebrows, surprised. "Yes. It's practically dulcet." She looked at the men but they were still cringing. "They still hear the other voice?"

The Gold Wife nodded.

"So they can hear you. They could not hear the other voice, the one named Persephone."

The Gold Wife nodded. "She did not wish to speak to them."

"Why does she wish to speak to me?"

"I don't know, but when I felt you in this place, I was awakened. I have not seen you in centuries. Not since Raven came back here. We left together when he returned for Wilgefortis."

"Why do I not remember you?"

The Gold Wife looked into Catriona's eyes. "Because your eyes are the wrong color."

Alexander lay back on the floor in the tent, then realized that position would be decidedly uncomfortable in very short order. He shifted his bonds and sat up, leaning against the pole supporting the tent.

He tried to figure out a way out of this. He reached out with his Power of Sovereignty to find anyone with fealty nearby, but the locale of a bandit camp turned up no Oaths. He shook his head at his wishful thinking. *Did I really believe there could be a spy among them, just waiting for a chance like this?* Clearly, the strain of his recent losses was taking its toll.

His mind wandered back to Caratia again and the nightmare that came from his obsession. He still felt Catriona in his heart, but he also felt the void left from her explosive escape from it. She had seen into Duncan's mind, had seen Alexander's sins. That was why he had no trouble confessing them to Tanglwyst. Why hide it at that point? He knew beyond all doubt he would never be allowed to set foot in Catriona's land again. Legend had it all Mandians were exiled from Caratia centuries ago and they could not even cross the border. Although he had found a way around that before, he believed his own boots would encounter that same barrier now.

The only thing to survive had been the woman arrested for his brother's murder and even she had escaped his grasp. He wasn't certain what he planned to do with Tanglwyst if they had returned to Patras. There was enough evidence for him to believe she was drugged and manipulated, possibly as far back as the days before the Ball. He frowned remembering that decision. He chose to stay in his room that night instead of go down to the ball and had, in the process, forgotten all the time he and the lady had spent becoming friends.

He took a deep breath and thought about it, about *her*. Tanglwyst had been as lonely as he when they started talking. He recognized the sadness of rejected love. Granted, they were both reunited with their lovers but he still could not believe the woman of whom he had become fond would choose to spend her time with a drunken pugilist. Catriona either.

He blinked at the realization his first thought of jealousy there was over *Tanglwyst's* attention and not Catriona's. Well, he *had* told Brigit he chose her. It was to be expected he would start putting her first over a lover who abandoned him. He closed his eyes and leaned his head against the pole. He felt out Tanglwyst's fealty, trying to find her. The dream before had indicated she was in the Papal City. He wondered if she got inside safely.

A faint beacon of an Oath called to him across the miles. He knew instantly it was hers. The pale blue glow was still there but it looked almost as bright as the fealty light itself. Her dedication to the country and Crown were waning, almost gone. For all he could tell, the only reason the bit remained was because of their exchange of the Power.

It still baffled him someone who plotted the murder of the king could have an Oath of Fealty still intact. It was the only reason he could transfer that Power to her while he was still alive. He was sure the Power would go to Alan if he died, though it might go to Tanglwyst now. It was one of the pieces of evidence Alexander had of Tanglwyst's intentions and innocence. She was not responsible for the attempt on Charles' life.

She was responsible for the one on Catriona though, and that alone was reason for Alexander to exile the woman. A month ago, that would have been enough to have her head and body on the walls of the city alongside Elizabeth's. Back then, his anger would not have been sated without blood. Alexander sighed. There seemed to be a lot of that in regards to Catriona.

Alexander started to nod off and he decided not to fight it. For years, in his dreams, he was reunited with the woman he loved. He let sleep take him so he might do so again.

Tanglwyst entered a room with a lavish bed and furnishings. A young page brought in her saddlebags and she gestured to the floor by the bed. She asked him something but Alexander couldn't hear anything. The young man nodded to a desk near the window and she thanked him. She went to the desk after he left, then opened the drawers until she found a graphite and a sheaf of paper. She sat at the desk and put the graphite to it. He expected her to start writing a letter, but instead, she began drawing. As he watched, a familiar sight formed on the page.

She had seen an amulet.

Alexander woke at the thought, images of the lady being ravaged by the shadows tearing apart his dream. Dusk had settled and he heard the inhabitant of the camp preparing dinner. The tent flap moved aside and a burly man set a plate of cooked rabbit before him. He stood and started to leave.

"Wait. My hands are tied behind me. How am I supposed to eat?"

The man looked stern. "Like a cur." He left.

Alexander looked at the food, his mouth starting to water. One thing he knew about rabbit, you didn't want to eat it cold. "I shall have to lodge a complaint about the service around here."

He leaned over and began tearing apart the carcass before him.

James looked at the sky. "It's getting late. We should set up camp."

Michael gestured to Catriona, talking to the Gold Wife. "What about her?"

"We can't get to her and she can't get to us. I'm going to read through the journal and see if I can find an entry about this Gold Wife or about Raven."

"Myrgen mentioned someone named Raven to me, when we had a chance to catch up. He is a mage."

"That explains why he's in my father's book." James stopped, realizing he had just formally acknowledged Alistair as his father, not his uncle.

James knew the journal had spoken of the Gold Wife and Raven, but he couldn't remember what it said. Searching through it would take his mind off the fact that one of their party was now sequestered away from him. He wasn't sure if it was a good idea to move on, but that was premature to consider. The journal might help get them in the area or at least get Catriona out.

"I'll make camp. You research." Michael unpacked one of the tents.

James nodded, sitting on the ground. He looked at Catriona again, still talking with the Gold Wife. Hopefully, she wouldn't leave their sight.

"What do you mean, my eyes are the wrong color?"

The Gold Wife straightened herself. "I'm not the Keeper of your memories. It is not for me to say."

"Then who *are* you to me?"

"A servant of the Land, like you. I represent the Magic connection, just as you represent the one of Death."

Catriona shivered. Something about the way she said "Death" felt *true*. "What *can* you tell me then?"

The Gold Wife looked her over. "How long have you been here this time?"

"Been where?"

"Here, above the dirt?"

Catriona started to answer but then realized she had no memories past about twelve years ago. "I came out of a wood a dozen years back. I had an accident, we think, shipwreck maybe. I can't remember before that."

"Where?"

She looked south. "Latia, south of Mande."

The Gold Wife looked towards Caratia. "The last time I saw you, you were there, in Caratia. You were blonde, because you had come back here in York, twice. Raven made a mistake."

"What," she shook her head, "what *mistake*?"

"He revealed who you were too soon."

Catriona reached up and rubbed her eyes. She hated vague clues. She decided to read the Gold Wife and find out what was going on.

She opened her eyes and looked the Gold Wife up and down. She had scuff marks and dust on her, in some places stopping her from looking like gold and more like silver. She had a faint odor of water attached to her, and earth with actual life in it. *Was she buried?* Catriona dismissed the idea. She didn't have mold or dirt, just dust. There was a mustiness that seemed like storage.

But she got no secrets. There may be a soul in this creature, but it was wiser than her. It hid everything better than she could extract it.

The Gold Wife looked at the archway. "Your friends are settling in for the night. We should do likewise for you."

Catriona looked at the house nearest the archway. "I can stay there. It's best for me to stay where we can talk."

"I don't think so. I think it would be better for you to come with me."

"Why?"

"Because now that you're here, it's possible all this destruction can be reversed."

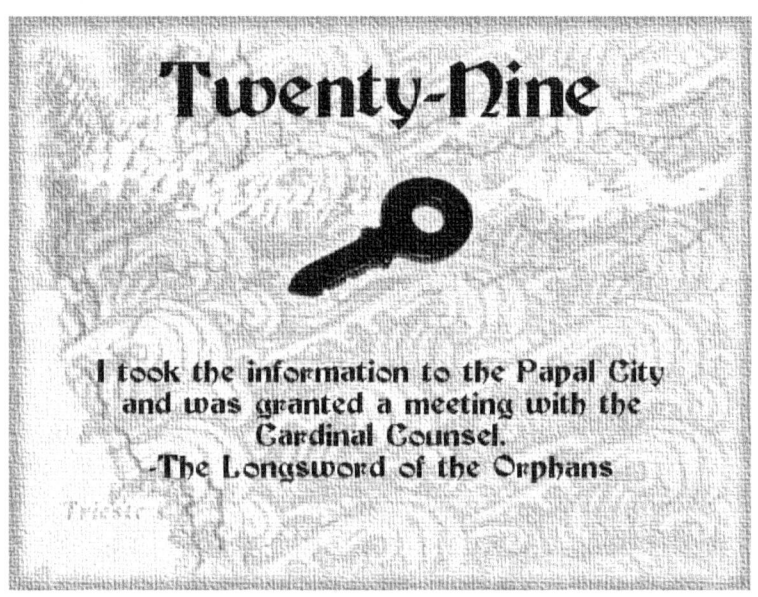

Twenty-Nine

I took the information to the Papal City
and was granted a meeting with the
Cardinal Counsel.
-The Longsword of the Orphans

Alexander spent the next day drifting in and out of sleep. When awake, he checked on everyone. His mother was passing away from Cliffbase, probably heading home. He thought about calling to her but the idea that she had left Patras unguarded bothered him more than his current circumstances. If she stood by the throne of Mervolingia, none would dare try to usurp it.

He checked on Gomez, who seemed to be spending time in St. Giles. He was in one area most of the time, probably investigating a crime or talking with nobility. He envisioned him at a desk with noble after noble coming in to get the special sashes that had been made, marking girls and women who were worthy of Alexander's scrutiny. The original plot had been a ruse but Alexander found he might need that assistance now.

He checked on Dominic, who seemed to be very busy. He was all over Patras, from one end to the other in any given day. Once, he thought he saw the fealty light far from Patras right before he dozed off but when he woke up, Dominic's light was in Patras so Alexander thought he might have overlapped Dominic's and Tanglwyst's lights. In none of the visits could he actually see the people he looked in on, even when he was about to doze off.

Except one.

When he focused upon Tanglwyst's light, he could see her. She spent the day after she awoke talking to a cardinal, whom she hugged. She went out into the Papal City and spent time shopping. Next time he dozed off, a servant was putting her new clothes away in the wardrobe. Though she had several outfits to choose from, for some reason, she seemed reluctant to get out of her traveling clothes. Instead, she worked on the drawings of the amulet.

This worried him. He didn't want her to get hold of one and if he was too late, he didn't want her falling prey to the same addiction that had claimed both him and Duncan.

Duncan.

He felt for the assassin's light but couldn't find it. Had he strayed so far into the darkness that his oaths no longer shone? It was either that or the man was dead. Alexander wasn't sure which would be better. The monster that tore into Tanglwyst was no longer his friend or her lover. When Alexander got out of this, he was going to have to hunt Duncan down and get him cleared of the poisonous amulet, hopefully before he suffered mass damages again.

He dozed to look in on Tanglwyst and saw her writing letters at the window seat. They were business inquiries, some heading to Patras, some to St. Giles. None of them were to Dominic but were instead to an Othon of Burwick and an Isabella D'Medici. Another was to Preston Crowley in St. Giles. He didn't know how to warn her about Gomez being there so he hoped this Preston person could be discrete.

She had a good head for business, it appeared. She was savvy enough to have private funds and stashes of business resources even in the Papal City. Apparently, she owned several shops there, and paid a large tithing to the church to keep herself in their graces. It worked because she was having no trouble functioning in her new surroundings. According to the letters, she had a meeting with her grandfather later that day.

She was drinking tea from a simple pot on the table by the window seat. He had been paying so much attention to the letters he hadn't even noticed it at first. He remembered the fancy tea party she set up for them back in Patras. The set had been silver and elaborate. He had delighted at the intricate griffin motif and had planned to use it often throughout the winter. Then he saw Alan in Emmy's room and all his plans dissipated like the steam in her cup.

She stopped writing periodically to gaze out the window at the city but he could see the forest where they were from this vantage. He could even see a tiny plume of smoke a day's ride from her, rising through the tree tops. Her eyes lingered there as she drank her tea, then she would return to her letters.

He focused upon the name Preston Crowley and found a light there in St. Giles. He was not far from Gomez but was definitely more active. Not as active as Dominic, but not far behind. Alexander checked on Dominic and found him far from Patras again. He seemed to be heading to St. Andrew. That was good. He needed to handle the situation with the noble down there, Rochefort. Someone did.

He returned to find her removing her breeches as a maid held a robe for her. He opened his eyes, forcing himself awake. It was inappropriate for him to see her unclothed. Probably going for a bath. It had been a while since she had such a luxury. Being on the road did not afford such joys but it meant she would be busy for a few hours.

Another meal was brought in and Alexander noticed everyone was different. The guard at the door, the one feeding him, the one escorting him to pee. His captors let him loose to answer nature's call, which was the only reason he still had fingers. Otherwise, they would have dropped off by now. Each guard who retied him did it in a different way so he couldn't get the knots figured out. The variety of skills these people possessed impressed him more with each encounter. They knew how to hold a hostage. This time, his bonds gave him a bit of freedom to possibly slip his hand in front of him so he tried to move his hands under his rear to the front.

He rocked back and he lost his balance and hit his head on the pole. Stars burst around him and he passed out.

Octavius stood by Estelle's tree and gazed at her sleeping form. Whatever Raven had done to his eyes, it was a blessing. He could feel her presence and it put him at ease. He had not realized how unhappy he had been until he saw her there. He touched the bark near her face and she shifted a little in her sleep, leaning into the touch. His heart broke and he felt hot tears rappel down his cheeks.

He didn't want to leave. He didn't want to go to the far reaches of Mervolingia in pursuit of some Fae. The only Fae he cared abot was right here. He gripped one of her branches, holding her hand. He felt the leaves caress his skin, and she smelled like cherry blossoms. The tears came faster.

They were never returning to the *Enigma*. Once she was released from this tree, she would be taken from him. If she wasn't, then she wouldn't be allowed to return to the ship that was almost her death. Octavius wouldn't allow it. He loved the crew, loved his captain, but he loved his wife far more. He wouldn't let that happen again.

He looked around. He was happy here before. He only left to protect Estelle. But she had followed him anyway and Catriona had facilitated it. He had been appreciative, and they had spent a good, long time at sea. It was time to move on from that life now.

He looked at his hand and saw that it was turning a little… *barky*. He frowned, not sure what was happening at first. When the first tiny bud grew from his thumbnail, he understood. He smiled at his wife, then wrapped his arm around her. Her branch encompassed him, bending easily with him. His feet grew very stable as he felt them embed into the ground and intermingle with her roots. He turned his face so his lips met hers.

As the last of the daylight left the sky, Octavius was once again in his wife's arms.

Raven came into the clearing with Estelle's tree, holding a piece of some fleshy fruit. Humans weren't supposed to take food or drink from Fae but Raven could. Then Octavius could take the fruit from him and it would be safe! Raven was almost sure that would work.

"*Octavius. I have food.*" Raven's call echoed through the trees but got no answer. He was about to call a second time when he saw the tree with Estelle in it. "Oh."

A second tree had joined with hers, as if they grew almost from the same root system. They wound around each other, her around him as much as the reverse. He was still a little mobile but that would fade by dawn. Raven could have reversed the magic, but that seemed cruel.

It was a unique solution. It did mean Raven was on his own again. That was discouraging. Lauriel was still back in Caratia and although he might be able to call his trusty companion to him, it was smarter to wait until he was back on the main continent. It looked like the trip to St. Giles was not as pressing as it had been an hour ago.

Raven toasted the couple with the fruit in his hand and took a bite, then went back to reveling with his father.

Tanglwyst followed her brother to the office of the Pope. It was later than she had expected. Caiaphas opened the door and they saw another cardinal speaking with an older, burly monk. The foyer of the office was beautifully furnished with crisp, white woolen armchairs, but both men were standing. Their backdrop was a set of gigantic oak doors carved with scenes from the lives of several saints.

The men looked at Tanglwyst and the monk took a breath of distaste and fingered the symbol of St. Thomas at his chest. Caiaphas bowed to them.

"Cardinal Erminio, so good to see you. Brother Fausto, you look well."

Erminio returned the bow. "Who is your companion, Cardinal Caiaphas? I do not think we have met."

"This is my sister, Lady Tanglwyst de Holloway."

Erminio bowed, then gestured to the monk. "This is our esteemed librarian, Brother Arnaldo Fausto, my lady."

Tanglwyst curtsied to the men. "I am most honored to meet you both."

Fausto frowned. "What can we do for her, Cardinal?"

Caiaphas glanced at his sister, then back to the older man. "She has a meeting with the Pope."

The cardinal put a hand to his own chest and the holy symbol there. "With His Holiness? What business could she possibly have with Him?"

"He's my grandfather." Tanglwyst was not surprised at the treatment she was getting at the hands of the men. The Papal Palace inhabitants were notoriously misogynistic.

"So? What does that have to do with it? And you will speak only when spoken too, *girl*."

Caiaphas took a deep breath. "Well, I suppose that's for His Holiness to decide, since he is the one who requested the meeting."

The great carved doors opened and a man in a monk's robe, younger than Fausto but older than Erminio, stepped out. "Ah, good. You are all here. Please, come in."

He led the way to the great desk, also of carved oak, cluttered with saints and paperwork. A small, venerable man sat behind the desk, but he rose and cantered around to the front when he saw Tanglwyst. "My dear girl! It is so *good* to see you. Please, come in. Make yourself comfortable. Brother Vito, please bring some wine for our guests."

The other monk bowed and went to a decanter to the side.

"Now, come, tell me about your trip. I see that Duncan got you here. Is he still around?"

Tanglwyst looked around. "No. I got here on my own. He…" She didn't know how to tell what Duncan had become, according to Alexander. "I'm not sure where he ended up."

Pope Gregory frowned. "That's too bad. I tried to summon him earlier but I did not get a reply. I fear the worst, my dear."

She swallowed and nodded. "So do I."

"Well, I got your letter you sent up. What's this meeting about?"

She opened up the sheaf of papers she brought with her and showed her grandfather the pictures of the amulet. "This item was on a man who attacked me. I have seen it before and was told, by Duncan, it was a holy artifact."

Brother Fausto looked at the drawings, then at Erminio. Caiaphas looked as well, but showed no reaction.

Gregory nodded. "Yes, it's one of ours. He attacked you?"

She nodded. "He took me to a room with no access except that amulet, which could take us anywhere. I took it from him and left him in the room."

Cardinal Erminio looked at her. "You *used* a holy relic?"

"I had to, to escape." She looked back at Gregory. "He was going to kill me."

Gregory patted her hand. "You did the right thing, my dear."

Erminio cleared his throat. "Where is this relic now? I trust you are here to return it?" He held out his hand for the amulet.

252

Tanglwyst shook her head, ignoring the hand. "I lost it in the catacombs under the palace in Patras. It made me sick."

"You *lost* it?" Erminio was aghast. "After tainting it with your," he waved a hand at her body, "*womanhood?*"

Caiaphas frowned. "Oh please, Erminio. She didn't stuff it inside her for safe keeping."

That made Erminio shudder in disgust but it quieted him.

Gregory looked at Fausto. "Do you have any books on this, Master Librarian?"

Fausto took the simple drawing Tanglwyst did of the amulet. "Well, it's hard to say from such a rudimentary sketch, but I will see what I can find." He took the drawing in two fingers like it had a disease.

Gregory was nonplussed. "Please do. I would appreciate a report by tomorrow eve."

Fausto looked at the Pope with surprise, then at Tanglwyst with scorn. "Of course, Your Holiness. I'll begin at once." He bowed and left the room.

Erminio looked at his superior. "What can *I* do, Your Holiness?"

"My granddaughter will be staying with us for a while. Please make sure she has someone to aid her and gets anything she needs."

Again the aghast face. "Your Holiness? *Here? At the Papal Palace?* Surely she'd be more comfortable elsewhere."

"Are you insinuating that there is a nicer, more hospitable place in all the world than my own home, Erminio?"

The cardinal swallowed, realizing his implication. He bowed. "Of course not, Your Holiness."

Caiaphas cleared his throat. "Grandfather, I put her up in a room on the fifth level already. She came in last night."

Gregory perked up. "That sounds perfect. Make sure she is taken care of. This lady is the owner of the Tanglwyst Trading Company."

Erminio's face changed from judgmental to downright cheerful. "Oh really? Well, that's different. I am *very* familiar wth your level of devotion, my Lady. Please, forgive my earlier behavior. I feared you were a common strumpet."

Tanglwyst did her best not to shake her head in wonder but failed utterly. "I'll try to find it in my heart."

That was taken as absolution by Erminio. "Oh good! Then we will be friends after all." He bowed to the Pope. "I'll see to the arrangements at once." He likewise left.

Caiaphas let out a hidden snicker. "By the Saints."

Gregory nodded. "Oh, I knew *that* would do the trick. Pure Mandian accountant, that one." He turned back to Tanglwyst. "Was there anything else, my dear?"

She thought hard about telling him about Alexander, how he had gone mad under the Power of Sovereignty, how his obsession with Catriona had almost cost the kingdom his life. But in the end, she couldn't bring herself to tell them of his crimes. She still had hope that he would return to the person she had met during the winter.

"Not yet. I would like to explore the library, though."

"Be my guest, literally. Whatever you need." He looked at her brother. "Caiaphas, please show Tanglwyst where the Library is."

Caiaphas nodded and held out his hand to escort her away. She hesitated, but went with her decision to not reveal Alexander to the man who could strip his crown in a single ceremony. She hugged her grandfather, then took her brother's hand and left the great room.

Thirty

He said it might be a trap to stop me from getting out if I ever did return.
-The Longsword of the Orphans

Catriona stepped up to the barrier. "Hey."

James looked up from the book and Michael tamped in the last spike of the tent. James stood and came over to the archway. The Gold Wife was watching from a distance. "What's going on?"

"I'm going to head inside the main building. The Gold Wife says there may be a way to reverse this wasteland, turning it back into real earth again."

James looked at Michael who came over, dusting his hands. The large Nubian glanced at the golden figure. "Can you trust her?"

Catriona glanced over her shoulder. "I have no idea. But I can't stay trapped in here."

James' eyes narrowed. "That's exactly what this sounds like: A trap. There's probably a pile of bones from the last wanderer who came across this place."

Catriona shook her head. "I doubt that, not with such a specific method for choosing who is allowed through the barrier."

"Just because someone *says* the cheese in the mousetrap isn't poisoned doesn't mean that's true."

Catriona understood his meaning. The Gold Wife did not have to be honest, and Catriona had an uneasy feeling about this place. It was very possible that these cottages held devoured prey. With there being no connection to the Land here, she would be relying on some pretty dirty fighting if it came to that.

Michael nodded. "What about your gift?"

Catriona shook her head. "Doesn't work."

"Because she's metal?"

"Because she's older and wiser than me by ages. I can't read a thing." She glanced back over her shoulder, then at her companions. "If I don't come out in a day, you need to go on without me."

Michael and James both protested at once but Catriona put a finger to her lips. She lowered her voice. "I know that's not a good plan, but you have a job to do, James."

"*My* job is to protect *you*." Michael pointed at Catriona. "I can't go back to Myrgen and tell him I left you in the ruins of a mage covenant in the middle of a wasteland."

"How do you plan to protect me?" She tapped her fist on the barrier.

"By making sure no one else comes in."

Catriona thought about it. The idea of Michael out here alone bothered her, regardless of his strength. There was only a limited amount of food and water. Eventually, he'd have to leave. Better to have him doing some good.

"No, you go with James. Make sure he gets home. After you are done with his quest, you come back here. I might have found out something by then."

James crossed his arms. "I don't like this."

"Me neither, but she says she can get me information about this." She nodded to the desert behind them. "You want to know what happened here, right?"

"Not that much."

She spread her arms wide. "Okay then, what have you got to get me out? You only have so much food. I don't even know if the food there could pass through here without being on me."

Michael reached over and tossed a chick pea square to her. The barrier bounced it back. He picked it up and gave it to a horse. "So, now we know about that."

"I don't think she wants me dead. She needs me alive. I won't starve."

"Yay." James sounded disbelieving. He looked over the barrier, then shook his head. "We'll give a few things a try before we go. I won't leave unless I have no other choice."

She nodded. "Understood. If I find anything, I'll come back and inform you."

They all nodded farewell and Catriona went to the Gold Wife. "Lead on."

The Gold Wife gestured to the tower up ahead. It was a ruin, and looked like it had taken several cannonballs to its structure. The tower seemed to be made of a single piece of polished obsidian, the top of the tower was strewn across the courtyard. Scorch marks, almost invisible until she got closer, punctuated the tower pieces. Once she was right up on the ruin, she realized there were no holes in it. It had simply blasted apart.

Two other towers were collapsed in on themselves, and they flanked the first one. The Gold Wife went to the base of the broken one and opened a door. Stairs descended and went through an area that was clearly a defunct bathhouse. Another door on the other side was open and footprints went through the dust from there to the outside. Inside was an elaborate water aqueduct, and several plant boxes long since gone fallow. Mirrors that conducted sunlight down to the greenhouse lay shattered on the floor.

As she passed, she felt the bottle Khudahar had given her tug at her belt. She glanced at the room and it tugged again. The Gold Wife did not notice and Catriona put her hand upon it to settle it. She didn't want it leaping off her belt and clanging on the ground.

The Gold Wife went to a closed door opposite the open one with the flower boxes, and unlocked it. It had a few magical locks as well, which bothered Catriona. She was *not* magical in nature and she would have no way to get past this area if the door was closed upon her.

"You have said several things that confused me. One of them is that I have been here before. How?"

"You were the First Dûcesa."

Catriona stopped. "The *First Dûcesa?*" She looked at the ceiling, shaking her head. "I think you have me confused with someone else. I am Stâpâna of Caratia, not the Dûcesa."

"That may be who you are now, but that's not who you were before. Don't worry. You'll remember sooner or later. You always do."

"Please. Explain this. How am I to help reverse this blight upon the Land here?"

"Well, that will become evident once we get you to the source."

She wanted to ask more questions, but she felt like it wasn't working. If she got an answer, she didn't understand it. She began walking again, following the Gold Wife through a storeroom with several shelves that clearly once held hundreds of varied items.

"How do I recover these memories?"

"There are stones that you eject when you die. They have gold flecks in them. If you touch them, you get your memories back."

Catriona frowned. "I have one of those stones. It is in the pommel of my sword. I have touched it often and never recovered anything like you are describing."

The Gold Wife looked over her shoulder. "Oh, that one isn't yours. That belongs, or rather *belonged* to your Stâpân, Slade Stormchest. It was later held by Raven Grasshair, who became your Stâpân after you died." She unlocked another door, this one going deeper underground. The Land was starting to have life again here and Catriona felt that thrumming vibration intensify.

"You see, when you die, you come back again. It can take any time from a couple days to seven, but never longer. Your Stâpân is the Keeper of your memories. It's his job to hold onto them and dispense them to you when the time is right. If you get them too fast or too soon, you can die. That's what happened to the Second Dûcesa. Raven told her who she was right after she rose up from the ground. She got a flood of memories, including the one where her Stâpân just died. It killed her all over again."

Catriona remembered the story of Slade and the Dûcesa. They had sacrificed being together to fight in the War against the Soulless. It was not permitted for the Stâpân to marry the Dûcesa. The Stâpân's role was to protect the people, not just one. She had always felt that story was horribly tragic, but she understood the message it taught.

The Gold Wife swept her hand over a candle, lighting it and illuminating another door. She opened it and continued walking. "Afterwards, he realized he wasn't supposed to reveal everything all at once. So when she came back again, he traveled with her to her home and stayed by her side until we determined she was ready. Then he gave her the memories and told her goodbye. I stayed with her until she died, then I returned here."

Catriona saw stones and symbols on the walls light up when the Gold Wife passed them. It lit the corridor that seemed impossibly long. "You mentioned before that I was a blond."

"Yes. When you die and go to ground, you return looking like a child of the previous incarnation, and a native of the land you rise from. Since the Second Dûcesa died in York, the Third Dûcesa rose looking like a child of York. This was strange for someone ruling over Caratia, but once she demonstrated who she was, no one doubted."

"How did she do that?"

"She built a castle out of living lava rock, using her will."

"Ashstone." Catriona shook her head. She knew that story too. "But how is the Stâpân chosen?"

"They also touch their memory stone. Then they too remember who they were before. But his stone has been lost. Slade went to a place of exile. He was not allowed to join the Land."

"You keep saying 'he'. Is it not possible for the Stâpân to be a woman?"

"Of course. You are one. So was I. In truth, it is the beloved of the Dûcesa that becomes her Stâpân or Stâpâna. The Third Dûcesa fell in love with Raven. It was the reason he left her. Once he found out that this was the course of action, he returned the sword to her and walked away from it. But to be honest, Raven was never one to stay with one woman too long. I was his beloved until Wilgefortis came along."

Catriona blinked, confused. This creature was made of metal. She was built like a blacksmith's wife. Why would a mage make a golem of gold to be his beloved? Especially this man. "Who made you?"

"A blacksmith many centuries ago, when metals were just being forged in heat. He had lost his wife so he made a monument to her for her grave. But he made it so lifelike, he could not part with it. He prayed to the Giver of Life to awaken me, but she did not listen. So he turned to Magic. A mage animated me, but she made me sentient. As someone made of minerals, the mage drew upon the power of the Land to give me that life, and it did. I am a servant, connected by Magic to the world."

They came to a dead end. Catriona could feel the Land alive and awake around her and she felt renewed. The Gold Wife turned to her. "It is time. Do you feel the Land?"

Catriona breathed in the air and exhaled. "Yes."

"Then access it. Move the opening here."

Catriona looked around and felt the earth in front of her to be the opening of which the Gold Wife spoke. She reached out and touched the wall. Runes glowed within it, surrounding her hands. Suddenly, the runes spun around her arms pulling her to the wall. The dead end opened up and a larger cavern filled the area. The runes lifted her into the air. The light enclosed her, caging her. The runes flowed into the ground around her and she felt her awareness flow with it.

Far away, she felt more than heard another voice, unknown to her, but familiar nonetheless, cry out in horror.

The Gold Wife looked at the Servant of the Land and confirmed that her life essence was going into the surrounding area. She could already feel the soil churning towards the surface. This one would saturate the land around the covenant and then, when she had revived this place, that renewing power would refresh all of York. Even if she died in the process, she would be reborn here, still held in place by the bonds of Magic. She was an infinitely renewable power source.

Then the Mages would return to Persephone. She knew Raven was still in the world. If York returned to life, he would come to see the covenant. Then they would be together again. Wilgefortis was long since dead, as was the Third Dûcesa. Raven had turned away the woman Clara who became a saint. There were no other lovers for him.

He would come home.

"You are released."

A haggard woman looked up from a heap on the ground. Her clothes were once vivid blue and her hair violet. Indigo eyes married the colors. With great effort, she lifted her gaze to Catriona. Then she looked at her hands and bare feet.

"Re…leased?"

"Yes. Your power was almost gone. I have replaced you with a better source. You may leave and return to your Fae realm."

The Fae maiden looked at the way out and tried to stand, but was too weak to do so. The Gold Wife watched Catriona for a few minutes, then turned and went back down the lit hallway. The maiden collapsed back on the ground, and looked at a place where the light was pulsing into the ground. She crawled to the edge of that light and stretched her hand so her fingertips were in it. Some of the light flowed up her arm, and she exhaled and closed her eyes.

James rubbed his eyes and looked at Michael. "There's nothing of use in here. The Gold Wife was a statue found in York somewhere. Raven brought it to life. He had it has his companion, though no one else could stand to be around it because of the screeching. Then the Land called her away for three years and she went. Disappeared right in front of him with no more explanation than that. He mourned her for six months, it says.

"That was when the Prince rode to Persephone and almost was killed by insects that were turned by the Soulless. Raven was able to get to a town in upper York and find a source that could vanquish the monsters. Embertwist closed off York so none could enter or leave it, containing the monsters, but the First Dûcesa and her Stâpân had just entered the country."

James waved his hand dismissively at the passage he was reading through. "This part is about the Soulless War. Afterwards, Raven felt guilty about killing the Second Dûcesa and took the Third to Caratia, where he ran into the Gold Wife again. She had been called to become Stâpâna when Slade attempted to step down. That's why she disappeared. He meant to be there for only a short time and returned when Wilge was giving birth to their first child. He left when the Land *again* called him to return to the Dûcesa.

"He stayed there until the Covenant told him Wilge was dying. He had been gone for fifty years by then. Geesh, this guy." James shook his head. "He returned with the Gold Wife, and told her that he would not go back to Caratia. His place was here. He gave Wilge a potion that healed her and stopped her from aging, then he never left her side again." James bobbed his head, "At least there's that. What's with this guy? He so lost that he can't keep track of how many years he's been gone?

"Anyway, the Gold Wife returned to Persephone after the death at sea of the Third Dûcesa. They did not get a fourth and no one knows what happened to the artifacts." He looked at Michael. "She's been here ever since, it seems."

"Nothing about the barrier?"

"It's powered by the source of the covenant's magic. If the covenant is threatened, it goes up. It takes mages to bring it down. Otherwise, it stays up until the threat is passed." James looked around. "With the land so lifeless, there were probably tons of threats. I wouldn't be surprised if the people in there starved to death. Bandits, the Church, scavengers. This place has likely been assaulted since the War, provided it ever came down afterwards."

Michael nodded towards the tower ruin. "Something brought that thing down."

"We'll walk around it tomorrow, get a good look at it. It might have just fallen down from age."

Michael nodded and they settled in for the night. Once they stopped moving and reading, he felt a low thrumming beneath him. It was like the vibrations Catriona mentioned. "Do you feel that?"

James nodded. "Catriona must have found something. She'll probably be along soon."

"How long do you want to wait up?"

"Well, a while at least. If she doesn't come back by midnight, there may be trouble."

"If there is, what do you paln to do about it?"

James closed the book. He looked at the low wall, then at the horses. "We may have to destroy the barrier."

"If we can't?"

He looked north. "Then we get someone who has been here before."

Thirty-One

I left and spent the next month in the Papal City, helping the guard, praying, and studying in the library.
—The Longsword of the Orphans

Tanglwyst wandered through a library, apparently not finding what she needed. She walked over to a nearby monk who explained something with a dour look. She was taken to an area and shown books on the Inquisition. The pages are centuries old and the bindings showed wear. She asked about something and gestured to her necklace, describing the amulets. The priest shook his head, held up a finger and left. She looked around the shelves, touching the books as she read the spines. She touched one and frowned, then went to pull it out.

The bookshelf shifted and the wall opened a bit.

She looked into the opening, then behind her as something caught her attention. She closed the bookshelf and turned, looking bored. The monk returned with an older priest. She repeated her gestures to the other librarian but he shook his head, his frown of disapproval dominating his face. He looked with disdain at the monk who brought him to her, then took Tanglwyst by the arm to the library doors. He tossed her out like a bar patron. She turned back to him as he closed the doors. Her eyes narrowed but her lips smiled.

She was on to something.

Alexander's eyes fluttered open. His head hurt and his hands were asleep from being under his hip. He shifted them back to behind him and sighed relief as he started regaining feeling. Moments later, relief turned to regret as the pins and needles arrived, but by the time it passed, his mind was already back to Tanglwyst. The bookshelf was interesting and he believed they were both contemplating what lay behind it. He sought her fealty orb again and determined she was back in her room.

She stayed in that area effectively immobile and Alexander found it humorous he might be awake while she could be sleeping. She started to move around again and half-sleep finally took him.

She opened the door to her room to find the younger librarian outside. He handed her an old tome and she smiled, curtsying her gratitude. The monk blushed and bowed, before leaving. She closed the door and set the book on the bed. She leafed through it, checking the illuminations on each page. She got her notes for comparison.

The travelling clothes from before were cleaned and folded on the foot of her bed. He wondered why she had not put them away in the wardrobe. Although he found her attractive in her breeches and shirt, seeing her in a gown again brought memories of the winter. She certainly knew how to flatter herself with color. This gown was ruby red which brought out her auburn highlights and lit her green eyes up with vivid life. She had fallen back into the habit of decorative hair binding which kept it from her eyes as she read over her notes.

Her reading was interrupted by another knock on her door. She hid her notes and the tome under her traveling clothes and opened the door. A valet brought in an elaborate tea service on a tray, complete with a very fancy gilt tea cup. She directed him to the table near the roaring fireplace and he poured her a cup before leaving. She retrieved her notes from their hiding place and brought them to the table but her attention kept wandering from her studies to the tea. She finally looked at the cup and sighed. He could almost feel her breath on his face.

She got up, taking the tea cup with her, and went to the window overlooking the forest. The full moon decorated the treetops and he imagined he could see the area where he was being held captive. Tanglwyst looked out across the woods, her eyes deep and distant. The steam from the cup rose, fogging the window and she drew a heart in the moisture. She put her hand on it, her eyes getting wet, then drew her

palm across it, oblitherating it. She looked towards Patras and he saw
her say something, something he realized he understood.
"*I miss you.*"

He took a deep breath, waking from the dream-state. She had looked
to Patras and said "I miss you." Could she have been talking to him just
then? Then he realized that Patras was also where she had been with
Nicolai and he sagged under the weight of regret.

It was ridiculous. Nicolai was a drunk and didn't deserve the
affection of *one* woman, much less two. When he had rid the world of
that slime, the air in Patras had gotten sweeter. Nicolai had been bedding
Tanglwyst while being jealous of the idea of Catriona and Alexander
together. His rage at possibly finding one of her hairs upon his pillow
and the attack in Rouen showed Nicolai's true nature. He had wanted
Catriona to be home, pining for him while he used Tanglwyst for
revenge. Alexander spat on the ground at the thought of his hands upon
the Lady.

But that wasn't how Tanglwyst saw it. He had stolen her beloved,
regardless of how unsuitable Alexander thought Nicolai was. The man
obviously gave her something and he didn't need to understand it. She
did, and he had decided his desires were greater than hers, that his heart
weighed more.

He sat up, thinking. His hands hurt a bit but he felt less interested in
his own pain and more in the pain he had put her through. Since Charles'
death, he had made one terrible decision after another and the damage
from the shrapnel was everywhere. He was glad she decided to leave
him. At least in the Papal City, she had family, her company, money. A
future. A life.

All he had to offer was death.

He closed his eyes and rested his head against the pole. She was
better off without him.

Tanglwyst looked into the empty cup and swirled the tiny residual
leaves in the remaining dregs of liquid. Her mind had time here to think,
but she tried not to let it out to wander too often. Repeatedly, it had gone

to Patras, and her time in Emmy's during the winter. She had felt such fondness for Alexander, and she had to keep reminding herself it had merely been loneliness that had drawn them to one another. They would never have been together otherwise, as evidenced by the way he reacted at the first hint of anyone else's presence.

No. Not just anyone's. Catriona's.

That was the part that stung the most. Tanglwyst had fallen to second place behind that woman over and over. Then logic would step in and remind her that Catriona held Tanglwyst's trust until that day she and Nicolai were reunited. Catriona had integrity, which was difficult to find in the world. Moreover, she always knew where to find it, a trick Tanglwyst did not know. The truth of it was that Tanglwyst *admired* Catriona, and that made these "betrayals" that much worse.

She got up and set the tea cup with the service. She got ready for bed and grabbed her notes, placing them in the tome for transport, and setting them on the night table next to the bed. She lay down, allowing the fireplace and moonlight to be her only company.

It had been quite a while since she had a bed to herself in a city, yet she had slept alone often the last month. She feared she must be getting old. She no longer attracted men like she once did. Ever since she turned away from this place to go find Alexander, her ability to get men to do her will had been minimized. She never knew what caused it in the first place, but she felt strangely at peace with the knowledge of its loss.

She thought about what she had learned so far. Her research into what to look for was turning out to ruffle some ecclesiastical feathers. This made her smile. She knew she was getting closer if folks were starting to block her. The bookcase opening had been very exciting. She couldn't wait to explore whatever was behind it. Since the placement was not near an external wall, she had no idea where it might be heading. The bookcase was actually near several others, all of them going to the ceiling. It was possible they were concealing a passage. No one would ever suspect one in the middle of a room.

She pulled her notes from the table and sat up, looking them over. Her commentary rambled a bit. Someone other than her might suspect it a code, but in fact, she just wrote what she thought. Luckily, she could understand the leaps.

Something that proved, at least to her, that these were undoubtedly made by the Church was the markings upon them. She remembered they seemed to be almost overlapping but she could make out one symbol with certainty: St. Giles.

Her home port was in the town named after him, and his symbol was on nearly every building and street. St. Giles was the first village south of the Black Forest, so the Church put protection symbols everywhere to keep out the Fae. Even her own winery had the symbol stamped on all the corks so she knew the symbol well.

Her question about the amulet and its connection to St. Giles stirred ire in Brother Fausto. Then again, he had seemed livid as soon as Caiaphas had introduced her. It was almost as if he had heard her name before. Since her grandfather was the Pope, she guessed that was the source, but now she wondered if there was more. Her name, Tanglwyst, was quite old, a family heirloom in fact. Without this name, she could not have the reach she had here, nor the business she had grown over the past twelve years. It all passed down only to daughters named Tanglwyst.

Tanglwyst Trading had an office in town, but the local laws prohibited an unmarried woman to sleep alone in a business. It assumed she was a prostitute if she did, but Tanglwyst wondered if the religious lawmakers understood a prostitute would hardly be sleeping *alone* in a place of business. Regardless, she had seen tactics like this before. Many times, laws were created to get rid of one family or one element, and the shakiest of foundations was the basis for the law. She studied some of them, but she always counted on Isabella's or Myrgen's advice when it came to pushing against those statutes.

Myrgen. She sighed. Her brother had left the Church and country, though that was probably safest for him. Alexander was not tolerant of Myrgen at present, but luckily, Catriona was. At least in her care, Tanglwyst was sure her brother was safe. It surprised her that she felt no more animosity towards Catriona. Myrgen had been unhappy for years, ever since the death of his son. It didn't surprise her at all that he would eventually leave the Church responsible for the boy's murder.

She remembered the horror of that night, the Grande Guarde Marcel commanding his troops to kill all Emilianites in Patras. Myrgen had made sure she was safe in an Augustinian church, then ran to his mistress's home. The next day, Tanglwyst found out about the slaughter of her nephew and the idea made her so sick, she had vomited.

267

It had been hard for her to give her tithe for the season after that. She was disgusted. Then the Pope was assassinated, and their grandfather elected. Gregory had made several changes and after that, she felt good about investing in the Church again. Now she was here, put up in the Papal Palace instead of sleeping on a cot illegally in an office. Her investments had paid off.

She needed to do her research before that clemency ran out. Those amulets were dangerous, and it baffled her to think something given out by the Church would turn the wearers into such monsters. The Scarred Man was clearly an accomplished killer. In contrast, Duncan was scary capable with a sword, but cheerful. She had no doubt he could cut someone's throat, but she didn't believe he would cut *hers*. But according to Tomas and Alexander, he had almost killed her.

Alexander.

She took a breath, looking at the tea service silhouetted against the flames of the fireplace. By the Saints, she wished he had not turned so foul. When he left her unescorted at the Ball, she had worried something was wrong with him. Later, she worried there was something wrong with *her*. In the end, it was definitely something wrong with *him*. The obsession, the lying, the murdering.

She shook her head. No, he was a lost cause, self-serving. Even after sharing the Power of Sovereignty with her, she was still nothing more than a subject to order about. She didn't know why she hadn't told her Grandfather about his transgressions, outside of not wanting to relive them. In the end, she figured he would exhibit this behavior when someone of higher rank than her was around to see it. You couldn't hide such a personality flaw for long.

She gave herself another minute of remembering the tea party and their closeness, then she closed that door in her heart again. She loved that feeling they had, but it was gone. She would miss him, as she had said at the window, but mostly because she knew he was not that man anymore.

A small draft brushed her cheek and she touched it. Her eyes were leaking at the thought of Alexander again. She wiped the tears from her cheeks with the back of her hand, put the papers in the drawer of the table, and turned away from the moonlit window to sleep.

Thirty-Two

They would have to be destroyed by fire...
-The Longsword of the Orphans

Catherine was exhausted, as was her companion, by the time the lights became identifiable as a roadside inn. Charles the Messenger called out, *"Your Majesty, we have to stop!"*

She pulled her horse to a trot, the animal wheezing from the forced march. The smoke in the air frightened her. It has become more prominent as they rode west. By now, she knew something massive was on fire in Bordeaux. Charles pulled up next to her and put a hand on her horse's reins.

"We have to stop, or the horses will collapse."

She looked at him, her eyes unable to hide the fear. "Bordeaux is *burning*. Can't you see that?"

"And what can you do about it?" His eyes showed earnest concern, but also logic. "You can't put out fires with a glance, can you?"

She looked west again, part of the sky glowing in the distance like a city, in an area no city existed. "I have to do something."

"What? Tell me what you plan to do and I will help you." His tone was a slap to her face, though he could not raise a hand to her.

She stuttered back and forth between the glow and her friend. Finally she closed her eyes, defeated by his sense.

He didn't gloat or push the issue, but he did take her reins and lead the horses at a walk to the inn. A stableboy, a man, and a woman all stood on the porch of the inn, watching the glow to the west. They turned when the pair rode up to the inn.

Charles nodded to the west. "How long has that been going on?"

The man glanced back. "We noticed the smoke smell earlier today. It looks like the vineyards might be burning."

"Is that common during this time of year?" Catherine tried to quell the ripple of fear in her voice. "I understand sometimes farmers burn to refresh the land quickly."

The woman shook her head. "Too big. You don't burn more than you can control. Every hand on the vineyard couldn't control a fire like that."

Catherine felt her fear swell, then dissipate. Talking with these folks helped. They had been keeping an eye on the matter and knew more than her. From here, she could monitor the situation and contact the highway guards. Even send messages to the capital to mobilize troops. They would not get there for days, but they could be there to help with repairs and burials. If was horrid to think in such terms, but Charles was right. She did not have the ability to call down rain or fold earth over a fire.

"Is there a room available? It looks like I might be here a while."

Gomez sat at the desk with the sashes, his fingers digging into the wood. The sashes for Alexander's potential brides were in a neat stack in a wooden box to his left and a ledger of names was to his right. The ink in the pen was dried up now and had soaked through the rare book with empty, lined pages. The tip was stuck to the paper. His right hand shook from holding the pen in the same place for over a day. His brow would have been sweating if he had any moisture in his body.

The head of the City Guard stood a few feet from him in mid-stride, bent over with a sash in his hand halfway to standing. The young maiden who dropped the cloth was turned, looking over her shoulder as Sergeant Jamie South had called out to her, revealing the drop. Originally, her gaze had been one of quiet bemusement and Gomez had noticed her attention to the young man as more than passing interest. Now, having been in these positions for hours, everyone's gaze showed wear and fear.

A line of folks stretched into the night, suitors for the future king's hand. Gomez's job had been very specific: To look in the towns and find good, kind women to wear the sashes. They did not need to be royalty or nobility. It was a chance to reward young women who might go overlooked in society for not having the right bloodline.

It was also a good cover for investigating the case with the Scarred Man. He had been able to talk easily with any citizen about any subject he liked. He actually had a few potential prospects for noble marriage, should Alexander need a set of names for some future project.

That was when the world had stopped and the smell of fires had begun. He had seen people running into town and the second their feet touched the city line, they froze, like all the other townsfolk. Several of them saw the demarcation of the spell and stayed out of it. He could still see many of them milling on the edges, exhausted and covered in soot. More than one had turned south to get help.

Gomez saw a single figure come through the city line, his armor polished to a reflective gleam. He took off his helmet at the city line, then walked across, his chin in the firm set of a man who has spent his existence in a military role. His hair flowed in an inhuman way, too beautiful to be real and Gomez decided he had nodded off. His face was bereft of beard but that did not stop him from having an age of experience etched in his coal colored eyes. The soldier stopped outside the City Guard office, just to Gomez's left of the line. The man bowed.

"Your Majesty. I am here to represent Corrigan Starshadow, the Midwinter King."

An amazing voice came from just out of sight, but clearly right outside the building. "General Bartolemaus Johner. I was wondering how long it would take you to get here. The Midwinter King is not coming?"

"He has sent me on ahead, Your Majesty. Is the Voice of Command not enough for your mission?"

"Of course. Forgive me, my lord. I did not wish to offend."

The soldier gave a slow blink of judgement, then looked at the surrounding populace frozen in their daily lives. "A suspension spell?"

"It seemed the best way to control a populace."

"You did not stop the environment though. Several are dead from your neglect."

Gomez heard a sigh and imagined the owner examining her manicure. "Undoubtedly, but it *is* an invasion, General. They took my daughter and will not return her."

"Someone here kidnapped the Princess of Krakte?"

"Not *here,* per se. But I have gotten word that my daughter was slain by the upcoming king. I have sent letters for a month requesting her body be returned to me but there has been not a single response. This monster seeks a wife among the country folk, yet refuses a royal request from a grieving mother. Since he has not come to me, I am going to him. Once I take this lovely little hamlet, I will move on to the capital city itself."

The soldier nodded. "That sounds reasonable. I am certain the Fae Lord of Summer will support your endeavor. Until he arrives, I shall mediate." He nodded to the person who owned the voice and stepped into the room with Gomez. He nodded to the guardsman.

"You appear to be representing the royal in question. I am General Bartolemaus Johner, second in command to the Midsummer King Corrigan Starshadow. I need your compliance in this manner in order to discuss terms."

Gomez couldn't move but he realized this was his chance. He conveyed his compliance with his eyes. The General nodded and Gomez could finally move. The rest of the people stayed secured and he could see Sergeant South trying to break the spell through sheer will. If Jamie got free...

"I am Gomez de Santander. I represent King Apparent Alexander Angloume."

"Good. We shall negotiate then. Your Majesty?"

An elegant woman walked into view. Her long brown hair fell in soft curls, doe soft eyes and luscious lashes decorated a demure face. Full, rich lips drew the eye down her face to a long neck and defined clavicle. She moved with the grace of a great cat, certain in her footfalls, and in her ability to recover from any unexpected misstep. A gown of emerald velvet draped her tall frame, gold and green jewelry gracing every option. Upon her head was a crown of gold and emerald, the crest of Krakte emblazoned upon the front.

General Bartolemaus gestured to the creature beside him. "This is the Queen Sovereigna Berenger. You overheard our conversation and you know why she is here."

Gomez conveyed his understanding.

"To release your people, I must extract your word that you will do your best to minimize the loss of civilian life."

Gomez tried to frown but barely moved at all. *Of course he would minimize the loss of life.*

"Good. Your Majesty, please release them."

Sovereigna waved her hand and everyone in the area moved. Jamie South drew his weapon before Gomez even saw him and he stabbed at the Queen. Bartolemaus produced a glaive of incredible size from nowhere, the blade thrusting through the guard's chest without the general even looking at him. Sovereigna didn't even blink.

The girl with the crush on Jamie screamed his name. Bartolemaus flicked his wrist and the glaive disappeared as instantly as it arrived. Jamie dropped to the ground, a lifeless *splat* as the blood hit the floor with him. The people in the street likewise screamed, or yelled, backing away. Gomez looked at the General, awaiting instructions.

"Tell your people to return to their homes and no harm with come to them. Attack us, and they die."

Gomez looked past the couple and walked on unsteady knees to the doorway. *"People! Listen to me."*

A few people grabbed others, calming them down. Gomez's voice seemed to carry to every ear.

"Return to your homes, tend to your injured and dead. Go about your regular lives. The King is coming here soon. He will deal with this."

The people, crying, frowning, and angry, moved to the sides. The obligatory rebels stayed in the streets. "What is he going to do?"

"He will talk with the Queen of Krakte and negotiate to save your lives."

Some of the rebels' family members tugged at their clothing, most of them went, a few with no one to tug on them lingered. He turned back to the General and Queen. "What now?"

The General bowed. "I will be your representative in this matter. You need someone to negotiate on your behalf." He turned to the Queen. "Return to your encampment, Your Majesty. I need to speak with my ward."

The queen nodded, then flowed from the room like smoke.

Gomez looked at the dead man on the ground and the wailing girl draped over him. "What do we do now?"

"You may tend to your dead and wounded. I can meet you in the morning to discuss terms."

The general didn't wait for an answer, but left the room. The girl tried to spit on him as he passed but missed. Gomez knelt beside her, her body reeking of urine. He realized many people might have lost control of their bladders and possibly bowels in the last day. The streets would be a nightmare of indignity.

"Amelie, you need to go to your family. Make sure they are alright."

She looked up at him with blood smeared clothing and nodded. "My little sister..."

"Go to her. I'll take care of him."

Several guards ran into the room as she left. Gomez motioned to one. "Get her home. Then see to your own families."

One guard stepped over to the body. He was short, but solidly built. He knelt beside the Sergeant.

"Squire Asher, my lord."

"Don't you have family to see to?"

"I'm afraid not, my Lord. I'm an orphan. Joined the guard to keep from starving two years ago."

Gomez looked around the office. There were commendations from the crown. One of the letters upon the wall was signed by Gomez himself, and was made out to Asher of St. Giles. Not even a last name. "You look like you might be the next ranking officer here, Asher."

Asher looked at Gomez. His blue eyes and light brown hair complimented his youth, and those eyes showed concern, then understanding. "You might be right, sir."

"We need to see to the Sergeant here, then to the people. I don't think either of us will be getting any sleep tonight."

Ce'Nedra rubbed her eyes and set the knife down. "There. I'm done."

Henri and Felix looked up from the table. Sylvaine stirred on the bed, but did not sit up.

"What do you need from us, my dear?" Henri got up but Felix just turned in his seat.

"I'm going to pour my energy in here, then, I'll probably collapse. You'll need to break the holy symbol after the Fae one is lit."

Henri nodded and took the dulled knife from her hand. She put her hand on the final symbol and said some words under her breath. The symbol flared to life, then dulled in the presence of the other one. Henri broke the symbol, then stood. "Can you pick her up and put her on the bed? I'm afraid I can't."

Felix nodded, not looking at Henri's stump. He got to work on Ce'Nedra while Henri used his remaining strength on the last of the holy symbols. Felix made sure the lady was comfortable, then came to help Henri, if necessary. It wasn't, but Henri was glad he offered anyway. They set the knife on the table, and Henri dropped onto the chair.

"Well, we got our survival out of the way. Now what?"

Felix rubbed his eyes. "I can't even think right now."

Henri shook his head. "Me neither."

Felix looked at the bedding the women had sacrificed for their comfort. He drooped over to it and lay down. Henri let him, because he had no intention of heading to sleep while the others did. The other night, before Ce'Nedra had gotten the wayfinder symbol finished, he had awoken to what he was almost sure was sulfur. It had not returned but he wasn't willing to risk anyone's throat getting cut in the night.

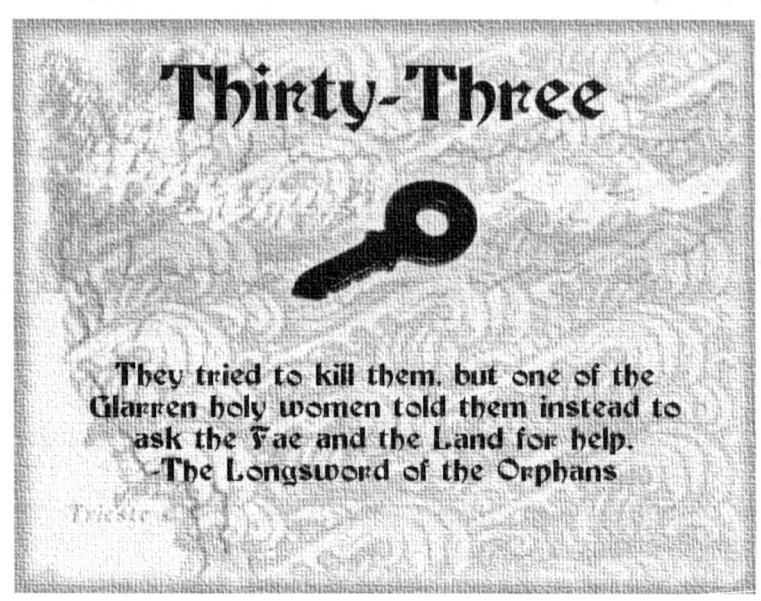

Thirty-Three

They tried to kill them, but one of the
Glarren holy women told them instead to
ask the Fae and the Land for help.
—The Longsword of the Orphans

Myrgen was restless. He had a sense something somewhere was wrong, but he couldn't place how, or even where. Part of the problem was that it also felt somewhat *right,* like something that *had* to be done, he just wasn't going to like it. Another part of the problem was that he felt like he was ill-equipped to deal with it right now and that, if he had simply done *something,* he could have mediated this whole situation. He just didn't know what that something *was.*

Myrgen looked at the dozen stones on the desk in his room, where he had been pacing for the last couple hours. They were so similar to the Heartstone, but they didn't react the same. When he had touched the one Anika wore, he had seen everyone in the room through the eyes of the Dûcesa. Each person was good, rich, kind. Every woman was beautiful. It was as if every foul person had been expelled from Zara, and only the truly good folks were allowed to stay. Judging from the people he had met in Mande, he thought that might not be far from the truth.

Anika was right. He needed to go to the Meditation Chamber. It was time to ask the Land what these meant, what these were. He scooped them up and put them back in the leather pouch. He saw the Stâpân's sword in the corner by the bed where he had set it. The pommel was gone and had not resurfaced. It was comforting to him because it meant the Land fully expected Catriona's return.

He grabbed the sword and put it on. If he was going to be going to the Chamber as Stâpân, he needed to make sure he was wearing all the regalia. The Onyx Key was still at his neck, laying over his heart as she had always done. He checked his appearance in the mirror and was a little disturbed by how unkempt he looked. After he returned from the meeting, he would be taking a bath. He contemplated taking it first, but realized that would just be stalling.

He passed by the Great Hall, where a few folks still lingered. A couple from the kitchen were practicing their dancing. He stopped for a moment to watch them as they went through the moves to Korabushka. At the end of the round, he went to his knee and she went across it and they attempted to kiss. He faltered and she slipped a little, causing them both to laugh. His heart swelled with pride that perhaps he had added a level of difficulty that would last.

He felt someone walk up beside him and he didn't have to look to know it was Anika. She watched the couple enjoy the interlude, then reset to try again.

"It seems you have made an impression, my dear."

He smiled. "It appears I have. At least I have one good thing I have left in this world." He reached down and took her hand, then bent to kiss it. "Thank you for showing me this world, for showing me *her*."

Anika patted his hand, then furrowed her brow a tiny bit when she looked at him. "You sense it too?"

He inhaled and nodded. "I'm going to speak to the Land. It's giving me some clue, but I can't understand what it is. It's like there are…" He shook his head. "*Threats* isn't right. More like," he paused trying to find the right word and failing. He shrugged. "I can't place it. I just have a feeling that knowing more would help."

"You learn to live with the fact that the Land may have things in motion that you can't see, because it is the *Land.* It touches everything." She looked at the dancers. "We don't always know what the Land has in mind for us, but we have to trust that it has a purpose for it. Any time I am allowed to play a part in that scheme, I am grateful. It means I was essential to the outcome of that story."

He watched the couple turning and clapping. "When I followed the Augustinian Church, I never felt that. I never felt Heaven had a great

Plan and I was doing something to further that Plan. After the Massacre, I realized Heaven had nothing to do with it. It was the *Church*, it was *men,* not Heaven that was at work there. No greater purpose or entity, just power, greed. Pride.

"But here, it's all personal. Everyone here is a part of this. We all have a place in the world, and it isn't just to breathe the air or till the earth. We are all essential."

"We're all part of the dance." She looked at him again.

He nodded, because she was right.

Her eyes were dampening, which, for some reason, made his go glassy as well. She patted his hand. "I'm so very glad you came here, Myrgen."

He tried to say he was too, but his voice gummed up in his throat. Instead, he hugged her and she hugged him back. He sniffed back the tears, and she patted him on the back. He took a step backwards, separating.

"I'm going to head to the Meditation Chamber. I have the feeling I need to talk to the Land."

"About the stones you found?"

He nodded.

"Do you need this one?" She reached up to touch the Heartstone.

"I don't honestly know."

She unclasped it from her neck. "Take it, just in case."

He took it. It was strangely inert in his hand. "Are you sure? It's the symbol of your position."

"That's the amazing thing about my position. I didn't choose it, it chose me. If I let it go and it returns to me, then nothing has changed. If I let it go and it is gone, then my part in this story has also changed. In the end, it was never *my* story it was telling."

She touched the Heartstone as he held it and he saw the beauty again. It was *her.* That was what made it work. If she didn't touch it too, he didn't see what the stone had to show him. He smiled, his eyes dry again, but with purpose. He bowed and turned back to his task, giving one final glance to the dancers.

He went to the tower where Catriona had gone to commune with her deity. The hallway loomed before him, and the doors even more so. He thought about turning back, but he felt there was no time like now. He would never be more prepared.

Myrgen touched the doors to the Meditation chamber, half expecting them to stay closed. He wasn't sure if he felt like the Stâpân simply because Catriona said it was so. The Stâpân didn't seem like a deputy position someone could appoint. The key was a good indicator, but he still hadn't seen the pommel stone for the sword. He wasn't even certain he could call the White Granite Sword to him anymore.

The doors opened despite his doubts, and he moved into the chamber. The air was dry and hot, like boiled stone. There was a glow ahead and clearly a turn in the passage, hiding the bulk of the chamber from the door. His heart thudded but he swallowed his uncertainty and entered the room. The doors didn't close, which made him feel better, but he also knew that anyone not allowed would be repelled. That made this room very safe in a siege.

He walked around the corner and raised his arm to protect his eyes and face. The heat was intense but the overwhelming part was the *presence*. He tried to keep his feet under him but instead fell to his knees under the weight of it. This was the home of a force so immense, it could dismember him into fragments accidentally. He would be dust, breathed in and expelled without notice. This was humbling and he did not know how Catriona did it.

He remembered why he was here and took his feet. He definitely felt this entity could answer his questions, provided he could get its attention. The survival instinct in him said not to do that, but he needed answers. He stepped forward and took a knee.

"My…"

He realized in the middle of his greeting he had no idea what to call this. There was no gender so Lord or Lady was inappropriate. Had he ever heard Catriona call it anything other than The Land? Calling it The Land sounded ridiculous in his head, where things usually sounded great before they left the mouth. He felt beyond unprepared for this venture now and wondered if he should simply go before he was crushed beneath the weight of his embarrassment.

He glanced back, then stood and took a step away towards the door. This was the best choice by far. He continued to back away until he saw the doors. The urge to run to them overwhelmed him and he bolted. The doors slammed closed and he was thrown back by the force of it. The stones tumbled from his pouch and spilled out onto the ground. They melted like butter on hot bread, soaking into the soil. The gold flecks dissolved, whatever they were lost forever. He turned back to the hallway as the barrier between him and the Presence crumbled away. The chamber opened to him and he felt exposed.

His voice left him. All his emotions were thrown at the entity in defense: fear, anger, hatred, cowardice. The entity burned them all away, leaving raw nerves. After a few moments, those were gone too. He felt flayed. His innards were exposed and destroyed as superfluous. His bones became ash. He could not understand why he still had thoughts.

A great voice filled the room, almost too big to understand. He had to let his brain absorb it and decipher the sounds. It felt like a foreign language.

No. Not foreign. Simply not familiar.

He was raised Augustinian. He knew the languages of Karma and the Emilianites. He *understood* other cultures, other dialects. This was like hearing a language he knew about, had heard of, but had only seen written. He didn't know the *voice*.

He listened and after a moment, *he heard.*

James opened his eyes, a fear shooting through him. He sat up, aware and searching the darkness. The fire was ebbing low and he heard a snore from Michael. He was leaning against the wall, arm across his raised knee. This was a problem, because Michael was the most diligent and trustworthy man James knew. He didn't fall asleep on watch.

The moon was full and he could see well in that bright-as-day glow that somehow never interfered with sleeping like the sun could. He heard something before he saw it. Rustling, within the covenant. It didn't sound like the rusty footfalls of the Gold Wife, which was a relief in itself. That creature just felt wrong. No, this was something else.

He stood and looked beyond the barrier, to as much of the courtyard as he could see. Still nothing. He walked around the small, disintegrating house by the archway and saw more of the yard, but still nothing to cause the sound. He looked at Michael, and decided to leave him be for the moment. James walked around to the north side of the wall where he could see the fallen top of the main tower. There was a door open there, and faint light came from some source within. The sound was coming from inside that room.

He crouched to the ground and waited, staying low and out of sight. The sound continued to grow and after about ten minutes, the source of the rustling appeared. At first, he wasn't sure what he was seeing. It was something moving along the ground, like a snake. There had been no wildlife since they had entered York proper, so the presence of an animal here would have been puzzling. Then the tip of it rose above the top of the stairs leading down to the door and he saw what it was.

Ivy.

Heart-shaped leaves of green and yellow crawled across the grounds. Another shoot found purchase on the doors and began their rise to the ruin still standing. More began slithering out of the doorway and up the stairs, groping in the night air. By morning, the place would be covered with them.

He stayed low, in case they were sentient, or being guided by someone, and made his way back to Michael. He was a little worried the man wouldn't respond to attempts to wake him, but he needn't have. James' first jostle brought Michael fully awake and aware. James put his finger to his lips and Michael refrained from making any noise.

James cupped his hand behind his ear, then pointed to the other side of the wall. Michael frowned, listening. When he heard it, he turned and peeked over the wall. James wasn't sure how long it would take for the plants to get far enough to be seen from here, but he decided to break camp nonetheless. This was important enough to go to Gloriana about.

Michael came over and James put a finger to his lips. Michael nodded and they worked with little noise but lots of speed. James saddled the animals, save Catriona's, while Michael struck camp. When they got the tent down, and on the pack horse, Michael looked at the courtyard. His eyes widened and he took a step forward, disbelieving. James had seen it and didn't need to be more spooked by the event. He needed to abandon one of their group to an unknown fate and he didn't want to think about that any more than necessary.

He knew he couldn't save her from out here. He mounted his horse and looked at Catriona's. The saddle and tack were valuable enough to steal, but if he saddled it, there would be damage to the animal, even if it made it home. You couldn't just leave a horse saddled indefinitely. If it stayed here, she would have to escape in the next day for the horse not to have problems unless he unhobbled it. He got the feeling the horse would know when the wait was hopeless.

He contemplated taking the animal as a gift, but he doubted Gloriana would use something so pedestrian. Fae had a different way of doing things. Would it return to Caratia on its own? He looked at the courtyard and from his higher vantage, he saw the tower was now one-quarter covered. There was no time to discuss it.

He turned his horse to the north. Michael frowned. James decided to risk talking. He had no way to communicate an idea this intricate. He did keep his voice low, though.

"Remove the hobbles."

Michael looked at the horse, then back at his companion, searching wordlessly for an explanation.

"I'm leaving it behind. Chances are this area will be covered by dawn. If it creeps beyond the barrier, then the horse will have food. If it doesn't, the horse will go home."

"Are you sure it can find its way from here?"

"It's a horse from Caratia. It knows the way better than we do."

Michael swallowed, then removed the hobbles. "That will alert them back home that there is a problem."

James glanced at the growing foliage. "With any luck."

Michael tossed the hobbling length to lay beside saddle and bridle, then mounted up. They looked at the growing green of the fallen tower, then to each other. James nodded north.

He kicked his horse and they rode off.

Raven looked up from his Fae wine, not sure what he just felt. Something somewhere was thrumming the air.

No. Not the air.

The *earth*.

It was known to him. It was old. He closed his eyes and tried to feel it, but it was too distant and he had water to bypass. It was white noise, which in most cases would be soothing. Not this time.

He got to his feet. There was a portal to Sovereignlumin here, as all the Fae Lords possessed. That portal would lead to other protals, enabling him to avoid the divine strongholds altogether. There were fewer portals to the Fae realm these days. There used to be small rabbit holes and bird's nests all over the world. Then the Soulless War happened and the Church tore them all down. Now only the strong doorways survived, and none were sronger than those to the resting place of the Father of all the Fae.

He gave a final glance to the Wedded Tree, as he now called it in his mind, and bid farewell to Octavius and Estelle. They were safe, for now. Corrigan would protect them, and in all the realms, none could do a better job. If the Lord of all Warriors couldn't stop a threat, that threat was the end of the world. He looked around and found the doorway to Sovereignlumin. Strangely enough, it was hidden in a bird's nest. Raven marveled at the peculiarity of the choice and stepped through.

The great tower that was the mausoleum to the Father of Fae speared the daytime sky. It was always daytime in the Fae realm, unless it was important for it not to be. He wasn't sure who made those decisions, but he noticed it this time because the light was bright and yellow instead of being bright and blue like it was a second ago.

He heard a howl he recognized and returned it with great joy. A few minutes later, Lauriel bounded across the fertile fields surrounding the tower. Raven stooped to catch the mighty hound and was naturally bowled over by the beast. The Fae wolf licked his face in that way dogs do.

"I'm glad to see you too. So, you decided to wait it out here?"

Lauriel stepped back and sat down. Raven nodded. "Probably best. There's something coming. Did you sense it?"

The wolf looked at the tower.

"Ah." Raven nodded. "Is she awake yet?"

Lauriel shook his head.

"Merrick still with her?"

Lauriel nodded.

"How does he look?"

Lauriel lay down and licked his foot.

"I suppose that's to be expected." He sat on the ground by his companion. "Corrigan was sending me to St. Giles. Do you know where that is?"

Lauriel snorted.

"Octavius said it was north. That's probably right. He was a really smart person."

Lauriel's ears swiveled.

"Oh, no. He's not dead or anything. Actually very sweet. He became a tree too! Isn't that interesting?"

Lauriel stood up and shook, then sat back down and bit at an itchy spot on his right flank.

"Of course he'll be alright. What a thing to say." Raven looked to the tower. "It seems Gloriana's realm is northerly. So we need to find someplace that way to come out." He stood and Lauriel stood as well. He looked around and saw something glowing off to the west of the Tower.

He walked to the far side from where he was and followed a path he was sure he had seen before. All roads led to Sovereignlumin in the Fae realm, but this one was particularly familiar, like maybe he had made it. It wasn't a recent creation, though. This one was old. He saw the giveaway light of a crossover portal and he and Lauriel stepped through.

He looked around at several ancient plant boxes and strange plumbing, broken mirrors on the ground. The boxes were alive with ivy and a few small trees were starting to push their way through the dirt ceiling. The whole place was covered in recently disturbed dust. A beautiful four-poster bed made of living wood, the domed canopy blossoming willow leaves from every pore, took up a quarter of the room and he felt his heart thud a single time in his chest.

Wilge.

He went to the bed they shared and touched the greyed covers. She had died in this room, and he had been forced to let her. She chose not to take the longevity potion again, and the toll on her body was fast and heavy. She had stayed with him for one hundred and fifty years. That was far longer than he deserved. He had not felt love again in the hundred or so years since.

A sound drew his attention and a rusted figure entered the room. She stopped in the doorway, her golden body stunned into immobility. He turned and smiled.

"Gold Wife!" He went to her and hugged her.

She broke out of her fog. "Raven."

He stepped back, wincing. "Whoa, my friend. Screeching?"

She cleared her throat and he felt the magic of her voice settle upon him, like an old mantle. "Forgive me, my love."

"You gave someone else your soft voice?" He crossed his arms, happy. "Who is it? Is he good to you?"

"She. And it is not important now."

"*She?* Interesting. Well, don't take it away from her on my account. I'm certain your new lover would be quite upset to find it in my care instead."

The Gold Wife walked over and put her arms around him. "I believe it is my choice to whom I give that voice."

She kissed him and she was warm and sensual, like she had been when they were lovers. That level of intimacy was powerful, and not to be given lightly. But he was in the room where the love of his life passed into the Dreaming. He could still feel her in this place, hear her laughter and feel her fingers in his hair. It was here he delivered both their children, on the very bed where they made them. Yes, he had shared it with the Gold Wife before he shared it with Wilgefortis, but once he married, he had never felt the need or desire for another touch but hers.

He pushed away, stepping back.

The Gold Wife blinked, as if confused. "My love?"

"Wife," the term sounded too intimate in his ears, so he tried another, "*Gold.*" He frowned. "No, that actually sounds too formal, like I'm using your last name, even though it's actually your first." He put a fist on his hip. "Didn't we have a name for you, like an actual name? The one the blacksmith gave you."

"His wife was Fruzsina."

Raven snapped his fingers. "That's right." He frowned. "But it wasn't. We didn't want you going by another's identity for you. You *chose* a name. What was it?"

"You don't remember my name?"

"It's been three hundred years, my friend. A man, even a mage," he snorted, "*especially* a mage, is entitled to forget such things." He wagged a finger at her, his eyes searching the ether for the moniker. "But you're right. I know this and it's rude to say I don't. Give me a second."

He tapped his finger to his head and pretended to think. Her name was Marica, but when she arrived, he noted that this place was different. It *felt* changed. Persephone was abandoned, not because it died, but because all mages had to go underground. The covenant and its inhabitants had been taken through the Fae realm to safety, spread throughout the world so as not to be associated with magic. Whatever was here now was not what was here before.

He paced and walked out into the old bath area. He had set up the aqueducts and heaters himself. He noticed the door to the old storeroom was open as well. This was where all the portable magic sources were kept, though he knew there was nothing left there now. Different things had inherent magic to them and if a mage knew how to use it, it made spell casting easier. It was also necessary for anything used by a non-magical being. Potions, wands, any artifact had to have a physical manifestation. Hence the stained glass on the *Enigma*, or the pitch that kept it sturdy and young.

He walked into the room and the Gold Wife followed him. There was a magic active in this place. Small seeds that had fallen from herbs or flora on the shelves were sprouting, hours away from digging into the wood to demand the ancient nutrients still housed there. He continued to the back of the room, the thrum he had heard before getting stronger. He saw the passage open and he realized he had never known this part of the castle was here.

A golden hand stroked his shoulder. "Raven?"

He frowned at the opening. "Hm?"

"It's not important. I know you. It will come to you. Let's go back to the bedroom."

He turned to look at her. Her eyes were expressive to him when her voice was smooth. She was practically transparent, if one knew to look. Right now, she didn't want him to go through that opening. He looked at it and went forward, sliding out from under her touch.

The symbols illuminating the passage were ancient magic, as if from the beginning times. They were so simple, they seemed faulty. Mages now overcomplicated things, except him. Of course, when he thought "mages now", he was really talking only about himself and one other. Oh, it was possible Snow was still alive. She was from Yokotama. But it was far more likely she had become air like all her ancestors. Merrick was the only mage still walking the earth.

The passage opened to a cave that was lit with impressive blue light, similar in feel to the ancient magic. Suspended in the air was a woman that kind of seemed familiar, but he couldn't place her. The coils of light around her fed into the soil around the room and roots were winding their way down her arms and up her legs.

"Oh Marica. What have you done?"

Thirty-Four

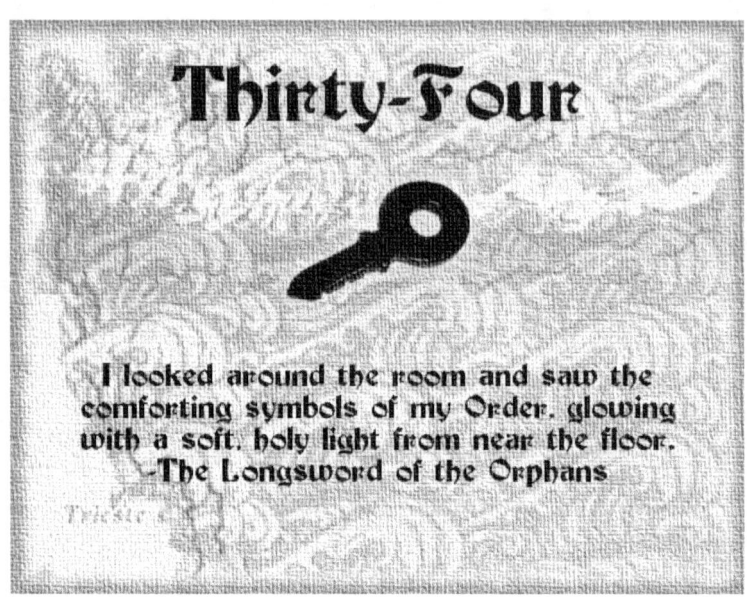

I looked around the room and saw the comforting symbols of my Order, glowing with a soft, holy light from near the floor.
— The Longsword of the Orphans

Tanglwyst rolled onto her back and moved her hair out of her eyes. She looked at the night, the moon far on its trek across the sky. The fire had died down too, so the light in the room had lost its main contributors. She nodded.

Good. It was time.

She got dressed, her nap refreshing her. The library had closed but Caiaphas had slipped her a key to the door when Gregory had told him to show her the way. She had not yet revealed to either of them what she was after, but she intended to let them read her notes when she had a good study compiled. The fact that a there was a secret passage in the center of the library was exciting, and it took her but a few minutes to get into her traveling clothes and be ready.

The halls were mostly empty but there were guard patrols walking their rounds. She had yet to find a place where they were just sitting, conversing between strolls. It was like they had some sort of sacred calling to walk a lot. She doubted she would be stopped, per se, but she didn't even want to be seen. If any of the cardinals were watching her, she didn't want their informants to have anything to report.

She saw an opening in the patrol rounds and slipped from her hiding place behind a statue of St. Raymond. Luckily, there were numerous niches like this in every hallway, if she needed to hide. She checked the intersection, then got to the stairs and made her way down to the library floor. Guards were talking in front of the doors and she rolled her eyes. *Of course. Now, they decide to congregate.*

She tried to listen to the conversation but she couldn't quite make it out. She was very vulnerable on the stairs, so she stepped into another statue niche, this one of St. George, and waited for them to move along. It took almost an hour. Finally, they bid farewell and she heard four sets of footsteps moving, two passing her on the stairs, two going away on the far side of the doors. She waited until she could not hear voices nor boots before moving from her spot.

She slipped up and unlocked the door as slow as she could, to minimize the noise of the tumblers. If Brother Fausto slept in the library, she didn't want to wake him. She got the door open just as she started to hear boots descending the stairs, and slipped inside, the door closed before anyone passed. She listened to the extreme quiet of the room, searching for anybody stirring among the stacks and seeing if she could hear people in the hallway. She could detect only the faintest of sounds when the booted guards from the stairs passed.

She slipped between the rows of bookshelves to the center, checking the long rows for any lights. The place had multiple windows streaming moonlight into the room so she could see, but there were also tons of shadows as a consequence. If anyone showed up, she would become motionless in one of them until the threat passed.

She made it to the bookshelf with the passage, and opened it with a glance first for librarians. She had no idea what she would find down there, but she hoped it would be tomes on the artifacts she sought. Stairs descended into darkness and she frowned. She had not brought a lantern or a candle or anything to see with. For some reason, she completely expected there to be torches or lanterns wherever she went.

A board creaked and she heard rustling. She stepped into the passage and pulled the bookcase closed. There was a handle with a latch on this side and the stairs spiraled down. She went down them, the dark lessening as she did. There was a faint glow down here and she could see it once she let her eyes adjust. The sound of water flowing like a town fountain filled the room with gentle laughter.

The glow came from a pillar covered in intricate markings, emerging from the center of a large basin. There seemed to be a wellspring here but as she looked around, there were no ways for the water to leave the basin. It wasn't stagnant, far from it. It looked cool and refreshing. The writing on the pillar shimmered in unearthly light, dancing with itself on the surface of the water.

She looked around the room and saw a dozen vaults with symbols upon them. She recognized them. They were the symbols on the amulets. Each vault had the symbol on the outside, but then it had the components of the symbols above it. Tanglwyst touched them, realizing the reason the symbols were strange and yet familiar. They were these stamped on top of each other.

They're saints. Brigit, Walburga, Raphael, and Nicholas the Woodworker. Healing, food, light, and travel.

The next vault had the symbols again, but in a different order. She checked and the order was unique for each vault. There were only a dozen here, but there could have been more, easily, the order of symbols have multiple combinations. Two of the rooms had all the symbols glowing, adding to the light in the room. On one of the two vaults, the glows were faint, as if suppressed.

She stepped back, then realized what these were. They were the rooms the amulet took you to, the ones with no way out. It made sense. No one would disturb them here and the Papal grounds were about the holiest connection you could get. She couldn't figure out which ones she had been in, but she knew the insides of two of them, which was probably one more than any of the amulet holders knew. These seemed keyed via combination to one specific amulet.

She put her ear to the wall of the vault with the dimmed symbols and listened but couldn't hear anything. If they were as sturdy as they looked, the walls were a foot thick or more. She doubted she could communicate with anyone inside. She thought about the last person she saw in one and realized she didn't want to communicate with him anyway. Let him rot. But the Saints help whoever found that amulet she dropped.

If the Scarred Man was still trapped here, he was either dead, or had gone silent. In a place as quiet as this one, any screams, even ones inside a block of stone, would have had a voice. She could strike the outside to rouse him, but preferred rapping on it when she had someone with her. To do so now could give her away. The library upstairs was at least as quiet as here and she had no idea how well sound carried.

She wondered if the symbols were glowing so faintly *because* he was inside and dying. She had put him there two or three tendays ago. If he was somehow still alive, she didn't want to be here when he was released.

She walked back over to the fountain and bent to it. The water smelled fresh and she tasted some. It was exquisite. She had never tasted fresher water in her life. It was restorative. She drank and found every ache in her gone, without so much as a flicker of doubt. Even the sore neck and bruises from sleeping on the ground in the forest were gone. She felt certain she could sleep well and deep now.

She looked at the pillar to see if she could make out the words there and realized that she could. They, too, were Saints. There was Teresa, after whom her grandmother was named, and Thomas, patron of scholars. She identified each one until she got to one she had never heard of before.

Clara? Who's Clara?

She looked again and saw, at the base, right above the fountain, were the words *The Registry of Saints. If Heaven Writes It, It Is True.*

Registry of Saints? That couldn't be right. She could almost have sworn some were missing, but there was also Clara, who she had never heard of. She didn't know whose registry this was, but it wasn't Heaven's.

Either that, or it wasn't the Church's.

She frowned. Why would the Church have a different listing of Saints than Heaven? What would be the gain?

She wanted to ask someone but she wasn't quite sure who. She clearly couldn't ask Brother Fausto. Maybe Caiaphas could check into it without endangering himself or her. She would see about that tomorrow. Now, she had to get out without alerting anyone. The trip in was hard enough. Without being able to see, she was risking opening the bookcase when someone was right there. She hoped she could listen at the door and hear outside.

She pressed her ear against the door and didn't hear anything. It *was* pretty late, well after midnight. If she stayed down here much longer, she would run into folks rising at baker's hours. Right now though, everyone should be asleep. She clicked the catch and risked a tiny opening to hear better. The rustling she had heard before was not there now, so she opened the bookcase a little more.

Light came through the crack and she scanned the opening to make sure it was the fading moonlight and not a lantern. Then she opened it enough to slip out. Just as she closed the passage, she stepped on a squeaky board. The rustling she heard before happened again and a light flared at another part of the library. It started moving, and she had to be clever to make sure she wasn't seen.

She heard Brother Fausto grumbling where she was before, so she moved as fast as silence allowed to the front doors. She opened them and checked the halls. She heard footfalls and voices which worried her. She could also hear Fausto sniffing around for her. She got only a moment between when she couldn't see Fausto and couldn't hear guards.

She stepped out, then locked the door behind her. Fausto probably had the key, but the time it would take him to get it unlocked gave her a chance to get away and hide. She went to the stairs, peeked up, then ran up the stairs. She dodged a few more guards before making it back inside her room. She locked the door and leaned against it, her heart thumping.

She had done it. She had found a secret of the amulets. Not all of them, but if the vaults were there, that meant there was more information on them. This did confirm that the Church created them, or at least sponsored their creation. She didn't think that was necessarily a bad thing, but it did bother her that the Scarred Man had been sponsored by the Church.

Maybe he stole it.

Maybe. No, probably. That would explain it. She heard no one coming down the halls, demanding her head, so she stepped away from the door. The adrenaline rush was abating and she was feeling fatigued. She sat at the window seat, and took off her boots. She looked out the window again and this time, she really could see a tiny flicker of orange-yellow in the trees. She smiled. Alexander would be asleep now, and she should be likewise.

Brother Fausto thought he heard the door to the library close. He rushed to open them, but the doors were locked, just as he had left them. He glared around the stacks of books. He had heard something and had been wandering the aisles for twenty minutes, looking for the source.

Mice were a terrible problem in libraries but these halls had long since been enchanted to repel vermin. He wished the spell repeled that wretched female as well.

He shuffled over to the center shelves where he had removed her before. He wanted to take the books with the amulets in them and put them well out of reach.

"Do I know of any books with these amulets in them?" His muttering gripes echoed through the aisle. "What an insult. Of *course* I do. I've been librarian here for four decades. I've read every book in here."

He looked over the shelves and pulled three books from them. He thought about putting them on the topmost shelf, then he got a better idea. He went to the secret passage door and reached up to the book that was the catch. His hand stopped as he saw it was tilted out, not flush with the other books. Not much, but enough to show it had been moved. He looked around, then tugged at it.

The room below had not been entered by him since the last Feast of St. Brigit. Every year, the papal City held a great service upon her Feast Day. The pope blessed wine and passed it among the attendees. The closest rows paid a lot of gold to be in those seats because the first barrel of wine was always made from the water from the Fountain of St. Brigit, though this was known only to a few Cardinals and Fausto. He would often sneak a second barrel made from the water a little farther down the communion line, just to ease the pain of those less fortunate. The books in his hands told the tale of the fountain and why the Papal City was built here.

They also told other secrets that a nosy bitch didn't need to know. Women were forbidden from holding any sort of status or office in the Church outside of convents. Fausto believed women were lesser beings, the burden of birth was his proof. A horrid ordeal filled with pain that often killed them, like it had his mother and sister. Even with herbs and several different methods designed to minimize the agony, there was always blood, filth, and screaming.

The first time he had heard his mother giving birth, he was barely old enough to remember. She was screaming in pain and he had gone in to see why. A midwife was there, pressing on his mother's massive stomach, and there was feces on the floor, covered in blood. He screamed at the horrifying sight and his father had rushed in to get him. Her screaming went on for hours and haunted his nightmares for days afterwards.

When he saw his new baby sister, he was confused as to where she came from. His father told him that this was the reason his mother was in such pain. A year later, it happened again. This time, it went on for most of the night, and in the morning, there was a baby brother. This happened every year for a decade. His mother became fragile and each time the screaming went on for less time. Twice, there was no new sibling, just a wooden box for the ground. Eventually, his mother broke under the torture and she died.

Within a few years, his sister became large of stomach and when she started screaming in pain, he fled the building. She couldn't handle the torture like their mother could, being much younger and smaller, and then there was a wooden box for her as well as the sibling she didn't give him. The house had no other women and there was no annual torture after that. They lived in peace, though on occasion, other women became large of stomach in the village and screamed in the night.

When the time came for him to choose a wife, he knew he wanted nothing to do with this practice. Taking a wife meant torturing and he wanted none of the screaming and blood. Instead, he asked if there was a place where women never were, and he was given a chance to be a librarian at a monastery. This was bliss. No women, no torture. No death after hours of screaming and bloody human waste.

Now this female had entered his world, his sanctuary. Although there were books in here about anatomy and childbirth, he had only skimmed them. He had no interest in the inner workings of women or children. If she stayed, she would become large with child and fill these halls with screams and blood. He would not allow his sanctuary to become a torture chamber.

He went to a wall by one of the defunct vaults and pressed a catch on a cabinet. Inside was a hollow with other books in it and a long wooden box. He removed the box and put the books within. He was about to put the box back inside, then he stroked it. Inside this was a solution to the problem. He opened the box and pulled out a silver dagger. The pommel was a strange stone. It was a perfect sphere and swirled black and clear, like ink in water.

As he touched it, his eyes took on the same quality.

"Yes," he watched the light glisten off the blade, "this will solve the problem nicely."

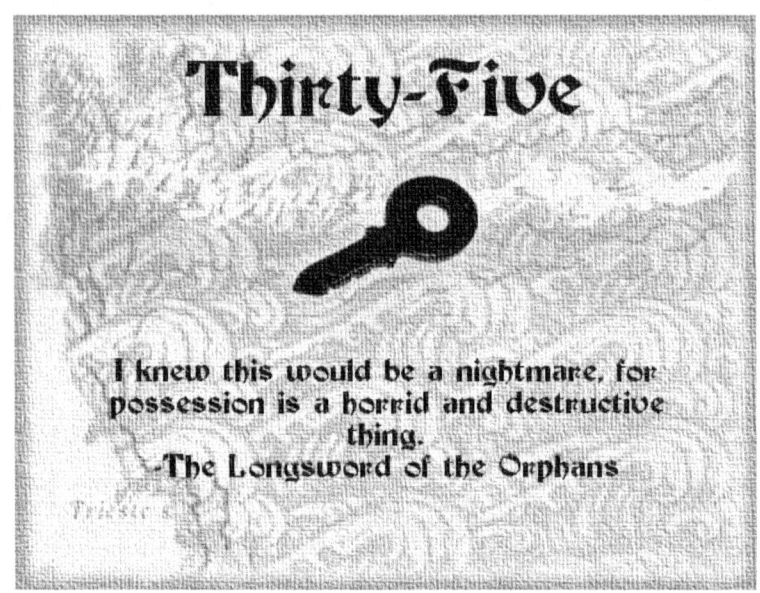

Thirty-Five

I knew this would be a nightmare, for possession is a horrid and destructive thing.
—The Longsword of the Orphans

Alexander opened his eyes, having actually *slept* for the first time in a while. He had started the night watching Tanglwyst, but when she retired for the night, he had left her side. He felt like he was there with her, or she here with him. The distance was not as depressing as the lack of hearing her voice. A new guard came in and Alexander again marveled at exactly how many people called this little encampment home. For having such flimsy dwellings, they were practically the population of a small village.

The food was simple fare again and Alexander wondered as he ate the animal (squirrel he thought), that the other bandits would be protesting giving him food when he wasn't earning it. His ransom had better make it worth their while. Of course, he had no idea if a ransom was even coming. Catherine was gone from the capital, as was Gomez. Dominic was in St. Andrew, last he checked. He had no idea who was around to govern with everyone else absent. He didn't think Dominic had taken the time to even appoint a deputy.

He checked on Dominic and found him back in Patras done with whatever business he had with St. Andrew. Something about that bothered him but he would think about it later. He checked on Gomez, who seemed to be moving about more today. Catherine was in a single spot on the way west. She should be home in Patras in a couple days. The capital had its caretakers back so Alexander relaxed and decided casually to look in on Tanglwyst.

She was in bed, a tray of food across her lap. The servant boy from before was tending her fireplace. She ate bread, sausage, and cheese, and drank tea. He watched her for a bit, then went to the window seat to gaze at the city. Folks were bustling about and the market looked inviting. The springtime sun was warm outside his tent so he imagined it was warm in her room.

He watched the servant leave and as soon as she was alone, she moved the tray off her lap. She got out the sheaf of papers from the drawer and her graphite. She started writing with such fury, he got curious and read over her shoulder.

Last night, I made my way to the area under the library here in the Papal City. There is a book on the eastern case, sixth shelf, that has a brown binding. The thing that caught my attention about it is that it had wear at the top of the book, but nowhere else, like people start to pull it out but then change their mind. A lot. I tugged at it and the bookcase moved. Inside was darkness and a set of stairs spiraling down.

The area under the library didn't seem lighted at first, but there was, in fact a faint glow as I descended the stairs. I went well after midnight so the Librarian, Brother Fausto, would be more likely to be asleep.

Alexander started. *She went somewhere on her own? What if something had happened to her?*

What if it had? It was not like he was in a position to rush over and thwart an attacker. He was an observer in her life, by his own choice. He had sent her away. He almost felt like, had he not been so driven by fear, she might have talked him out of that. She might have been willing to stay with him and help him through this mess. In the end, he wanted her safe and she was not going to be in a place like this. Of course, if she continued to explore without him, she might not stay safe.

Under the palace, I discovered several important things. First, there were large vaults with no openings. They had symbols on the outside that represented the Saints Walburga, Raphael, Nicholas the Woodworker, and Brigit. I had seen these symbols before, when I was in the room

297

Duncan took me to with the amulet. They were also stamped on top of each other on each amulet. I believe these symbols attune only one amulet to a room. Otherwise, people with amulets would be overlapping. If the missions each were sent on were clandestine in nature, knowing the other players could be problematic. The rooms would also be much larger and have more beds in them if they housed more than one person.

Only two amulets are in effect right now and one of them seems to be fading. I have no way of knowing if the amulet Duncan used was linked to one of these rooms, but if so, that room's symbols are no longer active. It still concerns me that two amulets still function. I wonder what room Alexander's amulet connected to?

His heart thumped for a beat when he saw his name written in her hand. He shook off the slight smile that forced itself on his lips.

It also worries me that Duncan was attached to one of these amulets. They serve the Church, not the Crown, and are corrupted. Alexander was served by Duncan as his assassin, but what if Duncan wasn't there for Alexander? What if Duncan was there for the Church in case Alexander didn't comply with their wishes?

Alexander stepped back. Duncan had access to the Crown before Alexander, as well as after Charles died. If he had a room with no exits, Duncan could have imprisoned anyone with no hope that they would be found. Duncan had once said he served the Church, then the Crown. Now he knew that Duncan would have cut Alexander's throat, or put him in a prison to die if the Church had given the nod. Had that been why he rescued Tanglwyst, at the Church's behest? What did the Church want with her?

Alexander was uneasy now. He thought Tanglwyst safe in the Papal City. If the Church saw her only as a pawn in their game, she was expendable. He thought of the movements Dominic had been making. He had recently thought the young Mandian lord was in the Papal City but when Alexander awoke, Dominic was right back in Patras. Dominic had gone to St. Andrew and back in a day and now Alexander realized why that bothered him.

That trip took a couple days by horse.

He closed his eyes and felt for the light that was Dominic. He found the man in the palace at Patras, center of the city. He focused upon that light and watched it. If it went anywhere in an instant, that would be the proof.

Tanglwyst detailed the information about the fountain and the pillar in her notes, then set the papers aside. She wasn't sure where she was going to send these notes when she finished. She could give them to Caiaphas. He would know what to do. Then again, so would her grandfather. On the other hand, she could tell them directly. No need to entrust them with her research, especially when this was the only copy. If Fausto got them, he might get touchy and she didn't want him knowing about her excursion into the basement.

She remembered that there was someone new on that pillar below. *Clara*. It also seemed like there was someone missing, but she couldn't tell who. She felt like the missing Saint was practically shouting out to her, but she couldn't place it. She needed another trip down, this time with a Manifesto.

She looked at the notes again. The only person she could think to send them to was not receiving messengers, at least not traditional ones. She smiled, thinking she could make a trek up the pass to the Drum and Nightingale, but if she were going to do that, she might as well just walk the notes right up to him. It would serve him right for sending her away.

She set aside her revenge fantasy regarding Alexander and instead placed a clean sheet of paper on the innermost page of writings. Then she put them in the book and closed it while she got dressed. She could go down to the library now, but she didn't know how many visitors it got in a day. She decided to go and see. If she got a chance to enter the basement, she would, and would simply wait it out, exploring the area until dark. She needed time to compare the entries in the Manifesto to those on the pillar anyway. She took the copy from the nightstand drawer. She realized she needed a satchel for all her notes and thought about heading to the market, but she would do that after she found out how many people flocked to the library during the day.

She opened the chamber door and headed to the library.

Alexander worried he would get bored, keeping track of Dominic but every time he thought about going back to Tanglwyst, he thought about that man having an amulet. Maybe it would't change the young D'Medici at all, but if it did, Dominic could do a lot of damage. Then he remembered what the shadows did to Gwen's body and his resolve solidified. He saw someone near him, Nina, but they did not seem to be engaging. He removed all other distractions and focused upon Dominic.

Then it happened. When there were no other lights near him, he disappeared. Alexander searched for him and found him in *Mande*. That was all he needed. When he returned to Patras, Alexander was going to remove Dominic from that office, and possibly imprison him in his own vault. He would have to be very careful not to become a prisoner himself.

With that resolved, he returned his attention to Tanglwyst. He went to his semi-dream state so he could see her. She was in the Library again and had a new satchel resting on her hip. She went near the bookcases in the center and he looked around like he could be her guard if she decided to try to enter the basement. He saw the younger monk, the one who brought her the other book, wave to her from down the aisle. A few other folks wandered among the stacks.

She spoke to the younger monk and tapped a copy of the Manifesto she pulled from her satchel. He nodded and motioned her over to another series of shelves near one of the windows. Near this area were a few tables with pedestal lanterns screwed into them. The older, sour monk that had evicted her the evening before scowled from a nearby desk. She smiled at the man, then sat down with her back to him. Alexander smiled at the snub as much as the older monk sneered.

The younger man came back with a few older versions of the Manifesto, and he and Tanglwyst talked about a few of the tomes. The young man had that sweet initial blush of embarrassment that comes from forbidden attention and Alexander looked at the older monk to see if he noticed. He had, but from Alexander's vantage, the older man also seemed to be doing something. His eyes grew dark, like he was contemplating something terrible.

Alexander decided to try and move closer to the man. The monk had no fealty to Mervolingia and Alexander feared he would return to his body if he strayed too far from Tanglwyst's side. Still, something about the older man worried him. He stepped closer, watching Tanglwyst. As he did so, he started to feel less solid in the library. That was odd since he wasn't solid at all, but he *felt* less present. He still couldn't see what the older man was doing with his hands so he stepped a little closer.

Whenever Alexander looked up at Tanglwyst, he felt more *there*, so he tried something. He kept his eyes on her, but walked backwards to the older man's desk. He thought of her, her laugh, her direct manner of conversation, the way she had played with Emmy. He remembered how frightening she had been when she threatened his life in the inn after his confession, but that he had also trusted her in that instance to do what was best for the country. He remembered her sleeping, and reading here at the palace.

The front of the monk's desk passed his hip and Alexander narrowed his eyes in concentration.

He thought about the time he had kissed her in St. Andrew, how he had made himself vulnerable in order to break a Fae spell. He thought about how he owed her a dance and that he had been such an ass for leaving her alone at the Ball after all they had been through. He thought about how he had wanted to kiss her, but had decided he would instead do that at the Ball, in front of the whole court. There had been a perverse joy in embarrassing his mother and all the sycophants with such an action. In the end, he wouldn't have gone through with it, but he had enjoyed the idea.

The back of the desk passed his hip and he glanced down at the monk's hands. They were in a drawer in the desk and grasping a silver dagger. The hilt of the dagger was a perfect sphere of clear stone and inside blackness was swirling like ink in water. Alexander heard the scream of the Shadows touching the dagger, encased in the pommel. His eyes flicked up to those of the monk and he saw that same blackness taking over there.

Alexander snapped back into his own consciousness, his heart thudding in his skull. Tanglwyst was going to die. If the monk got her alone, if he thought he could get away with it, he would kill her for her arrogance. Alexander managed to stand with his bound hands and stepped outside the tent, looking to the guards.

"Where is Tulio?"

The guards looked at each other and Alexander repeated his question with more authority. Tulio stepped from a large tent twenty feet away.

"What is going on? Why is the prisoner out of the tent?"

"Tulio, the Lady is in danger, the one you found in the woods. I need to get to the Papal City as quick as possible."

Tulio folded his arms. "Is that so? And why should I care about that?"

"You got her in the night, put her in this tent with no restraints or extra guards and have not, as far as I can tell, pursued her. You care about her."

Tulio frowned, the guards around him shuffling and glancing at one another. "Well, that's a rather inconvenient observation."

The guard outside the tent raised his chin. "How can you know she is in danger? You've been here the whole time."

"I've..." He tried to figure out how to explain without sounding insane. "I'm her king. I hold her fealty. I can sense this."

The bandits rolled their eyes and went back to their business. Tulio waved a hand at the guard and the man grabbed him and started to move him back to the tent.

"*Wait.* Fine, I dreamed it."

The activity in the encampment stopped and all eyes turned to him. Tulio stepped over to him. "Dreamed it?"

Alexander frowned, surprised that carried such weight. "Yes. There's a monk who has a dagger, the pommel of which swirls like ink in water. From what I can tell, he plans to use it on her."

That phrase changed everything. Tulio shouted to gather the horses and the guard behind Alexander cut his bonds. His sudden freedom caused him to stumble and he rubbed his wrists and shook out his arms as a horse was brought over. Three bandits joined them but Tulio raised his hand.

"Stay here. Secure the camp. I'll take care of this." He climbed on, then reached down for Alexander and pulled him onto the horse in front of him.

The bandits nodded.

"I apologize for the intimacy, but they will need the horses." Tulio shook the reins and the horse leaped forward.

Thirty-Six

We returned to the Papal City to find the place sealed to all outsiders.
-The Longsword of the Orphans

As they rode, Tulio's look was intense, like he was playing something through in his mind and did not like the outcome. He did not vary his gaze to his surroundings and Alexander found his dour look unsettling on his portly, naturally cheerful face. Discontent would be an unwanted visitor to that place, and this look was well beyond displeasure.

They rode through the day and Alexander was relieved to see Tanglwyst's fealty still shining like a beacon through the forest. He didn't understand why she still maintained her fealty after Alexander's confession. He hoped that the time she spent as Sovereign had show her the burden and given her perspective. Whatever the reason, he was grateful for the light to guide him to her.

As evening loomed, he heard the bells far away, calling the faithful to Mass. They must have been enchanted by Heaven to carry this far, and the sound tried to reassure him. He hoped it meant she was going to Mass, surrounded by hundreds of people. What he feared was that it meant the library was emptying of witnesses.

He felt Tulio shudder at the sound. "What?"

Tulio looked at Alexander. "Bad memories."

Alexander noted that the determination in his captor's voice mirrored his visage and did not delve. As darkness settled, Tulio pulled to a stop. He nodded to Alexander. "Is she still alive?"

Alexander nodded. "I can feel her."

Tulio looked to the city. "Can you find her in there? Can you track her?"

Alexander looked as well. "Yes."

Tulio glanced around, then closed his eyes and shook his head once. "Then let's get in there."

"You don't have to go. You can return to your men. We'll come back once she's safe."

Tulio snorted. "I believe you would, but that's not it. I just have an aversion to such places as this."

"Then why enter?"

Tulio looked at Alexander and for the first time since they started this mad rescue, his old self returned. "The challenge, of course."

Alexander smiled. *Damn it. I really like this man.*

The Papal City shimmered in the night, lanterns dotting the windows in every surface. It looked like stars laid out on a blanket. The Papal Palace was shining, stained glass casting jewel tones into the dark from the tower. Alexander felt around for Tanglwyst and found her on the ground floor. That was both good and bad, because although it made access a little more direct, it suggested she wasn't going to Mass.

"There. Ground floor. Center of the palace from the looks of it."

Tulio shook his head. "You don't make it easy, do you?"

Alexander shrugged, smiling. They continued on towards the city, and got to the gate. The City Guard were checking everyone coming in.

Tulio frowned. "What are they doing?"

Alexander shook his head. "I don't know. I've never been here before."

"What's your plan?"

"I don't suppose you know of any back ways in? I could stride in with full regal arrogance. I doubt they'd stop the King from entering, it would look bad to the pilgrims. But then of course I would be watched the entire time. Not conducive to a rescue."

Tulio looked at the city, smiling. "There are always back ways into a place. This way."

They walked to the road into the city and crossed it casually, not to draw attention. Once on the other side, Tulio glanced around the forest. "Good thing it's still Spring for a few more days. This wouldn't be possible in a ten-day." He closed his eyes and whispered something. To Alexander, it sounded like "Where there's two wills there's two ways..." Tulio opened his eyes and skirted the city wall away from the gate. Alexander heard water rushing ahead of them. A large grate covered a culvert, spilling grey water over a stony area.

Tulio smiled as he approached, then stopped, frowning. "Hmm. That will be a problem."

"New grate?" Alexander raised an eyebrow.

"Not quite." He turned to Alexander. "Look, I need to prepare you for something. The Papal City is different from most places in the world. Certain things are *stronger* and others are considerably weaker. So, just, be aware."

Alexander refrained from pointing out that nothing Tulio said felt like it was preparing him for anything, "As you say. I will follow your lead."

As they moved closer to the grate, Alexander felt his connection with Heaven grow stronger with each step. He wondered if this feeling would continue to grow as they progressed into the city, or if, for some unfathomable reason, this culvert was blessed.

Tulio went to the grate and looked over the edges. He moved some bits of metal around and the grate fell open. Tulio gestured for Alexander to enter, then followed the King inside.

As they entered the sewer system, Tulio pulled his scarf over his nose. "You know how to find her, Your Majesty. Lead the way."

Making a conscious effort not to inhale through his nose, Alexander reached out for Tanglwyst with his mind. She was still in the same place but Alexander was having trouble seeing her. He was fully awake, so all he could do was find her light. He couldn't tell if she was hurt or scared. He couldn't tell if anyone was sneaking up behind her. This gave his steps urgency, and he started to run.

He came to a T in the hallway and looked around, trying to see a slope or opening that would indicate the tunnel turned towards the palace. Tulio came up and looked as well.

"What is it?"

Alexander looked at his companion. "I need to go forward from here. I can't tell which path will do that."

Tulio closed his eyes and mumbled the line about two wills again. His cheeks twitched when he finished, and the scarf fell from his face. His cheeks, once round and jovial, were now sharp and well defined. His dark eyes, still brown had a more feminine appearance and his frame was slighter, more nimble. Tulio pulled the scarf back up and tightened it.

Alexander's eyes widened, then narrowed. "Tulio?" Was the low lighting in the tunnel playing tricks with his vision?

"Pay it no mind, King. I told you things would be different inside." He jerked a thumb to the right. "This way."

Alexander drew no attention to the slight change in the bandit king's voice. He took the right tunnel. He touched his face discretely, wishing he had a mirror. He wondered if his features were changing too.

"This woman, why do you care about her, King?"

Alexander's step halted for a moment before resuming its normal pace. Tulio had asked what Alexander had been trying to determine himself.

"She helped me get through a difficult time and I didn't really appreciate it. I cast aside her good will. Yet, when I needed it again later, she did me an even greater kindness." He smiled. "She withheld it. Shook me out of my pathetic stupor and a spiral I had no chance of getting out of on my own. And how did she do that? *She left.* She did all this by *not being here.* She made me do it on my own. I couldn't have done it with her, and I couldn't have done it without her. I owe her something for that."

"You sound ridiculous. Giving thanks to her for your own accomplishment? I doubt she would be tolerant of such talk."

"Maybe not, but I'm going to make sure she hears it nonethless."

Tulio put a hand on Alexander's shoulder, turning him. The hand on his shoulder definitely held a man's strength. "This sounds like an arrogant royal who feels entitled to another person's emotions, another's life. I've seen your type before, King. You might say, I've watched people like you my whole life."

Alexander looked at Tulio's eyes. They weren't jovial. They were sharp, intense. And... *familiar.* "Do I *know* you?"

Tulio stepped closer. "Do you? Do you see the people around you? Or are they expendable, like this woman?"

Alexander didn't flinch. "I have been an absolute fool. I have pursued a woman who didn't want me based upon a single desperate night. I turned my back on my family, my country, even my faith trying to recapture that one night. Now, I need to *stop* being a fool long enough to save the one person who has had the nerve to slap me out of it. Please, Tulio. Let me save this woman's life."

Tulio scrutinized Alexander, a gaze as unsettling as Catriona's had been but he stood his ground. Finally, Tulio released him.

"Fine."

He pushed past Alexander and continued down the sewer. Alexander noticed the man's footfalls made no sound and did not disturb the water's surface more than a breath's ripple.

Tulio turned down the tunnel. The holy aura was destroying the illusion, chewing at it like a mouse at a bag of bread. The longer she was in this place, the more would be revealed. She didn't know if she trusted Alexander, but she had watched him grow up in that castle in Patras. What happened in Cheryb all those years ago had driven Alexander to become the healer he was. That was saying quite a lot in that environment of deception and blood.

The Sinister Glove looked at Alexander. The boy she had watched grow into a man had rejected the politics of his bloodline. She had noted his turn to the healing arts and his desire to end pain rather than cause it. She saw his faith enhance him instead of rule and imbrue him. He was what was best in men.

Tanglwyst had been a special project for the Glove. She had wanted this woman to survive and had seen to it. But in the end, she had not needed the Glove's help. She had fought off a Fae spell to warp her. When the Glove had noted the presence of the spell, she had told her boss. They watched the situation, ready to interfere when necessary. They hadn't needed to. The Spell was fought off and the perpetrator put down by Alexander himself.

That was the spark of a firestorm altogether.

Once Tanglwyst was recovered, the Glove had a different mission. There was another trapped in this cursed city and he was more important than any human. Even her two favorites.

"How long were you in Patras?" Alexander trailed behind him.

Tulio looked at Alexander. "What makes you think I was in Patras?"

"You have contempt for me. That means you've seen me at my worst. I've done a lot of terrible things but I can think of only one that's bad enough to make someone this mad. The St. Michael's Day Massacre."

Tulio didn't respond.

"My mother tricked me. She tricked us both."

"I know."

Alexander stepped in front of the man. "How?"

Tulio glanced behind them. "I'm an expert at deception. I can see it in people. It's why I'm helping you." He looked at Alexander, his eyes almost beautiful. "You're not lying."

Alexander swallowed, then shook his head. "No, I'm not."

"And what about her? What about this woman we're helping? Why her?"

Alexander knew the answer. "Because she's important to me."

"Why?"

"She understands me. She knows me."

"Why?"

"Because..." Alexander closed his eyes. "Because, I love her."

Tulio was silent, and when Alexander opened his eyes, expecting the Bandit King to scoff, he discovered he was alone. "Tulio?"

The man poked his head out of the wall a few feet away. "This way."

As Alexander followed Tanglwyst's protector, he couldn't ignore it anymore. The robust man from the forest was now a lithe creature, feminine in nature. He was about to say something when the person before him stopped.

Tulio looked around. "There. I see an opening."

They ran to the area where some light was filtering through a grate in the ceiling. The grate was about a foot across diagonally and Alexander shook his head. "I can't fit through that."

"I can." Tulio stepped on Alexander's knee without any weight and sprang to the ceiling. He used his momentum to move the grate, shifting quieter than Alexander thought possible. He slipped up inside and bent down, reaching in. "Here. Give me your hand."

Alexander reached up, not understanding what Tulio had in mind. Tulio frowned and seemed to exert himself and Alexander squeezed through the grate. The room was a sauna, large tubs with steaming water. The air was thick with it. Alexander could hear people in it but he couldn't see another person.

When he got into the room, Tulio's hair had acquired a grey streak and he was sweating, but not from the sauna.

"Once Tangl is safe, I have some questions." Alexander nodded to the streak, then pointed into the room. "This way."

They went to the door and opened it, taking care to be very quiet. A couple of guards walked by at the end of the hall and they waited for the footfalls to fade before they left the room.

"Where is she?"

Alexander focused. "She's that way. I think she's still in the library. She doesn't know it's a trap."

They ran through the hall, scouting ahead. They turned a corner and saw the older priest from his dream going into the doors he saw before. He looked at Alexander and scowled out of habit. Alexander wondered what the penance was for pushing a priest down a flight of stone stairs. He didn't get the chance to find out.

"That's him. That's the one with the dagger."

The sound of Alexander's voice echoed down the hall directly to the monk, who turned, his eyes growing wide.

Tulio crouched. "Well, so much for being sneaky."

Alexander looked for Tanglwyst and saw her light inside that room. "Stop!"

The monk looked at the doors in his hands, then smiled, ducking inside. Alexander's Power flared, his fear forcing it out to protect him. Tulio backed away, his façade dropping completely. The priest's eyes grew wide, then the doors were closed. Suddenly, alarms went off within the entire palace, huge bells ringing out the word "Fae! Fae!"

Tanglwyst heard the doors to the library close and the lock *clank* into place. She got up, looking around. Brother Fausto was nowhere around and neither was his assistant Brother Netuno. Netuno had managed to get her seven Manifestos from the last seven hundred years. Apparently, a new Manifesto was made at the turn of the century, and Netuno hoped to help write it this time. He knew more about the Manifestos than she had ever thought possible. She wanted to take him down to the Pillar. She hoped that was him locking the doors.

She took her information and piled it together, then put it in her satchel. She stacked the books together and looked towards the aisle of books leading to the center of the library.

"Brother Netuno?"

She heard scuffling, and her heart started thumping in her chest. It wasn't Netuno's walk. That was Brother Fausto's. Fear blanketed her and she slipped to the shadows of the stacks. She saw Fausto come to the area where she had been, glaring at the books left on the table. She held her breath as he scanned the shadow where she hid, but he didn't seem to see her. He went to the desk and pulled out a dagger from a drawer. The pommel swirled and she knew she needed to get out of there.

Thirty-Seven

Dew armaments were in place, large
ballistae and archibuses dotted the towers
of gold and white marble while guards in
new white and gold tunics emblazoned
with wards patrolled the streets.
-The Longsword of the Orphans

Boots running across tile caught the attention of the pair. Tulio looked down the hall and then back to Alexander. "Help her! I've got these."

Alexander nodded and ran, pulling at the door. It was locked. He looked at Tulio, whose hair was now short and almost white. She turned brilliant white eyes on Alexander.

"Ok, *you* hold them off. I'll get the door."

Alexander spread his hands. "Hold them off with what?"

She ran over to the door, pulling out a lockpick set. "Not my problem. Improvise."

Alexander rounded the corner and slumped against the wall, rubbing his head as the guards came into view. He pointed further down the hall, "They came from behind. Took the priest with them."

He hoped the panic in his voice would convince them his story was true, not make them realize he was lying and unarmed. To be safe, he readied himself to attempt to wrestle away one of their weapons if need be. The three guards started down the direction Alexander indicated, then one turned around to ask if Alexander needed help. His angle was such he saw the woman picking the lock to the library and gave a shout to his companions. As they turned back, the woman Tulio opened the lock. Alexander rolled to his feet and ran to her.

Tulio looked at their assailants. "You go. Save her. Get her out of here."

Alexander looked over his shoulders at the guards as he moved into the now open door, "What about you?"

"I plan to get them to chase me. Trust me," she smirked, "I'm very good at it." She pushed Alexander into the library and he heard he door lock behind him.

Thoroughly mystified at what was going on with 'Tulio', he shook his head, scanning the room quickly for Tanglwyst. She was moving towards the center of the library, moving fast.

"*Tanglwyst,*" he ran through the bookshelf aisles.

"Alexander, get out! He has an amulet dagger!"

Alexander heard her scream as a solid *thunk* sounded deeper in. He heard footsteps running and a sound of a heavy click in the center of the room. There was a struggle and he heard a slap, then someone falling down stairs. He looked down all the paths for fallen books and saw something much worse: blood.

No.

He ran to the center of the room and found the bookcases all standing flush together. He put his hands up and pushed but they did not move. He screamed in frustration. She was going to die and he was going to be mere feet away from her when she did.

Then he remembered her description. Eastern case, sixth shelf, with a brown binding that's worn at the top. He looked around and found it. He tugged on it so hard it came off the shelf, revealing a metal lever, but the bookcase popped open.

Sounds of a struggle raced up the stairs to him and he hurried into the room with the Pillar. Tanglwyst was on her hands and knees, trying to stand. The older monk was standing over her, pointing at the Pillar. In his right hand was the silver dagger Alexander had seen before.

"You wrote this here, Little Witch? You were down here, snooping, *defiling* this record? Even His Holiness will call for your execution for such a thing. But he won't have to see it. Once I deal with you, I'll cut that blasphemy out."

Fausto raised the dagger and Alexander vaulted onto the man. His Power flared as the dagger's pommel cast out vicious black smoke. He pinned the man's forearm with his shoulder. Fausto stabbed Alexander, the tip searing as it carved into his shoulder blade. The angle wasn't enough to really penetrate but Alexander didn't want to feel more. This already felt unnatural.

Tanglwyst shook off the previous attack and moved towards the wrestling couple.

"Stay back. The dagger has those shadows from the amulets."

She looked around for a weapon but there was nothing loose enough to wield. She looked down, then took off her satchel and knocked Fausto across the head. He dropped the dagger.

Fausto wrenched his arm from under Alexander's shoulder and threw him off. He rolled, getting to his feet, and recovering his weapon. The monk looked at the King with eyes dark with zealotry.

Fausto looked at the glow surrounding Alexander and gave an unsettling smile. Alexander moved in front of Tanglwyst to shield her. The shadows flowed around the monk's hand and his eyes were swirling with black.

"Sovereignty. You really *are* well connected, woman. But that Power is in your hands, boy, by the Church's Will, not yours."

The monk muttered some words and Alexander's protection vanished. The shadows in the pommel screeched in delight. Alexander's strength fell away and he dropped to his knee, holding his head against the painful screams of the monsters in the dagger. Their calling was foul and he felt like he was breathing and swallowing tar. Worse, it told him to murder the woman at his side, to hold her still while they cut her throat and consumed her soul. Alexander fought it, but it took everything he had to do so. Fausto walked by Alexander and to his true victim.

Alexander grabbed the man as he passed, turning him away from her.

"Run…"

Tanglwyst kicked Fausto's knee from the side, and the man crumpled in a howl of pain. The dagger hit the ground and she kicked it away from the fight. Alexander punched the man in the diaphragm, knocking the wind out of him and taking him out of the battle for the moment. Tanglwyst took the chance afforded her and Alexander. She tugged him to the fountain and scooped water from it onto his shoulder.

The pain washed away like mud in a waterfall. He looked at her in wonder. "What *is* this place?"

She focused upon his wound. "The Fountain of St. Brigit. It's why the Papal City is in this place and not somewhere that makes more sense."

He looked at the Pillar, his breath taken away by the beauty and holiness of it. The glow from the names was too similar to the glow from the Power. He tried to spur it to life, but the Power was gone. He looked at the monk who was starting to recover.

"We need to go."

They moved away from Fausto, up the stairs. The latch on this side was broken, the case now hanging open. She looked at him. "Did you do this?"

"I panicked. I thought you were about to be killed."

She shook her head. "What are *you* doing here?"

"Saving you."

"Why did you think I would need saving?"

"I saw him with the dagger." Before she could ask any more questions, he moved her into the library. He could still hear the call of the shadows. "We need to get away from here. I can still hear those things. They were…" He tried not to alarm her but there was no way to tell her what they wanted him to do without scarring her sleep.

"Let's find my grandfather. We'll tell him everything. He's in town…"

He grabbed her shoulder. "No. Look, Tulio is here too, and he's distracting the guards while I get you out of here. You can write your grandfather or request an audience later. Right now there's a madman with a shadow dagger that wants to kill you. I can't protect you anymore. We have to go."

She looked about to chastise him, undoubtedly for endangering Tulio with this, but she held her tongue. "We're gonna have a conversation about this tomorrow."

"And I will be happy to have it, my lady. Right now, the doors to the library are locked and the keys are downstairs. How are we getting out of here?"

"I have a key!" She felt her pocket, then rummaged in her satchel. "which I apparently left in the drawer in my room." She shrugged. "I didn't think I'd need to unlock it again."

He looked around in a slight panic. "Any other exits?"

She looked to the west end of the library. "Well, there are windows over here. They are an option, but I'm not sure how much of one."

They hurried to the western wall and she opened a set of stained glass shutters. He looked out and saw what she meant. The drop from here was into sunken gardens, which took this from being a four or five foot drop to the ground to being a leg-breaking fifteen or twenty feet. There weren't even any hedges or shrubs beneath the window to break their fall. Even a pond would have helped.

They heard Fausto muttering curses and Alexander made a decision. The Church may have the ability to take his protection but his *healing* was a gift from Heaven itself. He hugged Tanglwyst to him and fell out the window as Fausto came screaming around the corner.

He tried to twist to take the brunt of the impact but there was so little time. They hit the ground with their shoulders. He felt his arm and collarbone break and his head smacked on the grass. His hip cracked and his knee screamed in pain. Tanglwyst yelped as she suffered similar injuries.

"Shhh. Lie still."

Fausto looked out the window above them and Alexander caught the motion out of his peripheral. He went limp, his arms falling away from her. He tried to stay very still, like the damage was fatal or at least debilitating. The vile cackle from Fausto's throat struck around them, but Tanglwyst didn't flinch. The monk pulled his head back inside and closed the shutters. Both of them let out their breath, then she squeaked in pain.

"What in Hell is wrong with you?" She shifted onto her back, muffling another scream.

"Hush. Lie still."

He reached for the healing energy and was not denied. It started to go to his own wounds but he pulled away. He pushed it into her, seeking out the damage. Her shoulder and collar bone was also broken but she had struck a small rock as well and had a skull fracture. Her pelvis was cracked and her hip dislodged. He spread the mending glow throughout her body, cleaning the pain and destruction like blowing dust from a shelf.

She exhaled and looked at him, confused. She sat up as he sat back, her eyes flushed with wonder. "How…?"

He held up a finger to stay her questions and she complied. He flushed his own body with healing energy and was very happy to discover he could do it. The thought had occurred to him that he might be able to heal others but not himself. If that had been true, it would have changed the situation completely.

He looked at Tanglwyst. *Well, not completely. I would have still healed her, but she would have survived without me. She doesn't need me. I need her.*

The pain subsided and the broken bones mended. He made sure he got it all, then also exhaled, getting to his feet. He helped her stand, then dusted off the formerly-wounded shoulder.

She resumed her question. "How..."

The sound of heavy hoof beats struck above them and they looked up. Tulio was on the back of a horse, riding across rooftops. They jumped to the wall which seemed barely wide enough to hold the beast.

"That's my horse! Who's that on his back?"

"Uh, Tulio."

The pair rode around, dodging swords and attempts to unhorse her. Tulio saw the couple and raised a hand in greeting. "Get out! We'll meet you outside!"

"Fae Sympathizers! Arrest them!" Guards pointed to Alexander and Tanglwyst.

"Time to go." Alexander looked around.

"How?" This seemed to be her new favorite question.

"I need to find a way to the sewers but I can't go the way I came."

"This way. I saw a gardener retrieve a fallen tool today. He went underground then back out. The grate may not be closed."

Tanglwyst led him through a rose bush to the sewer grate as the sound of galloping hooves cantered around. The couple dropped into the sewers and he grabbed the grate, replacing it. He looked around, getting his bearings. "I think I know the way."

He took her hand and ran down the sewer tunnel. Soon, he saw the T and turned right onto the tunnel that led to the exit. They hurried out, then looked back. Alexander wanted to signal Tulio that they were safe but Tanglwyst tugged him along.

"They saw us go into the grate. This is clearly how you got in. They know we're out. Run."

"Archers! Ready the Fae Arrows!"

The Glove looked at her Lord, his illusion of being a horse not valid before her eyes. "Fae arrows?"

Embertwist-Bedlam looked at her. "Looks like they want us to go."

"And I was having such a *nice* visit."

The Glove patted Bedlam on the neck and the pair moved into position. Bedlam ran at the wall. He leapt and sailed over it.

He heard a loud *thuwunk* from a tower nearby and then his neck was wet. He landed on the other side of the wall and ran off into the nearby shrubbery. He was about to turn towards the forest when he felt the Glove slide from his back. He turned around and saw a large arrow protruding through her chest. The horse wheeled and Embertwist abandoned his horse-form. He knelt beside her.

"Glove? Glove, we can't stop. They can still hit us."

"..Go... I'll be right...behind you..."

He picked her up, the arrows flying around him. He jumped on a couple in midflight, using them as springboards. They hurt his feet, as cold iron often did but he got away from them. He threw up a shield of briars to hold them off while he tended to his lieutenant. Cries came from the palace and a bell continued to sound in a high tower.

He set her down and went to grab the arrow from her chest. The iron burned his hand.

She waved him off. "I got it."

She was human, with special Fae gifts like the armor, her eyes, her weapons, and others he had long since forgotten he had given her. She grabbed the arrow and pulled it free, tossing it aside.

"You're lucky you have not fulfilled your contract with me."

"You're lucky I care."

They stood and she looked back. They heard another *thuwunk*, this one louder, and she turned. "What now?"

A large iron bolt from a ballista soared through the air. Embertwist looked up in time to dodge but his feet were burned and it slowed him. Just a fraction, but he was going to be hit.

The Sinister Glove, his beloved companion for hundreds of years, moved into place to deflect the bolt, standing sideways to give the lowest profile. She put up her hand but the bolt cut through it, the iron bypassing all the Fae protections she had. It pierced her palm, then travelled through her arm, riding the bone and cutting away the flesh. It pierced her chest, the impact blowing apart her ribs in a spray of bone and blood. It continued its destructive path, cutting open her lungs and heart before emerging on the other side.

It embedded in the ground an inch from him, splattering her life across his boots. She hit the ground in a splat, her upper body no longer attached to her lower one.

"Glove!"

The briars he put up for protection responded to his grief as if unbidden. They grew, ripping the ground to pieces. The thorns impaled the archers and guards that were caught in the path, churning through them like teeth. Bodies were lifted into the air as the thorns grew around the entirety of the city. They meshed together into a solid mass until they covered even the ramparts of the Papal Palace. Roots thrust into the ground, ripping it as well. The briars stopped at the wall, but they blotted out the sky.

Embertwist collapsed. Summer was supposed to be a tenday away, but he had just spent nearly all his power. He looked at the briars, then made a decision. He raised his hand and poisoned all the thorns to the last, above and below. His energy expended, he turned the season to his brother Corrigan, and knelt beside his friend. The grass and flowers grew up around her, putting her back together, but she did not mend. He felt the pull, and bowed his head.

The Land opened and embraced her into it, and a plethora of stunningly beautiful flowers grew wherever she had touched. The scent caressed him and he fell across them, weeping.

Alexander and Tanglwyst looked at the dome of briars growing up to cover the city.

"Grandpa..." She turned to run back into the briars but Alexander grabbed her.

"Don't. You can't get to him anymore." He looked up at the overgrowth. This didn't seem like a barrier of Heaven. It seemed like a different sort of magic.

"It's almost like a fairy tale. You know the one? With the briars that sealed the kingdom and hid the princess from the world."

"I remember one about a poison and a death-like sleep. True love's kiss."

She reached out to touch the thorns and he gently grabbed her hand. "Let's not test the tale, okay?"

She looked about to question, then nodded. "No, you're right. No one really believes in true love anyway." She looked at the now solid barrier, then to the woods. "We should be on our way. Tulio will likely head to the encampment."

"We should return, make sure they made it out alright."

She frowned. "You want to return to an encampment of thieves who were holding you ransom?"

"I promised I would. I want to be a man of my word."

She looked skeptical but then cast a worried glance back at the briars. She nodded and gestured for him to lead the way.

Thirty-Eight

He said he would destroy it, and we
believe him capable of this.
-The Longsword of the Orphans

"So you *do* remember my name."

Raven looked at the Gold Wife. "Of course I do, but you wanted to hide this. What are you doing to her?"

"What she was designed to do: I am having her serve the Land."

"Who is she?"

"She is the Dûcesa."

Raven turned to look at Catriona, her unconscious form limp. "No." He looked at the coils. "What is happening to her?"

"She is replacing the power source for this covenant. The old one was drained."

He turned to the Gold Wife, angry. "So you imprisoned her here?"

"Every source has been imprisoned. The previous one was trapped here for millennia, put here by your Fae Lords. You even know her name, since the covenant is name for her."

"Persephone?" He looked around. "What happened to her? Where is she now?"

"I released her. As I said, she was spent." She gestured to Catriona. "This one will last a long time. One of the nice things about being immortal."

"You can't do this." He looked around. "If she turns... Where is her Stâpân?"

"Gone. They left earlier. Just rode away like she didn't matter. They even left her horse to die waiting for her."

Raven knew the Stâpân would never leave his Dûcesa's side, especially this one. This was the woman to whom Myrgen was being drawn. He remembered now, as a cat in St. Andrew, seeing her every year. On her last visit, there was some sort of vigil held for the man on the docks. This woman, captain of the ship Octavius married, had watched over Myrgen all night, surrounding him with lanterns.

He had shown Myrgen the cave because the Land had put it in their way. He had not been sure if it was supposed to be a lesson for Myrgen, or for himself, and had treated it as a teaching opportunity for both. Now he knew the lesson was Myrgen's for certain. He was supposed to gather the memory stones. He was supposed to awaken as her Keeper. He was supposed to be here. If Raven awoke her, or if she awoke on her own, she could die.

Even if the shock didn't kill her, the draining of her life essence would. Marica was right, she would renew, but she would change. Raven liked Myrgen, and he remembered liking this lady too. He didn't want Myrgen to endure what he had when the Second Dûcesa died.

He turned from her, his gaze on the Gold Wife unwavering. "Release her."

"Can't. The bindings are unbreakable by me."

"Then how did you release Persephone."

"I simply brought a better source to the bindings. They sensed the value in her and took her of their own volition."

Raven was angry at the Gold Wife's lack of empathy. It wasn't that she didn't understand what she was doing. She *did*. She just didn't care. *Why didn't it take the Gold Wife?*

True, the Dûcesa had a title, but so did the Gold Wife. She was the first magical artifact struck by the very first mage in the world. She was older than most civilizations, and there was a power that came from longevity. The longer you were around, the stronger that tie to the world. He looked up at the ship captain.

This woman was worth more than the Gold Wife.

He looked around. "Where is the previous captive?"

The Gold Wife looked around. "She appears to have taken her leave."

"You took an immortal being that was imprisoned millennia ago and just turned her loose on the world?"

"She didn't matter." She stepped up to Raven and tried to put her arms around his neck.

He stopped her, grabbing her hands. "Stop it. You either don't know what you've done here or you don't care. Either way, I'm not interested in being intimate with you." He threw her hands down. "I can't be with someone capable of this."

She stepped back, her eyes filling with fury. She opened her mouth and she was suddenly solid and sharp. She screamed and her voice became knives, eviscerating his soul. He covered his ears and dropped to his knees.

She stopped. "Clearly you need some time alone to think. This seems as good a place as any." She stepped back through the doorway into the chamber.

Raven tried to move but his body ignored his commands. The Gold Wife's voice resonated off every surface. Even Catriona stirred a little from her coma.

"This place held a magical creature captive for over four thousand years. It can definitely hold the likes of you."

She stepped back through the opening and sealed the door.

Catriona saw the old Augustinian church before her and looked around. She realized this meant she was unconscious but she didn't realize how that had come to pass. She had been talking to the Gold Wife and... She shook her head. There was far too much to sort out there. This was a good thing. Father Benjamin would help with this.

She went to the doors, remembering the lesson from before. She entered, no longer afraid of experiencing the non-memory. In fact, in light of the comments of the Gold Wife, she wanted to see it.

She felt herself falling, the warmth of a hand at the center of her back still lingering as she dropped. The ground thrust towards her, and she hit, torso first. Her body snapped like branches in a storm, rent from the tree to pierce the air and soil, cascading to the stone floor in a cacophony of crunching ivory and bursting blood vessels. She felt the pain of impact at first, then her neck hit, and she felt nothing else.

Dust from the stone filled her nostrils, cut with blood and the taste of metal. One of her teeth fell down her throat, stabbing into the side of her windpipe. Her body came to rest, and she saw the light above silhouetting the heads and shoulders of her attackers. Then the heads disappeared, one by one, leaving only a rectangle of light. Stone on stone scraped the air and the light receded, becoming smaller and smaller.

Before the light could fade, she cast her gaze about the room for the first time. Near her was a smoky stone with gold flecks in it, thousands of them. She mustered her remaining strength to try and touch it. It was near her right hand but her body did not respond. Her neck was broken and she was paralyzed. She could see she was also bleeding out. The tooth she swallowed had pierced her jugular and her mouth was filling with blood. As the last light went away, she wondered why she saw this scene. How many more were there like this?

She had died. The Gold Wife said it happened periodically. When it did, she would change. She would recover her memories when the Keeper deemed it appropriate, but it seemed like she might be able to recover them on her own. The Gold Wife had called her Death, and she knew beyond measure that she was right. She died, but didn't. It made the vision make more sense, the reliving the incident. If she had died over and over, then this might have been a sacrificial place.

She looked around for Father Benjamin and found him where she usually did. She sat in a pew to wait for him to finish praying and actually looked around at the church. The walls were dark cherry wood, rich crimson in color and very highly polished. The altar was snow white marble, almost shining in contrast. The widows were stained glass, showing a series of Saints doing various holy things. There were eight, four on each side. She didn't know them but they had names under them. On the right were Brigit, Giles, Clara, and George. On the left were Michael, Gabriel, Raphael, and Uriel. These had wings, where the others did not.

It still made no sense that a Land worshiper would have an Augustinian Church in her mind. She remembered the church, and the priest, but these were apparently not the memories of which the Gold Wife spoke. They weren't fatal. Apparently, Raven just telling her about her memories made them come back fast and hard enough to kill her. Was that the intention of the Gold Wife? To kill her?

That seemed counterproductive. Her life essence was necessary to heal the land here. She could feel it healing, growing new life. She didn't want to die but she also didn't mind it if this was the outcome. York was a desert where a fertile land used to be. It deserved to be restored.

Father Benjamin came over to her and sat down. "How can I help you, my child?"

She gestured to the walls. "What is this place, really?"

Father Benjamin looked around. "It is my home here."

Catriona's eyes narrowed. "That's not what I mean and you know it. Why is this place here?"

Benjamin swallowed, his skin paling.

She frowned. *He looks… nervous. Scared.*

"I don't know."

He lied. He just lied. Sort of.

"You know something."

He turned from her scrutiny, and she felt him do something new: He blocked her from seeing something. It was like when Duncan resisted showing her what Alexander had done. She pressed, and his eyes turned persistently *away* from the doorway.

"There's more there, isn't there?"

"Catriona, you need to rest. You are being drained."

It didn't matter. He didn't want her to see something in the doorway.

She stood, looking at the entrance. If she died so often, if *that* was some sort of sacrificial place, then there had to be another time that took her life a little more slowly. One where she didn't land neck first.

She wondered if she could guide the vision, control it.

She walked to the exit and left the church. She turned to look at it again and Father Benjamin stood. He seemed to understand what she meant to do. She couldn't tell if he approved or not, but it really didn't matter. He was trapped in there. He could keep her out in an extreme circumstance, he had done it before, but she wanted to test this. She stepped back through the doorway.

Show me.

She felt rough hands upon her, a dozen, but she didn't know why they were hurting her. She had come to their village because someone was sick, very, very sick. They were suffering. Why weren't they letting her help them?

Three others had the lid to a large sarcophagus mostly off and were holding it, straining against the weight.

"Let me go to her! I have to go to her right away! She's suffering!" She struggled, trying to fight her assailants, but there were too many. They hefted her up, the walls of the room, cave, painted with images and incantations. The symbols were strange. She had never seen such things. Then she was plummeting. She twisted, trying to land differently. She succeeded, shattering her pelvis, then ribs. She broke both legs and her right arm as they struck the ground. She saw five stones on the ground around her when one of her ribs pierced her heart.

She stepped through. Five stones.

She left, and reentered.

She had a head wound this time, and she was starting to come to. Then she was falling. Eight stones before impacting face first.

She left, and reentered.

Nine stones. She could still move. Lower legs unresponsive but she reached out for one of the stones. Then something else fell on top of her.

Something else? They dropped something else to make sure she died? What had she done wrong? She looked at the doorway again, getting more and more angry. She knew she had a duty, she had someone who was desperately calling for her help. She could feel it in everything she was, every part of her. Why were they stopping her?

She stepped back through and saw Father Benjamin had fallen to his knees. He was crying, sobbing. She could also see a glowing door behind him. It was strange, but familiar. It was very important too. She looked at the threshold, her spirit refusing to let this go. She stepped through.

She was in pain. An arrow was piercing her lung. Again, the dozen hands but this time, she looked at them. She noted their faces. She saw light brown hair, blue eyes, beards. Clean clothes of homespun linen and wool. Elaborate embroidery of geometric shapes. No hats, but hair insisting there had been a few worn. She looked at the chamber as they entered. The paintings on the left wall were of this process, over and over. She counted eleven times. On the back wall were words, old and hard to read.

On the right was a man. He was nailed into the wall, his blood being collected in a bowl by another man. The collector took the blood and moved over to the wall with the writing to continue doing so. She looked at the man on the wall and she knew him! He was hers.

He raised his eyes, his skin so very pale from loss of blood. The others lifted her above the pit and she got a hand free. She clawed one across the face, then she was falling. She spread out to have the impact more distributed and then relaxed. She hit hard and bounced this time. She still felt many bones break and she knew she would not survive it, but she was conscious and mobile. There were a dozen stones around her and she reached for one.

Then, something hit the ground beside her. It was her man. She knew him, knew is beautiful eyes. His body was drained and he was almost unconscious before he was dropped, so he had done what she was not entirely successful at. He had hit the ground limp. He was also broken, was also dying, but he reached out to touch her face. His hand was cold and bloody.

"I love you, Bringer."

She knew him. She touched his face. Her breath was fading but she would not die without him knowing this. "I love you, Hunter. I will see you again."

"I don't think so."

"I will. This will never happen again."

She kissed his palm. His blood tasted of copper and iron. It was all she could do. They faded from life in each other's touch.

Catriona fell to her knees. This atrocity was unacceptable. These people were *murderers.* She looked at Father Benjamin but the door behind him was gone. He reached out for Catriona.

"I'm sorry. I'm so, so sorry."

That's when she saw it. Ancient scars so old they had faded from sight. But now she saw them. He had scratches across his face.

"You. You did this to me, to *us. Why?*"

"I left after that time. I couldn't do it again. But your mark stopped me from dying. Regardless of how many times I tried, you refused to take me. Eventually, I gave up trying to die. I became a member of the Church, trying to get forgiveness. I figured if you refused to take me, maybe Heaven would... I don't know... *override* your decision. But it didn't work. It never worked until I met you again.

"I knew who you were immediately. When I first saw you, my scars stung and I knew you. I couldn't let you suffer again, not again. I helped you with your delivery, and got you out of there. But it wasn't until I was willing to die to save your son that you forgave me. You released me from my curse, but not from your side."

He gestured to the church around them. "You wanted to know what this was. It's my prison. I can't leave because I need to give you something. You need to go, you need to find him. When you do, you'll understand. *But come back.* You must come back. Please."

Catriona looked at the walls around her, the wood stained with the blood of those who made a different choice. Windows showing scenes of people who did not matter. An altar stained with blood disguised as grace. She hated it, and she hated him. He was no friend. He was a murderer, putting her to death over and over. He had captured her beloved and helped torture him, bled him so they could draw on a wall with his life force.

He had touched her son.

Her eyes flared and her fingers became claws. She stormed toward him, his eyes pouring rain. She grabbed his beard and turned his head into the light. There, barely visible.

Not for long.

Her claws raked across his face, opening the old wounds.

Apparently, this was a day for such things.

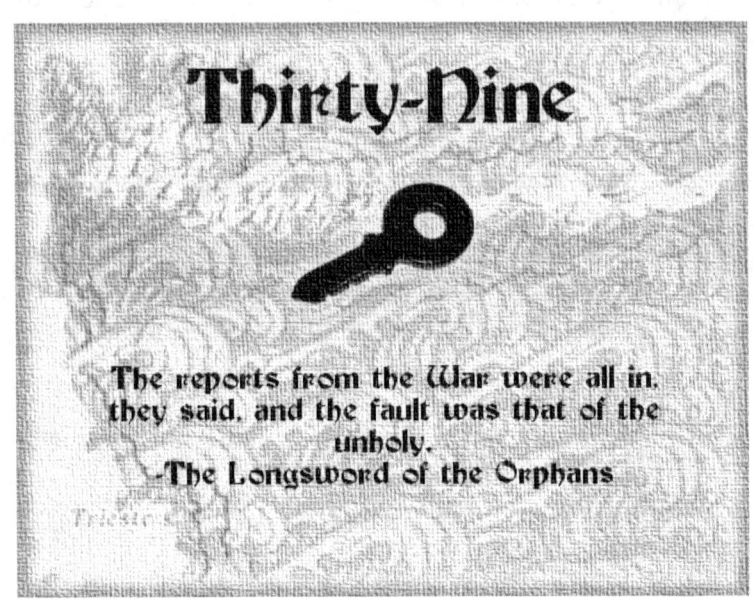

Thirty-Nine

The reports from the War were all in,
they said, and the fault was that of the
unholy.
-The Longsword of the Orphans

Catherine looked up from the desk she had purchased for this room and motioned for Charles the Messenger to come in. He bowed.

"Your Majesty, the guards you requested are here. And I have another messenger now."

"Good. I need you. Sit."

She motioned to a chair near the end of the desk. She had several papers and a quill next to it. She pushed an inkwell she was using so it was halfway between them.

"I need you to record what the guard tells us. This will need to go back to Patras, but not before a copy is made to send up the mountain at Cliffbase."

Charles nodded. He realized it was no longer just the future king being away on a wife hunt. Things were happening. She would deal with them, but Alexander needed to know. He also understood he would be the one taking these missives to the top of the pass. She wasn't going to trust anyone else.

The guard came to the door and poked his head in. Charles waved him in. Catherine sat straight, imposing even while sitting.

"Your Majesty, this is Gerard Masson. He is a patrolman for the road between here and St. Giles. He just returned from that run."

Catherine nodded. "What can you tell me about the fires to the west, Gerard?"

The guard took a knee before her, having been told by Charles and the other patrolmen who he was about to see. "Your Majesty. The vineyards that are prominent in Bordeaux have been put to the torch. The city of St. Giles has a spell upon it that immobilizes anyone within its borders. When I had left, the inhabitants had been frozen for almost a day. It took me another day's ride to get here."

Catherine's normal demeanor showed no fear, but her eyebrows gave a slight twitch in concern. "Are they asleep? Dead?"

"They are not. In fact, I fear it's worse than that. They are not only alive, but aware. They are merely stopped in the middle of whatever they were doing. They cannot speak, but I saw the eyes of those near the border. One was near a fire, reaching for a child that was falling. The parent had... hold of the... child... but had not pulled it from the fire's proximity when the spell took hold." He was crying, the image too horrible for his heart.

Catherine closed her eyes against the vision, then took a breath to steady herself. "What caused this spell?"

"We couldn't tell. The fires began, the people at the vineyards fought them, but they were lost. I spoke to one of the people heading to St. Giles on my way to report. They were going to send a message to their Mistress, Lady Tanglwyst de Holloway."

"I feared it was that lady's holdings. Those were the property of the Crown until her trial. So she obviously wasn't hiding there or in town or they would not have been sending a message to her. You said it took you a day to get here. That's with resting for the night, correct?"

He shook his head. "Sleep was not a thing I sought nor would it have graced me, my Lady."

Catherine nodded, a sympathetic sigh leaving her chest. "Understandable, my good man. I fear I will be likewise after your tale."

"I apologize for that."

She raised her hand. "I needed to know."

Gerard waited.

Catherine exhaled. "Thank you. Please wait downstairs."

"Yes, Your Majesty." He rose and left the room without turning his back on the Queen Mother.

She shuddered.

329

Charles nodded. "I feel the same."

"That poor family. The loss of the child was bad enough. I cannot think what it was like for the mother."

"What could do such a thing?"

Catherine leaned forward on the desk. "I can think of a spell that might do that, but it would take a powerful caster. One like that?" She shook her head, then looked at Charles. "That's Fae magic."

"Fae? But St. Giles is guarded against such things. It's on the edge of the Black Forest and there are symbols to St. Giles everywhere."

"That's why it would take a very powerful caster." She glanced at the paper. "Write that tale down. All of it, including the child. Then make two more copies. One will go to Gomez, one to Alexander. We'll keep a copy with us. How long will that take?"

"Give me an hour for the ink to be dry."

She nodded. "Make it so. I want these on their way to the recipients before dawn."

Persephone stumbled through the woods outside the Fae gate from the covenant that bore her name. She fell and had been laying there when the green-haired mage walked by. She knew him, for how could someone forget a creature like that. She watched him and his beast enter the portal, but could not see where they went from there.

The mage had never met her. She had never met any mage personally. She had only been able to watch them, see them through the bonds. When they fought the monsters that destroyed the soil, she thought the bonds might weaken, assuming they were held by the Land. Fae were connected to the Land so it was easy to connect the two, and a couple of the mages had magic that overlapped those disciplines.

That was not the case, however. The bonds were something else. Something older. When the dark woman had entered the room, the bonds flew to her as if they had been waiting for her. Like they were designed to hold her specifically, and that Persephone was merely a place holder. She was discarded.

It was harder than she expected. She had been attached to the area for so long, she didn't understand what freedom was. She almost had not left the room. When she sensed the magic portal, she went through and became overwhelmed by the light, the colors, the smells. She lay on the ground, trying to sort it out. After a few moments, she fell asleep.

Now she awoke, and she felt better. She could think, though the idea of being away from the covenant bothered her. She hated being trapped, had always tried to escape, but now that she was out, it was far too much. She did not remember heat of the sun, the feel of the cool grass, the scent of the flowers. She saw and heard, nothing more.

She lifted her head and looked around. In the nearby sky, a white spire pierced the treetops. There was a window in the top though it was too far to see anyone in it. She stood and moved towards the tower.

There were doors on every side and she did walk around to check. There was a symbol on each door and she touched it. It almost seemed familiar, like a face in the fog, then she lost the sense. The effort to see the potential memory exhausted her and she sat down against the wall until she felt better. The stone was comforting, not too warm from the sun, not too cool from being stone. She felt better just being in contact with it. After a while, she got to her feet again. She opened the door before her and entered the hall.

The entry to the tower was enormous, far larger than possible from the outside. There were four doors within the tower spaced between the outside doors. One had a snowflake on it and was frost-covered. One had green leaves and flowers growing around the jam and the door itself looked like a rainbow through mist, with a raindrop as its symbol. Next to it was a small set of rocks in a stack with water coursing down them. Another had a sun and was made of metal, gold and brass gleaming and glinting in the hall. The fourth had pumpkins and apples beside it and had leaves turning red, gold, and orange. The symbol in it was a basket of vegetables.

She walked to each door, touching the symbols. The autumn door felt different. When she touched it, it had a heartbeat. She tried the handle, but it was locked.

There were stairs that wound around the tower, almost decorative in nature, and they seemed to go all the way up. The ascent was daunting in her current state. She started breathing heavy just thinking about it. She looked at the apples and realized they were food. It surprised her. She had forgotten about food since the covenant was deserted. She remembered a Fae that took care of the ale in the basement stores and wondered if he was still around somewhere.

She picked up one of the apples and bit into it. It was glorious. The flavor was sweet and crisp, and she devoured it as if she had not eaten in millennia. Which, when she thought about it, was probably true. The food was restorative, more than a simple apple would be to anyone. This was special food, spiritual somehow.

She looked at the water across the hall and went to it, kneeling beside it. She bent her lips to it and found the same properties as the apple. She had not realized she was thirsty until she was quenched.

She looked at the stairs with renewed sense and started climbing. The first stairs were only wide enough for a single person, and not a very large one at that. Had she more mass, she would have had to press her back against the wall and side-step her way for the first lap around the room. They had no railing for the first three turns around the room, but then a small lump began on the outside of the stairs, growing taller with each step. The stairs also grew wider at that point.

After ten steps, the lumps were poles coming up to about her waist, where they started growing buds. The buds turned into flowers, which turned into other branches. By the fourth turn around the building, a railing of intertwining white branches caressed her palm.

At the seventh turn, there was fruit forming on the branches, and moisture collected in leafy cups. She drank from one and believed it must have been from the spring below. She picked one of the fruit, a fleshy pear, and held it in case her strength started to wane again. She felt fine now, but the tower continued for a hundred turns and she did not want to take the offerings for granted.

She stopped to rest at about ten turns and thought this might be a good idea as a plan of action. The tower was very tall, taller than she thought originally. But then, it was smaller on the outside. She ate her pear and sat on the steps, marveling at the wonder around her.

She repeated this five more times, drinking the cup water, eating a piece of fruit (it was different every time), and resting every ten turns. After that, she felt tired, and thought about leaning against the wall to sleep. Then she envisioned tumbling in her sleep and falling down the stairs. That was not a comforting thought so she pressed on.

She got two more turns and rested on the stairs longer. She was not hungry anymore. She drank because she needed to. Sitting on the stairs was more important and she started to feel that exhaustion she had outdoors. This worried her because she was far too high for safety and far too close to the top to stop. She started to rest for longer after each turn, until she got to the sixty-fifth one.

The stairs changed then, with a landing and benches. The benches were padded with pillows, in brilliant colors similar to the doors below. A berry bush grew in the center of the landing. She laid down upon the bench and fell asleep.

She awoke when she heard a strange noise, one from so long ago, she could not place it. There was a small, feathered beast sitting in the berry bush and the sounds seemed to be coming from this creature. They were high pitched, but decorative. She found them pleasant but difficult to sleep through. She stood and stretched, then went to the berry bush. The creature flew away and landed on the railing heading towards the top. She gathered and ate several berries and drained an equal number of water cups before returning to her task of climbing.

It occurred to her to wonder what would be up there, and to wonder exactly why she was doing this. Mostly, she wanted to do something new, and this was very new. There were so many fragrances. Each flower was a new scent and they made her very happy. The taste of each fruit was new and she reveled in them as someone who had never experienced this, which she did not think she had. The feel of the railing, the pillows, the flowers, the air were all intoxicating.

She got to the point in her journey where she could see the top and it was exciting. The chirping creature had stayed with her, just moving ahead of her. She felt a sort of companionship with the thing and wished she could touch it. It looked soft. It spoke to her in its musical voice and she started assigning thoughts to it, though it was very unlikely it had those. She watched the approaching apex with increasing anticipation and stopped eating or drinking or resting.

When she got to the top, the stairs emptied onto a great stone floor. In the center was a stone box with a man laying upon it. The man was wearing flowing robes of gold, silver, and gemstone colors. Upon his head was a brilliant crown that looked like the woven bannister that protected him. It was made of white metal, thin but strong and moving like wind in the clouds. His eyes were closed and his hands were clasped upon his chest.

She stood next to him and touched his hands. Tears ran down her cheeks. Her voice filled the room when she finally spoke.

"Lumin…"

"Your Majesty, we have arrived at the Teeth."

Cipriano looked at his ship's captain. "Drop anchor. Ready the longboats."

The captain bowed and left. Cipriano went to a sealed case about three feet long and a foot wide and used a pin on his desk to prick his finger. There was a small well on the top of the case and he squeezed his finger until it dropped enough blood to fill the well. Once it had enough, the blood disappeared, absorbing in streaks into the wood. A lock formed upon the front and he opened it with a key.

Inside was the prize, the tool by which he would conquer Caratia at last. He lifted the White Granite Sword from its resting place and inspected it. The tip was still blackened from where it had fought shadows, and still stained red over that from where he embedded it in Boots. It seemed to truly be turning away from its pristine reputation the more he tainted it.

He smiled. This would likewise taint it further. By the time he got within sight of Caratia, this thing would no more be connected to the Land than he was.

He went out onto the Main Deck where his soldiers were gathering. He could feel the sword trying to escape, to twist from his grasp but he did not let it. The men were on the main decks of the several ships and he climbed to the upper deck to be within sight of them all. He nodded to the soldiers on his ship and they proceeded to the longboats. The other ships saw this and did likewise in a ripple effect.

There were two hundred men, each armed with an amulet and special swords that would not lose their edge. At six per boat, thirty-one needed to be deployed to get everyone on land. He didn't care about the boats after they got within sight of the shore. They only needed to get to the other side of the Teeth. Once there, they could teleport to land and invade. He could practically see it from here but he knew the lore. The Teeth had a magic that did not yield to outsiders.

Cipriano was no longer an outsider though.

He motioned for the longboats to come up alongside him. Once there, his rowing team moved him up to the Teeth. Large fins sliced through the water on the other side, each one a man high and shiny black. The men in the boats started shifting nervously, which irritated Cipriano. He had chosen these men personally from all over Mande. They were the strongest, smartest, best combatants the country had. He did not approve of them doubting him.

Well then, it's time to ease their fears.

He touched one of the stone spires with the White Granite Sword.

The spire shuddered, then rumbled beneath the waves, making an opening. The fins changed course and headed for the boats. He dropped the tip of the sword into the water. The great sharks turned aside and fled.

The men on the ships were silent for a heartbeat, then cheered, as did those on the ships. He touched more of the spires and dropped them into the sea until his fleet could pass. He moved the cheering longboats forward and the ships raised anchor.

The Invasion of Caratia had begun.

Forty

I handed it to her and looked at the angel.
-The Longsword of the Orphans

Myrgen felt his feet reconstruct beneath him, felt his heart grow in the air, then spawn a chest before it began again to beat. He became whole again. He was rebuilt, and he felt the stains of his previous existence burn away. He didn't feel bound by fear or pain any longer. He knew.

He knew his place in the world and that place was valued. He thought he understood before, but he realized he had only been shown the outline of that. It had been enough to solidify his love of this country, this place, these people. He knew he loved Catriona, and he knew that if not being with her was the sacrifice for being Dûce, then he would not step onto that stone when the time came.

The most interesting part of this was that none of that had changed. What *had* changed was his feeling of purpose. He didn't feel like an outsider, like a convert. This was his essence. It had always been thus. Now he knew the life he had before had simply been treading water until the moment when his real life began.

He looked down and saw the pommel stone to Catriona's sword. He knelt and placed the sword she had entrusted to him on the ground next to it. The stone flashed and became part of the sword again. The Land rumbled in approval.

He touched the stone and closed his eyes.

Hunter had managed to live twenty-seven years without ever meeting the Bringer of Death. He spent his days in the mountains, hunting and skinning. He returned to the village only to bring them meat and furs. They had built him a dwelling, despite his protests. The Elder had told him it was important to the people he served. Hunter had a bed with clean sleeping furs, a table with two chairs, a fireplace, a basin and cloths, and shelves on the mud brick walls for his dishes. A heavy wool drape with a very detailed felted hart in full rack hung before the opening that was the entrance.

The Elder stood beside him, looking around. Hunter looked at him. "Your husband, you said he is ill?"

The Elder nodded. "Yes. He has been getting worse for some time now. I believe the Bringer of Death should be arriving in town soon." The man put his hand on Hunter's shoulder. "I would ask your help, my friend."

"You have only to ask and it is yours."

"Our children are old as well. We do not have any capable of this. Will you please bear my husband to the Resting Place?"

Hunter could not deny the Elder his request. The children he spoke of were the orphans of the village, parents lost in hunting accidents, from illness, bad luck, or battles against thieves. They were leftovers from a more dangerous time, but they had not suffered losses like those in two generations. The Giver of Life had visited several times since then, gifting the village with health, prosperity, and babies.

The Elder was right. His children could not carry the body of their parent.

"When is the Bringer due?"

The Elder opened his mouth but then a bell rang outside. He smiled. "It appears she approaches now."

"The Bringer of Death is a woman?"

"The Bringer of Death does not make that choice. It does not need to."

Hunter stepped outside with the Elder and waited. He felt apprehensive, like he needed to prepare for a monster or bandit. In the shimmering light of the approaching dusk, she stepped from the twilight into the area before Hunter's home.

She had very long black hair that curled along her shoulders and back. Her clothes were made to travel. Boots were sturdy but showed wear. A cowl covered her head which she pushed back when she approached. Her skin was dark and beautiful, like the eyes of a doe. Her eyes were sparkling green, as if stars were given color. She bore no weapon, no animal to ride and carried no pack. She did not even have a walking stick.

She did not look at him, but bowed to the Elder.

"You have called for me."

The Elder returned her bow. "We have. This way."

He led the Bringer down the village. All the people came out to see her and bowed in reverence. She did not look to them, her attention bent upon her charge in the home ahead. The Elder's dwelling was marked with a felted drape dyed with blue and yellow spirals. The Elder pulled the drape aside and the Bringer entered. The Elder motioned for Hunter to join them, then entered after the younger man had passed.

The Bringer went to the bed in the room and sat on the edge. The Elder's husband opened his eyes and smiled. He reached up and touched her hand.

"You came."

Her smile was full and genuine. "You called for me." She stroked his aged brow. "Are you ready?"

He looked at his husband and the Elder stood next to the bed. His husband held his hand, then nodded to the Bringer.

She stroked his face and he shuddered. His body breathed in deep and out, then the life expelled from his lungs. He relaxed entirely and the tension in the room disappeared. The Elder patted his beloved's hand, then set it upon his chest. The Bringer stood and stepped back to give Hunter room to get the body.

The Elder's husband was on a special fur that was made just for this occasion. Hunter folded the fur across the man, and tied the thongs across that to hold it closed. There were five along the body to swaddle him. Once he was bound, Hunter picked him up. The procession walked out of the hut, followed by the others in the village.

They walked to a field of flowers at the end of the village and the Elder stepped to a place, and pointed. Hunter placed the body on the ground where the Elder indicated. The Bringer stood beside the body and waited until all were there to say goodbye. When he was ready, the Elder nodded to her.

She lifted her hand and the ground shifted to bring the body within it. It flowed around the body like water and when it was consumed completely, a patch of beautiful orange flowers with purple centers grew where he entered. The villagers sighed and smiled. Even Hunter acknowledged the sight. He was an expert in these woods and had never seen such flowers.

The Elder took the Bringer's hand. "Please join us for the feast in my husband's honor. Hear the tales of his life and revel with us."

"It is not my nature to linger."

"Then take these gifts with you." He handed her some jerky, fruit and bread."

"I am honored. Go, remember your loved one."

She looked at Hunter and bowed to him, then turned and left town, heading south.

"She's just going to go into the dark now?" Hunter was confused.

"It is not her nature to linger."

"Then why did you offer?"

"Out of respect. Without her, our loved ones would linger in pain and sickness. She releases their life to return to us later. We want her to return, and we want her to feel welcome. We also understand if she does not wish to stay. Her presence means someone among us had died. People can behave badly when they lose someone they love, especially if it is sudden."

Hunter looked after her, and thought how lonely her life must be. She raised her cowl and disappeared into the night.

Within the year, the Elder grew likewise ill. The next time Hunter returned to the village, he was met with a request to visit the man. He pushed aside the drape on the door and knelt beside the bed.

"You wanted to see me?"

The Elder turned weak eyes upon Hunter. He reached out and touched his face. "You came, my friend. Thank you. I wanted to wait. Please, stay in town a few days."

The Elder's strength waned then, and his hand dropped slowly to the bed. Hunter stood and looked to the Elder's oldest child, a daughter.

She smiled, but her eyes were wet. "He will call the Bringer, but he said he would not call until you came home. He wanted you to bear him to the Resting Place like you did our other father."

Hunter looked at his friend, then nodded. "Of course I shall. It is my gift to them both."

He stood at the edge of the village, right in front of his home, when dusk came. The oldest daughter was beside him. She looked at his house.

"Does the drape keep the weather out?"

He glanced at her, then at the drape. "Oh. Yes. It is very comfortable. The hart on it is very detailed. I'm very impressed."

"My son and his wife made it. They were trying a new technique. I'm glad it worked."

He saw the figure coming through the shimmering twilight and smiled. The bell was rung by her husband, who was on top of their home, watching for the Bringer's arrival. The bell let the village know to come to the street. "She's here."

The soon-to-be new Elder looked out and took a deep breath, letting out in a slow measure.

The Bringer of Death entered the village and stood before the pair. The daughter bowed.

"You came."

"You called me." Bringer looked at Hunter, bowing to him. "We meet again."

"I, too, was called."

Bringer smiled, then turned to the daughter. The trio walked to the Elder's hut, again with the village assembling outside. The endeavor went as the last did, a gentle repose that removed the pain and anguish from the house. There was a relief, a quiet joy, at the release. The daughter spilled tears, as did her family. Hunter swaddled the Elder and bore him to the Resting Place. He laid him beside his husband and a patch of blue and gold flowers sprang up where the ground took him. The flowers mingled with the orange and purple ones.

The daughter bowed. "Please stay and join our feast. Hear the tales and revel with us."

"It is not my nature to linger."

"Then take these gifts." She gave the Bringer food, and a couple pairs of woolen socks.

The Bringer took them and bowed, a glance given to Hunter, then went on her way. The daughter returned to her family. Hunter watched Bringer leave again, but this time, he went to her before she passed from sight.

"Excuse me."

Bringer turned to look at Hunter. *"Yes?"*

He gestured to the village. *"Please, join us. It is dark and the wolves in the area have been active of late."*

She smiled. *"I do not fear the wolves."*

"You have no pack, no shelter. Stay and at least see the dawn."

She looked in his eyes with merriment. *"You do not need to fear on my behalf. I am the Bringer of Death."*

She reached out and squeezed his hand. He flinched, but her hand was warm, soft. Her eyes grew a little sad at his reaction, and she let go, retrieving her hand.

"It is not my nature to linger." She put up her cowl and walked away.

He cursed himself for flinching. That was probably why she didn't stay, because people feared her touch. He remembered the Elder taking her hand and nothing ill had befallen him. He considered her a friend and a vital part of the village workings. Next time, Hunter decided, he would not be so foolish.

Hunter began spending more time in the village. He put hooks upon his walls for his weapons and traded furs and leather for things like ceramic bowls and ewer for his water. The stone mason had installed a hook for a kettle in the front of the fireplace and he got a pounded metal pot to hang from it. He spent time gathering herbs in the forest when he hunted, as well as roots and mushrooms. He dried the herbs and sometimes the mushrooms if he was going to be gone for more than a week, though he did that less and less.

It was almost a year before the call was made again. An older person got sick and their cough would not dry out. The sickness was more sudden than the Elder or his husband, and the village did not have time to prepare. Hunter looked at twilight for the Bringer, but several days passed and she did not come.

He wondered if it was perhaps not as bad as he thought, so he visited the sick villager. He heard a great cough, each one spewing blood on the old woman's face. Her husband was in tears as he wiped away his wife's bloody spittle. He looked at Hunter.

"Help us."

Hunter went to the Elder. "Why have you not summoned the Bringer?"

The Elder was crying. Her husband was rubbing her back. He looked at Hunter. "The offerings we made fell into the fire. We have nothing to give her."

Hunter raised his eyes to the sky. "Call her. I will handle the gifts."

He went to his home and set about cooking a stew. He looked at the gift he had worked on since their last visit: a new pair of boots. He did not know the size of her foot so he made them to be adjustable. The fur was inside, to cushion and keep her warm, and they were tall enough to cover her knees. He didn't know how much she walked in the woods but they would save her from scrapes from bushes.

He stepped outside, looking as the sun was setting this time. As he hoped, he saw her figure entering the village. The bell tolled. He smiled. "You came."

Her eyes glittered. "You called me."

"I've been waiting for your return. I want to apologize for my behavior on your last visit."

She frowned. "I don't understand."

He reached down and took her hand. It was warm and soft. He looked at her again, and her own eyes took on a wet look. She blinked them back and nodded to the town.

"Where do I need to go?"

He gestured to the village, then accompanied her through town. She did her business, the Elder and his wife looking on, nervous. When the woman was committed to the ground (her grave grew flax), he nodded to the Elder and approached Bringer.

"Please, stay with us and celebrate this woman's passing."

She smiled, their ritual well known by now. "It is not my nature to linger."

"Then please come with me. I have your gift at my home."

She studied him a moment, then nodded.

He held out his hand for hers. The village watched this and a murmur went through the town of wonder and surprise. It did not lessen when she took his hand.

He escorted her to his home and showed her the boots. The Elder clutched her chest in gratitude when she saw them. Bringer did similarly, surprised at the level of effort given to this gift. She raised her hand in refusal.

"This is too great a gift. I cannot accept it. Others will decide this is necessary and will not call if they don't have the proper gift."

The Elder looked at Hunter, ashamed. She realized she had fallen into that trap. She had let the woman suffer for days because the gift was gone.

"Then this is a gift from me. For my rudeness during your last visit."

Bringer smiled. "That I shall accept." She looked around and then sat on the ground, starting to tug at her own boots.

Hunter gestured to his hut. "I have chairs. And this way, I can adjust them if need be."

She looked at his hut. She nodded to the drape. "This is beautiful work."

The Elder smiled, then got an idea. As Hunter escorted Bringer inside, the Elder ran off to her son's home.

Hunter helped her into the boots, then offered her some stew while they waited for the Elder to return. The lack of other people set Bringer's mind at ease. After a bit, the Elder poked her head into the room, carrying a blanket under her arm.

Hunter waved her in. She unfolded it and displayed a field of stars on a dark woolen blanket. Bringer took it in her hands. It was soft and supple.

"This is beautiful. The designs are very intricate."

"It was a gift from my children. I would like you to have it."

"I couldn't."

"You must."

Bringer looked at the blanket again. "What about you?"

The Elder smiled, wiping the tears from her eyes. "That's the beauty of this. They are here in this village. I can get another creation by them."

Bringer hugged the blanket to her, her eyes spilling as well. "I am so honored. Thank you."

The Elder took Bringer's hand and pulled her to standing, then hugged her. "You are welcome here anytime. I promise I will never again let another suffer."

Bringer was surprised, and returned the hug as if she had never gotten one, but had always wanted it. They two women stayed like that a few moments, then the Elder released her.

"Join us. Hear the tales of our friend."

Bringer looked at Hunter. "Will you be there?"

"I will, for you."

She reached out and took his hand. She set the blanket upon the chair, beside her old boots. Together, the three left the hut and went to celebrate the life of their loved one.

Myrgen opened his eyes, not sure why the memories were pausing there. Then he heard the pounding on the door. He looked up at the Land and bowed. The Land had released him from the memories to handle the task at hand. He went to the great doors and opened them. Rose, the girl who cleaned his room and taught him to dance, was panting in fear in the hallway. She was holding a pot by the handle and had obviously used it to pound upon the doors. There were several dents in it.

"The Dûce and Dûcesa need you. There are boats in the Sea of Blood!"

Forty-One

This would free the monsters to destroy
the world, for they did not care if one
were man, beast, Fae, or mage.
-The Longsword of the Orphans

Myrgen went to one of the windows in the tower, Rose on his heels. He saw large ships breaching the Teeth and flotsam on the water a bit closer. He couldn't see detail because they were too far away. He looked down into the city when he heard a few shouts and screams. In the courtyard of Ashstone, men were appearing from nowhere and drawing swords upon those they found. Myrgen saw three people cut down, one of them was a lady from the kitchens.

He turned to Rose. "Where are Drake and Anika?"

"They went to the city. They wanted to check with the harbormaster to see who was due to arrive."

Myrgen saw the man in the courtyard disappear and then show up on the nearby rampart. He drew his sword. "Do you know where the Granite Bow is?"

"Yes."

"Bring it here. And get everyone in the castle into the Meditation chamber."

He pushed out the door to the ramparts and flicked his wrist, sealing it behind him against the intruder. The man looked decidedly out of place. Black hair, dark eyes, this man was *Mandian*. How was that possible?

Myrgen didn't care. He knew something this intruder did not: He was easier to question when he was dead. Myrgen swung his sword and ran the man through.

Myrgen pushed the sword through him and shoved him off by disposing of him over the side into the courtyard. The man's body crunched and several folks looked up to see Myrgen. Several more Mandian soldiers popped into the courtyard and Myrgen shouted for their attention. He stamped his foot and the courtyard shook, knocking the invaders to the ground. Several Caratians seized the moment to stab their assailants.

Myrgen looked to the city and saw Drake and Anika battling in the streets. They had called their personal weapons to them. The Granite Bow was not in Drake's possession. The doors behind him opened and Rose was dragging the great bow, barely able to lift it. People were running behind her to head down into the Meditation room. Myrgen took it from her and kissed her forehead.

"See to the others." He hefted the bow easily and she nodded, relieved. The doors were closed and again sealed against anyone of Mandian blood.

Several men appeared on the ramparts away from Myrgen and he drew the bow. An arrow of stone and lava appeared in the bow and when he released, it flew, spitting molten rock along the path. It embedded in an invader, searing him like he had just entered a volcano caldera. He didn't even have time to scream before he was dead.

The men around him didn't even realize their companion had been killed, and teleported to the courtyard below. Myrgen fired two more arrows, picking off the ones at the back. By the time he got to the last one standing, the man turned around to find he was alone. He had approached the doors to the interior of Ashstone and found them solid. He screamed at Myrgen and teleported to the wall.

He ducked behind the crenelatons, getting cover from the castle itself. Myrgen didn't like the idea of the castle shielding this man, and apparently, the castle didn't like it either. The crenelation dropped, exposing the area where he had been, but he was gone. Myrgen looked around but didn't see him.

He moved to the front wall. These people would go where they could see. He looked at the wall then jumped off. The ground did not harm him, nor claim him, and he put his hand upon the wall.

"Seal them in."

The Onyx Key glowed and the wall grew, covering the top of the castle and all the windows in stone. Myrgen ran to the town square, firing as he went.

Tib opened the study door when the castle sealed. He had not realized they were under siege. Rose was yelling at people to get to the Meditation room and staff and populace were rushing to comply. She saw him and waved him over. Then a blade protruded through her chest from behind her and she fell, dead. A Mandian man climbed the stairs from outside and saw Tib before him.

Tib ran back into the study and looked around. There was a sword in the hands of one of the statues and he went to it, trying to wrench it from the stone. The hand released it, and he swung on the room.

No one was there. He had even neglected to close the doors. He listened and heard screams coming from down the hallway where everyone was. He also heard a sound like metal hitting stone. He ran to the hallway, his eyes wet as he passed Rose's body. His foot accidentally caught on her hand and she shifted. She slid down the stairs and rested at the bottom with a *slutch* sound.

Tib wiped his face, then turned to the hallway leading to the Meditation room. He heard more people shouting and screaming, and recognized all the voices. He ran, screwing his courage up. They were sealed in with a killer and he needed to protect his family. He saw the killer cut down a man who was fighting him off with a broom. The killer cut the handle in half and swung at the man (Mathias, from the stables), as Tib screamed at him.

The killer turned at Tib and thrust his sword at the young man, spearing him through the shoulder. Tib cried out, hitting the man in the arm. The arm dropped off, that hand's sword still embedded in his shoulder, but the other sword swung at Tib. Mathias drove the half stick into the side of the killer's head, shoving grey gunk out the other side. The killer spun, and his other sword hit Tib in the neck.

Tib dropped to the ground in two pieces.

Myrgen moved steady towards the Town Square. He shot lava into invader after invader. Though several townspeople were saved, he continued not to find the man he saw on the wall. He hoped he hadn't gotten inside before Myrgen sealed the castle.

The streets were wet and bloody, most of the blood soaking into the ground. That which did not ran to the lowest place in town, the docks, as if on a sluce. He called out for Drake and Anika but didn't find them. Another arrow went down the street and then he heard the *boom*.

He turned as a cannon ball flew in front of him into the square. He heard a scream, a man's scream, and he ran to the sound. He heard Anika cry out as well, but hers was in rage. Myrgen entered the square and saw Drake down, his legs crushed by a smoking cannonball. Several more shots fired and buildings splintered around them.

"Anika!"

"Myrgen! Stop the cannons!"

He did as bidden as several more cannons were fired. He shot the ships with the lava arrows. The ships he could reach caught fire but there were several out of his range. He turned to look at Anika, stooping to see to Drake. He heard another boom and suddenly, the world turned red. His hand holding the bow stung and he hit the ground, hard. A cannonball had hit the bow, shattering it.

No cannon is that accurate.

He looked at the cannonball on the ground and saw it was not smoking. It was exuding shadow. Tendrils licked the remains of the Granite Bow, staining them black.

He turned to look at Anika and saw a man appear directly behind her. He stabbed a white sword through her before she knew he was there.

Myrgen's rage caused him to stand and he stumbled towards the scene.

Forty-Two

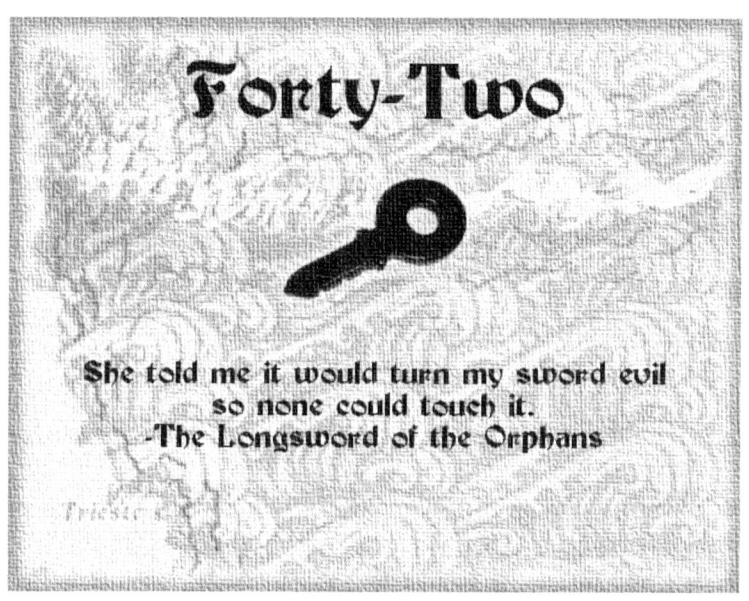

*She told me it would turn my sword evil
so none could touch it.
-The Longsword of the Orphans*

Cipriano pulled the Granite Sword from Anika's body, her blood soaking into the ground. He kicked her over to the side. Drake roared at the loss, dragging himself towards the King of Mande. His useless legs did not stop his ire and he gripped the soil. Cipriano turned on Myrgen as he stumbled towards the invading king.

"Ah! The Stâpân! Thank you so much for the use of this blade. I could never have gotten here without it."

Myrgen glanced around but did not see Entivia anywhere. "I never gave that to you. How did you get it?"

"I took it from Entivia's warm, dead fingers. It was my right. She tried to assassinate me with it. I can't have that from my subjects. Breeds revolt. But I have learned much from the study of this blade. Since it is an artifact of the Land, it bypasses all the precautions set up by the First Dûcesa. My blood didn't matter, nor did the blood of my men. The Teeth let us through like we belonged here."

Myrgen snarled. He drew his own sword and came at Cipriano. He felt the Land guiding his steps, telling him exactly how to fight the man. He saw Drake crawling to Anika and did his best not to be distracted by that. Not now.

Myrgen feinted left, but felt his move was telegraphed and Cipriano didn't fall for it. There were a few more stabs and Myrgen parried them. Rage started to overtake Cipriano but then he looked at the Granite Sword and smiled, calming. Myrgen felt the Sword communicating with Cipriano, protecting him.

"You are quite the failure, Myrgen, letting this Sword make its way to Mande. You didn't even know what you were giving up. It is telling me everything. It told me about you taking this office. It told me about Catriona leaving. It told me about everything I needed to take over this country and rule it. It also told me you Land people will do anything you are ordered to, so long as you have the authority of one of these weapons."

Cipriano brought the full weight of the Sword to bear upon Myrgen and drove him back. Myrgen parried a blow coming at his neck, but the weight of the Sword increased, driving him to his knees. Cipriano stood over him, gloating, and Myrgen felt his collarbone shatter under the weight of the Sword. He screamed out, falling to his hands and knees, his sword skittered just out of reach. He knew he was probably about to die, and so did Cipriano. He pushed Myrgen all the way down, his bloody shoulder wound draining into the ground.

Cipriano lifted the sword and plunged it through Myrgen's shoulder, disabling his right arm. He pulled out the bloody blade from the gushing wound and stepped back, surveying his work. There was a rumble, and a smoky quartz Stone, shot with streaks of living orange rose from the ground near Cipriano. He looked at it, then at the Sword. He smiled.

"Well now, that's interesting. According to this Sword, all I have to do is stand upon this stone to be selected as Dûce." He started to walk over to the Stone, turning to point the white and red blade at Myrgen. "Now I know what you're thinking. How will I rule two countries at once? Easy." He pulled the chain around his neck and revealed the shadow amulet Boots had worn.

"I have a whole *box* of these."

He nodded to his men and every sailor he brought with him had an amulet around their neck. Myrgen's blood ran cold into the ground. He touched the Amulet to the Sword and the black tendrils wrapped around it, bruising it. Cipriano kissed the bloody part, and stepped back onto the Stone.

The fire within it flared, lava bursting upwards to surround him. The molten stone consumed the amulet at his neck in a fiery instant as Cipriano screamed in pain. In that moment, Myrgen understood. He turned to look as every sailor burned in lava spouts that encompassed only them. The Land knew about the amulets, knew what they represented, what they would do. It had tricked Cipriano here, to its heart, and had him bring them all. It was the only way to destroy them.

The spout of flame consumed the amulets, but it didn't spare the soldiers. They died instantly, so quick, he doubted many of them knew it had happened. Then, every Mandian sailor was spit into the air and propelled in the sea. Several of them landed upon the ships beyond Myrgen's reach, breaking through the main deck and catching it on fire. Bodies flew into the sails, lit up the ropes and torched the wood. Anything not attacking the ships went into the Sea of Blood. Fins the size of people cut through the glassy surface of the water and churning bloody brine flew into the air as righteous jaws destroyed the bodies.

Myrgen turned back to Cipriano who was still locked onto the Stone. His body was roasting slowly as his screams of agony filled the air. The Granite Sword was still clutched in his hand, mostly because he could not let go at this point. Myrgen reached out for it and summoned it to him. It disappeared from Cipriano, down into the ground and came up immediately beneath Myrgen's left arm. He smiled, grateful to hold it again.

"I'm sorry, my friend. It just appears the Land needed you more."

The Sword formed into a crutch to help him stand. To his right, stone legs formed around Drake's lower body, attaching themselves to his waist above the sword cut. They bore his weight. He bent down and picked up his beloved Anika. He carried her over to the center of the Town Square as Myrgen watched a Stone rise beneath the grass. Another rose not far from him, and he knew what this meant.

A final blast of lava disintegrated the King of Mande and the heat vent blew the chunks and ash into the sea. The Stone he stood upon faded away, leaving the other two. Myrgen limped over to the Stone near him and stood upon it, held up by the Granite Sword. He looked around at his grateful countrymen and women, his family. They moved forward, crying, as they saw what was happening to their defenders.

He looked at Drake holding Anika's limp body across his arms. The Heartstone dangled from her neck, hovering over the Stone. Blood dripped from it a little, going so close to her open eyes, they looked like tears. He took a breath, and held Myrgen's gaze as they felt the Judgment come. The earth opened beneath Myrgen's feet and he was consumed.

Appendices

Appendix A: Characters of the Saintlands

Alan Moriarity: Catriona's son. After his Naming Ceremony, Victor Tiberius Morganosa

Alexander Angloume (ANG-loo-may): King of Mervolingia, Alexander succeeded the Throne after Charles. Alexander is also the Duke of Anjou, the family lands of the Angloume house.

Anika Heartholder: Dûcesa of Caratia and adopted mother of Catriona.

Antoinette: Cook in the mornings at the Patras Royal Palace.

Alistair MacGlarren: In service to Gloriana, the Midwinter Queen, Alistair is also the bloodline heir to the throne of York. The original Black Sparrow, he retired from this position after succeeding in learning about Tanglwyst's pirate operations. He stopped when Catriona, his former lover, found out. Alistair is also the father of James and Gwen. Since his death at the hands of Duncan McVryce, he has been serving Karma in the afterlife.

Anika Zapolya- Dûcesa of Caratia. Holder of the Hearstone.

Archbishop Alonzo de Patrone: Archbishop of Patras.

Artemisia: Mythical name of the Moon and mother of the Sea Goddess Calista.

Black Sparrow: Notorious pirate who attacked the Tanglwyst Trading Company. Taken out by Catriona Moriarity.

Bringer- An entity of Power that has been missing for centuries. Counterpart to Giver.

Catriona Moriarity (CAT-tree-OH-nah MORE-ee-AR-it-tee): Stâpâna of Caratia. The Stâpâna is the Protector of the Land's People in the country of Caratia, the second highest rank in the country. The Stâpâna is chosen through a secret ritual known only to those in Caratia. Lover of Myrgen.

Charles Maximillian IX: Former King of Mervolingia, ruler and instigator of the St. Michael's Day Massacre.

Dominic D'Medici (DOM-uh-nik dee MED-ee-chee): Fiancé of Gwen. As Acting Chancellor of Mervolingia, he is in charge of all funding and expenses for the entire kingdom.

Don- A general title of noble station. In Augustinian countries, it means Lord.

Drake Zapolya: Dûce of Caratia. The ruler of Caratia can be either male or female and is chosen directly by the Land through a ritual involving several trials and finally culminating in a ceremony in the town square of Zara.

Duncan McVryce: A notable member of the Back Streets of Patras, Duncan has played a role in several events involving members of the Royal family, the Augustinian church and Tanglwyst's interests.

The *Enigma-* Catriona's ship, it houses a Fae spirit named Estelle, that is the daughter of Corrigan, the Midsummer King. Estelle is wife to Octavius.

Entivia "Boots" Malatesta- Horse in the Stable of Assassins owned by Giovanni Sangiardo.

Father Benjamin: A priest in service to Marco Giovanni, he was killed helping Catriona escape her captivity in the breeding pans of the Giovanni estate.

Giver- An entity of power being held captive in Heaven. Counterpart to Bringer.

Gomez de Santander: Head of Alexander's personal guard, Gomez began as a guard at the Giovanni estate.

Gweneviere "Gwen" Douglas (GWEN-eh-veer DUG-lus): Handmaiden of Catriona, Gwen has the distinction of being her most trusted companion. Daughter of Alistair and Gloriana, twin of James.

James Douglas- Captain of the *Crimson Veil.*

Johannes- Bo'sun on the *Enigma.*

King Henry II: Father of Francois I, Charles, Alexander and Margaret, husband of Catherine, Deceased.

Lawrence of Cleves- Keeper of the Watch on the *Enigma.*

Marco Giovanni: Mandian Count and head of the Apolodorus family, Giovanni almost married his cousin to secure a large financial conglomerate but murdered his son and then committed suicide the tenday before his wedding, leaving the Apolodorus fortune to his oldest child. Father of Dominic.

Michael - Myrgen's Nubian Slave. A very large man who is fiercely loyal to Myrgen.

Morgan Wolf - Viscount in St. Marguerite, and Myrgen and Tanglwyst's brother.

Myrgen "the Grey" de Sablonierres (MUR-gun dee SAB-yon-air): Former Chancellor to Mervolingia, he was accused of the regicide of King Charles. Wandering the world in search of his path, he is Catriona's lover.

Nicolai Moriarity - Husband of Catriona Moriarity and father of Tib. A guard in the Patras Palace. Dead by poison.

Nigel - King Charles's Castellan before Myrgen.

Nina Richelieu - Gardin of the Royal Palace at Patras, she is Gomez' second in command.

Octavius - First mate of the *Enigma* under Captain Catriona Moriarity, husband to Estelle.

Pope Gregory - Head of the Augustinian Church.

Princess Isabelle - A Mandian Princess of marrying age

Princess Marie-Elizabeth - The daughter of Elizabeth and Charles.

Queen Elizabeth of Krakte - Queen of Mervolingia, married to Charles Maximillian IX. Mother of Marie-Elizabeth. A school friend of Tanglwyst's along with Adriana Capaletti

Queen-Mother Catherine D'Medici - Mother of Charles and Alexander. Married to Henry II.

Tanglwyst de Holloway (TANG-gul-wist dee HALL-oh-way): Owner of the Tanglwyst Trading Company and Catriona's secret partner. Sister of Myrgen and Morgan Wolf.

Thessius- Glarren member of Catriona's crew on the *Enigma*. Former First Mate to Ramerez on the *Crimson Veil*. Quartermaster on the *Enigma*.

Tristram Wulfschlager - Captain of the *Righteous*, one of Catriona's ships.

Urien Atredes - Husband of Tanglwyst de Holloway, a Latian Merchant who owns The Atredes Trading Company, which along with the Tanglwyst Trading Company controls 73% of the Mervol - Mandian trade.

Ûr- Caratian form of noble address

Wilgefortis- The wife of Raven Grasshair, she was also the Baroness of Conterbury in York and the Seneschale of Persephone during the Soulless War.

William- Navigator on the *Enigma*

Appendix B: The Augustinian Calendar

The world of the Saintlands has four seasons, and those are the purview of the Fae Lords. Embertwist Apocraphix, the Vernal Monarch, rules over spring, Corrigan Starshadow, the Midsummer King, rules summer, Calpurnia Allegheri, the Autumnal Sovereign, reigns over fall and Gloriana Talnig, the Midwinter Queen, rules winter.

The combat these lords, the Church originally invoked the Archangels against them. These were sufficient but as Heaven gave the Church the Saints, these former humans were invoked in addition, adding to the strength of the protections against Fae trickery. The saints were originally celebrated upon the day of their ascension and delivery by Heaven into the Rolls.

However, 300 years ago, the Church, in the aftermath of a great war, decided to write down a formal calendar, honoring saints for their purviews instead of their date of ascension. This was to battle non-church beliefs, unify the masses and establish lines of Church control.

Pope Richard I told the cardinals to which he assigned this task to begin the year prior to the apex of Gloriana's control, so as to get ahead of the rise of her power. The Cardinals discussed it and Cardinal Cosimo of Pardua offered up Genevieve, invoked against disasters, to start the year. Richard approved and the calendar was begun.

Genevary became the first month and the months were divided into 31 day sets with 10 day tenday. In the center of the month, the 16th, is the Devotional Day, where all work stops for a day to pray and invoke the saints of the month. This strengthened the divinity in the realm, repelling anything not Heaven related. Although the new calendar reorganized the role of Saints during the year, many days are still known by the saint who ascended upon that day, though the Archangel's days were established during the Augustinian Calendar.

Months

1St: Named after Saint Genevieve, **Genevary** 16 honors Sebald, Martin of Tours, and Raphael the Archangel. Genevieve is invoked against disasters, which abound in the Saintlands during the winter. Sebald once burned icicles in a poor woman's home to produce heat. Martin of Tours cut his cloak in half to give to a naked beggar. Raphael brings the heat of the sun and dawn to battle freezing cold.

2nd: Named after Saint Vitus, **Vitusary** 16 honors Medard, Catald, and Barbara. Vitus is invoked against storms, but is also the Patron saint of dancers so balls abound in Vitusary. Medard is invoked against bad weather because he sheltered the beautiful queen Angelica, granddaughter of Saint Marie Angelica, when she fled the intrigues of the Mervol court during a storm. Medard gave his own tent so she would be safe and dry. An eagle sheltered him from the weather, creating an umbrella for him as he rested. Catald cured the ill and is invoked against plagues, which often abound from bad weather. Barbara was saved when lightning struck her attackers during a siege.

3rd: Named after Saint Florien, **Florias** 16 honors Vincent, Jude, & John of Nepomuk (bridges & flooding). Florien is invoked against floods, a common problem in the Saintlands the third month. Saint Vincent Ferrer is the patron saint of builders, often put to work during this time. Jude helps the hopeless. John of Nepomuk strengthens bridges during floods to save the towns.

4th: Named after Saint Elmo, **Elmos** 16 invokes Fiacre (gardeners), Phocas (market gardeners), and Uriel the Archangel. Elmos starts the sailing season, so Saint Elmo, patron saint of sailors marks this month. Fiacre and Phocas bring the first harvests from winter, began indoors or in warmer climes to feed the masses while Uriel protects the people from the lies and trickery of thieves.

5th: Named after Saint Walburga, **Walpurgisnacht** 16 invokes Valentine, Rose of Lima, & Theodore of Sykon (reconciling the unhappily married). Walpurgisnacht 1 allows the young and amorous to

361

pursue each other unhindered and as such, this month marks the beginnings of many marriages. Valentine honors true love. Rose of Lima honors florists and flower growers. Theodore, known for his counseling skills, reconciles the unhappily married, reminding them of the way they felt their first month of marriage.

6th: Named after Saint Wilgefortis, **Vilgfort** 16 honors Felicity (women wanting sons), Monica (wives), & Marie Angelica (nun who married). Felicity is invoked by women wanting sons, usually royals, due to her miracle of delivering sons whenever she was a woman's midwife. Monica honors wives as she was Heaven's example of a perfect wife and Marie Angelica was a nun who married for the sake of the world. A vision held that Marie Angelica would have a daughter who would alter the church and though she was a nun, she was persuaded to leave her vows to fulfill this vision. Her daughter, Tanglwyst Angelica, inherited a powerful shipping company which was destined for the hands of a corrupt Church. Her sacrifice honors all women who must abandon their own dreams for the sake of a greater good.

7th: Named after Saint Maurice, **Maur** 16 honors Elizabeth (war), Clara (savior in the Soulless War) and Michael the Archangel. This is the season of war, and thus, the people invoke Saint Maurice to keep their soldiers safe while away from home while Elizabeth is invoked to find peaceful resolutions to wars. Clara was a woman whose role in the Soulless War enabled the plague to be destroyed through the spreading of soil she had walked upon, preventing the plague from crossing it. Michael fought the creatures of Hell to preserve the faithful during the great wars.

8th: Named after Saint Francis, **Franco** 16 honors Hubert (hunters), Andrew, and Sebastian. Saint Francis honors all animals and those who tend them. Hubert honors the hunters. Andrew the fishermen and Sebastian protects archers.

9th: Named after Saint Thomas Aquinas, **Aquin** 16 honors Ivo, Augustine, and Albert. The season of scholarly pursuits, Aquin honors those who devote themselves to study. Ivo honors lawyers. Augustine honors theologians and his ideals of Heaven are the basis for the Augustinian Church. Albert honors scientists and herbalists.

10th: Named after Saint Benedict, **Benedine** 16 honors Gabriel the Archangel, Giles, & Margaret. As this is a time of darkness descending upon the land and things turning cold, people were often creating tales of ghosts and fear. Those who had died in the wars of the summer or in the professions of the year were often "seen" wandering the desolate places during this month. To counter these tales of fancy, the church brought in their strongest saints against fear and superstition. Saint Benedict fought his greatest fear, being homeless, and opened his home as a shelter. As such, he is their patron saint. Giles protects against night terrors. Margaret defends against those being attacked by devils, enabling their escape. Gabriel the Archangel heralds Heaven's will, driving away doubt and fear.

11th: Named after Saint Ferdinand, **Ferdin** 16 honors All Saints (Fer 1), Eloi, and Anne. To celebrate the survival of the month of fear, All Saints Day was noted as the first Church holiday. It also honors those responsible for the greatest achievements of humanity: Ferdinand for Engineers, Eloi for jewelry and metal smithing and Anne for pregnancy.

12th: Named after Saint Brigit, **Brig** 16 honors Cosmas & Damian, Raymond, and Roch. A most notable saint, Brigit was one of the first saints ascended to Heaven after giving her life to heal others. Her blood created a fountain by which those who were ill or damaged could be restored. This fountain is in the center of the Papal Palace in the Papal City. Cosmos and Damian are conjoined twins who became doctors. Raymond honors midwives. Roch is invoked against epidemics.

Weekdays

Day 1: Honorasday: named from Honoratus, for bakers.

Day 2: Bernaday: Named after Saint Bernadette, shepherds.

Day 3: Rufinasday: Named after Saint Rufina, potters.

Day 4: Simproniday: Named after Four Crowned Martyrs, stonemasons.

Day 5: Julianusday: Named after Saint Julian, boatmen.

Day 6: Vincentsday: Named after Saint Vincent Ferrer, builders.

Day 7: Wencesday: Named after Saint Wenceslas, brewers.

Day 8: Genesday: Named after Saint Genesius, Actors & Comedians.

Day 9: Columbasday: Named after Saint Columba, poets.

Day 10: Dismasday: Named after Saint Dismas, undertakers.

Appendix C: Religions

Augustinian (AHG-us-TIN-ee-uhn)

The Augustinians believe God made the world and made Heaven. God set up the ability for Man to ascend to Heaven body and soul by doing good works. If a human is good enough and helps enough people, they can become a Saint. Each Saint in the Augustinian Rolls was once a human and their name appears in the Heavenly Roster when they ascend. The Heavenly Roster is a book kept in the Papal City on the Official Altar in the center of the Cathedral under constant guard.

In the 1300s, the Church stopped acknowledging new names in the Roster after The War of the Soulless which they blamed upon the heathen religions. The reason cited for this denial was the War made it difficult to believe all the reports of ascended Saints. At the time, it was unknown by the populace about the Heavenly Roster but after the declaration and an investigation by nobles outside the church, this information was revealed to the public. Regardless, once the Pope responsible passed away and the scandal was uncovered, the new Pope acknowledged the updated Rolls and the new Saints were canonized.

The main Tenant of Faith in the Augustinian religion is the Saints are the world's connection to Heaven. It is only by praying to the Saints that one can communicate with Heaven. It is against the Laws of the Church to pray directly to God, bypassing his appointed representatives, to make requests, though one can offer praise unto Heaven without invoking a particular Saint. However, if one prays to a particular saint for guidance or assistance and they receive it, it is against the laws of the Church to not acknowledge the Saint who answered the prayer.

Emilianite (uh-MEEL-ee-uhn-ITE)

After the War of the Soulless and the Scandal of the Unacknowledged Saints, a group of followers broke away from the

Church. Citing corruption in the dictations of the papacy, it was determined that apparently the Church could communicate directly to Heaven without the help of the Saints since they refused to acknowledge the Saints received in the Rolls. They called these Saints "the Abandoned Children" and called themselves Emilianites, after Emilio, the patron Saint of abandoned children.

The Emilianites believe that man cannot be trusted with the will or intent of Heaven through a conduit, for that can be hidden or destroyed. Instead, they believe man can be more assured of correct information if he prays directly to Heaven. If Heaven wants the Emilianites to pray to a Saint, they will communicate that Saint's name to all the Faithful. Until that happens, the Emilianites will pray directly to Heaven. Since the Scandal of the Unacknowledged, no Emilianite has ever noted a Saint's name being given to them. As such, they continue to offer prayers only to Heaven.

Land Worship

The Maker split in two, creating the Heavens and the Land. Both are sentient and great entities unto themselves. Heaven holds the Well of Souls and deals with all things ethereal such as dreams and thoughts, ideas and concepts. The Land deals with all things physical, be it body, plant or liquid. If it can be held, it is the purview of the Land.

When the body dies, the Land takes it into itself and dissolves the flesh, leaving the soul. The soul is filtered and cleansed of the sins of its life and when all the sin is gone, the soul that is left is returned to the Well of Souls. The Land interacts with the people on a daily basis, feeding them, clothing them, healing them. They trust the Land and count on its gifts for life.

Calista's Call

Oceanus, Father of Waters, was alone and lonely. He wandered across the world without drive or direction. Sometimes, to relieve his boredom, he would slice through a mountain or sink an island he made but in the end, he was aimless and alone. Then, one night, he heard a stirring song. It beckoned him from across the Land and he fell upon a beach, kneeling before the singer. A beautiful maiden of silver hair and glowing pale skin sat naked on the beach, her voice filling the night. He crept up behind her and she saw him and screamed, then grabbed her clothes and fled to the sky.

Every night, he went to the beach to fall upon the shore, begging her to return. He brought her gifts from the sea and faraway lands, creatures and stones, wood and plants. Eventually she peeked from behind the curtain of night and slowly emerged, a little more each night, until she fell in love with Oceanus and they made love upon the beach. They created a daughter of rich blue skin like her father and glowing white hair like her mother. They called her Calista and the salt from their tears of joy at the sight of her soaked her, making her touch turn water into salt water.

Calista watches the sea and keeps her secrets and those of her followers. She is a fickle goddess though, and prone to fits of fury that can seem unprovoked. When she is happy or dealing with honorable people, her hair is the white of sea foam. Mermaids gather the honored dead and if a sailor is a good follower, Calista recognizes them and grants them the ability to live underwater as merfolk in her cities. Her dolphins and sea mammals guide ships through treacherous areas and are always signs of her pleasure.

But she has her primal side as well and when dealing with the dishonorable, she sends her teeth to rend them. Her hair turns bloody red and her sharks and sirens call the evildoers to their destruction. If there is an argument in ship at sea and sharks arrive on the scene, it means someone in the fight is lying. If a criminal is sentenced to death at seas, the sharks will take him, but if the criminal is remorseful, they take him to the depths where he becomes a Marked One and serves Calista for as long as they breathed air. Sirens call the unjust to the sharks' maws so if one hears a siren's call, the heavier the sins on their soul, the harder it is to resist them.

If a body is rendered with fire at death, Calista will know them not and shall cast their spirit out of her mouth to walk the earth forever.

The Ancient Ones

Sovereignus was a good king. He loved Magic so much, that he mated with her, and fathered the Fae. The Fae were everywhere. They were the merfolk in the sea and the harpies in the air. They were the pixies and dryads in the trees and the white-furred talking animals in the snows. All the magical creatures, great and small, frolicked in the love of their mother and father. The Fae loved humans and played with them, guiding them to good places and punishing the lazy or wicked with their games and tricks.

But then a sickness came, one that threatened all the magical creatures. Dark men captured the Fae, torturing them to find the sources of Elemental magic. Sovereignus roared and rode to war against these dark men and felled them. In the battle, he was mortally wounded and returned home to die. He gave to his four eldest his power, divided as to their gifts.

To his youngest son Embertwist Apocraphix, he gave the powers of Spring. The Vernal Monarch is the quintessential thief and like a thief, it comes in the night, stealing the cold of winter and revealing the living things beneath her skirt. To his oldest son, Corrigan Starshadow, he gave the powers of Summer. As the Midsummer King, his paladin nature marches forthright towards the good and just.

To his oldest daughter, Calpurnia Allegheri, he gave the powers of Autumn. Calpurnia so resembled his beloved Magic, she channels the gifts of change and harvest during her reign as the Autumnal Sovereign. To his youngest daughter, Corrigan's twin, he gave the power of Winter. Gloriana Talnig, the Midwinter Queen, uses the cold to stop disease and preserve and heal, but also to punish the wicked and delay the unjust. The children split and went to different parts of the world to preserve their realms from the followers of the Dark Men, but each season, they return to Sovereignlumin, the great Tower That Watches All to transfer the power of the seasons.

Karma

Karma is all about balance. For each act, there is an equal and opposite reaction in a person's life. As they get closer to the end of their life thread, they can find themselves bound by the threads they have thrown. Negative acts cause sticky threads, positive acts throw stabilizing threads. If a soul has cast more sticky threads than stabilizing, they can be caught up in the negative and it will strangle them. Thus are many of the symbolic gods of Karma multi-limbed creatures.

The Primordial Egg

The Primordial Egg twitched and cracked and from the shell, four Dragons emerged. They opened their mouths and breathed forth the world. The Earth Dragon formed land and grass, ore and metal, wood and dale. The Water Dragon formed oceans and rivers, lakes and streams, snow and ice. The Fire Dragon breathed the sun and stars to warm the world. And the Air Dragon gave life and the moon. As all things came from magic, all creatures upon the world were magical, and all things communicated with one another in the combined tongue of the elements.

But then, a threat loomed on the face of all and it tried to conquer the magic in the world. It's flashing sword and violent means crushed all but its own belief, slaying the dragons in the world. The Elemental Dragons Rose against it, but to destroy the threat meant to destroy all they loved as well. Instead, they seized their followers and sealed them away in special places. The Earth Dragon hid the giants and Dwarves in the mountains. The Fire Dragon hid her faithful in the ash and lava. The Water Dragon took her children and gave them the ability to breathe water. And the Air Dragon took his children to the sky, to the place between life and death.

At first they spoke aloud to one another, but monsters found their hiding places, so the Dragons broke the world and spoke only in secret languages so none could find their whereabouts. The Earth Dragon spoke through entrails and omens, the Water Dragon through storms. Fire claimed its own hypnotic power and Air spoke through the dead. Together, they all keep the legends and the magic safe, making certain that only those who wish to keep magic in the world can find them.

Fang and Claw

The practice of having an animal choose to join with a person's soul to guide them is standard practice in the followers of Fang and Claw. They also believe in the consuming a part of the animal allows for that animal's superior quality to enter the consumer.

As a rite of passage, warriors of the tribes will hunt a dangerous animal with which to partner. Shaman may not be led by a dangerous animal, but by a wise one such as Snake or Owl. And those who become the Seers find themselves in the company of spiders.

Appendix D: Countries

Caratia (CUH-ray-SHEE-uh)
Capital City: Zara
Native tongue: Caratian (CUH-ray-SHEE-uhn)
Dominant Religion: Land Worship

Glarren (GLARE-uhn)
Capital City: Kilmory (kill-MORE-ee)
Native tongue: Glarren
Dominant Religion: The Ancient Ones

Krakte (KRAHK-tuh)
Capital City: Austra
Native tongue: Krakten
Dominant Religion: Augustinian, Emilianite, the Ancient Ones

Latia (LAH-tee-uh)
Capital City: Cheryb (SHARE-eeb)
Native tongue: Latian (LAH-tee-uhn)
Dominant Religion: Calista's Call

Mande (MAHND)
Capital City:
Other Cities: Pardua, Floren, Roma
Native tongue: Mandian (MAHN-dee-uhn)
Dominant Religion: Augustinian

Mervolingia (MER-vole-LIN-jee-uh)
Capital City: Patras
Other Cities: Rouen (ROO-en), St. Giles, St. Andrew, St. Marguerite
Native tongue: Mervol (MER-vol)
Dominant Religion: Augustinian, Emilianite

Nubia (NOO-bee-uh)
Capital City: Leeus Brul (lee-OOS bruul)
Native Tongue: Fangspek
Dominant Religion: Fang and Claw

The Papal City (PAY-puhl)
Capital City: None
Native tongue: Mervol
Dominant Religion: Augustinian Church Seat

Toledo (toe-LEED-dough)
Capital City: Tuscan
Native tongue: Toledan
Dominant Religion: Land Worship

York (YORK)
Capital City: Landen
Other cities: Canterbury, Kent, Oxford, Cambridge
Native Tongue: Yorkish
Dominant Religion: Emilianite

Yndia (YIN-dee-uh)
Capital City: Yantap (YAN-tap)
Native tongue: Yndian
Dominant Religion: Karma

Yokotama (YO-ko-TAH-mah)
Capital City: Kūki doragon
Native Tongue: Yokotaman
Dominant Religion: Dance of the Air Dragons

About the Author

     Tonya Adolfson has been a member of the Society for Creative Anachronism since 1988 and has met thousands of people with very interesting personas. Many of these people have made it into these books and she is grateful to them for enriching her life.

     Tonya lives in Boise, Idaho with her husband, two children, two housemates, four cats and three dogs and yet, strangely, the house is actually pretty clean.